新东方口译考试培训班指定辅导用书

汪海涛 邱政政 主编

Interpretation

中级口译笔试
备考精要

邱政政 徐兰 钱春雷 张驰新 编 著

世界图书出版公司

上海·西安·北京·广州

图书在版编目(CIP)数据

中级口译笔试备考精要/汪海涛,邱政政主编. —上海:上海世界
图书出版公司,2004.10(2008.9重印)

ISBN 978 - 7 - 5062 - 7087 - 8

Ⅰ. 中...　Ⅱ. ①汪...　②邱...　Ⅲ. 英语—口译—水平考试—
自学参考资料　Ⅳ. H315.9

中国版本书图书馆 CIP 数据核字(2004)第 097650 号

中级口译笔试备考精要

汪海涛　邱政政　主编

上海世界图书出版公司出版发行

上海市尚文路 185 号 B 楼

(公司电话:021 - 63783016 转发行科)

邮政编码:200010

常熟市大宏印刷有限公司印刷

如发现印装质量问题,请与印刷厂联系调换

(质检科电话:0512 - 52621873)

各地新华书店经销

开本:787×1092　1/16　印张:21.25　字数:300 000
2008 年 9 月第 1 版第 8 次印刷
ISBN 978 - 7 - 5062 - 7087 - 8/H·542
定价:32.00 元
http://www.wpcsh.com.cn

序　言

进入二十一世纪，中国国际化进程日益加快，成功加入 WTO，主办 2008 年奥运会，承办 2010 年世博会成为中国与世界进一步接轨的重要标志。城市经济的快速发展、上海的广阔市场和经济平台吸引着成千上万的外商来沪投资，各类国际商务会议和文化会展在沪召开日益频繁。在上海发展需要的紧缺人才中，中高级口译人才首当其冲；在大批懂外语的人中，精通口笔译的人才奇缺。《上海口译岗位资格证书》考试的诞生，大大激发了广大学生和市民提高英语技能的学习热情。近几年口译考试参加者猛增，已经通过大学英语四、六级考试的学生纷纷准备挑战口译考试，加强了课外英语学习，而更多的白领也纷纷利用双休日参加各类口译辅导。2004 年口译考试报名者突破 6 万人次，而 2005 年 3 月一次考试的报名考生更多达 3.3 万人，已经超过了上海本地今年考研的人数，"口译热"掀起了一个又一个外语学习高潮，影响遍及到了长江三角洲的各个地区。

上海新东方在外语培训方面一直声名远播，除了在出国考试、四六级考研和听说口语方面有良好的口碑，2003 年打造出了高品质的口译旗舰系列课程，迅速赢得了市场的赞誉和普遍认同。仅 2004 年一年上海新东方学校就汇聚了 11,293 名口译学员。除了上海本地复旦、同济、交大、财大、华师大等各高校的学生外，还有一批来自于苏州、杭州、南通、无锡、南京和温州的学生，甚至有学生不远千里从安徽、福建、湖南、湖北、河南、山东、广东赶到上海新东方学习。

新东方口译培训的成功，不仅源于新东方十年发展积累了通过各类考试的成功秘籍，更在于我们为口译课程配备了雄厚的师资团队。其中新东方口译专家顾问团的 6 人组均为国内外口译界泰斗和知名专家、教授。新东方针对教学的"分项突破法"设立了口译五大教研组：听力、阅读、笔译、口语和口译教研组定期召开课程研讨，编写图书和学术文章。新东方口译明星讲师团由 36 人组成，除汇聚了世界名牌大学英语语言文学或英汉互译硕士或博士之外，还包括两名联合国会议高级同传、3 名美国和加拿大政府特聘的高级同传和 3 名欧盟认证同传。

经过长期的教学研究和课堂实践，新东方中高级口译教研组隆重推出了"中/高级口译考试备考精要"系列图书，共分四册。其中邱政政、Jessie Zhang 老师创作的《中高级口译考试词汇必备》收集了 12 个章节的中高级口译百科词汇，信息量充足，覆盖了大量口、笔译常用词汇和表达，紧扣时代脉搏，展现当代中国政治、经济发展特色，涉及到中西文化的方方面面，分类介绍，便于记忆，实战利用率高，填补了口笔译词汇图书的空白。附录部分编选了历年考题中听力、阅读出现的高频词汇，使考生在复习时能够抓住重点记忆。两位老师执笔的《中/高级口译口试备考精要》则分不同场景和话题，给出了丰富的应答思路和地道的口译语言，大量的情景语言分析让读者直接熟悉了实战的方方面面，应对考试时能够胸有成竹。《中级口译笔试备考精要》和《高级口译笔试备考精要》则由新东方口译教研组名师邱政政、郝斌、张弛新、肖逸、David Qian、徐兰和郭中宝共同创作，各分听力、阅读和笔译三个版块，将听力、阅读和翻译理论和实践范例溶为一体。通过各个章节的系统论述，历年考题的典型题型与解题思路变得清晰透彻。新东方应试策略与学术研究的闪光点层出不穷，尽现纸上，使得"全攻略"系列成为教学过程不可缺少的辅助材料。

需要强调的一点是，任何一种考试都不能只以考试技巧和高分作为最终目标，尽管新东方帮助了无数的学员赢得了高分，但我们反复强调扎实的语言基本功和过硬的英语应用能力，并在课堂上展开丰富的口译情景训练，中高级口译学习是无数学生走出英语学习的平原向高峰登攀的重要过程，是对学生综合能力考察的重要标准，我们期待的是这批同学在挑战考试成功后，能够把外语当成一种熟练应用的工具，能够进一步进行各类专业和业务知识的积累，最终成为上海经济高速发展过程中所需要的高素质科技和商业精英。

上海新东方学校校长　汪海涛
2005 年 5 月

目　录

听 力 篇

阅 读 篇

翻 译 篇

Interpretation

听

力

篇

第一章　语　音

语音，或者说学会正确辨音，不仅是正确理解听写填空内容的第一步，也是顺利完成所有听力试题所必需的能力。我们之所以要把语音放在备考必需能力的第一项，是因为语言是有声的，对语言的感觉首先是通过人的听觉。对英语的语音不够敏感，听力很难得到质的提高。

Without a very solid foundation of pronunciation，your English listening can not go far.

在中级口译听力考试中，英式英语和美式英语兼有。大量地道、生活化的美音，对于大多数以英音启蒙的中国考生而言，不能不说是一大障碍；而对于考过托福或者喜欢观看美国电影或电视剧的考生来说，"拿腔拿调"的英式发音又或多或少听起来不那么顺耳，影响了他们对听力题目的理解。

以下分析将帮助考生迅速掌握语音部分的难点。

第一节　同音及近音

由于一些考生平时很少把文章用英语朗读出来，不能分辨相同或相近的音，或者本身对于某些单词始终发音不准，因此在听音的时候容易造成理解上的错误，例如：sale, sell 和 sail 这三个单词的发音非常相像，而且 sale 和 sell 的意义也十分相似，因此很容易造成误读。

再请看以下例句：

正：The teacher corrected the paper yesterday. 老师昨天批改了试卷。

误：The teacher collected the paper yesterday. 老师昨天把试卷收上去了。

两个句子，其他成分都相同，只是动词的区别，便造成了语义的极大区别。理解这句话出现偏差，主要是考生平时分不清[l]、[r]这两个辅音。

这样的例子很多，比如 fifty 和 fifteen，ninety 和 nineteen 的读音都非常相近。而这些往往是听写填空中的高频考点。考生应明确区别分别以[ti:n]和[ti]结尾的数字。

请考生参见以下同音/近音词，并注意总结其他常见词汇：

quite	相当	quiet	安静地
affect	影响，假装(v.)	effect	结果，影响(n.)
adapt	适应	adopt	采用
angel	天使	angle	角度
contend	奋斗，斗争	content	内容，满足的
context	上下文	contest	竞争，比赛
principal	校长；主要的	principle	原则
dessert	甜食	desert	沙漠
sweet	甜的	sweat	汗水
costume	服装	custom	习惯
champion	冠军	campaign	战役
pray	祈祷	prey	猎物
cite	引用	site	场所
compliment	赞美	complement	附加物
council	议会	counsel	忠告
dose	一剂(药)	doze	打盹
emigrant	移民(到国外)	immigrant	移民(从某国来的)
immoral	不道德的	immortal	不朽的
assure	保证	ensure	使确定
inspiration	灵感	aspiration	渴望
story	故事	storey	楼层
expand	扩张	expend	花费
commerce	商业	commence	开始
through	通过	thorough	彻底的
steal	偷	steel	钢
loose	松的	lose	丢失
stationery	文具	stationary	固定的
personnel	人事	personal	个人的
statue	塑像	statute	法令
phrase	短语	phase	阶段
mission	使命	mansion	大厦
vision	视觉	version	版本
gasp	喘气	grasp	抓住
delicate	微妙的	dedicate	献身
idle	空闲的	idol	偶像
lapse	流逝	elapse	消逝
source	水源	sauce	酱汁
vocation	职业	vacation	假期
blossom	开花	bosom	胸口
bullet	子弹	bulletin	公告

collar	领子	color	颜色
eminent	杰出的	imminent	逼近的
median	中央的	medium	媒体
suite	套房	suit	一套衣服
path	路径	pass	通过
cause	原因	course	航程
tenth	第十个	tense	紧张的
formal	正式的	former	从前的
faith	信念	face	脸
serious	严重的	series	系列
knight	骑士	night	夜晚
two	两个	too	也
knows	知道	nose	鼻子
seize	抓住	sees	看见
sea	海洋	see	看见
sale	卖(n.)	sell	卖(v.)
assent	同意	ascent	上升
contact	接触	contract	合同
metal	金属	mental	神经的

第二节　美音和英音的区别

　　在中级口译考试中，多数使用的是美国英语的语音，也有少数语段仍然使用英音朗读，而中国传统英语教学采用的却是英式英语及其音标。因此，许多考生只习惯于听英音，一旦记忆中的读音与听到的不同，就会导致单词辨认失败，而最终造成听力的失败。

　　在听力考试中，反应速度和准确程度至关重要，即使是一秒钟的时间甚至只是一个单词的差别也要争取，每个单词辨认的正确与否都能在很大程度上影响你的分数，因此必须要多读多听，熟练区别美音与英音以及其他容易混淆的发音，才能在考试时提高反应速度，考出高分。

一、元音

　　英音和美音音素的最大差别在于元音音素，以下列出几个例子，请大家进行比较：

1. 字母"a"出现在 -ss, -st, -th, -ff, -ef, -nce 等前面时，美音把 a 读为[æ]，而英音读作[ɑ:]

	美音	英音
can't	[kænt]	[kɑ:nt]
last	[læst]	[lɑ:st]

	美音	英音
mask	[mæsk]	[mɑ:sk]
chance	[tʃæns]	[tʃɑ:ns]
advantage	[æd·væntidʒ]	[əd·vɑ:ntidʒ]

此类全真词还包括：

answer, advance, after, ask, banana, branch, castle, commander, example, fast, France, glance, glass, half, last, etc.

2. 某些单词中的字母 "o" 在美音读为[ɑ]而在英音中读为[ɔ]

	美音	英音
bottle	['bɑtl]	['bɔtl]
popular	['pɑpjələ]	['pɔpjulə]
knock	[nɑk]	[nɔk]
politician	[ˌpɑli·tiʃən]	[pɔli·tiʃən]

此类全真词还包括：

odd, lock, pot, sock, watch, fog, mock, nod, solve, rocket, shop, etc.

3. 美音和英音的元音在其他一些单词中发音亦不同：

	美音	英音
either／neither	['iðə／'ni:ðə]	['aiðə(r)／'naiðə]
borough（市镇）	['bʌro]	['bʌrə]
thorough（彻底的）	['θʌro]	['θʌrə]
tomato（番茄）	[tə·meitəu]	[tə·mɑ:təu]
schedule（日程表）	['skedʒul]	['ʃedju:l]
epoch（新纪元）	['epək]	['i:pɔk]
leisure（空闲）	['liʒər]	['leʒə]

二、辅音

在辅音方面，英音与美音的相同之处大于他们之间的不同之处，但也有一些差别，例如在/t/这个发音上，当这个音素是组成音节的第一成分时，发音是完全一致的。例如，table, together 等，但是当/t/夹杂在两个音中出现时，美音中就会出现变化，这个音不再发为/t/，而是发成浊辅音/d/。因此，如果仅仅根据听到的音，往往比较难辨认出正确的单词，例如 writing 和 riding，在英音中完全不同，可是在美音中，两者几乎没有什么区别，这就给考生的辨音带来了一定的困难。让我们来看看相同的例子：

	美音	英音
city	['sidi:]	['siti]
better	['bɛdə]	['betə]
pretty	['pridi:]	['priti]

此类全真词还包括：

waiter, winter, actor, yesterday, chapter, etc.

> 总的来说，英音和美音虽然总体区别并不太大，但是仍然在细微之处存在差异，如果考生在考试时第一次接触，往往会造成疑惑，影响心情，最后降低整体水平的发挥。因此平时对于全真试题和《听力教程》一书的听力材料需多加练习，熟悉发音区别，从而在考试时将该干扰因素排除在外。

第三节 连 读

在听力材料中，由于朗读者语速加快或为了方便，往往会出现连读的现象。这不仅是英语中的一个特殊现象，也是很多中国学生练习英语听力中的一个难点。往往由于句子中两个或几个单词发生的连读，造成误听或无法理解。

连读主要出现在词义连接较为紧密的意群中，例如冠词与名词，数词和名词，动词与副词，连接词与代名词之间，如果前一个词以辅音结尾（大多为辅音，少数情况下为元音），后一个词以元音开头，则这两个词很容易发生连读。值得注意的是，由于连读主要出现在一个意群中，因此语义自然停顿的地方不用连读。

连读的类型大致可以分为两大类：

第一类，前一单词的辅音与下一个单词的元音连读

例如：

in an hour	give out
not at all	ice or water
look after	pull out
lose aim	take off
an apple	pop out
hot and cold	think over
write essay	at ease
same area	finish up
squeeze us	take it easy

. . .

第二类，前一个单词以元音结尾，下个单词亦以元音起始

在这种情况下，一般较为多见的前个单词结尾的元音包括/iə/ /juː/ /ɑː/等，而且在拼写时，最后一个音节中往往有 r 这个字母存在。在读音时，考生可想象在两个元音间加入[r]的音，将两个元音的发音连接起来，即能发出较为标准的连读。

例如：

as far as	cheer up
pure eyes	hair oil
difficult or easy	cry over spilled milk
...	

> 考生可跟读听力磁带中的对话并模仿其中的连读单词句子，举一反三，熟悉并掌握连读的发音规律。

第四节　爆破失音

爆破失音也是英语语音中的特殊现象之一，如需在这方面获得突破，考生应该对于其原理有所了解。爆破失音一般指的是当一词以辅音中的爆破音（包括/b/、/d/、/g/、/k/、/t/、/p/等）结束，后面的词语又以爆破音、破音或擦音、鼻音（考生可将此处各类发音理解为辅音，以便于操作）等开始时，前一个词中的爆破音发生失爆现象，即该音节不发音，诵读者在该拍停顿后，发下一个词的音。

在以上各爆破音中，又以/t/和/d/发生失爆现象较为常见，列举如下：

first class　　　　　　　last chance

next day　　　　　　　one thousand people

tight schedule

...

当考生练习爆破发音时，应特别注意最常见的两种现象：

第一，当前一词以/t/结尾，后一词以/t/或/d/开始，则前面的/t/音失爆：

例如：

Have you finished it today?

What do you prefer?

Please lift the bag.

在这些连接词中，前一个词的/t/音都不发，只稍作停顿。

第二，动词否定式的缩写形式中，结尾的 t 不发音。

例如：

He mustn't do it.

You needn't pay for it.

I wouldn't let him go.

You don't know him.

Mary shouldn't call him at work.

在这些句子中，所有的结尾/t/都失音，造成停顿。而英音和美音的一大区别，即can't 在英音和美音中元音的发音不同，再加上美音的读法中发生了失爆现象，造成了在听写填空和听力理解中大量对于文章描述的答案是否正确，出现确定或否定两种截然不同的理解。

要克服这样的难点，主要可以通过三种方式：一是对于英语文章进行大量的模仿跟读，熟悉失爆现象；第二，主动记忆失爆原理，诵读掌握；第三，在做题过程中，根据上下文语义，积极理解。

第五节 语 调

语调是英语语音中极为重要的一个部分，它具有特殊的表意作用。说话声调的上升或下降，声音的高亢或低沉，表达了说话者对于事件的不同态度、感情、口吻和意图。

在英语语言中，降调通常表示命令、推测、赞同等感情或用在语义完结、语气肯定的陈述句中，例如：

命令：(降调)

Give me that key now.

语气肯定：(降调)

I will never hurt you.

而升调往往是用在表示疑问、怀疑、期待或表达说话人欢快的心情时使用，例如：

May I help you?

Are you sure you want to stay alone?

有趣的是，同一句子运用不同的语调所表达的意思也完全不同，例如：

Are you serious? (升调，表明对于说话者前面所提内容的疑问，希望了解答案)

Are you serious? (降调，表明对于说话者前面所提内容的不相信，相当于否定)

我们可以通过重复听力理解篇章题的语段，特别是对话语段，熟悉并体会语调在不同语境下的变化和所表达的含义。

第二章　听写填空

掌握了基本的"M7"英语听说学习法，攻克了语音难点后，让我们一起开始对中级听力考试的各个部分进行分项突破。

中级听力测试中的第一项就是 Spot Dictation——听写填空。首先让我们来看一下做题要求：

Part A: Spot Dictation

Direction: In this part of the test, you will hear a passage and read the same passage with blanks in it. Fill in each of the blanks with the words you have heard on the tape. Write your answer in the corresponding space in your ANSWER BOOKLET. Remember you will hear the passage ONLY ONCE.

根据对试题要求及考纲的分析，听写填空部分的主要特征如下：

> 一篇文字内容，长度约为 300 词，语速为每分钟 130 个词左右，在该篇文字内容中标出 20 个空缺部分，要求考生在全面理解所听内容的基础上，准确填写出试题中所播报的空格内容。每格所填词语或短语长度以 4 个词为限。每次听写内容播放完毕后，有大约 3 分钟的时间供考生填写及检查所填内容。文章内容题材广泛，体裁多样，体现时代性、实用性。例如电脑和网络的作用，青年人职业的选择等。

从听写填空的题目要求可以看出，此种测试考查的不仅是考生的听力水平，还包括了短时记忆、笔录及准确拼写等能力。与此同时，由于在 Directions 中，明确了每一段文章考生只能听一遍，这对考生提出了较高的要求。在准备这一部分考试时，考生应时刻牢记。

> 听前准备——四大工作
> 听时记录——精听速记
> 听后检查——七个重点

在下面的文章中，我们将就提高听写填空能力所需要的知识及技巧进行分析。

第一节　听前准备

听力文章播放前，大约有将近一两分钟的时间留给考生，这段时间包括了录音播放 Directions 这一部分。很多考生以为这段时间只需要定神静坐，等待正文开始朗读就行了，可恰恰是这段时间，可以帮助很多考生大幅提高听写填空的正确率。考生应始终记得，听写填空部分是中级口译笔试部分的"得分库"。这部分共 20 个空，每个空 1.5 分，共 30 分，因此两个听写填空的得分相当于做对三题听力理解，相当于完整的一句句子翻译，或是半段文章翻译，因此提高该部分的得分意味着提高听力部分的整体得分，进而增加考试通过的可能性。

在听前准备中，考生应完成四大工作，以确保得到高分：

一、掌握主题大意

在打开考卷，阅读听写填空的文章后，考生应立即完成对第一句的语句特征及整体大意的分析。应该说，由于考生在平时的准备中已对快速阅读有了训练，因此在 10 – 15 秒之内对该段的内容大意就能做出判断，比如，到底该段文字是描述事件的记叙文，还是对某一论点所作的评论；他的风格是用词简单平实，还是使用大量形容词进行描绘。而第一句可以马上帮助考生进入对于整体大意的分析。

整体大意分析这一步骤主要是为了通过了解该篇文章的主题，迅速调动考生脑海中和该主题联系较为紧密的相关词汇，从而变被动的接收词汇为主动的挑选词汇。以下段为例：

The development of the Space Shuttle has dramatically reduced the cost of sending loads into space. The Shuttle takes off from Earth _____ (1), and lands again like a huge aircraft. It can transport not only its own _____ (2), but also passengers, and has a huge _____ (3), which is capable of carrying large satellites or a space _____ (4).

在此段中，阅读完第一句后，我们可以马上发现该段的主题是有关 Space Shuttle（宇宙飞船）的，而且该篇内容应该是有关宇宙飞船如何便利了宇宙飞行的一篇记叙文。因此，我们马上想到了和宇宙太空这一专题相关的一些词汇，例如：

astronaut（宇航员）　　　　　the Solar System（太阳系）
rocket（火箭）　　　　　　　　spacecraft（航天器）
ascend（上升）　　　　　　　　descend（降落）
…

这些单词相对来说在日常生活中使用频率较低，我们如果猛一听到，可能会反应迟缓或停顿。但是如果主动回忆起了相关单词，就会大大增强考试时的信心。事实上，上述主动回忆起的单词中超过一半是该篇听写填空中所需要填写的答案。

二、填空内容分析

这一步不仅是听前准备的重要一步，也是保证该部分成功的关键步骤。在这一步中，我们要对听写填空的文章进行通篇略读并对相关空格的内容及其在文章中的格局进行判断推测。

我们通过以下两套考题，详细阐述怎样进行听前准备中的填空内容分析：

As long as we are in a relationship, there is the potential for lasting happiness as well as for serious conflict. This applies at work, _____ (1), and at home. The simple fact is that relationships are not always _____ (2) sailing. Conflict can lead to anger, hostility, and further conflicts. On the other hand, it can be used as _____ (3) for solving problems.

For example, you can handle conflict by _____ (4) that the problem exists, smoothing it over, or trying to overpower the other person. These, of course, will _____ (5) win or lose situations. But when you resolve conflict through collaboration and compromise, you can achieve _____ (6) situations. In today's lecture, I shall outline a few steps on _____ (7) transform a conflict into a solution in which both parties win.

First _____ (8). Explain the problem to the other party. You should _____ (9) the conflict. It's hard to fix something before _____ (10) on what is broken.

Second, understand all points of view. Set aside your own opinions for a moment and _____ (11) to understand the other points of view. When people feel that they have been heard, they're often more _____ (12).

Third, brainstorm solutions. Dream up as many solutions as you can and _____ (13) them one by one. This step will require _____ (14). Talk about which solutions will work and _____ (15) they will be implement. Your solutions need to be acceptable by both parties, so you should be prepared to _____ (16). Later, you'll need to review the _____ (17) of the accepted solution. If it _____ (18), be open to making changes or _____ (19) to bring about a new solution.

Finally, implement. When you both have _____ (20), decide who is going to do what by when.

1. 分析篇章大意：

通过阅读该段文字的第一段，我们可以比较明确地了解，该篇文章是关于如何处理人际关系的。整篇文章的布局在文章开头就提到：As long as we are in a relationship... "只要我们身处各种人际关系之中，就有可能遇到长久快乐和严重冲突。无论你是身处工作、还是家庭都存在这样的问题。事实上，人际关系总不是风平浪静。人际关系中的矛盾不仅会带来敌意和愤怒，更有可能导致进一步的冲突。但是也可以利用其解决问题。"

很明显，下面的文章一定是说明人际关系中的矛盾如何更好地解决。果不其然，第二段通过举例，说明"如果否认问题的存在或单纯地想要压倒对方，只会导致一方的胜利和另一方的失败。但是如果通过合作和妥协解决冲突,你可以获得另一种局面(未知内容,尚未填入)。今天的讲课主要是说明怎样将冲突转化为双赢局面的几个步骤。"

对这一段的分析进一步说明上面的推测是正确的,接下来的第三、第四和第五段按顺序解释了作者介绍的分步解决矛盾的方法。至此,文章的结构清晰地展开为:

人际关系可以使人快乐,也会导致冲突→你的解决方式决定了人际关系处理的结果→作者建议的四步解决人际关系矛盾法

2. 预测空格信息

掌握篇章大意后,对于空格具体内容的预测就相对简单了,在第 1 个空格中,This applies at work, ＿＿＿＿＿(1), and at home. 这句话明确表达了三种地点的并列,且已经叙述的内容分别为工作和家庭,对于大多数人的生活范围来说,我们可以大致预测空格内容为与学习相关的地点表述。而第 2 个空格中应该是对 sailing 这个词的修饰,因此要填入一个形容词。在第 3 个空格中,作者通过 On the other hand 这个词语的使用,清楚地表明接下来的句意与上句中"Conflict can lead to anger, hostility, and further conflicts"的对比转折,因此可以猜测作者想要表达的意思是"Conflict 可以被用来解决问题",因此可以填入的单词包括了 chance, way, measure, opportunity 等等。

在第二段中,作者认为"否认问题的存在＿＿＿＿＿win or lose situations."这里存在一种明确的因果关系,因此在这个空格中可以填入表达因果关系的连接词,这样的词当然存在很多(请见附录句子逻辑关系列表),根据该空格的前后语法分析可以得知,能够填入的词包括 lead to, cause, result in 等。此外,该句后立即跟上的一个 But 提示了我们下一句是对上一句的彻底颠覆,故而当第 6 个空格中又出现对于 situation 的形容时,我们立即可以想到是 win or lose situation 的反面,即我们常见的"win-win"situation。在该段最后一句中,作者陈述"I shall outline a few steps on ＿＿＿＿＿(7) transform a conflict into a solution in which both parties win."根据上下文的连贯性猜词悟意,在这里应填入表示"怎样"转化的词语,例如 the way to, the measure that can, how to, which we can 等等。

其他较易判断的空格包括第 8 个空格中,由于 4 个段落的起始均为动词性词组,因此该空格亦应为动词性词组,并且每段第二句中都对该动词性词组进行详细阐述,因此该段第二句也是说明该步骤的内容——解释问题的存在,根据上述两点可以判断,第 8 个空格中应该填入与"解释问题"语意相近的词组。

答案:

(1) in the classroom   (2) smooth

(3) a powerful opportunity   (4) denying

(5) lead to   (6) win-win

(7) how to   (8) state the problem

(9) clearly define   (10) both of you agree

(11) take the time   (12) willing to listen

(13) evaluate   (14) time and honesty

(15) how difficult　　　　　　(16) make compromise

(17) effectiveness　　　　　　(18) doesn't work

(19) be ready　　　　　　　　(20) agreed on a solution

让我们再来看一篇文章，进一步了解怎样预测空格内容：

Doctors are starting to believe that laughter not only improves your state of mind, but actually affects your entire physical well-being. Britain's first laughter therapist, Robert Holden says: "Instinctively we know that laughing helps us _____(1) and alive. Each time we laugh we feel better and more _____(2)."

A French newspaper found that in 1930 the French laughed _____(3) for nineteen minutes per day. By 1980 this had fallen to _____(4). Eight per cent of the people questioned said that they would like to _____(5). Other research suggests that children laugh on average about _____(6) a day, but by the time they reach _____(7) this has been reduced to about fifteen times. Somewhere in the process of _____(8) we lose an astonishing 385 laughs a day.

William Fry, a psychiatrist from California, studied the _____(9) on the body. He got patients to watch funny films, and monitored their _____(10), heart rate and muscle tone. He found that laughter has a similar effect to _____(11). It speeds up the heart rate, increases blood pressure and quickens breathing. It also makes our _____(12) muscles work. Fry thinks laughter is a type of _____(13) on the spot. Laughter can even provide a kind of _____(14). Fry had proved that laughter produces endorphins-chemicals in the body that relieve pain. Researchers divided _____(15) into four groups. The first group listened to a _____(16) for twenty minutes. The other three groups listened to either an informative tape, or a cassette _____(17) them, or no tape at all. Researchers found that if they produce pain in the students, those who had listened to the humorous tape could _____(18) much longer. Some doctors are convinced that _____(19) should be a part of every medical consultation, as there is evidence to suggest that laughter stimulates the _____(20).

这篇文章的主题十分明确，笑容有益健康，并解释其原理和试验。让我们再试着对第二和第三段的空格进行预测：

刚看到第 3 个空格时，没有人可以知道应该填什么样的内容，没有关系，让我们继续往下看，French laughed for nineteen minutes per day. 而第 4 个空格很明显是对于前一个数字的变化，因为 By 1980 this had fallen to _____，这个数字已经降落到一个更少的数额了。接下来的对比关系立即让我们明白了第 3 个空格中需要填写什么内容，因为 Other research suggest that children laugh on average about _____(6) a day. 在这里，作者将成人与儿童笑的频率进行了比较，因此我们可以大胆推测第 3 个空格中也应填入 on average 这个词。同时，第 6 个空格应该是关于"笑的时间长短"这样的信息，在下一句中，我们得到了具体的提示，but by the time they reach _____(7) this has been reduced to about fifteen times. 很明确，第 6 个空格中应该是"一天笑的次数"。有趣的是，在该段最后一句中，明确表示"Somewhere in the process of _____(8), we lose an astonishing 385 laughs a day."那么 385 加上 15，我们就可以立即填入 400 times，而这个也就是第 6 个空格的内容。

第三段列举了三种笑在人的身体上可能产生的反应，第 10 个空格需要考生填入其中的一种，而在下一句中，文章写道"It speeds up the heart rate, increases blood pressure and quickens breathing." Breathing 明显是 muscle tone 的一种表现形式，heart rate 已经出现，那么在空格中就应该填入 blood pressure 一词。而第 16 个空格前的 listen to 一词框定了后面可填的内容，我们常用的 listen to 的内容无非是 radio, program, 或者 tape 和 cassette. 而第 17 个空格前的内容印证了只有 tape/cassette 才是正确答案。与此同时，cassette 作为一个较容易拼错的单词，如果考生在考试时提前发现下文的提示，可以避免在听写时过分紧张而影响情绪。

我们可以发现，当提前阅读一篇听写填空文章时，可以根据文章上下文的连贯性和平行性(coherence and parallel)，语义的一致性(consistency)，语法规则的准确性(accuracy)，并熟练利用排比、转折、因果等句子和文章关系，对于空格内容的各种可能性进行预测和排除，直至篇章完善。

答案：

(1) feel healthy   (2) content

(3) on average   (4) six minutes

(5) laugh more   (6) four hundred times

(7) adulthool   (8) growing up

(9) effects of laughter   (10) blood pressure

(11) physical exercises   (12) facial and stomach

(13) jogging   (14) pain relief

(15) forty university students   (16) funny cassette

(17) intended to relax   (18) tolerate the discomfort

(19) humour   (20) immune system

请完成下列真题，进一步练习词语预测的能力：

1. The Conservative and Labour Parties have controlled _____(1) for the last fifty years, but today neither party can any longer be sure from which class or _____(2) its support will come. Not long ago you _____(3) the working classes always to vote for the Labour Party. The word "labour" means "hard work"—especially hard work _____(4). The Labour Party is the party which is supposed _____(5) the "working man." You would also have expected the _____(6) classes to vote for the Conservative Party. The word "conservative" means "keeping things"_____(7). The Conservative Party is supposed to be the party which represents _____(8), businessmen and the self-employed. In some respects traditional British "class distinctions" are becoming _____(9), and you can be less sure how people will vote. Many members of the middle class _____(10)

答案：

(1) the political scene   (2) income group

(3) would have expected   (4) with the hands

(5) to represent   (6) upper and middle

(7) as they are   (8) property owners

(9) less clear   (10) support social reform

2. ... The reason for this is that computers cannot think as _____ (4) . For example, imagine that a computer is given the information that _____ (5) has four legs and that a dog has four legs. The machine might well _____ (6) when producing a list of suggested living-room and dining-room furniture.

But today, groups of _____ (7) in the United States, Japan and Europe _____ (8) a new type of computer. These new models will be incapable of making such _____ (9).

Instead of being programmed with lots of unrelated _____ (10), the new computers will contain knowledge of subjects that are _____ (11). The machines will then _____ (12) items of information, and will be able to reject conclusions that do not _____ (13).

These new computers will already know that dogs are animals that _____ (14), bark, wag their tails and chase other animals. By comparing _____ (15) with features of living-room and dining-room furniture, the computer will conclude that a dog is an _____ (16).

Even a present-day computer could _____ (17) if given enough information and enough time. But it has to consider _____ (18) one at a time before selecting the best. This means that it would _____ (19) for even the most powerful computer to reach a _____ (20).

答案：

...   (4) human

(5) a table   (6) include a dog

(7) computer scientists   (8) are working on

(9) simple mistakes   (10) pieces of information

(11) related   (12) compare and contrast

(13) make any sense   (14) eat bones

(15) this knowledge   (16) inappropriate selection

(17) make this choice   (18) alternative solutions

(19) take days   (20) simple conclusion

三、标注段前段后空格

在考试时，考生往往会发现这样的问题，好不容易把一个空格中的单词全部填出，继续往下听的时候却发现已经漏掉了下一个空格中要填的内容。而且这样的现象往往出现在两段互相衔接的地方。例如：

. . . the other is the pure joy of physical exhilaration which is part and parcel of every trek or
_____ (6). If we fail to exploit both _____ (7), we are the losers.

While enjoying the former, we have moved into the realms of the latter _____ (8).

在这篇文章中,第6、7和第8个空格紧密相连,留给我们反应的时间非常之短,因此这类空格也是考生大量失分的地方。

> 考生需要在听前阅读的过程中,对于段落衔接处出现多个空格相连的情况,及时作出明显的标记,以便提醒自己在听到上一段结尾的地方,尽量利用缩写或其他的方式尽快记录完前一个空格,并将注意力立即转移到下一个空格的内容上。

再以下一段落为例:

. . . Shuttle flight, stay as long as necessary, and then return at his or her _____.
It is difficult to imagine the _____ created by the Shuttle.

这两个空格之间的间隔是非常之短的,在当年的考试中,大多数考生都完全没能记录或无法记录完整后一个空格的内容。如果掌握了上述方法,利用阅读时做出的显著提醒标记,则在听该段落时我们已经准备好利用缩写,简写等方式快速记录前一个空格,当听到 convenience 一词后,可将其缩写为 cv 或 conv,之后,注意力立即转移到后一个空格上。

四、了解空前空后单词

很多考生在考试的时候很紧张,始终绷着一根弦,因此在听写的时候,坚持认为能够记下越多单词越好,一旦空格出现,即飞快填入所听到的 3~5 个单词,等到写完往下看时,却又发现空格后已经印出了填写的最后几个单词,不仅让人觉得懊恼,也浪费了时间。为了避免这种情况,

> 我们应该利用阅读的机会,大致了解每个空格,特别是第一段中的每个空格,之后的第一个单词,从而避免重复填词。这不仅节省了考生的脑力,同时也节约了时间。

除此以外,有些考生还存在这样的情况:在辛辛苦苦地填完所听到的内容后,突然发现找不到文章念到哪里了。等到找到当前正在朗读的内容后,发现已经遗漏了一个或两个空格的内容。要解决这个问题,

> 我们也需要在阅读时了解空格前的一个单词,这个单词会起到警示音的作用,即使你找不到现在读到哪里了,如果你听到空格前的单词,就能立即帮助你排除杂念,记录所听到的内容而非继续盲目地在文章的内容中寻找当前句。

第二节　听写填空

在听写填空测试的过程中,我们应始终掌握"精听速记"的原则。一般来说,两个空格之间的间隙应相当于中上水平,拼写速度稍快的考生应该能在有效时间内填写完整个空格内容,因此不必过分担忧时间来不及的问题。

相反,被很多人忽略但又很重要的问题是:一旦一个空格的内容没有完全听清或听不懂,就开始手足无措,或是在填写空格的时候发现单词的拼写卡壳了,就死盯着这个空格不放。这两种情况都可能会导致下一个空格的听写失败,严重的还会导致整个听写填空部分的失败。

因此,考生应特别注意:

> 当一个空格播报完,已经过渡到了下一个空格的范围内时,如果前一个空还未填完,就暂时放弃它或利用速记的方法快速记录,集中精力转入下一个空。等到全文听写完毕后,再将前一个空的内容补充完整。换句话说,前一个空格的内容填写不出,已经少了 1.5 分,如果再因此影响了下一个空格的填写,真的是顾此失彼,两头不着杠。

在平时的练习中,我们在记单词,特别是字母较多的单词的时候,应该采取一些速记的方法。绝大多数人没有接受过速记训练,仅仅为了参加中级口译考试而专门进行专业速记的训练也没有什么必要。我们这里所说的速记,指的是使用一些固定的词头或缩略语,甚至使用自己独特的符号等,起到记录内容、提示自己的作用。找到适合自己的速记方式需要大量的练习。我们在下面列举了一些方法,供大家参考:

怎样使用缩略表示

英语当中缩略词使用的频率很高,如 IMP: important, ASAP: as soon as possible。很显然如果能熟练掌握缩略词,会对考试大有裨益。

当然,简单记忆缩略词和他们所代表的单词意义不大,因为这样的词不一定能在考试时出现在你的即时反应中,因此,掌握以下的四种方式可能更为有利:

☞　拿掉所有元音

MKT:	market	MGR:	manager
MSG:	message	STD:	standard
RCV:	receive		

☞　保留前几个字母

INFO	information	INS	insurance
EXC	exchange	IOU	I owe you

I/O   In stead of

☞ 保留开头和结尾几个发音字母

WK   week   RM   room

PL   people

☞ 根据发音

R   are   THO   though

THRU   through

根据上述规则，考生可参考下表，找出最适合自己的速记方式：

缩略词	原词	缩略词	原词
APT	apartment	ACC	accountant
ACDG	according	ACPT	accept
AD	advertisement	ADS	address
ADV	advice	AMAP	as much/many as possible
AMT	amount	APV	approve
ASAP	as soon as possible	BAL	balance
BLDG	building	CERT	certificate
CFM	conform	CNCL	cancel
CNF	conference	CMI	commission
CMP	complete	CMPE	compete/competitive
CMU	communication	CONC	concern/concerning/concerned
COND	condition	CO.	company
DEPT	department	DISC	discount
DPT	departure	EXCH	exchange
EXPLN	explain	EXT	extent
FLT	flight	FNT	final
FRT	freight	FYR	for your reference
GD	good	GUAR	guarantee
H.O.	home office	INFO	information
IMPS	impossible	IMP(T)	important
INCD	include	INDIV	individual
INS	insurance	INTST	interested
I/O	in stead of	IOU	i owe you
IVO	in view of	MANUF	manufacture
MDL	model	MEMO	memorandum
MGR	manager	MIN	minimum
MKT	market	MSG	message
NCRY	necessary	NLT	no later than
OBS	observe	OBT	obtain
ORD	ordinary	PAT	patent

缩略词	原　　词	缩略词	原　　词
PC	piece	PKG	packing
PL	people	PLS	please
POSN	position	POSS(BL)	possible
PROD	product	QLTY	quality
QUTY	quantity	RCV	receive
REF	reference	REGL	regular
REP	representative	RESN	reservation
RPT	repeat	RESPON	responsible
SEC	section	SITN	situation
STD	standard	TEL	telephone
TEMP	temporary	TGP	telegraph
THO	though	TKS	thanks
TRD	trade	TRF	traffic
TTL	total	U	you
UR	your	WK	week
WL	will	WT	weight
XL	extra large		

　　在这里举出的例子仅仅是较常出现的一小部分词语，考生应在平时的练习中注意总结，并经常对其含义进行记忆，以免出现在考试时使用了一种速记方法记下一个单词，却在事后检查希望补充完整时发现完全无法回想出该缩写所对应的单词。

　　除此以外，希望考生在听写填空内容播放的过程中，

> 放弃希望从头到尾听全并理解整篇文章内容的想法。听懂并理解该篇文章的内容并不是这类题型的要求。我们需要做到的只是在听写过程中，听懂并填出空格所在句的内容。在听写的同时，我们无法也没有必要去听懂没有空格的那些句子在说些什么。如果努力要抓住所有内容，只会让自己过分紧张。

第三节　听后检查

　　听后检查在中级口译的听写填空中不仅非常必要，而且是必须的一项内容。考纲明确指出需要考查考生的笔录及准确拼写等能力，对于填写内容是否能够准确拼写并最终得分就需要依靠听后检查这一工作加以保证了。但是听后检查也不仅仅局限于拼写这一项内容。很多考生通过听后三分钟的全面检查，捡回了很多分数，包括书写太过潦草，漏词错词，忘记大写，等等。

> 根据我们对于高频考点的总结，在听后检查中，考生必须完成对七大重点的总结，以确保得到高分。

一、漏词

因为每个空格的内容并不只是一个单词，往往可多至 3 至 4 个单词，而这些单词也不全部是实义的名词、动词或形容词等，因此很容易发生一些漏词的现象。考生需要利用自己的语法知识及词汇储备，及时发现这类问题，并补充所漏的单词。

例如：

The professor had urged the student to _____ today.

当考生听到录音时，明确听到的是 finish 一词，但是如果我们直接将 finish 一词填入，就会产生问题：当 finish 一词后不跟所指代的对象时，可以表示该人"完蛋了"，当然，这个教授不会让他的学生都完蛋了，因此，finish 在这里应该使用它的及物用法，即在 finish 一词后面加入 it 一词，表示"完成工作"的意思。那么为什么 it 一词在听力原文中完全听不到呢？这是因为 it 一词与前面的 finish 和后面的 today 一词分别发生了连读和失爆现象，当读到该词时，我们只听到了停顿一拍，而没有听到确实的单词，因此造成了漏词。但值得庆幸的是，按照语法规则，通过对该空格内容的检查，我们可以找到这个潜在的漏词。

> 除了这种由于特殊语言现象造成的漏词外，其他漏词的情况还包括：
> - 在名词前遗忘弱读的定冠词 a 或 the；
> - 遗漏如 at, out, on, in, to 等加在名词之后的介词；
> - 遗忘代词，如 it 等。
>
> 通过语法和考生语感的检验，我们可以顺利完成查出漏词的任务。

二、拼写错误

由于所给记录的时间太过仓促，可能会造成单词的拼写错误，

> 考生应将所填所有空格内的单词进行核对，特别是那些较长和较生疏的单词。

例如，在单词中，何时使用双写，何时使用 ie 而不是 ei，还有一些意义相近容易混拼的单词，都是需要特别注意的地方。

很多考生在日常生活中很少手写英语单词，大多通过电脑输入。如果使用电脑输入英文文章，在拼写错误的单词下通常会主动显示拼错的内容，提示使用者进行修改，不仅如此，电脑还具备自动更正的功能。这的确省了很多检查的功夫，但是当你参加中级口译考

试时,并不存在这一条自动浮现、提示出错的红线,因此我们需要在平时少用或不用电脑提示的自动更正,而更多地通过培养自己视觉识错的能力,找出自己容易出错的高频点,严加注意。

下列单词为经常出现且容易拼错的考点,包括(划线部分为通常拼错的部分):

accidentally	license
accommodate	judgment(请对比 management / arrangement /
acknowledge	acknowledgement)
acquire	lightning
acquaintance	maintenance
amateur	maneuver
apparent	millennium
calendar	miniature
category	neighbour
changeable	noticeable
collectible	occasionally
column	occurrence
committed	pastime
conscience	perseverance
conscious	possession
consensus	preferable
discipline	precede(请对比 succeed 和 supersede 二词)
embarrass(ment)	principal / principle
experience	privilege
explanation	pronunciation
foreign	questionnaire
fulfill	recommend
guaranee	ridiculous
harass	remembrance
hierarchy	referred / retcrral
humorous	restaurant
ignorance	schedule
immediate	their / they're / there
indispensable	threshold
intelligence	twelfth
its / it's	vacuum
jewelry	weird
leisure	

希望考生不仅能准确拼写上表单词，还应多做总结，增加经常易拼错的单词，以进一步提高。

> 临场检查拼错单词的另一个小窍门就是在检查时从右往左按音节倒过来进行拼写，并和第一次所拼写的单词进行核对。当然，如果在平时练习时，不能注意到一些常错的单词，倒过来正过去拼一百遍也是没有用的，呵呵。

三、大小写

检查单词的大小写首先想到的是专有名词的大写。专有名词包括人名、地名、国家名、组织名、机构名，等等，此外可能出现的还包括书名的大写、节日名称首字母大写及最容易疏忽的句首大写。

因为大家对于常见的专有名词大写应较为熟悉，在此仅提出值得注意的一些特殊要点：

1. 节日：

(1) 多个单词组成的节日名称需要将每一个单词的首字母大写，如 April Fool's Day，Children's Day，National Day，等等。

(2) 勿将一个节日名称拆为两个部分，如 Thanksgiving → Thanks-giving 或 Thanks Giving

(3) 如节日名称的首字母大小写较为相近，请务必明确表示大写的方式，以免阅卷老师在无法辨认清晰的情况下，将该格分数扣去，这样的单词可能包括有 Christmas，Valentine's Day，Spring Festival，Lantern Festival，等等。

2. 政治特殊词汇

中级口译考试较为喜欢出与政治、经济类相关的文章，因此注意一些政治特殊词汇的首字母大写也是十分有必要的，例如：

(1) 政党名称和特殊团体名称需要大写，例如：the Trade Unions，the Conservative Party，the Labour Party

(2) 政治专门词汇在被特定化后需要大写，例如：Bill，First Reading，the Parliament，Congress 等等。

(3) 人物的职务放在人名前时，需要大写，例如：Premier Zhu，President Hu

由于中级口译的听写填空需要将最终答案填写在答卷纸上，因此很容易忽视大写的句首字母。为避免这种情况的出现，同时也为了避免在答卷纸上进行反复涂改造成阅卷时的不当扣分，大家可以在做听写填空时，首先将内容填写在空格内或空格上方，在最后完成后统一搬移到答卷纸上。这样做有几个好处：

第一，不会遗漏空格或填错格；

第二，不用反复于试卷与答题卷中，免去眼光腾挪的过程，节约时间；

第三，避免了在答卷纸上填写完上一个空格后，找不到下一个空格方位的情况出现；

最后,可以及时发现需要大写的句首字母。

四、同音/近音但异形/异义

由于大量英语单词发音相近或相同,在听力考试中容易引起理解错误,这需要考生平时多积累,也需要对于词义进行准确把握,因为即使读音完全一致,如果考生完全了解一词的含义,就可以根据上下文的内容排除错误单词项。我们曾在语音一章中举出了很多例子。

> 熟悉常见同音/近音单词,将帮助考生在遇到这样情况时,通过对于上下文的理解,判断出正确的单词。在听写填空部分中,由于给予考生反应的时间较短,因此无需过分拘泥于听到的是相同发音中的哪一个单词,记录中只需将所听到的单词记下,即使搞错了,在听写短文朗读完毕后的 3 分钟间隙中,可以根据上下文的意思理解进行订正,从而保证答案的正确性。

五、时态及语法

考生应检查所写内容的词法和句法等结构是否符合英语时态及语法规则。例如,动词第三人称单数,过去时及非谓语动词形式等。需要注意的考点包括:

(1) 非谓语动词形式要注意经常发生的单词音节弱读和失爆,这往往具有极高的欺骗性,需要小心;

(2) 动词与 to 联系使用时,注意该动词是否应根据该篇文字的总体时态使用 -ed 形式。因为在很多情况下,动词 -ed 形式与 to 的结合导致了 -ed 不发音,从而迷惑了考生;

(3) 第三人称单数的动词要记得加上 -s;

(4) 如果发生助动词或情态动词的连读,应根据上下文的时态将其表现出来,例如:they've,I'd rather,you'd better,he's fine,等等。

对于最后的通篇检查来说,十分有必要根据全文所用的时态来判断空格内单词的正确形式。要记住,凡是所写的句子加入空格单词后在语法上明显有错误的,一定是空格内的单词发生了差错,因此考生可根据已经掌握的语法知识,适时修改。

> 注意:如无法判断空格的时态,可根据听写填空段落的第一句话的时态来判断,所有听写填空段落的第一句话都无空格,属于时态的标志。

六、单复数

单复数是很多人刚刚开始接触英文时就已经掌握的内容,在此不再赘述。但是在中级口译中,需要注意以下三个问题:

● 常考名词的不规则单复数变化;

- 单复数形式分别表示不同内容；
- 通常／必须以复数形式出现的名词。

1. 常用的单复数特殊变化，例如：

这类不规则变化的名词很多，不胜枚举，考生可以通过阅读各类语法书中名词一章相关内容加深印象。

单 数	复 数	单 数	复 数
Photo	Photos	Piano	Pianos
Tomato	Tomatoes	Hero	Heroes
Mouse	Mice	German	Germans
Species	Species(单复数同形)	Basis	Bases
Emphasis	Emphases	Phenomenon	Phenomena
Medium	Media	Criterion	Criteria

2. 单数和复数名词分别表示不同内容

分清这部分名词单复数所分别代表的含义不仅能在听写填空中起到很大的作用，还能在 statement(单句理解) 和 listening and translation(听译) 部分起到极大的作用，例如 premise 这个词，单数形式出现时，往往表示前提的意思：

The premise for me to accept this offer is to give me a satisfying salary.

(我接受这个工作的前提是给我满意的薪水。)

而 premises 较多地用来表示场地、房屋。例如中级口译的 sentence translation 曾经考过下面这一句：

As he intended to expand his shop, he made an offer for the premises next door.

译句：他希望扩大店铺(的规模)，所以出价购买隔壁的房屋。

如果我们拘泥于 premise 单数的常用含义而忽视了对其复数形式不同含义的理解，根本就无法翻译出上面那句话。

让我们共同来记忆以下较为常用的单复数异义名词：

advice	忠告	advices	消息
ash	灰烬	ashes	骨灰
authority	权威	authorities	当局
blue	蓝色	Blues	忧郁
colour	颜色	colours	旗帜
content	容量，内容	contents	目录
compass	罗盘	compasses	圆规
custom	习惯，风俗	customs	海关，关税
experience	经验	experiences	经历
force	力	forces	军队，兵力

green	绿色	greens	蔬菜
ground	土地	grounds	根据,理由
iron	铁	irons	镣铐
letter	信,字母	letters	文学
manner	方式	manners	礼貌
minute	分钟	minutes	会议记录
pain	痛苦	pains	辛苦,努力
oil	油	oils	油画
premise	前提	premises	房屋
sand	沙	sands	沙滩
spectacle	景象	spectacles	眼镜
step	步骤,脚步	steps	台阶
time	时间	times	时代
troop	群,队	troops	军队
water	水	waters	水域,海洋
work	工作	works	工厂

3. 通常/必须以复数形式出现的名词

考生应明确一些特殊的名词通常或必须以复数形式出现,因此在拼写时应该及时加上表示复数的 -s,例如 scissors, trousers, pants, glasses, spectacles, make friends, clap/shake hands, take turns, congratulations, make repairs,以及 the Olympic Games 等。

七、听不懂/听不清的单词

相信这部分内容也是很多考生极其关心的话题。每次在考试过程中,似乎总有那么几个空格中的某个单词无法清楚听到,或是完全听不懂它的内容。考生往往会为此紧张,进而又使得更多的内容听不进去或听后面的内容时,反复回想刚才所听到的东西,这样就会造成恶性循环,而使听力总体成绩受到影响。

其实,在听的过程中,单词听不清或听不懂是肯定有的现象,关键在于怎样使用一定的技巧解决这个问题。

我们应该将听不清或者听不懂单词分为两种情况,即:

- 听者所听到的单词实际并非生词,而是由于语速、连读、失爆等现象使该词对于听者变得模糊,从而产生理解障碍。但是一旦将该词写出,听者能立即反应出正确的意义。

- 所听到的单词听者完全不认识,即使将该词以书面形式写出,听者也无法回忆或完全陌生。

解决这两种情况的方式其实完全相同。在听到一个不熟悉的单词时,不要暂停默写的过程,苦苦思索该词的来龙去脉,也不要立即放弃该格的填写,转攻下一个空。我们可以试着根据该词的发音,快速写下该词的音标或利用常用的拼写形式代表该单词的发音。

写下该词的发音后,不应再眷恋于此空格,而应立即转向下一个填空。在整段听写完成后,考生可再回到该格,根据以往掌握的构词知识和刚才所遗留的读音拼写,试用最常用的字母组合根据读音规则拼写出这个单词。

如果属于第一种情况,那么在大多数情形下,完成这一步后,已经能够根据上下文的意思回忆起该词的含义和正确拼写。

但是如果属于第二种情况,那么考生更应放手一博。如果放弃拼写这个单词,则分数一定被扣,如果试着使用常用的拼写,可能倒会猜中正确答案。

例如:

Some doctors are convinced that _____ (19) should be a part of every medical consultation, as there is evidence to suggest that laughter stimulates the _____ (20).

在第 20 个空格中,应该填入 immune system,而这个 immune(免疫力)并不是一个常用的单词,因此很多考生在听到该单词后一时反应不出,便苦苦思索,但最后不但没能写出该单词,也耽误前文的检查工作。其实,如果在听写时一旦发现这种情况,就可以立即根据读音规则拼写出 imun,且根据"i 后面的 m 经常双写"和"元音发长音代表开音节"等规律,可以拼写出正确答案 immune。

综上所述,我们只要能够遵循:

听前准备——四大工作:预览全文内容,掌握文章大意,预测空格信息,语意猜词造句

听时记录——精听速记:辨听诵读信息,快速反应默写

听后检查——七个重点:遵循语法检查,适当运用想像

就能在最后达到完善全文内容,成功取得听写填空部分高分的目的。

第三章　听 力 理 解

听力理解 (Listening Comprehension) 为中级口译听力考试的第二大部分，该题型共 30 道题，每题 1 分，共 30 分，占听力总分的三分之一。

听力理解部分对于中级口译考生的要求是：
(a) 能逐句理解，听懂说话者的主要含意。
(b) 能听懂交际场合中各种英语会话和讲话。
(c) 能听懂诸如政治、经济、文化教育、语言文学、科普方面的一般性讲座等。
(d) 能听懂同样题材的广播或电视短篇。

根据上述考纲要求，我们可以发现，对于不同题材的听力材料，实际考查考生的能力要求是不一样的。对于交际场合——也就是普通人日常交往的场景——中级口译不仅要求考生能够听懂所有的对话内容，也就是能够彻底了解讲话者或对话双方的含义，而且要求考生能够理解说话者某些没有直接使用语言表达，但通过语调、对比及反问等隐含的语意。这类题材考察的题型多种多样，不仅要求考生了解宏观的主题，还要考生掌握具体的细节。考点分布十分散落，使得考生防不胜防。

与此相比，对于政治、经济、文化教育、语言文学、科普等专业领域的考查难度就相对较低了。以中、高级口译考试都较常出现的政治经济类文章来说，文章本身逻辑清晰，条理分明，总体选用单词难度适中，考点一般均为文章当中的直接信息，无需考生过多猜测作者的态度或喜恶。在这类文章中，通常令考生望而生畏的是大量不了解的专业知识和专业词汇。

中级口译考试希望通过该部分的考查，最终达到测试考生通过听力理解获取信息的能力。

听力理解部分所有试题均为选择题，每一节听力材料后有一至数道选择题，每道选择题后有 15～18 秒的间隙。要求考生从试卷给出的四个选择项中选出一个最佳答案。录音语速为每分钟 150 词左右。听力材料有单句，也有讲话、对话（采访）、广播、讲座等类型。根据听力材料的不同，听力理解部分中有两种不同的题型：

- 单句理解（Statement）：单句长度为 20 词左右，结构上不超过两个分句，例如两个简单句或主句与从句。要求考生在听完一句录音后，在提供的四句句子中选出与所听到的句子意思最为接近的一句。
- 篇章理解（Talks and Conversation）：在这一部分中，顾名思义，共有两大类型的篇章，一种为讨论某一专题或题目的对话，难度适中，内容题材与日常生活、工作或学习有关，尤为多见的是学生之间或同事间有关学业、业余爱好及工作内容的相互讨论。第二大类文章为讲话、讲座，内容为演讲者或教师就某一科普或社会专题所作的一段讲话。这类篇章内容多种多样，我们会在下文中对其进行总体分类，逐个击破。

以下，让我们就单句理解和篇章理解两种题型分别讲解考题分类、常考考点、攻题技巧及必备知识要点。

第一节 单句理解

单句理解部分共 10 题，每题 1 分，共 10 分。该种题型在平时的各类考试中较为少见，因此许多考生在刚刚接触该种题型时，觉得无从下手。让我们首先来看一下做题要求：

Statements

Directions: In this part of the test, you will hear several short statements. These statements will be spoken only once, and you will not find them written on the paper; so you must listen carefully. When you hear a statement, read the answer choices and decide which one is closest in meaning to the statement you have heard. Then write the letter of the answer you have chosen in the corresponding space in your ANSWER BOOKLET.

在本题型中，每个单句只读一遍，理解该句意思后，在答卷所提供的四个选项中选出与所听到的句子意思最为接近的一句。

> 换句话说，statement 这种题型不仅考验了考生的听力理解能力，还考查了 paraphrase 的能力，也就是即时对英语语意进行同义置换的能力。

让我们举一个例子，开始熟悉这种题型：

I can't imagine why Paul hasn't arrived for the meeting. He was due to be here before now.

(A) I know why Paul hasn't arrived although he was due earlier.

(B) I can't understand why Paul is here.

(C) Paul is due to pay for the meal ticket.

(D) I don't know why Paul is late for the meeting.

在考生听到的听力原文中 I can't imagine why Paul hasn't arrived for the meeting 实际上

体现了说话人的一种埋怨,而非真正的无法想像,也就是"我真不知道 Paul 怎么会迟到"。然后说话人进一步表述"他早就该到了"。将原句与四个答案比较,(A) 选项虽然表述了 Paul 早该到但未到这层意思,但却误加"我已经知道原因",因此是错误的答案。(B)选项错误,因为说话人无法理解"Paul 为什么在这里",明显与原句意思相悖。(C)选项出现了完全无关的信息 meal ticket(饭票),天知道这个词是从哪里来的,可能是出题人出到该题时肚子饿了,因此认为考生可能会将 meeting 一词误听为 meal ticket,当然,我们是绝不会上当的。由此,只有(D)才可能是正确的答案"我不知道为什么 Paul 开会迟到"。

通过对于上题的分析,我们可以发现,

> 只要能在 4 个选项中发现一个与原句最为接近的句子,就是我们应该选择的正确答案。需要指出的是,正确答案中并不需要包括原句中的所有信息,只要这个句子与原句的意思不相违背,并在 4 个选项中与该句最为接近(即使只是一部分),它就是正确的。

让我们来看这个例子:

The editor in chief called in question the accuracy of the figures in the draft report of the financial news.

(A) The editor didn't know that the figures were accurate.

(B) The editor expressed doubt about the accuracy of the figures.

(C) The editor questioned the reporter about the accuracy of his article.

(D) The editor had telephoned someone and requested for a draft report.

首先我们可以发现,在 4 个选项中,都省略了原句有关主语的部分信息,将 editor in chief(主编)改为 editor(编辑),但是这并不影响句子的意思表述。第二,原句中的 financial news(财经新闻)在答案中也消失得无影无踪。但是,我们仍然能够很快的选出正确答案,因为该句的考点为 call in question 这个词组,下文中只有 express doubt 可以表示"质疑"的含义。正确答案正是(B)。有些考生错选了(A),请注意"不知道数字是否准确"和"对数字的准确性提出怀疑"是有区别的两个概念。

通过上面两道例题的练习,大家应该对于 Statement 这种题型有所了解。同时不知考生是否发现一个特点:在该题型中,4 个选项都很冗长,通常达到每句 10 个单词左右,加在一起就意味着考生在两个单句理解的 15~18 秒的间隙中,需要阅读约 40 个单词并做出正确选择,时间看来并不充裕。更要命的是,这 40 个单词所组成的 4 个句子还会有各种意思上的重复,如果考试时不是神清目爽,很有可能就被灌了"迷魂汤",选不出隐藏在里面的正确答案。因此,首先让我们来学习一下怎样阅读 Statement 部分的选项。

一、选项阅读

选项是听力信息的重要体现,因而也是我们重要的信息来源。我们通过对选项的提前阅读、解析和思考，就能提前了解听力内容，从而在聆听过程中抓住重点。那么，应该怎样进行选项的阅读呢？

1. 时机把握

大家都知道，单句理解的 directions 要求考生等到单句朗读完毕后，再读四个选项，然后决定哪一个是正确答案。对于有的人来说，这样没有什么问题，但是对大部分人来说，如果这样做题，即使学习了再多技巧，如果时间不够，用不上的话，对于解题已经是没有意义了。因此我们要先读选项，然后听题，继而直接选出正确答案，这样的做题方式我们称之为"逆向判断"。

2. 解题步骤

- 当录音中开始播放 Directions 时，就立即开始阅读第一题的 4 个选项，阅读时注意搜索 4 个选项中共同的人名、地点、时间、动作等。这些共同信息将对你的听力理解有所帮助，你甚至可以通过反复出现的共同信息开始拼凑可能出现的听力单句。

□ [技巧提醒 1:注意及时圈出选项中的互异信息和惟一信息]

- 当单句开始播放时，立即停止看题，集中精力聆听录音。

- 单句播放完毕后，根据在第一步中所听到的内容以及圈出的特异信息，迅速找到正确答案，进行选择。

□ [技巧提醒 2:如果无法当场选出正确答案或在两个内容中徘徊，应该立即完成两项工作:

　　◇ 排除肯定错误的选项，提高选中正确答案的概率。

　　◇ 简单记下所听到的肯定正确的信息，等到整个单句理解部分完成或整个听力部分播放完毕后，再回过来选出答案。此时虽然已经过去了一些时间，但由于已经排除了肯定错误选项，又有笔记的提醒，可以充分利用再次选择的机会]

□ [切忌:反复纠缠于一题，会延误下一个步骤的进行]

- 快速填写答题纸或在答卷上圈出正确答案，回到上述第一步，开始阅读下一题的选项。

使用这种"逆向判断"的好处是，一方面你能够及时得到与对话内容有关的线索，同时，在大量的阅读练习中所培养的快速扫视和归纳能力可以帮助你熟悉可能听到的单词或意群，从而用阅读能力加强听力能力。第三，能够帮助你及时找到需要听到的重点，从而减少考试时的焦虑急躁。

可能有的人会问:这么长的选项，即使采用了上述做题的方式，似乎还是来不及，那应该怎么办呢？

要解决这样的问题，就需要使用阅读时的三大法宝:

第一，纵向而非横向。 在冗长的选项中，有很多共同的信息，而这些相同的信息在各个句子中所处的位置也大致相同，通过纵向的快速扫描，考生可以在 1 秒钟，甚至更短的时间内寻找到即将出现的单句的有关线索。这样阅读，速度比横向理解快得多。

第二，重复需要记忆。在四个选项中的反复重复信息需要进行短时记忆，因为这些重复信息一定是单句中的某个部分，所以提前熟悉并记忆可以帮助你主动辨认单句的各个成分。

第三，区别一定标明。注意各个选项中的主要区别。在每个选项中，都会出现一些不同的名字，地点或者不同的动词。这些不同之处就是你在听的时候需要张大耳朵，一字不漏的地方——也就是该句的重点。同时非常重要的一点是：如果你在某个选项中发现了和另外三个选项中完全无关的信息，而该信息属于句子中的主要成分，并且在单句中也出现了该特异信息，则我们可以毫不犹豫的排除该选项，原理很简单：出题人一定想把选项隐藏的越深越好，如果在原句中出现了一个特殊信息，而该信息只在某一选项中出现，那么不用理解整句句子，仅凭突然蹦出的一个单词就可以选出答案，怎么能够体现考查的目的呢？用句俗话说，这种做题的方法就是"听到什么，不选什么"。

为了掌握上述方法，让我们来看个例子：

(A) Mr. Johnson lied.

(B) Mr. Johnson admitted he had lied.

(C) Mr. Johnson denied that he had lied.

(D) Mr. Johnson insisted that he had not murdered the liar.

首先，纵向扫描发现单句的主语必定是 Mr. Johnson，然后争论的焦点就是他有没有撒谎。相信这一点大家都能判断出来。然后我们突然发现，在(D)选项中出现了一个特殊的信息 "murder"，这个血腥的词在前面 3 个词中间都没有出现，让我们对它心存怀疑，当听到原句：

"Mr. Johnson insisted that he hadn't lied about his whereabouts the night of the murder."

哈！我们又再次听到了这个 murder，立即毫不犹豫的在 D 选项上画个大叉，如果这就是正确答案，岂不是小看了我们的智慧？而通过理解单句中的 insisted...not lied 我们可以判断出该题的正确答案是(C)。

好了，既然我们对于选项的阅读已经有所掌握，下面让我们进入 Statement 的题型分类讲解。

二、单句理解分类讲解

无论是 1997 年首次中级口译考试的听力真题，还是最近的一次考试，单句理解中都有一些反复出现的题型，掌握这些题型对于这个部分的成功与否起着至关重要的作用。以下总结的八大题型是需要考生所必须要掌握的。不夸张地说，考试时，如果你已经对这八大类题型滚瓜烂熟，那么到时候你只需要守株待兔，对号入座就可以了。

1. 虚拟语气题型

虚拟语气绝对是单句理解的常青考点，每次考试至少有一题虚拟语气的理解，例如：

If you had consulted with the board of advisors, you wouldn't have started the dress code campaign in the company.

(A) I think you should have talked to your advisors.

(B) I'm interested in your advisors' cocktail party.

(C) I wonder if you have finished with your champion.

(D) I'm curious to know why you haven't been consulted.

原句的意思是"如果你和顾问商量过的话,就不会在公司里搞这个活动了。"而它背后的含义是,你没问,你搞了这个活动(现在出问题了。在下面的 4 个选项中,(A) 选项中的 should have done sth. 表示了该做而没做,因此这个就是正确答案。

再看一题:

If I knew Peter's telephone number, I wouldn't have to write this letter.

(A) I don't have a telephone.

(B) I don't have to write Peter a letter.

(C) I don't know Peter's telephone number.

(D) I know Peter's telephone number, but not his address.

原句的意思是"如果我知道 Peter 的电话号码,我就不用写这封信了。"背后的含义是:我不知道 Peter 的电话号码,信我也写了。正确答案是哪一个呢? 就是(C)选项:我不知道 Peter 的电话号码。

两题做完,大家一定觉得很没劲,为什么? 这种题型太简单了!

永远的一个固定结构:

"*If (somebody) did / had done something, somebody wouldn't do / have done something.* "

　　而正确的答案呢? 就是"反向选择",即从相反的角度来理解整个句子表达的意思,换言之,就是对于条件句中听到的信息反着说,将单句中的字面意思进行否定,并且正确答案往往有个标志:一般表现为否定句形式。

举个例子:

这一次让我们先看这 4 个选项:

(A) I knew Smith wanted to sell his computer, but I didn't buy it.

(B) I didn't buy Smith's computer, because I didn't know he would sell it.

(C) I bought the computer without knowing it was Smith's.

(D) I'll buy the computer as soon as Smith decides to sell it.

如果我只告诉你原句是一句虚拟语气的句子,你能选出正确答案吗? 当然了! 很明显,(B) 就是正确的答案。原句是:

"I'd have bought Smith's computer if I had known he was selling it. "

对付这类题目,大家只要在本题型练习中选择几句例句背得滚瓜烂熟,就能立刻建立起对这类题目现象和本质的准确认识。

当然了，我们除了虚拟语气的一般形式外，还要掌握以下几种虚拟语态的常见变体：

- I wish
- If I were you
- If only
- Had someone...

题型练习：

1. Had he realized the possible consequences, he wouldn't have made the suggestion at the committee meeting last week.

   (A) He didn't know what would happen if he made the suggestion.

   (B) He didn't feel nervous after he had put forward the suggestion.

   (C) He realized that the committee members would not adopt his suggestion.

   (D) He considered it important to talk to the committee members first.

2. If Jack could have fixed the lamp in the hallway, he wouldn't have called in an electrician.

   (A) Jack could not repair the lam and it was repaired by an electrician.

   (B) The lamp was so badly damaged that Jack had to buy a new one.

   (C) Jack didn't ask an electrician to repair the lamp, although it was badly damaged.

   (D) Jack could repair the lamp himself, but he didn't bother and called in an electrician.

3. Peter'd never be studying mathematics if it weren't required.

   (A) Mathematics isn't a required course.

   (B) He's never met the math student before.

   (C) Peter is taking a mathematics course.

   (D) They will never require mathematics.

4. If we had your phone number, we would have called you on our arrival.

   (A) We knew your phone number, so we called you.

   (B) We didn't know you were at home, so we didn't call you.

   (C) We didn't want to disturb you, although we had your phone number.

   (D) We didn't have your phone number, so we didn't call you.

答案：1. A   2. C   3. C   4. D

2. 数字题

数字题在中级口译中包括的类型很广，包括时间、日期、价钱、号码、航班等等。一般来说，数字题有两类，一种是"直接答案型"，即在一个句子中出现两个以上的数字，而在4个选项中只针对其中的一个数字，考查考生是否能够明确辨音。这类题目不需要运算，直接就能判断答案，但是考生亦需注意两点：

- 区分数字的相似读音，例如 thirteen/thirty, eighteen/eighty，此类数字由于读音相似，稍不注意就容易出错。
- 辨别两个数字分别指代的对象，适当的时候可以作出标记，以免张冠李戴，答非所问。

数字题的另外一种题型就是"计算型"，这种题型要求听者根据所听到的句子和数字，进行适当的运算后才能得出正确答案。此类题目的特点是解题不能通过选择单句中出现的某一个数字达到。此类单句所表现的特征是单句中所听到的数字一般在选项中都会出现，但所听到的数字往往都不是正确答案。

让我们来看一个实例：

The plane was due at 9:30, but has been delayed half an hour.

(A) The plane will arrive at 10:00.

(B) The plane will arrive at 9:00.

(C) The plane will arrive at 10:30.

(D) The plane will arrive at 9:30.

像这一题，就需要考生进行简单的计算，要求考生具有快速反应能力，熟练掌握英语中时间表达的方法，并作出推算，9点半误点半个小时，因此正确答案是(A)。

接着来一题难度稍高的题：

About one-third of the sixty invited guests failed to show up at the dinner party.

(A) Thirty guests came.

(B) Forty guests came.

(C) Twenty guests didn't receive their invitation cards.

(D) More guests came than were expected.

这一题很有趣，转了两个弯，先是表明60的1/3，那也就是20个客人了，这是第一个弯，然后再次转折说这20个人都没来。那么在选择答案时就要将60减去20得到最终的答案，也就是一共来了40个客人，选择答案(B)。

要做好这类题目，考生需要培养对数字的敏感度，例如在有关数字计算时，我们就必须了解常用的表达方式：

小数和分数	0.25	• zero point two five • point twenty five
	1/3	• one third • a third
	3/8	• three eighth
	1/4	• a quarter
数位的表达	千/百万/十亿	• thousand/million/billion
数字计算	多/少	• more/less
	加上	• add/addition/plus
	减去	• subtract/minus
其他	两倍 三倍	• twice/double • triple

在时间方面，我们需要掌握两方面的信息，特殊时间的表达方式和改变时间的词汇运用。

- 包括：
  - ☐ 整点：8 o'clock sharp／8 o'clock on the hour／8 o'clock on the strike
  - ☐ 两个特殊时段：at noon／at midnight
  - ☐ 提前和延误：以半小时为例，可用：
    - ◇ half an hour early
    - ◇ early by half an hour
    - ◇ half an hour ahead of time
    - ◇ half an hour ahead of schedule 等
    - ◇ 其他表示提前和延误的词还包括：

提前	· ahead of time
	· in advance
	· beforehand
	· prior to
延后	· delay
	· put off
	· postpone
	· prolong
	· behind schedule

题型练习：

1. The Company quoted a price of 100 dollars a piece for the summer dress. But after much bargain, we got an offer at 25% discount.

   (A) We need to pay $25 per piece.

   (B) We need to pay $50 per piece.

   (C) We need to pay $75 per piece.

   (D) We need to pay $125 per piece.

2. The closing of the textile factory, with two thousand workers being laid off has doubled the unemployment rate in that town.

   (A) The population has doubled in that town.

   (B) Many people were hired because of the new factory.

   (C) The unemployment rate in that town is now twice as high.

   (D) Despite the closedown, the unemployment rate remains the same.

3. We had expected the repairs to cost us no more than fifteen thousand dollars, but the maintenance company charged us twice as much.

   (A) The company charged us 5,000 dollars.

(B) The company charged us 10, 000 dollars.

(C) The company charged us 15, 000 dollars.

(D) The company charged us 30, 000 dollars.

4. Twice as many tickets for the Auto Show could have been sold, but the exhibition hall has only a capacity for 500 visitors.

(A) No more visitors can be allowed in the exhibition hall.

(B) The exhibition hall can hold slightly over 250 visitors.

(C) Five hundred visitors wanted to see the Auto Show.

(D) More than one thousand visitors saw the Auto Show.

5. Two years ago we paid only 10 cents for one page of this brochure, but now it costs double that amount.

(A) Now we pay 5 cents.

(B) Now we print half-size pages.

(C) Now we pay 15 cents.

(D) Now we pay 20 cents.

6. The plane for Los Angeles was supposed to take off at noon, but due to a minor fault in one of the engines the flight was delayed for 2 hours.

(A) The plane left two hours before.

(B) The plane left at ten o'clock in the morning.

(C) The plane left at two o'clock in the afternoon.

(D) The plane left at four o'clock in the afternoon.

答案:1. C   2. C   3. D   4. A   5. D   6. C

3. 转折(but)句型

每一套单句理解题中都会有一两道这类题型,这类题型的解题关键是:

> 努力听懂转折词 but 后面的内容,因为这个地方是永远的考点。考生如果无法将转折词前后的全部内容都听出来,只要能理解其中一点,问题就不大;因为可以通过对听出部分进行否定的方式猜测 but 所带来的转折。

让我们看看下面的例子:

We tried to persuade him not to go to Australia, but in vain.

(A) We told him not to go to Australia and he took our advice.

(B) He didn't listen to us when we asked him not to go to Australia.

(C) We tried to persuade him to go to Australia, but he said he didn't want to.

(D) We said that he could do well in Australia, but he was not convinced.

这一题很多考生由于不了解 in vain 这个词组表示徒劳无功的含义,所以选不出正确答案,其实按照上面的方法,否定前面的句子就可以得到正确的答案(B)。因为:我们想要说服他,但是说服不了——也就是,他没有听我们的。即使无法对前句使用否定的方式,考生也可通过合理的想像,使用自己的中文能力将句子补充完整,例如:

Linda thought we ought to go ahead with the project, but Peter thought the contrary.

(A) Like Linda, Peter preferred to be in the country.

(B) Both Linda and Peter were in favour of the project.

(C) Unlike Linda, Peter was against the project.

(D) Peter told Linda that the concert had been cancelled.

如果在考试时,你没能听出 Peter 后面的词语,没有关系,试着想像这句中文句子:

"Linda 认为我们应该继续进行这个项目,但是 Peter ＿＿＿＿＿＿＿＿＿＿"。

在横线当中,你认为应该填什么呢?第一想到就应该是"不同意"或者是"反对"吧?所以以 but 引导的转折句一点也不难攻破,关键就是掌握"第一否定,第二想像"的原则,就可成功解题。

此外,请注意其他表示转折关系的词语,例如:

- however   - otherwise   - on the contrary

题型练习:

1. Mr. Carter, who promised to lend us $1,000,000 for the setting up of the laboratory, backed out of financing the project at the last minute.

(A) Mr. Carter made a last minute decision not to fund the project.

(B) Mr. Carter was the last to find out the errors in the report.

(C) It was Mr. Carter's car that backed out of the finance department last night.

(D) There were more mini-cars sold because of the financial crisis.

2. Ordinarily we can drive into the city in less than one hour, but today it took us an hour extra because we ran out of gas halfway there.

(A) It took us about two hours to drive into the city today.

(B) The city is a two-hour drive from here.

(C) We must carry an extra tire with us when driving.

(D) We had to run for an hour because our car broke down.

3. The MBA program of that well-known university I attended last year was rather difficult, but I got a lot out of the courses there.

(A) I was the last to know about the MBA program.

(B) I learned a great deal from the MBA program.

(C) I misunderstood only the most difficult part of the program.

(D) I dropped out of the program because it was difficult.

4. At first, the Chairman didn't intend to attend the opening ceremony, but he changed his mind at the last minute.

(A) The Chairman didn't attend the ceremony at the last minute.

(B) The Chairman refused to attend the opening ceremony at the last minute.

(C) The Chairman never changes his mind at the last minute.

(D) The Chairman made a last-minute decision to attend the ceremony.

5. High school graduates should by all means go on to college. But they should first of all think about what they want to get, or need to get out of a college education.

(A) Only those high school graduates with excellent skills can be admitted into colleges.

(B) No matter how difficult it is, high school graduates should at least try twice to get themselves into colleges.

(C) Students should consider what they want to learn in the university.

(D) Once in the university, you will feel superior to those drop-out students.

答案: 1. A　　2. A　　3. B　　4. D　　5. C

4. 否定题型

并不是你听到了 not,就一定是否定,也不是你没有听到 not,这个句子就不是否定句。这句话听起来像绕口令。其实这是因为否定题型,包含了完全否定、部分否定、双重否定等几类。

完全否定指的是下列几种表示绝对否定含义的情况:

- 用否定词 no, none, nothing, never 等;
- 使用 not any 或 not any 与 thing, where, body 等搭配;
- 其他表示否定含义的单词,例如:
  - ☐ fail to do something
  - ☐ far from
  - ☐ too... to
  - ☐ the last ... to do sth(绝不 ...)
  - ☐ deny
  - ☐ 使用动词的否定前缀,如 un, im, in 等。

部分否定指的是使用一些表示程度低的词描述对象,但不是否定该事物的全部,例如:

I seldom go there.

He can hardly understand it.

I barely know Tom.

这些都是表示对于该事件的部分否定。

需要注意的是,我们需要在完全否定和部分否定的情况下区别一个特殊的词组,就是用 not 与表示"全部"含义的词联接时,对于对象只是部分否定,而非全部否定,例如:

Not all children enjoy the trip. (Obviously, some enjoyed, some not.)

Not everywhere is decorated with a Christmas tree. (At least somewhere is decorated,

Hallelujah!)

I do not always go to the Casinos (That's because I don't always have money.)

双重否定是第三种重要的否定形式，是指在句中出现两个表示否定的成分，从而表达肯定的含义。例如：

She seldom goes out without her red dress. （她几乎是穿红的才出去。）

No one is unwilling to be a volunteer. （人人争当志愿者。）

双重否定还存在一种特殊形式，就是 cannot...too 和 cannot...better(比较级)的搭配，前者表示的意思是"越……越好"或者"无论怎样……都不过分"，后者表示肯定的意思。例如：

You cannot eat too much. （你吃得越多越好。）

I cannot agree with you more. （我太同意你说的了。）

考生在做题时，只要能够注意在原句中表示否定的成分以什么形式出现，就能顺利完成考题。

题型练习：

1. Within the past century, scientists have been trying unsuccessfully to find a real cure for the common cold.

   (A) Scientists have found a cure for the common cold in the past century.

   (B) Scientists' discoveries were often misunderstood by the common people.

   (C) Scientists have yet to discover effective ways to conquer the cold virus.

   (D) Scientists have been unable to explain the cold climate in the past century.

2. Those instructions are so complicated. I don't see how anyone could ever figure them out.

   (A) The figures on those instructions are difficult to see.

   (B) The instructions are illogical and incomplete.

   (C) I don't know how people can understand those instructions.

   (D) I can't look at anyone else's figures.

3. Let's not sign the memo until we have a lawyer look at it.

   (A) A lawyer should sign the memo.

   (B) We should get legal advice.

   (C) We have seen a lawyer.

   (D) Let's wait for a lucky sign.

4. The company replied that they were unable to deliver the spare parts until the end of January.

   (A) The company was unable to order spare parts.

   (B) The company was short of cash for delivery.

   (C) The parts would be considered genuine.

(D) The parts could be sent in late January.

答案：1. C　　2. C　　3. B　　4. D

5. 因果关系题型

因果关系题型和转折题型一样，很容易辨认，因为它往往是由标志性的因果关系连接词所引导的：

A lot of people nowadays have muscular problems in the neck, the shoulders and the back that are really due to stress and tension in their work.

(A) Hard work often brings about discomfort in parts of the human body.

(B) If you are nervous, you may hurt yourself in performing this kind of task.

(C) Those staff members who work back to back are hard on each other.

(D) This exercise is to relax your muscles in the neck, the shoulders and the back.

这一题考查的是表示因果关系的 due to 与正确选项中的 bring about 的对应关系，考生只要能够辨认出 due to 这个关键词，就能选出正确答案。

Because of the increasing population migration to other residential areas we decided to close down our branch in that downtown district.

(A) We stopped operating there when people began to move out.

(B) Our branch in that area was closed because of the public holidays.

(C) We set up a new branch in that area to meet the population growth.

(D) We decided to close down despite the increase of population.

该句开始的 because of 点明了这是一个因果关系句。在做这样的句子时，考生只要完成两个步骤就可以顺利完成：

因果关系题解题关键：

- 第一，分别定位原因和结果，如上题中原因是 people migrate，结果是 we close our branch；
- 第二，在答案中寻找分别 paraphrase 的原因和结果，例如在正确答案中 (A) 中，people migrate 变形为 people move out，而 close down 变形为 stop operating。

表示因果关系的连接词还包括：

• because	• therefore
• so	• since / as / for
• as a result	• thus
• accordingly	

请继续练习下列例句：

1. Betty missed a week's work because she was down with a bad cold and was advised by her doctor to stay at home.

(A) Betty brought a week's work home because of the cold weather outside.

(B) Betty was absent from work seven days while recovering from a cold.

(C) Betty did not have enough time to recover from a bad cold.

(D) Betty felt quite weak for seven days after she had caught a bad cold.

2. Mrs. Green couldn't attend the opening ceremony last Tuesday because she had to meet the CEO from our Chicago headquarters at the airport.

(A) Mrs. Green had to rush to the airport to meet the CEO for Chicago.

(B) Mrs. Green refused to attend the opening ceremony in Chicago last Tuesday.

(C) Mrs. Green was scheduled to see someone from Chicago last Tuesday.

(D) Mrs. Green didn't accept the CEO's invitation to work in Chicago at last.

3. Your letter was delayed because you forgot to notify the post office of your change of address when you moved.

(A) The post office was slow in delivering the letter.

(B) You failed to give your new address to the post office.

(C) The post office didn't process the change of address fast enough.

(D) You forgot to write your new address on the letter.

4. Mrs. Green resigned from the committee yesterday because her proposal to close the downtown branch was rejected.

(A) Mrs. Green signed when she heard the suggestion.

(B) Mrs. Green rejected the committee's suggestion.

(C) Mrs. Green quit when her idea was not accepted.

(D) Mrs. Green didn't accept the signature.

答案: 1. B   2. C   3. B.   4. C

6. 让步状语从句题型

让步状语从句(Adverbial Clause of Concession) 在单句理解中出现的频率也较高,

> 攻克这类题型的关键在于谨记让步状语从句的定义: 在从句内容的前提下, 主句的情况依然出现。

例题:

Although Doctor Carter is a very busy man, he often takes time to have a cup of coffee with his colleagues.

(A) Doctor Carter avoids the company of others whenever possible.

(B) Doctor Carter is too busy to have a cup of coffee.

(C) Doctor Carter is a quite sociable person.

(D) Doctor Carter is a lonely man, according to his colleagues.

这句话可以分解为，即使 Carter 医生很忙 (从句内容——前提)，他仍然抽时间和同事们一起喝咖啡(主句内容——仍然出现)。因此，答案应该选择 C，他善于社交。

在上题的基础上，我们可以发现，做让步题型时的关键在于：1) 置换引导从句的连接词，2)认清主句内容并在选项中寻找相同项。

请继续练习下面这个句子：

Although Miss Brown has less teaching experience than other faculty members, she is one of the best instructors in the college.

(A) Miss Brown is one of the best teachers because she has taught longer.

(B) Miss Brown has the best experience of all the college instructors.

(C) Miss Brown does not have enough qualification to teach in the college.

(D) Miss Brown is an excellent teacher in spite of her insufficient experience.

根据上面所说的做题步骤，我们首先寻找是否有 although 置换项，立刻发现 in spite of，第二步检查两句主句意思是否相符，选择(D)项，就这样完成了漂亮的解题过程。

下面补充一些引导让步状语从句的常见关键词：

- although
- even if
- in spite of
- nevertheless
- though
- even though
- despite

题型练习：

1. Never have I been more willing to cooperate! Although I was a chief executive officer, I am now an assistant.

   (A) I've never been a cooperative person.

   (B) I'm very ready to cooperate now.

   (C) I'll be a corporate executive.

   (D) I never want to be an operator.

2. Lena wants to give up office work to concentrate on her MBA courses, even though she has been quite successful at her job.

   (A) Lena has trouble with office work.

   (B) Lena doesn't like her colleagues in the office.

   (C) Lena intends to become a full-time student.

   (D) Lena gets on very well in her MBA studies.

3. Although Jenny and I have many differences of opinion, we usually get along well most of the time.

   (A) Jenny and I do not get along because of our differences of opinion.

   (B) Jenny and I usually get up early most of the mornings.

   (C) Jenny and I can generally have a harmonious relationship.

(D) Jenny and I do not get along because we make no effort to do so.

答案: 1. B   2. C   3. C

7. 建议和个人意见题型

人都是很自我的动物。因此在考试时，如何顺畅表达自己的建议和意见也是很重要的一个部分。在单句理解中，这类题型往往以下列方式出现:

- I am afraid . . . /I think. . .
- Why not . . . /Why can't . . .
- How about. . .
- Let's . . .
- You should/Maybe you should/You'd better

I'm afraid you'll have to revise and type the memorandum of understanding a second time.

(A) Typing the memorandum is sometimes unnecessary.

(B) You will understand it if you read the memorandum a second time.

(C) The first draft of the memorandum is not satisfactory.

(D) The first draft of the memorandum is better than that of in the second time.

这类题目的考点无非两类:

- 将说话人的意见 paraphrase 后，看考生是否还能识别;
- 利用提出的建议/意见，表达对于过去状态的不满。

这一题就属于第二种情况，要求重新修订备忘录，表达了对于第一版的不满意，因此答案应该选择(C)。

题型练习:

1. I think the applicant lacks the necessary qualifications for the post as a computer programmer in that hi-tech corporation.

   (A) I don't think he has the qualifications for such a post.

   (B) I am not sure if he has enough money to pay his college tuition.

   (C) He is not qualified to teach in the advanced Computing program.

   (D) He takes courses in Computing because he needs more qualifications.

2. If George wants to do an outline of the proposed project, why don't we let him?

   (A) Why doesn't George want to write out the outline?

   (B) Why do you think George can't do an outline for us?

   (C) If George wants us to do an outline, he'll have to ask us.

   (D) Since George is willing, he should be allowed to do the outline.

3. May I suggest Friday for our trip to Hong Kong?

   (A) We must go to Hong Kong on Friday.

   (B) We would be allowed to go to Hong Kong on Friday.

   (C) Friday is the only day I can manage for the trip.

(D) Friday would be a good day for us to go to Hong Kong.

4. I think my assistant will fill you in on what happened at yesterday's committee meeting.

(A) My assistant will give you some forms to complete.

(B) My assistant will schedule today's committee meeting.

(C) My assistant will ask you what happened at yesterday's meeting.

(D) My assistant will give you the information you missed.

答案：1. A   2. D   3. D   4. D

8. 词组/习语题型

终于，我们学习到了单句理解部分的最后一种题型——词组/习语题型。对于很多人来说，这种题型是最为头痛的，因为你永远不知道他的考点会出现在哪里。而英语学习到了这一阶段，似乎应该掌握的词组和习语也是纷繁芜杂，千头万绪，不知从何入手。以我们最常见的 take 这个词为例：

- take after: 表示"与……很相像"
- take down: 可以表示"记下,写下",也可以表示"拆掉,取下"
- take...into account: 把……纳入考虑范围，和它相同意思的还有 take sth. into consideration
- take turns: 轮流
- take up with: 成为朋友

我们在这里只是举了几个简单的例子。这类考题，考生如果不熟悉短语的意思，就很难做出正确判断，因此，希望大家能够在平时拓展自己的阅读范围，尽量多地接触英语语言中的各类表达方式。此外，非常重要的一点是，《听力教程》应该是词组/习语中学习非常重要的一个部分，历年有很多考题都出自于此书。如果无法在短时期内记忆大量陌生词组和习语，考生可以阅读《听力教程》中的单句理解相关部分，并参阅本书随附的《常用词组习语表》。

题型练习：

1. Just between you and me, Mary is shortlisted and has made an appointment to see that personnel manager next Tuesday.

(A) Mary had made an appointment to see the personnel manager last Tuesday.

(B) Mary has been applying for a job and is going to see the personnel manager next week.

(C) Mary is shortsighted and cannot see that personnel manger in the next office.

(D) Mary didn't get that job since she was rude to the personnel manger on Tuesday.

2. I am glad that Florence has made it and join us in this reception, especially at such short notice.

(A) Florence has made this reception possible.

(B) I don't mind if Florence comes to the reception.

(C) Florence didn't get enough notice to come to the reception.

(D) Florence was able to come to the reception.

3. Mr. Carter, who promised to lend us $1, 000, 000 for the setting up of the laboratory, backed out of financing the project at the last minute.

(A) Mr. Carter made a last minute decision not to fund the project.

(B) Mr. Carter was the last to find out the errors in the report.

(C) It was Mr. Carter's car that backed out of the finance department last night.

(D) There were more mini-cars sold because of the financial crisis.

4. In the long run, Joyce proved herself a successful businesswoman.

(A) Joyce is so busy that she always runs for work.

(B) Joyce runs her small business herself.

(C) Joyce eventually became successful.

(D) Joyce's business had been successful for a long time.

答案: 1. B   2. D   3. A   4. C

第二节 段 落 理 解

在中级口译中，段落理解部分由 4~5 篇对话或篇章组成。对话部分的内容题材与日常生活、工作或学习有关。讲话及讲座的内容涉及科普或社会专题。该部分不仅考核考生的理解能力，而且还有对英语的记忆能力和思维能力。Talks and Conversations 部分的对话或篇章中，每篇有 4~5 个选择题（近年以 5 个段子，每段 4 个问题居多），共 20 道题组成。要求考生从四个选择项中选出最贴近听音原文的答案。此部分每题 1 分，共 20 分，占听力部分总分的 22%。

对于大多数考生来说，Talks and Conversations 可能是中级口译听力部分中最为熟悉的一个部分。高考、大学英语四级、六级，以及其他大多数英语水平测评考试中都有类似的题型。可是，经常有考生抱怨在做这个部分的时候，文章听得迷迷糊糊，或者是文章听清了，却分辨不出正确的选项。因此，如果一味多听，却不对做题过程中出现的问题加以总结，就无法解决上述问题。听力水平不仅与听力技巧和熟练程度有关，更是与听、说、读、写、译等方面的综合能力，以及对英美国家文化背景的了解程度有关。在开始此章的考点讲解前，我们首先要学习听力理解的"三步走学习法"。

"听力理解三步走"不仅适用于口译听力理解，还适用于托福、研究生入学考试和大学四级、六级等各类考试中听力理解部分。考生可以将这个方法贯穿于练习的始终，并结合下文对考点的分析来提高能力。

第一步: Pre-listening 听前

☞ 稳定情绪: 听力考试前必须 Maintain your confidence。不要因为一处的失误，影响做题情绪。

☞ 快速扫读选择项，预测、寻找记忆重点。若选项中出现人名、地名、数字、时间等时，要特别留心它们的对应事物。

考查考点和选项的对应关系是近年来的重要趋向。

第二步: While-listening 听中

☞ 思想集中: 听音的过程中要 concentrate on the task，但情绪也不可过分紧张。

☞ 有"化境"之感: 进行联想，把可能出现的内容和自己的知识背景结合起来，思想要介入到要听的内容中，使自己融入听力材料——Make a picture！

把抽象的文字变成形象的图画反映在脑海中。这样就有了动态图像的帮助，就有利于我们避开"直接翻译的无序性"，以至抓住了中级口译听力的主干而不是细枝末节，从而走出了"听了后面，忘了前面"的"怪圈"。

☞ 迅速笔记: 在听音中要利用预测时得到的潜在信息(人名、地名、数字、时间)，把握听音的重点，利用符号、图示等方法迅速做笔记，以促进有效记忆。

☞ 抓住关键词: 听音时的笔记很重要，沿着主题的思路进行归纳和总结。

☞ 耳眼并用: 就是一边用耳听，一边用眼浏览选择项，进行分析和归纳，做到听与浏览相结合，听与思考及记忆相结合，这一过程必须在短时间内完成。

第三步: Post-listening 听后

☞ 听完录音之后要迅速回忆和整理所听懂的内容。

☞ 采取排除法、归纳法等解题。

在掌握了上述的"三步走方法"后，让我们逐步学习相应的技巧:

一、逆向判断法

在做这部分题目时，我们仍然需要利用在上一节单句理解中所提到的逆向判断的做题方法，只是步骤与其稍有不同:

- 利用段落正式开始前的时间，采用纵向阅读方式[注意! 再次提醒]快速阅读题目选项，特别注意是否有下面将会谈及的主题题型和细节题型存在;

- 尽量利用这段时间看完一个段子中的 2～3 题，并用做题后的空隙阅读完第 4 题，也就是一个段子的最后一题;

- 当段子开始朗读后，立即停止看题，集中精神听段子信息，并就出现的下一节中将会介绍的高频考点信息适当做笔记;

- 当段子念完，问题提出后，再读一遍四个选项，如果在第一次阅读时，对选项的相

同部分已经比较清楚,则可直接纵向阅读相异部分,并选出答案;

- 即使无法直接选出答案,也要排除认为肯定错误的选项,并将可能正确的选项标出,以便在做完该段子的所有题目后,提醒自己就上下文内容重新对该题作出选择。

考生如果能掌握上述做题的方法,通过先看后听的方法,事先掌握段落中心议题,并在听题的过程中,对以下介绍的各个高频考点加以"特别关注",辅之以记录,则做题的正确率将大幅提高。

二、考点分布顺序

一般来说,段落考点的分布即 4 个问题的提问顺序是与段落本身的概念递进和逻辑发展齐头并进的。

让我们来观察下面这个例子中各个考点的分布:

> 换句话说,每个段落的 4 个问题,除了第一题可能是主题题型外,所有题目的排布应该与段落的顺序相同。

This is the final call for Olympic Airways to Athens flight number OA260. Any remaining passengers must go immediately to gate 2 where the flight is now closing. Olympic Airways flight number OA260 closing now at gate 2.

Scandinavian Airlines to Stockholm, flight number SK528 now boarding at gate 4.

Passengers to New York. British Airways regret to advise a delay of 35 minutes on their flight number BA175 to New York. That is a delay of 35 minutes on British Airways flight number BA175 to New York.

Austrian Airlines to Vienna, flight number OS455 now boarding at gate 8. Austrian Airlines flight number OS455 boarding now at gate 8.

Question No. 11. Where is this announcement most probably made?

Question No. 12. Which of the following statements is true about the Olympic Airways flight to Athens?

Question No. 13. Where is the Scandinavian Airlines flight scheduled to fly?

Question No. 14. According to the announcement, how much longer will passengers to New York have to wait?

Question No. 15. According to the announcement, at which gate are passengers to Vienna boarding?

11. (A) At an airport.   (B) At a railway station.

    (C) At a coach station.   (D) At an underground railway station.

12. (A) The flight is already closed.

(B) The flight is now closing.

(C) Its passengers are boarding at gate 4.

(D) All its passengers are on board the flight.

13. (A) New York.　　　　　　　　(B) Vienna.

(C) Athens.　　　　　　　　(D) Stockholm.

14. (A) A quarter of an hour.　　　(B) Twenty minutes.

(C) Thirty minutes.　　　　(D) Thirty-five minutes.

15. (A) Gate 2.　　　　　　　　(B) Gate 4.

(C) Gate 6.　　　　　　　　(D) Gate 8.

仔细观察问题的分布,我们可以发现,这个段子一共5题,而所问的5个问题,除了第1题为主题题型,其他4个问题,正好是按照文章的顺序,一段一个问题。而这也正是中级口译听力段落理解部分的出题规律,即先出现的考点先提问,按出现顺序排列。根据这个规律,如果你发现,当一题的信息你还没有听到,录音中却已经讲到了下一题选项的内容,就需要暂时放弃这一题,跟着段落的发展继续往下看。同时,考生可以利用这个小诀窍:

把每个段子所有题目的选项相连,应该组成文章的主干大意/故事大纲——注意:如果你的选项上下矛盾,一定有错误了!

三、高频考点

在段落理解中,一共有8种高频考点,下面我们根据他们各自的特点介绍解题技巧:

1. 主题大意题

中级口译的段子由于篇幅所限,均在开头清楚表明该段子的主题,因此考查考生是否能在第一时间理解文章内容的主题题型成为出题频率最高的考点。什么是段落主题?怎样才能找到它?段落主题也可理解为这个段落的中心意思,或者是体现这个段落的主旨和方向的核心意思。换句话说就是,你找主题的过程也就是确定这个段落的主要目的的过程。它是要告诉你一件事,还是解释说明,亦或是详细叙述?它是要与其他某事或某物作比较,还是要反驳某件事,亦或是就某点说服你? 凡此种种,不一而足。体现段落中心意思的主题句往往是段落的第一句。其后所跟的其他句子,提供支持这个主题句的全部细节。一种特殊的情况是当要讨论的是一个比较费解的意思,或者说当一个段落的目的是要说服你时,主题句有时放在段末。

掌握了这种规律后,我们知道如果能够抓住段落开头的1~3句,不仅能帮助理解整篇段子的内容,如果同时结合场景知识,往往还能达到事半功倍的效果。

[听力原文]

There is a great deal of land in the United States, but there are also a great many people. Where did the people come from? (下文省略)

Question: What might be the best title for this passage?

(A) Where the Americans came from   (B) The size of the American population

(C) Land in the United States   (D) American Indians

该段听力原文一开始就点明了段子的主题：美国地多人也多，这些人都是哪里来的？然后该段子分别叙述了印第安人与移民各自的来历。如果对于这一开头马上抓住，则对于下文结构已经能够了然于心了。

再比如：

[听力原文]

Today I'd like to discuss something new that botanists may be bringing us in the near future: plants that produce plastic. I am not talking about artificial plants made from plastic. I am talking about living, growing plants that produce a plastic-like substance. （下文省略）

Question: What type of plant is the woman discussing?

(A) Artificial plants.   (B) Plants in plastic containers.

(C) Plants that resemble plastic.   (D) Plants that produce a usable substance.

在这道题中，段落开头不仅明确表示了主题：一种直接能作为塑料的植物，还用随后的两句话排除了第23题中的另外两个混淆选项 B 和 D，这种植物不是塑料做的，是活生生的，可以产生和塑料相同的物质。

> **注意**：主题题型的选项一般较长，可以作为提前阅读时的一个信号。此外，如果在主题题型的某个备选答案中出现了文章中的某个细节，则可将这个选项排除出正确答案

2. 数字信息题

对段落中出现的数字信息的考查也是中级口译钟爱的考点，也是考生容易听错或听不懂的弱势所在。在过去的考试中，数字题的难度不高，一般不需要进行计算，即在文章中听到的直接数字就是正确答案。但是近年来，由于考生对于数字题总体掌握水平的提高，考查的难度也水涨船高了。现在的数字信息题有两大特点：

- 一个选项中至少有 2 个混淆项，或者除正确答案外，其他选项都是混淆项。混淆项的意思是，该选项中的数字在听力段落中都出现过，只是指代的对象并不是问题询问的主体。针对这种题目，考生应该在发现提到选项中的数字时，及时做好笔记，分清各个选项中数字的含义。

- 如果没有其他混淆项，则正确答案的数字需要经过简单运算才能够得到。解答此类题目时，考生需要特别注意在数字出现后，有无表示增加、减少或加倍等的信息。

让我们来看下面的例子：

Woman: Now let's go back to your first novel, <u>Stand up Kids</u>. When did you write that?

Man:　　Stand up Kids, yes, I wrote that in 1970, a year after I left college.

Woman: How old were you then?

Man:　　Twenty-three? Yes. Twenty-three, because a year later I went to Indonesia.

Woman: Mm. And of course it was your experience in Indonesia that inspired your film The Eastern Island.

Man:　　Yes that's right, although I didn't actually make The Eastern Island until 1988.

Woman: And you worked in television for a time too?

Man:　　Yes, I started making documentaries for television in 1983, when I was 36. That was after I gave up farming.

Woman: Farming?

Man:　　Yes, that's right. You see, I stayed in Indonesia for eight years. I met my wife there in 1975, and after we came back we bought a farm in the West of England, in 1980. A kind of experiment, really.

Woman: But you gave it up three years later.

Man:　　Well, yes. You see it was very hard work, and I was also very busy working on my second novel, The Gold Touch, which came out in 1985.

Woman: Yes, that was a best-seller, wasn't it?

Man:　　Yes it was, and that's why only two years after that I was able to give up television work and concentrate on films.

Question No. 27. When did the man write his first novel, Stand up Kids?

Question No. 28. How old was the man when he started making documentaries for television?

27. (A) When he was still at school.　(B) A year after he left college.

　　(C) When he visited Indonesia.　(D) After he made his first film.

28. (A) Twenty.　　　　　　　　　　(B) Twenty-three.

　　(C) Thirty.　　　　　　　　　　(D) Thirty-six.

在听力原文中，我们可以发现，出现了大量数字和年代，如果不在听的过程中做好笔记，就可能在最后导致做题的失败。

此外，考生可参见单句理解中的数字题一节有关计算的相关词汇及考点。

> 注意：如果在提前阅读时，发现数字题使用英语拼写，而不是阿拉伯数字时，建议立即在旁边用阿拉伯数字注明，以便在听题时，加快反应速度。

3. 信息来源题

这一类题型考查的是考生在理解段落的过程中，是否从朗读者的字里行间意识到该段子中所讨论的信息自身的来源。这类信息来源在原段子中往往只用一个字带过，一旦出现却占到段子考题分值的 25%，因此非常重要。例如：

"I was reading the newspaper and I saw this article about edible food packaging."

newspaper 这个词在整个段子中再也没有出现,但考题中就出现了"作者从哪里得到了可食用包装材料的信息?"。当年考试的很多考生都在这一题上失分了。但是,如果考生了解这一类信息来源题,并在提前阅读时发现出现了之后将列举的 7 类信息来源中的几类,则可在段子中,特别是开篇的句子中注意所提到的话题来源。这样有备而来,这类题目无异于送分。又比如:

[听力原文]

W: Did you read this magazine article? The information in it is unbelievable.

M: What's the article about?

Woman: It's about paper, specifically about how much paper Americans use up each year.

(以下省略)

Question: Where did the woman learn the information?

(A) from a textbook   (B) from the television

(C) from a periodical   (D) from a lecture

这道题不仅考查了在听力原文中是否辨识出 magazine 一词,还就词语的含义考查了考生将其置换为 periodical 一词的能力。

总结历年考题,信息来源常考答案共有 7 种。你只需排除未在下列七类信息中出现的选项,并结合所听到的信息,必可选出正确答案。

a) Newspaper: 报纸作为新闻的载体,是中级口译中最常出现的信息来源。以报纸作为信息来源的段子主题往往是新生事物或新型的技术发明。

b) Magazines and Books: 杂志和书本常会报道有关政治、经济、环境保护等具有一定深度的主题,其变体还包括:periodical 和 journal。

c) TV: 一旦出现,必定以 watch TV, TV program, broadcast 等形式出现。

d) Radio: 请注意例如像 Radio station, radio program 这样的提示。

e) Internet: 往往段落的主人公正在网上做有关的 research,并且有新的发现,将 Internet 作为信息的来源。

f) Class: 课堂也是重要的信息来源,这类变体包括:seminar, presentation, lecture 等。

g) Someone: 当然是从别人那里听来的八卦新闻了,包括老师、朋友、同事、亲戚,等等。

掌握了以上 7 类信息的来源,考试中的一大难点就迎刃而解了。

4. 因果关系题

这类考题的特征十分明显:如果考生在观察选项时,发现 4 个选项都是解释原因,无疑此题是对因果关系表述的考查。这类问题主要对原因进行提问,因此在听原文时要注意 because, for, since, as, so that, to, if...then 等引导的句子或短语。有些时候,这样的因果关系出现得较为隐蔽,因此考生要特别留意以下几个词组:

due to, that's why, that's the reason for

特别在考试中,如果考生遇到一些比较生疏的因果关系引导词,一定要分清何为因,何为果。以 as a result 和 as a result of 为例：as a result 是一个插入语，在他之前是事件的原因，之后是事件的结果；而 as a result of 恰恰相反，它的后面必须加入表示原因的短语。

但是，由于近年考题难度的提高，同时要判断一个事件的来龙去脉，理清其因果关系，或是对事件做出合理推断，光从一个短语或一个句子的表面来判断显然是不够的。我们应该从总体入手，理解听力材料的大意，在此基础上再去捕捉具体的信息。

让我们来看下面这两个例子：

第一个因果关系问题的例子是一道细节题，也就是在文中出现了直接的句子表明因果关系，它的问题是：

According to the speaker, what will happen to a program if it does not have enough viewers?

(A) It will then be revised by the director.

(B) It will be put on a different channel.

(C) It will be shown on the international airlines.

(D) It will no longer be shown on TV.

在原文中，就有这么一段话：

No matter how good a TV program is, if it does not have enough viewers, which is to say, if it cannot reach enough prospective customers, it will be taken off the air.

因此，只要选择表示不再播出的选项就可以了。

而在同年所考的另一个有关赛车的段子中，有这么一题"Why does the woman say that the man has led a dangerous life?"。这个问题的答案没有直接在文中出现。但是整个段落都是叙述那个男子由于太喜欢赛车这项运动，有好几次几乎在比赛或训练中丧生。因此，答案的选出就必须建立在通篇理解的基础上。

5. 作者观点题

在听力中，往往作者会对一种事物进行优缺点的比较，并给予一定的评价，因此总结段落中作者的观点成为了较多出现的考点。这往往包含了两种情况。第一，在原文中，作者清楚地以 I believe, I think, in my opinion 或 in my point of view 这样的句子表达了对某种事物的看法，此时要考生就作者的观点选择正确的答案较为容易。第二种是较为困难的，是作者自始至终没有对某种事物作出正式的明确的评价，而考题中要求就作者介绍的情况，推测作者可能的态度，这是难度较高的一种题型。当遇到这样的考题时，考生应回忆：第一，作者对于该事物优点进行了怎样的夸奖？对缺点进行了怎样的点评？第二，两者相比较，哪一个较占优势？ 或者换句话说，哪一个占据篇幅较大？第三，最重要的，作者在最后提出的是表扬还是批评？ 在大多数情况下，结尾部分的评价即为作者的观点。同时，考生也应注意，如果确实无法对于作者的态度作出评价，也应观察考题的 4 个选项中，有无两个 magic words：一个是 objective（客观的），另一个是 neutral（中立的）。

> **注意**：这两个只要出现在选项中，为正确答案的可能性极大。

6. 举例题

举例的识别标志很明显，大家也都很熟悉，无非是 for example, such as 等等。听力理解往往喜欢就文章的举例考查两方面的内容：

- 举例的细节
- 举例所要说明的问题

让我们来看下面这个例子：

Dog trainers have found that almost all types of dogs have equally good senses of smell. Even though different types of dogs have equivalent sense of smell, they are not equally good at different tasks. However, certain types of dogs are better at certain tasks because of other characteristics they have. For example, beagles are small and friendly, so they are often used at crowded airports to smell for illegal food products in luggage. German shepherds have quick reactions, so they are often used to smell for explosives such as dynamite. Golden retrievers work well in the cold, so they are often used to find people lost in the snow.

Question No. 28. What is true about the various types of dogs?

Question No. 29. According to the talk, what are golden retrievers trained to find?

Question No. 30. Why are German shepherds used to find explosives?

28. (A) Most have no sense of smell.   (B) They are all unable to smell drugs.
    (C) They have equally good senses of smell. (D) Most are quite unattainable.

29. (A) Drugs.   (B) People.
    (C) Luggage.   (D) Explosives.

30. (A) Because they are small.   (B) Because they are friendly.
    (C) Because they react quickly.   (D) Because they work well in the cold.

请大家注意划线部分：首先作者表明"有些狗由于其特性，特别擅长某类工作"。为了说明这一点，作者随后进行了三个举例：Beagle（小猎兔犬）are small and friendly，所以 used at crowded airports to smell for illegal food products in luggage。German Shepard 的反应快，so they are often used to smell for explosives such as dynamite。金色巡回犬 Golden retrievers work well in the cold, so they are often used to find people lost in the snow.

在题目中，两种类型的题目都被考到，应该说本题的难度不高，但是在当年的考试中，很多考生在这个对话中，3 个问题都无法确认正确答案，主要的问题是 3 种狗的名字不熟悉，造成了无法做好记录，选出答案。

其实，在做这类题目时，我们应该忽视具体举例事物的名称，如果不认识或没听过举例的对象，只要取其首字母，或任何你记得的代号来指代这个对象即可。这类题的关键在于清楚辨认所举例子从哪方面说明了举例的目的，掌握了这个细节也就完成了题目的要求。

此外，如果考生在听题时，听清了所有的举例，但没有抓到在 for example 前出现的举例所要说明的问题，这该怎么办呢？其实很简单，只要利用在小学语文课上学过的归纳段落大意的方法就可以了。回想一下，如果我把上面的 3 个例子放在你面前，你可以归纳出"狗的特点不同所以用途不同"这一点吗？

7. 正误判断题

这类题是对短文的具体细节进行提问，测试考生捕捉细节的能力，并要求考生有良好的短时记忆力。根据听力原文来判断选项的正误可分为两种情况：

- 选项是否正确
- 选项在短文中是否提及过

这类题目考生一定要听清问题，特别是问题中是否含有 NOT，以免答非所问。

要攻克此类题型，其实也很简单。首先，在阅读时警惕此类题型的出现，大凡正误判断题，四个选项的内容都是南辕北辙，各不相干，而且选项一般较长。如果考生发现这样的选项，就应该提前准备。

第二，在发现"疑似"的问题后，考生可在聆听文章的过程中，适当关注该题的四个选项。一旦发现有提到的选项，就立即进行阅读。一般此类选项与听力原文十分相似，如果发现有任何不符，立即将其做好标记。

使用这种方法，攻克这类题目简直易如反掌。让我们来看下面这个例子：

(A) There are more American Indians than Blacks in the U. S..

(B) A large portion of American Blacks now live in the southwest.

(C) The first immigrants to America were English and Dutch.

(D) African Blacks came earlier than either the English or the Dutch.

观察四个选项，发现内容均不一样，就应该引起警觉，在听力过程中按原文的内容进行标注，就能准确及时地选出正确答案。

8. 主次题

当段落理解篇章在论述几个问题或一个问题的几个方面时，提到其中最重要、最突出的一个，而且出现像 most, main, essential, primary 等表示主次关系的词语时，考生既要注意又要重点记忆。因为大多数情况下会对这些信息进行提问。主次题通常是由 what 或 which 引导的含有主次关系词语的句子来提问，例如：

What is the main reason for...

Which is the most important element in...

作此类题的技巧应和正误判断题一样，即养成边听边做的习惯，就不难选出正确的答案。

如果考生能够掌握上面所解析的 8 类考题，则段落理解的大部分考题就无出其右了。

第四章 听 译

听译 (Listening and Translation) 是中级口译中较为独特的一种考试题型，它要求考生在听懂和理解原话的基础上，译出英文原文的主要内容。在整个听译部分中一共有两种题型：单句听译和段落听译。

- 单句听译共有 5 句，每句长度为 25 词左右，在朗读一遍以后，停顿 45～60 秒钟左右，供考生翻译书写。
- 段落听译每段 80 词左右，语速约为每分钟 130 词，朗读一遍段落后有 150～200 秒的间隙供考生翻译书写。
- 听译部分的测试目的主要是考查考生的听力理解、短时记忆及翻译能力。

在历次考试中，听译一向被认为是难度最高、最不易得到高分的部分。这往往是由于考生对于该部分题型不熟悉，不知道怎样下手练习造成的。 但是往往这一部分也是通过训练，可以提高最快的一个部分。

根据中级口译考试委员会的大纲要求，听译部分的选材原则是：

"内容多种多样，难度宜适中。同时应选用以口语体为主的材料。"

通过分析大纲要求，我们可以发现，听译部分的单句或段落并不是靠难词取胜，而是强调文章的整体理解。此类题型的本质无非是将同声传译 (consecutive interpretation) 化为笔头练习。这一部分与口译部分的训练应该相辅成，同时配合对于本书翻译部分章节技巧的学习，就能帮助考生在高强度笔记训练和脑力灵活反应的基础上，达到大幅提高听译部分水平的目的。

下面，让我们进入听译技巧培养训练阶段。

第一节 语序训练

大家在学习了多年英语以后，应该已经发现英语和中文语言在例如思维方式、遣词用句等很多方面都有巨大的差异。其中一个显著差异便是语序上的不同。中文作为我们的母语，其表达方式影响了我们的思维方式。换句话说，正是因为中文语序与英语语序的不一致，导致了听懂英语并转换为你所熟悉的母语不是一个同步的过程。让我们举一个最简单的例子来看一看：

当你希望问"迎面走来的那个人是谁"时，你会用中文说：

"迎面走过来的的那个人是谁啊？"

而如果使用英语表达的话，句子就变成了：

"Who is that guy coming towards us?"

直译过来，在英语中我们听到的是：

"谁是那个人走过来朝着我们？"

这样的句子即使直接用中文讲给你听的话，你可能也需要几秒钟的时间才能够反应过来说话人大概是什么意思吧！更何况当我们在作听译的时候，还要先将这样的句子从英语理解过来。

英语语言的重点和中文不一样。中文习惯将所有的修饰成分统一放在所要修饰的对象之前，并在加入各种连结元素后将句子的所有成分堆放在一起，形成一句长句。这样的句子中，主语、谓语和宾语等主要句子成分被隐藏了起来，句子的主干结构变得模糊，因此在收听这样的句子时，意思并不是按词语划分，而是按照意群来进行划分。这就提高了对于理解的要求。

- 在做练习一时，希望大家首先将英语原文大声朗读出来，然后观察另一侧的中文，特别注意语序不同的地方，并逐渐掌握通常的规律。(中文的语序已经按照英文进行了调整)
- 在练习二中，我们只放上了英文原文，要求考生一边朗读，一边迅速发现与中文语序不同的地方，在脑海中按照英语语序进行大致的翻译。
- 练习三中所有的段落都是中文，请考生看着中文，迅速反应英语语序与其不同的地方，并进行大致的翻译。

相反，在英语中，较为习惯将修饰成分放在所要修饰的成分后面，以补语或各种从句的形式出现。在这种结构中，句子的主干凸显明确，方便理解，使得英语语言的逻辑关系极为清晰。但在某些情况下，由于修饰成分的增多和听者本身对于逻辑关系掌握不佳，就很有可能造成修饰成分指代模糊，造成理解错误的问题。

因此，语序上的巨大差异，是听译的主要障碍之一。在本节中，我们要通过熟悉听译真题的语序，再加上练习，逐渐建立根据英语语序理解原句的能力，并加快英汉互译的速度。

以下三个练习特供考生巩固上述技巧使用：

相信通过练习，考生对英语的反应速度将会大大提高。

练习一

I arrived in the United States ten years ago, but I remember my first day there very clearly. My friend was waiting for me when my plane landed at Kennedy Airport at three o'clock in the afternoon. The weather was very cold and it was snowing, but I was too excited to mind.

我到美国是 10 年前,但我记得第一天非常清楚。我的朋友在迎候着我当我的飞机降落在肯尼迪机场下午三点钟。天气很冷,下着雪,我却非常兴奋,一点也不在乎。

About seven out of ten people released from prison will be put into prison again sooner or later. Some people think this simply shows that once a person becomes a criminal he will probably remain a criminal. But it could equally suggest that being in prison actually makes people more likely to commit crimes.

大约有七成从监狱里获释的人会再进监狱迟早。有些人认为这正说明了一个人一旦成为罪犯,就可能永远是罪犯。但这也同样意味着进了监狱就会使人更有可能犯罪。

May I have your attention, please. The library is closing in a few minutes. Please return the reference books to the shelves they belong to. Those who want to check out reserved books for overnight use may do so now. Thank you very much for your co-operation.

请各位注意,图书馆就要关门了马上。请放回参考书到他们的架子上,如果要外借备用书籍以便当夜使用,现在可以办理(手续),多谢各位合作。

Thirty years ago, when I was a small child, my father arranged for me to spend two summer holidays at a farm in the countryside. He thought it would be good for me, and he was right. It taught me a great deal about the importance of independence. The place was so isolated that the owner's daughter, who must have been in her early twenties, said that she had never been away from home or seen a locomotive.

30 年前,我还是个小孩子的时候,我父亲曾安排我度过了两个暑假去一个农场,在乡下。他认为那有好处对我,他是对的。那教会我很多重要意义有关自立。那地方非常偏僻,农场主的女儿,当时肯定已是二十出头的说她从未离开过家门,也未见过火车。

练习二

1. Cambridge is one of the most important and beautiful towns not only in Britain, but also in Europe. Visitors all over the world are attracted by the quality of its buildings, in particular those belonging to the University and the unique atmosphere caused by the combination of rivers and gardens.

2. I think that this problem of teenagers getting into trouble with the law is mainly caused by unemployment. Because of the high level of unemployment, so many teenagers nowadays leave school and find that they have no chance of getting a job. As a result of this, they feel bored and are much more likely to get drunk and wandering around the streets with nothing to do, which can easily lead to trouble of one sort or another.

3. "Package holidays" are becoming more and more popular. The travel agency will arrange for the holiday-makers the transportation and the hotel accommodation and even order the food. That is why it is called a package holiday. Such holidays are usually very cheap. That is probably why they are so popular among wage-owners and pensioners.

4. What annoyed me most about parents is their inability to say "No". Few take the time to explain to their children why certain behaviour is wrong, and as a result children are

allowed to decide for themselves what they want to do and when to do it. They are allowed to stay up too late, watch unsuitable TV and have too many new toys. They don't need candies or toys. What they need is their parents' time, which seems to be in increasingly short supply.

练习三

1. 剑桥不仅是英国,也是欧洲最重要和最美丽的城镇之一。其建筑物的特色吸引着全世界的游览者,尤其是那些属于(剑桥)大学的建筑物以及那河流与花园汇合交融的独特气氛。

2. 我认为青少年犯法这个问题主要是由失业而引起的。由于失业率高,现在好多青少年毕业后发现自己与工作无缘。结果他们感到厌倦,更容易喝醉,在街上闲逛无所事事,如此,很容易导致这样或那样的麻烦。

3. "全包旅行"越来越流行。旅行社为度假者安排交通和旅店,甚至饮食。那就是为什么(这种假期)被称为全包旅行。这一类度假通常非常便宜。这可能是为什么全包旅行在工薪阶层和养老金领取者中那么流行的缘故。

4. 说到家长,我最恼火的是他们不知道该怎么说"不"。他们很少花时间向孩子解释为什么某种行为是错的,结果是,孩子们被允许自己决定做什么以及何时去做。他们被允许熬夜,看不适合他们的电视节目,并且拥有过多的新玩具。他们并不需要糖果或玩具。他们需要的是父母的时间,而父母的时间却似乎老是不够。

第二节 逻辑训练

在上一节,大家已经清楚地了解并体会了英语与中文之间的语序差异并作了一定的练习。当然,使用与英语语言语序完全一致的中文翻译是无法直接写在答卷上的,也不可能得到高分。上述练习的目的是快速提高考生对于英语翻译的反应速度——第二语言与母语之间的切换速度。当然,英语是一种逻辑性非常强的语言,在真正开始落笔翻译前,我们需要按照英文的逻辑关系,将句子调整成中文语序。

在听译考试中,当你听到较长的句子和段落时,不要立刻作笔记,因为即使你从句子或段落的开头就开始奋笔疾书,由于播报的速度快于你笔的移动速度,到了句子的中间部分,你就无法继续做下完整的笔记了。在这种情况下,我们应该做到的是把握主旨,记忆要点,在完整理解的基础上,利用以下两个步骤:

1) 理清句子逻辑关系,调整语序;

2) 适当速记关键点后,进行填充。

在本节中,我们重点学习如何掌握句子逻辑关系。

在中级口译的句子和段落中,出现了各种各样的逻辑关系,有由各类连接词连接起来的复合句,也有由主从句关系连接起来的复杂句。在听力练习部分,我们将主要就复合句的逻辑关系进行分析,并将其主要分为6大类。至于复杂句的逻辑关系及其翻译,大家可以参阅本书的笔译相关部分,以完成能力的综合提高。

注意:逻辑关系是阅卷老师分析你是否理解一个句子的关键,考生们在阅读并完成下列针对复合句的练习时,应注意体会英文的逻辑关系是怎样在中文译文中体现的,从而增强自身对英语逻辑关系的语感。

一、转折关系

转折关系出现的标示为:

- but
- otherwise
- in spite of/ despite/ although
- on the other hand
- however
- after all
- on the contrary

在翻译时,请强调翻出:

- 但是
- 否则
- 尽管……仍然/尽管……但是
- 却
- 毕竟,始终

注意:中文中没有对于在"尽管"后不得使用"但是"的规定,相反,如果少了这个"但是",就会觉得句子不完整。因此在翻译时,我们可以进行补充。

- 相反地
- 另一方面来说

让我们一起来翻译下面的句子:

1. I arrived in the United States ten years ago, but I remember my first day there very clearly.

   我10年前到过美国,但我仍然非常清楚地记得那一天。

2. The weather was very cold and it was snowing, but I was too excited to mind.

   天气很冷还下着雪,我却非常兴奋,一点也不在乎。

3. Some people think this simply shows that once a person becomes a criminal he will probably remain a criminal. But it could equally suggest that being in prison actually makes people more likely to commit crimes.

   有些人认为这正说明了一个人一旦成为罪犯,就可能永远是罪犯。但这也同样意味着进了监狱就会使人更有可能犯罪。

4. The fire broke out at about three o'clock, but by four the fire brigade had got it under control.

大火在 3 点左右烧了起来,可是到了四点,消防队已经控制了火势。

5. They must ask three or four professors to write letters of recommendation and request the university to send off transcripts of their undergraduate records. But, there is no guarantee of acceptance.

他们必须请 3~4 位教授写推荐信,并且要求毕业院校寄出他们的大学成绩。但是(即便这样),也不能保证被录取。

二、因果关系

因果关系标示词:

- because/ since/ for/ as
- so/ as a result/ thus/ therefore/ hence/ accordingly/ consequently

在翻译时,请强调翻出:

- 因为……所以/由于……
- 结果……/因此……

让我们一起来翻译下面的句子:

1. Young people today have few guidelines on which to base their choice of career. This is because they have no previous practical experience of employment.

现在的年轻人对于自己的职业选择没有什么方向。这是因为他们先前没有实际的就业经验。

2. She is now well over 70 and she really needs help, as my father died of a car accident more than ten years ago.

她现在已经 70 多岁,确实需要人照顾,因为我父亲在 10 多年前已经因为车祸死亡了。

3. It is easier to go downhill than to climb uphill, so it is easier to fall into bad habits than into good ones.

下山容易上山难,因此,染上坏习惯容易,养成好习惯难。

4. I won't be able to be present at the board meeting tomorrow because I have a dentist's appointment.

我明天与牙医有约,因此无法出席董事会。

5. In many schools, a small number of teenage students are so naughty and mischievous that they are totally out of control. As a result, teachers can no longer teach their classes effectively.

在许多学校,一小部分青少年学生调皮捣蛋,完全不受管束。结果是,教师无法把课教好。

三、举例关系

举例的标示词为:

- for example/ take...as an example/ for instance
- like/ such as
- in other words

在翻译时,请强调翻出:

- 例如/举例来说
- 诸如/譬如
- 换句话说

让我们一起来翻译下列句子:

1. Most people want to have some form of relaxation when they come home after a hard day's work, such as taking a hot bath or listening to some light music.

   大多数人在劳累工作了一天回到家后,都希望能休闲一下,诸如洗个热水澡或者听听轻音乐。

2. This mistaken conception is due to certain social conventions. For example, English people seldom shake hands except when being introduced to someone for the first time.

   这种错误的概念是由于某些社会习俗的缘故。譬如说,英国人很少握手,除非两人初次见面。

四、条件关系

条件关系的标示词是

- if/ if so
- otherwise
- unless
- in that case

在翻译时,请译出:

- 如果……就会……
- 除非……才会……

> 注意:在英文中,习惯将 if 引导的条件放在主句的后面,而在中文中,习惯将条件放在结果之前,请观察例句。

- 否则/要不然
- 在那种情况下

让我们一起来翻译下面的句子:

1. You can get a meal for about $5 or slightly more if you eat in snack bars or coffee shops. But if you eat in a hotel or a downtown restaurant, you are expected to pay ten times as much.

   如果你在快餐店或咖啡店吃一顿饭,你只需花5美元或再多一点;但是如果你在一个酒店或市中心的饭店用餐,可能要花上 10 倍的价钱。

2. In Britain, teachers are worried that their jobs may become impossible in the near future unless something can be done to restore school discipline in the classroom.

在英国,教师们担心除非采取措施来恢复课堂上的纪律,否则在不久的将来,他们的工作就不复存在了。

3. If I work there as something else, perhaps as a secretary or a post-office clerk, it means I have to take a drastic drop in salary.

如果我做别的工作的话,比如秘书或邮局职员之类的工作,那就意味着我的工资锐减。

4. The trouble with living in the country is that it's much too quiet. There aren't enough things to do, and there are so few buses that you cannot get into town easily in the evening if you haven't got a car.

生活在乡村的缺点是那里实在太安静了。 没有足够的事情可以干,而且公共汽车太少,如果你自己没有汽车,晚上就无法进城了。

五、比较关系

比较关系的标示有:

- than
- the (more) the (more)
- compare to

在翻译时,请译出:

- 越来越……
- 比……更……
- 与……比

> **注意**:在翻译比较关系时,如果在英文中由于上句提到了比较的一方而在比较句中省略时,考生应注意在中文翻译中是否要将其补上。

让我们一起来翻译下面的句子:

1. The more people there are and the worse their living environment, the greater the possibility for all kinds of social problems.

人口越多,生活环境越差,越有可能产生各种各样的社会问题。

2. The population of elderly people is increasing rapidly because people are living longer than before. This is especially true of developed countries.

老年人口的数量在急剧增加,原因是人们比过去更加长寿。 这在发达国家更是如此。

3. You will earn a 5 percent interest on this type of deposit account, which is higher than the average interest rate, but there'll be a penalty for early withdrawal.

(如果)你存这种定期账户,就能得到 5% 的利息,这比平均的利息率要高。但是如果要提前取款,就会受处罚。

4. A common misconception about suicide is that most people who take their own lives are old and near death. The truth is that those under 50 are more likely to commit suicide than those over 50.

有关自杀的一个错误概念是，认为自杀的大都是老年人或行将就木的人。事实上，不到 50 岁的人比 50 岁以上的人更容易自杀。

六、列举关系

当我们在翻译段落时，还有可能遇到有关列举的情况，例如：

- firstly... secondly... thirdly... finally
- besides/ in addition
- moreover
- next/after

在翻译时，请译出：

- 第一……第二……第三……最终
- 此外
- 而且/更有甚者
- 接着/然后

> **注意**：我们在翻译时，不仅要注意列举词本身的翻译，还要注意文章内容本身的互相呼应。

让我们一起翻译下面这段话：

Quiet, please. Quiet, boys and girls, Thank you. Now I have a few announcements to make. First, thank you to everyone who had worked so hard to raise money for our new gymnasium. All of your efforts are appreciated and I think you'll all agree that now we have a stunning new sports facility at this school. And also would you all just give a moment to thank Mr. Forster, who is retiring this year for his incredible twenty-five years of service to our school. I'm sure that you'll all agree that he's been widely appreciated all these years. Thank you, Mr. Forster.

请安静，安静，孩子们。谢谢你们。现在，我要宣布几件事。首先，感谢各位为新的体育馆积极募款。感谢你们的努力，我想大家会一致认同现在我校有了一座崭新的体育设施。还有，请各位借此机会感谢富斯特先生，他今年要退休，感谢他为本校长达 25 年的服务。我肯定大家都认为这些年来他受到了广泛的欢迎。谢谢你，富斯特先生。

第三节 速记训练

在上节中，我们介绍了听译部分的主要逻辑关系，在这里，我们要利用速记技巧，完成成功捕捉听译信息的目的。

使用速记技巧的三大原则：

- "脑记为主，笔记为辅"。简写符号和速记技巧只是帮助考生记忆和理解原文信息,但不能喧宾夺主,完全依赖简写符号进行记忆。我们应该时刻谨记:理解句子的逻辑关系,速记句子段落细节。

- "实用,快速,个性化"。简写符号因人而异,中英文兼可。只要能便于记忆和书写,最高境界就是寥寥几笔,却能最大程度地提醒考生相关信息。
- "坚持练习,产生条件反射"。开始尝试速记的考生往往还是抑制不住把单词写全的冲动。只有多加练习,才会熟能生巧。

在收听录音时,值得记录的细节包括:

- 数量:考生需要对于数字有敏锐的感觉,并能及时转换千位以上的数字。
- 各类地点:明确表示方位地名。
- 人物身份:人物的名字可能不会忘,但千万不要忘了身份,例如 prime minister, old headmaster, chairman of the board,等等。
- 惟一性及强调:例如 the only one, the most, no more 这样的词,都需要进行记录,以便在译文中准确体现。还有表示强调的 forever, always, usually,等等。
- 形容词:在句子中出现的重要形容词,也要适时记录,特别是在句子中惟一出现的形容成分,例如:fast and growing, important and interesting, difficult and challenging 等等。

在听译方面,很多考生也会抱怨:即使作了笔记,即使掌握了结构,自己的记忆力似乎还是"未老先衰",在句子翻译时,体现为翻了前半句,忘了后半句。在段落听译中更是如此,一旦录音播放完毕,恨不得生出 10 只手,迫不及待地快点将前面的句子翻译出来,以免遗忘。好不容易一路译到最后,却发现最后一到两句的速记怎么也看不懂了,或是刚听完录音时还记得,最后却忘个精光,只能和答卷"大眼瞪小眼了"。

要解决这样的问题,大家可以试验这样的方法:

- 在句子翻译中:
  - □ 前半句在听到录音后,迅速在大脑中翻为中文,并牢牢记住;
  - □ 后半句在录音播放完毕后,记住英语原文;
  - □ 开始翻译时,可以先将后半句译成中文写下;
  - □ 然后再将刚刚已经储存在大脑里的前半句中文写下。

    使用这种方法的好处是,由于前半句已经用你比较熟悉的母语记下,因此遗忘的速度会比英文慢得多,而后半句由于是 fresh memory 立即翻译,可以译出更多的有用信息。

- 在段落翻译中:
  - □ 边听边做记录;
  - □ 记录对象应该都是实义词,不要浪费时间记录了一堆代词或定冠词等;
  - □ 录音一旦播放完毕,不要立即火烧火燎地开始翻译;
  - □ 花 5～10 秒的时间将最后 1～2 句的意思较为完整地记录下来;
  - □ 之后再开始翻译整个段落。

使用这种方法，不但可以避免在翻译段落的结尾时，看不懂笔迹或是完全忘光，还能帮助你回忆起在开头和结尾之间——也就是中段部分的一些细节信息。放心，段落的开始人们总是记得比较牢的，而且考试时听译的时间是充分的，因此千万不要吝惜录音播放完毕后的那10秒钟。

那么，考生应该怎样开始速记呢？我们以几类单词为例，帮助大家逐渐掌握并发掘适合自己的方法。

一、地点

地点是听译中的高频考点，要求考生准确识别出主要国家的名称、首都或重要地点等，并能够进行翻译。如果要把每个地点的名称完整的记录下来，会很费时间。因此，考生应将以下地名相关信息的记录方法烂熟于胸。

1. 国名——使用首字母表示

K = Korea, US = the United States of America, SW = Switzerland，等等

2. 地名——使用固定字母或符号表示

例如：Rm 代表 room, Rd 代表 Road, Fwy 代表 free way，等等

3. 方位——使用方向符号表示

方位的记录在听译时是很容易遗漏的信息，但是如果借助简单的"卜"来表示东、西、南、北、中等方位，并利用地理学习的"上北下南，左西右东"，就可以简单的解决这个问题。

例如：the Republic of Korea（ROK，韩国），表示为"K̄"；相应的 the Democratic People's Republic of Korea（DPRK，北朝鲜），就可以表示为"K̲"；London，表示为 LD；Western Europe（西欧）表示为"│EU"，Eastern Europe（东欧）表示为"EU│"。

二、时间

1. 固定时间的表示

固定的缩写可以表示时间的单位，例如 wk(week), m(month), yr(year), hr(hour)，等等。

2. 时间区间的表示

翻译文章时往往需要表示 段时间，可以使用 (2m) 表示 for 2 months, since 2 months ago 等。

3. 时间先后的表示

考生可以在表示时间的缩写前/后加"."来表示，例如 2 weeks ago 可以写为". 2wk"，而相对的，2 weeks after 就是"2wk."。用这样的方式，既节约时间，又能清楚表示听到的信息，帮助翻译，何乐而不为呢？

三、其他常用速记概念

除了上述两大类例子外，我们还可以对下列常用概念进行速记：

☺	表示开心：pleasant, joyful, happy, excited, etc.
☹	表示不满、生气：unsatisfied, discomfort, angry, sad, etc.
←	表示来自于：be/come from, return, receive from, etc.
+	表示"多"：many, lots of, a great deal of, a good many of, etc.
$++(+^2)$	表示"多"的比较级：more
$+^3$	表示"多"的最高级：most
×	表示"错误"、"失误"和"坏"的概念：wrong/incorrect, something bad, notorious, negative, etc.
>	表示"多于"概念：bigger/larger/greater/more than/better than, etc.
<	表示"少于"概念：less/smaller, etc.
=	表示"同等"概念：means, that is to say, in other words, the same as, be equal to, etc.
( )	表示"在……之间"：among, within, etc.
≠	表示"不同"概念：be different from, etc.
~	表示"大约"概念：about/around, or so, approximately, etc.
╱	表示"否定"、"消除"等概念：cross out, eliminate, etc.
:	表示各种各样"说"的动词：say, speak, talk, marks, announce, declare, etc.
?	表示"问题"：question, issue，例如：台湾问题：tw?
√	表示"好的"状态：right/good, famous/well-known, etc.
	表示"同意"状态：stand up for, support, agree with sb, certain/affirmative, etc.
☆	表示"重要的"状态：important, exemplary（模范的）, best, outstanding, brilliant, etc.
↔	表示"交流"状态：exchange, mutual, etc.
&	表示"和"、"与"：and, together with, along with, accompany, along with, further more, etc.
∥	表示"结束"：end, stop, halt, bring sth to a standstill/stop, etc.

-ism	简写为 ^{m}	例如：socialism	S^m
-tion	简写为 ^{n}	例如：standardization（标准化）	std^n
-cian	简写为 ^{o}	例如：technician	$tech^o$
-ing	简写为 ^{g}	例如：marketing（市场营销）	MKT^g
-ed	简写为 ^{d}	例如：accepted	$acpt^d$
-able/ible/ble	简写为 ^{bl}	例如：available	av^{bl}
-ment	简写为 ^{mt}	例如：amendment	amd^{mt}
-ize	简写为 ^{z}	例如：recognize	reg^z
-ful	简写为 ^{fl}	例如：meaningful	mn^{fl}

在学习上述的方法后，结合在第三章听写填空中的单词缩略方法，将大大提高考生对于句子或段落的笔记速度，并帮助在翻译时回忆关键信息。

此外，在进行段落翻译的速记时，请考生始终牢记一个原则：

> 记录时,必须一个意思间隔为一行,分行记录,可以帮助回忆信息,分清段落关系。

让我们以下段为例,进行一个综合的速记分析:

原文:

Yesterday at 10 o'clock in the morning on the South Highway, a lorry overturned. The electronic goods in the lorry spilled onto the road. The driver was injured and was taken to hospital. The accident caused a big traffic jam and it was two hours before the road was finally cleared. It was later reported that the driver had broken both legs.

记录:

Yesterday at 10 o'clock in the morning on the South Highway	. d 10am Hwy
a lorry overturned	车 ∧
The electronic goods in the lorry spilled onto the road	Elec ↗↖↙ Rd
The driver was injured and was taken to hospital	D^{er} Inj→Hospital
The accident caused a big traffic jam	Acdt→X
two hours before the road was finally cleared	2hr→clear Rd
It was later reported that the driver had broken both legs	: D^{er} 2 Lg ×

根据上述方法,考生应在平时的练习时,多多积累,熟悉自己的速记语言,以取得这部分的成功。

第四节　译文的表达

训练听译的最后一步,是将我们所理解的含义转化成符合中文表达习惯的句子和段落,从而成功完成该题型的要求。

值得注意的是,很多考生忽略了这最后一步。他们认为只要能将句子的主要部分翻译出来,并堆砌在答卷上,就可以保证自己得分。这实际是一种错误的观点,让我们来看听译部分的评分标准:

Sentence Translation 部分一共 15 分,每句 3 分。评分标准如下:

- 内容基本正确,表达通顺,给 3 分
- 内容基本正确,表达较通顺,给 2~2.5 分
- 尚能表达一般内容的,给与 1.5 分
- 关键信息错误不给分

Passage Translation 部分一共 15 分,每段 7~8 分

- 语言表达占每段总分的 40%
- 内容占每段总分的 60%
- 内容错误不给分

从上述评分标准我们可以看出，一个句子到底能得到满分3分，还是2分，完全取决于考生的中文表达是否流畅、通顺，而非很多考生所理解的完全取决于英语内容的听写。这一点在段落听译中显得更加重要。中文的语言表达占到了整个段落总分的40%。换句话说，即使你段落中所有的信息一字不落全部记住，但如果你的中文译文支离破碎，让人不敢恭维，那么最高也只能拿到60%的分数。

下面，我们从6个方面分析一下，帮助大家熟悉怎样翻译出符合中文表达习惯的句子。

一、英语重结构，中文重语义

在逻辑关系一节中，我们已经提到，中文注重意群关系的表达而英语重在逻辑。具体体现在句子上，英语句子一般比较复杂，这主要有两个方面的原因：第一，考试要求句子要有一定的难度，不然无法检验考生真实的听力和翻译水平；第二，英语可以通过结构上的安排使许多层意思在一个句子中表达出来。下面我们先看一个例子：

And also would you all just give a moment to thank Mr. Forster, who is retiring this year for his incredible twenty-five years of service to our school.

在这句英文中，通过结构的编排，有条不紊的表达了几层含义：i) 向Forster先生表示感谢 ii) 他即将退休 iii) 已经在学校服务了25年。其中每层意思在中文中都可以是一句单独的句子。

从中文的表达习惯来看，句子一般不宜写得太长，修饰成分过多或过长会造成喧宾夺主、语义含混。我们先看一看这句话的直译：

"此外，请你们感谢即将在今年退休并为学校辛勤服务了25年之后的富斯特先生。"

这样的译文倒是很忠实，但在表达上却不像是中文，译者译的时候费劲，读者读的时候也费劲。现在我们把译文调整一下：

"此外，请各位借此机会感谢富斯特先生，（因为）在为本校辛勤服务了长达25年后，他即将于今年退休。"

很显然，调整后的译文给人更清楚、更顺畅的感觉。很巧的是，它与改写后的英语句子结构上更加接近，这说明中文不需要通过复杂的结构提高表达水平。只要意思清楚、正确，表达方式上可以有更多的自由。

二、英语句子长，中文句子短

由于英语重结构，汉语重语义，英语句子往往比较长，中文句子则常常比较短。这一点上述例句的翻译已经表现得很清楚。弄清这一区别之后，翻译时我们就可以"带着镣铐跳舞"，适当摆脱原文结构的束缚，这便是钱钟书先生所说的"get the meaning, forget the words"（得意忘言）。在这一方面，关键是要做好对英语长句的结构分析，把长句按意群切分成若干个小段。相关内容，大家也可以参见本书笔译中的相关章节。

三、英语前重心，中文后重心

所谓前重心是先说结果后说细节，先将句子中的主干结构提炼出来，然后再用从句进行修饰，而在中文里的后重心则是先说细节后说结果。回忆一下，是不是在中文里，才有这样的句子：

"伟大的享乐主义创始人，忠实的花钱者，极端热爱懒惰的，社会的寄生虫和家庭的拖后腿者×××今天终于破产了。"

呵呵，开个玩笑，但是从这个句子中大家可以发现，破产这个结果被放在了句子的最后，而同样的句子用英文来写，×××之前所有的细节都一定被摆在主干结构的后面以从句形式出现。

四、英语多引申，中文多具体

很多词放在英语的句子里，我们明明理解它是什么意思，但是如果直译成中文，就会闹笑话了。举个中级口译里段落听译里的句子为例，段落大意主要是阐述太阳能对于人类的重要性，其中有这么一句：

"The sun warms and feeds mankind."

这句话的意思很好理解，太阳的照射不仅温暖了我们，而且它照耀了地球上其他的植物和生物，帮助它们生长，而这些植物和生物正是人类的食物。但是，这句话直译就变成了：

"太阳温暖了我们，也喂饱了我们。"

如果这是真的，我们大家都成为了太阳能机器人了。在这里，英文引申了 feed 的含义，但是在中文中，我们要把它具化为：

"太阳温暖了我们，也为我们提供了食物。"

这不一定是最好的翻译方式，但是它忠实地表达了原文中 feed 这个词的含义。

五、英语多代词，中文多名词

因为英语句子结构较长也较为严谨，因此大量使用代词。中文虽然也使用代词，但使用频率明显不如英语高。由于这些代词起着很重要的作用，译成汉语时往往必须还原为名词。这看起来是加大了翻译的难度，实际上却是在考查你对句子的理解。遇到这种情况时，我们要注意句子信息的还原，把确切含义表达出来。

六、英语多被动，中文多主动

英语，特别是口语里面经常使用被动结构，而中文里却较少使用被动结构。面对这一矛盾，我们当然不能将每一个英文原句中的被动结构都机械地照翻，一定要根据具体情况进行适当的处理。

例如：

"In Britain today, almost half of the houses are owned by the people who live in them. About one third are owned by the local authorities, and the rest are rented from private owners."

在这里出现了 3 个被动结构，如果在中文里全部使用被动翻译，就会觉得句子的翻译味很浓，因此我们可以做这样的调整：

"在当今的英国，一半以上的房子归居住者所有，当地政府拥有三分之一，其余的要从私人业主处租住。"

这样的句子感觉就较为灵活。

当然，在翻译中我们还有很多问题需要注意，这部分内容大家可以参阅本书的翻译章节以取得更大的提高。

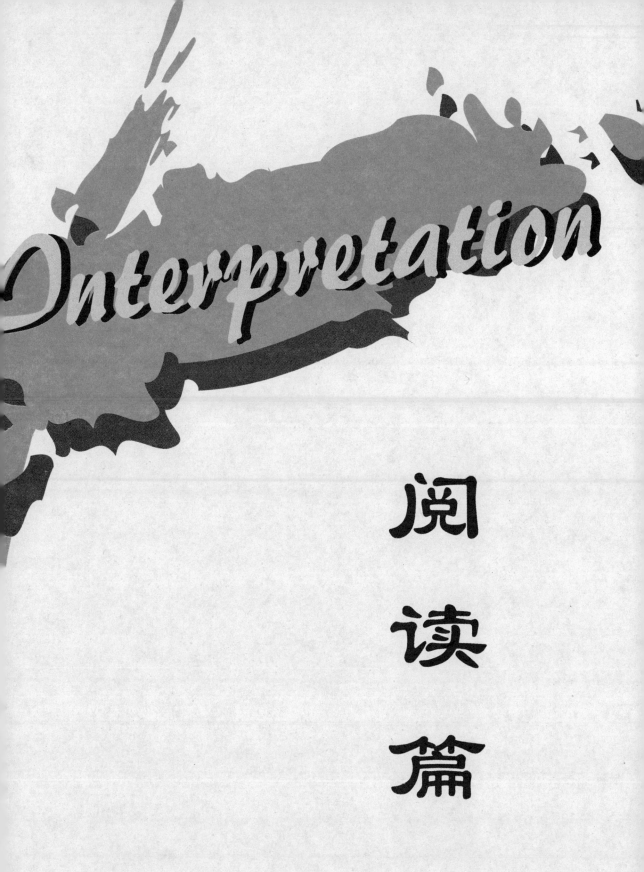

Interpretation

阅

读

篇

序　言

与其他国内英语资格考试相比,中级口译考试最显著的特点和难点自然在"译"上。而在笔试阶段的三种考试题型中,听力和笔译都涉及到了对考生在翻译的知识和能力上的测试,惟独阅读部分("Reading Comprehension")保持了传统的风格,从而使得考生们能够在复习训练中有较好的心理准备。毕竟,从初学英语,到参加中高考,以及大学四级、六级考试,中国的英语学子们对阅读理解这种考试形式已是烂熟,从某种意义上来说,每个考生都是一名"expert"。然而很少有考生可以自信地说自己已经能够得心应手地应付阅读理解考试,而作者在平时给考生做咨询服务时所遇到的大多数考生都表示阅读是自己的一个弱项,甚至作者同行们在休息闲暇之时都会不时地举出一两道阅读题,进行一番激烈的争论,小小地过把"争强好斗"的瘾,同时也借此来"sharpen their minds"。 由此我们足以看出阅读理解这种考试形式的难度和深度。

阅读理解所涉及到的知识面和所考核的能力架构是相当广泛的,最突出地表现在阅读和解题两方面:

阅读能力

宏观知识面:对各种文章体裁和结构及相关特点的掌握,对段落分布及相互呼应的敏感,以及对文章题材及相关背景知识的了解等。

微观知识面:对词汇、句型及其各种灵活运用的掌握。

技能面:正确阅读习惯的建立,对文章中心的快速定位,对主题和细节的正确区分,真正培养对"what to read, what not to read"的敏感,对作者观点和语气的判断,以及对出题点的推测等。

解题技巧

宏观知识面:对各种题型的辨识,以及对针对性的解题思路和方法的了解。

微观知识面:对题目在文章中定位的敏锐,对文章内容和选项、选项和选项之间的衔接等。

技能面:文章快速定位的技巧,正确选项的锁定技巧,错误选项的识别技巧,干扰选项的排除技巧等。

最终决定考生们阅读理解成绩高低的两个直接因素是考生的阅读速度（speed）和解题的正确率（accuracy）。换句话说，考生们只有将以上两方面（阅读和解题）的知识和技巧有机地结合在一起，并加以正确的运用，才能既节省时间，又提高正确率，在阅读理解测试中实现质的突破。

Relax！读到这里考生们无须为了众多的知识和能力要点犯愁。本篇的目的就是力图切实地做到"Make your lives easier！"。本篇在内容上注重突出其知识性、理论性、可读性以及实战性。本篇不仅涉及到了丰富的阅读知识，总结出了完整的理论体系，提供了行之有效的阅读和解题的技巧，而且还提供了最贴近考试的实战经验。

本篇的结构分布：阅读篇共分为三个章节。

第一章　概论——概述中口阅读理解的整体知识框架。

第二章　阅读技巧——这是攻克中口阅读理解的核心技能之一，通过对大量文章的分析，我们总结出了"定主题，理结构，抓重点，略细节"十二字阅读原则，为考生们展现了提高阅读能力的新天地。

第三章　解题技巧——这是攻克中口阅读理解的核心技能之二，通过对基本题型的讲述、特殊阅读题型的介绍、高效阅读理解的案例分析以及对综合试题的讲解等多角度、多元化的训练途径，阐述了各种帮助考生们制胜的解题技巧。

在学习完本篇之后，希望考生能够结合书中所提到的知识和技能架构，学会建立正确的阅读和解题习惯，再辅以大量有针对性的例证和练习，辅助技能的补充，模拟试题的历练，课外阅读的加强，和实战经验的交流，每位同学在阅读理解方面的应试能力一定会得到长足的进步，在中级口译考试的阅读理解部分实现高分必将指日可待！

第一章　概　论

在国内近 10 年来的英语学习热潮中，各种国内外的英语能力和资格考试一直是各种层次的英语学习者孜孜不倦的奋斗目标之一。而中级口译岗位资格证书考试也是在这一热潮中涌现出来的一个非常代表实力的资格证书考试。随着报考人数逐年递增，考试区域的逐步扩大，关注这个考试的考生也越来越多。 正所谓知己知彼，百战不殆。考生们常常会把中口考试与我们早已熟悉的国内英语考试，如四、六级考试以及知名的国外英语考试，托福、雅思考试做比较，希望加强对这个考试的了解。

下面我们就针对中口考试中的阅读理解部分，通过一些围绕这部分考试最常见的问题 FAQs (Frequently Asked Questions)来给考生们做一个概述：

问题一：中级口译考试阅读理解部分的考试形式和特点是什么？所占比重是多少？

中级口译考试分为两大部分，笔试和口试。考生只有通过了第一阶段的考试，即笔试部分，方能进入口试部分的测试。阅读理解（Reading Comprehension）排在听力测试（Listening Comprehension）之后，为笔试的第二部分。

篇章数量（大纲）

阅读部分共有 6 ~ 8 篇文章，均取材于原版的英文书刊杂志，试题形式为传统的选择题，要求考生在四个选项中选出一个最佳答案。

篇章长度（大纲）

阅读部分每篇文章长度约为 150 ~ 500 字，全套题目的总长度约为 2000 ~ 3000 词左右。

题目数量和分数比重（大纲）

整套阅读理解题目共有 30 题，每题 2 分，总分为 60 分。上海市英语中级口译岗位资格证书考试第一部分，即笔试部分的总分为 250 分，所以阅读部分的分数占到总分的24%。

> 提示：笔试部分的四种考试形式中，听力的总比例最高，为36%，阅读其次，为24%。但是听力题目形式分为三部分，各占总分的12%，且难度逐步增加，尤其是听译部分对考生的压力较大，故总体拿到高分的难度较大。 相比之下阅读部分题目相对集中，难度适中，且广大考生对题型也较为熟悉，故增加了考生拿高分的机会。这也提醒了考生们提高和保持对阅读理解的重视，争取在这部分尽量取得高分。

问题二：中口阅读理解考试中的文章有哪些特点？

中口阅读理解考试中的文章都选材于英语国家的报刊杂志，与其他类型的国内外英语考试相同。文章体裁大致可分为议论文、说明文、记叙文。议论文是针对一个观点或生活现象阐明作者个人观点的一种体裁，其中作者可以直接提出自己的观点并加以举例说明，或针对一个现有的观点予以否决，同时提出例证来加以论证，最后做出结论。说明文用来说明事物的特征和道理。记叙文记录人物生平、历史事件和生活故事。同时在记叙文中还有一部分描写的成分，多以地理、动物等自然题材为描写对象。另外，除了传统的文章（Essay）之外，考试的文章中还借鉴了一些国外移民类考试中训练生存英语的文体，如摘录、图表等。

中口阅读理解中的文章题材非常广泛，涵盖了政治、经济、社会、法律、人文、地理、科技、社会科学、自然科学、人类学、心理学、美学、天文、气象、生物以及生活常识等诸多题材。在这些题材丰富的文章中会适量地出现一些专科的名词和术语，增加了阅读的难度。

> 提示：无论文章的题材或词汇的难度如何，这都是属于文章内容（content）范畴之内的知识点。文章的题材千变万化，但是文章的结构（structure）却万变不离其宗，有相当的规律性。所以在分析文章的时候，我们除了要掌握作者的主要观点或叙述对象之外，更应该关注的重点是文章的结构组合、层次编排、行文特色、方能做到以不变应万变，真正做到对文章有效的理解。相关的阅读技巧会在第二章中详细介绍。

问题三：中口阅读理解考试的题目有哪些特点？

阅读理解考试的主要手段当然是：在理解文章的基础上解答一系列与文章相关的题目。中口阅读理解的题型主要分为四大类：

主旨题：考查一篇文章的主题，或作者的主要观点和写作目的；

细节题：考查一篇文章一个或多个局部的细节知识；

指代题：考查一篇文章中的指代词所指代的对象以及个别词句的解释；

推断题：考查在文章提供的知识基础上做出合理的逻辑推断的能力。

考题形式不同，考查的方向也有所区别，所以解题的思路和技巧也要有针对性。主旨题考查考生对一篇文章的宏观掌控能力，解题的思路是通过对文章的整体阅读了解作者的主要意图；细节题考查对局部细节的了解，需要考生通过准确地在文章中找出题目的对应内容来解答；指代题考查对文章个别词汇的理解，考点在文章中的位置已经给出，而解题的关键是根据上下文推测被考查词的含义；推断题则主要考查考生的逻辑推理能力，其覆盖的层面可以针对文章的具体内容，也可以涉及文章的组织结构、写作方法等。本篇在第二章中将进一步讨论针对各种题型的解题技巧。

问题四：提高阅读理解能力需要阅读哪些文章？

基于阅读理解考试文章的选材特点，考生们在平时的阅读训练中可以有选择性地阅读一些英语国家知名的报刊杂志。在选材上需要突出中口阅读考试在选材方面的多样性，广泛地阅读各种题材的文章。文章可以通过订阅或在 Internet 上搜索，图书馆也有一定数量的最新英语原版杂志。在中口阅读理解中有一部分文章的主题涉及到一些受到全球关注的时事话题，例如环境污染、生态环境（遭到破坏）、人口增长（过度）、种族歧视、媒体（犯罪暴力宣传）、健康指南等等。围绕这些话题来讨论的文章在主要观点上也都相对统一，比如使用新能源来改善环境、破坏生态环境必将自食其果、人口增长率必须严格控制、种族歧视根深蒂固、媒体"污染"影响青少年心理健康、疾病的预防、减肥、合理饮食带来健康的身体等等。考生们不妨有针对性地阅读一些相关主题的文章便可以大致了解到一些类似的话题和观点。

通过这些阅读不仅能够增加信息量和知识量，同时也可以运用一些我们下面要学习到的阅读技巧对文章进行分析理解，训练对各种文章题材和结构的分析能力。

问题五：文章读不懂，在规定时间里来不及答题怎么办？

相信为数众多的考生都深有体会，在阅读理解考试中遇到的最大的困难莫过于上面提到的问题了。原因何在，如何克服这个困难，其实也就是本篇所要阐述的要点。在阅读理解考试中，对文章的理解是以解答相关问题为最终目的的。在这个层面上理解文章，要求考生做到舍次求主，灵活机动。主可以是文章的主题和架构，次则为各段落的具体内容；主又可是论点，次则为辅助的论据；主亦可是段落中的意群分布，次则为个别词句的含义。总之，阅读旨在对文章做宏观了解，这样答题才会有充分的时间，同时又非盲人摸象，而是有的放矢地在原文中搜索必需的信息。阅读时要灵活机动，充分利用每篇文章的特点来帮助解题。最终还应具备对生词的容忍度和推测能力，既做到舍弃与解题无关的词句，又能够在必要的时候推敲词句的含义。时间和正确率的双赢来自高效、高质量的阅读。这也是本篇在下面的章节中主要讨论的话题。当然在培养和训练各种技能的同时，考生们仍然需要巩固词汇知识和积累英语国家的背景知识，这也是在复习过程中一个必不可少的环节。

第二章 阅读技巧

围绕着阅读理解的一个一直不休的争论便是阅读的顺序：先阅读文章，还是先阅读考题。许多考生都反映先读考题可以节省阅读时间，带着问题阅读文章可以做到有的放矢。但是同时他们发现，在解决了几道涉及文章局部知识的题目之后，对全文的结构和大意仍然一知半解，而如果遇到了涉及文章主题或中心思想以及跨段落知识点的题目时，解题便要受挫。通常这时他们会选择重新阅读文章，或根据自己对文章有限的了解猜测正确的选项。这样的做法或者延长了阅读时间，或者降低了解题的正确率。由此可以得出这样的结论：通读全文不仅是阅读的一个首要的步骤，而且更是考生们需要掌握和不断练习的一种重要技能。接下来我们就有针对性地来探讨一下如何在考试中阅读文章。

阅读理解考试永远是一个速度（speed）和正确率（accuracy）并行的赛跑，而中口的阅读理解部分就更是如此。很多考生经常说，如果再多给他们一些时间，就一定能读懂文章了。但是阅读理解恰恰考查的就是在一定时间限制内对文章的快速理解，同时在解答相关题目时根据对文章内容的掌握准确地找出正确答案。阅读文章不代表对文章进行逐字逐句的分析，理解文章也不等于对文章的各种枝干细节一概参透。即快速又有效的阅读方法需要遵循四大原则：定主题、理结构、抓重点、略细节。这四个原则也是考生们在练习阅读理解时必需的四种技能。其中前两种技能属于宏观技能，即把着眼点放在整个篇章的宏观布局上，高屋建瓴，统观文章的全局，抓住作者的写作目的和方法；后两种则属于微观技能，即斟酌文章的个别局部，细致入微，滴水不漏，既做到提炼局部的重点词句，又可剔除无关痛痒的细节描写。

完成了对文章的宏观理解之后，考生们已经可以略过其余的枝节内容直接开始解题。这样就节省了阅读时间。而在解题过程中凡是涉及篇章的问题，考生可以通过先前的阅读中所获得的信息迎刃而解。凡是涉及文章局部或词汇的题目，考生可以通过题干和选项中的提示回到文章中有的放矢地搜索相关的信息，从而提高了解题的效率。这种阅读——解题的方法既不影响考生们解题时获取必需的知识点，又从实质上提高了考生们的阅读速度。在中口阅读理解的考试中，考生只要能读懂文章，就一定能理想地答题。我们提倡考生们无论在复习或考试的过程中都要充分结合以上四个要点，这样才能从实质上提高阅读理解的水平。

第一节 确定主题

对于阅读考生来说,文章的主题是需要首先确定的信息。这样不仅可以直接了解作者写作的目的,也可以把握阅读全文时的大致方向,真正做到有的放矢地阅读。所以在面对一篇文章时,确定义章的主题是考生的首要任务。

一篇文章的主题,或者中心思想通常体现在主题句或中心思想句 (Topic Sentence) 中。换句话说,在文章中作者通常会用一两句话来概括其写作的主要观点和意图,文章的其余部分将会围绕着这个主题来展开。确定并理解了主题或中心思想句,文章的主旨便可了然于胸。

主题的方位:国内英语考试阅读理解部分的文章主要取材于英文原版书刊,而刊登在这些书刊上的大多数义章(Essay)在英语写作上均有一个共同的特点:主题鲜明,逻辑清晰。作者通常会在文章伊始就鲜明地提出自己的观点,然后分段展开讨论或叙述,最后对最初提出的观点加以总结。这是一种非常典型的行文方式。传统的阅读方法由此指出:文章的第一个段落是阅读时的一个关键点,尤其是对主题的确立更为重要。这种总结有着一定的普遍性,但是并不全面。在中口阅读的文章中,尤其是在近年来的题型中我们发现,主题的方位完全是多样化的,单单依靠首段来确定主题缺乏实战依据。这点是需要考生们格外注意的。在中口阅读的文章中,根据作者提出其主要观点的方式以及主题出现的相对位置,我们总结出了以下大致四种方式:直叙式、引导式、总结式、省略式。

一、直叙式

一种常见的提出主题的方法就是在文章的首句直接提出主题,我们称之为直叙式。接下来文章会围绕着这个主题展开讨论(议论文),或加以叙述(叙事文),或加以说明(说明文)。这样的方式使考生对主题一目了然。接下来无论文章如何展开,必将围绕着一条主线。所以考生可以依据这条线索去整理文章的框架和具体的细节内容。

例1:

A Japanese construction company plans to build a huge independent city-state, akin to the legendary Atlantis, in the middle of the Pacific Ocean. The city, dubbed "Marinnation", would have about one million inhabitants, two airports, and possibly even a spaceport. Marinnation, if built, would be a separate country but could serve as a home for international organizations such as the United Nations and the World Bank.

解析:本文为说明文。在文章第一小节的首句,作者直接提出了本文的主题(划双线部分),即一家日本的建筑公司计划建造一座类似于亚特兰蒂斯的海底城市。那么接下来文章必定围绕这个主题展开。第二句提到了这个城市预计容纳的人口数量和设施(capacity),而第三句话提到了这个城市的用途(usage),即可能作为包括联合国和世界银行在内的国际组织的总部。以下文章的内容必定围绕这整个城市的建造展开。考生便可以顺着这条主线确定接下来的段落和主题之间的关联。

例 2:

Many folk cures which have been around for centuries may be more therapeutic than previously suspected. A case in point is that of penicillin. Alexander Fleming did not just randomly choose cheese molds to study when he discovered its very important bacteria-killing substance. Moldy cheese was frequently given to patients as a remedy for illness at one time. Fleming just isolated what it was about the cheese which cured the patients.

Q: This passage is mainly about _____ .

(A) using folk medicine to replace modern medicine

(B) antibiotics in the field of medicine

(C) the effectiveness of folk remedies

(D) isolating antibiotics in cheese, sugar, and slime

正解: (C)

解析: 作者在首句就提出了有许多民间的治疗方法的疗效比我们想像的要更加好,从而奠定了文章的主题。接下来文章会围绕着这个主题来介绍哪些药方有什么样的疗效。

例 3:

Lincoln's now famous Gettysburg Address was not, on the occasion of its delivery, recognized as the masterpiece that it is today. Lincoln was not even the primary speaker at the ceremonies, held at the height of the Civil War in 1863, to dedicate the battlefield at Gettysburg. The main speaker was orator Edward Everest, whose two-hour speech was followed by Lincoln's shorter remarks. Lincoln began his small portion of the program with the words that today are immediately recognized by most Americans: "Four score and seven years ago our father brought forth on this continent a new nation, conceived in liberty and dedicated to the proposition that all men are created equal." At the time of the speech, little notice was given to what Lincoln had said, and Lincoln considered his appearance at the ceremonies rather unsuccessful. After his speech appeared in print, appreciation for his words began to grow, and today it is recognized as one of the all time greatest speeches.

Q: The main idea of this passage is that _____ .

(A) the Gettysburg Address has always been regarded as a masterpiece

(B) at the time of its delivery the Gettysburg Address was truly appreciated as a masterpiece

(C) it was not until after 1863 that Lincoln's speech was recorded in history

(D) Lincoln is better recognized today than he was at the time of his presidency

正解: (D)

解析: 文章伊始,作者提出了论点:林肯著名的 Gettysburg 演讲在当时并没有受到人们的重视。这个主题给了我们两个信息：(1)林肯的这段演讲在当时没有引起足够的影响，但是现在却闻名于世；(2)林肯本人在当时（执政）没有受到人们足够的关注，但今日却受到万人敬仰。接下来文章按照他的演讲从不受关注到受到赞誉的过渡展开。

例4：

Even as the number of females processed through juvenile courts climbs steadily, an implicit agreement remains among scholars in criminal justice that young male define the delinquency problem in the United States. We suggest two reasons why this view persists. First, young females are accused primarily of victimless crimes, such as truancy, that do not involve clear-cut damage to persons or property. If committed by adults, these actions are not even considered prosecutable; if committed by young males, they have traditionally been looked on leniently by the courts. Thus, ironically, the difficult conditions of female delinquents receive little attention because they are accused of committing relatively minor offences. Second, the courts have long justified so-called preventive intervention into the lives of young females viewed as antisocial with the reasoning that women are especially vulnerable. Traditional ideas of women as the weaker and more dependent sex have led to earlier intervention and longer periods of misdirected supervision for female delinquents than for males.

解析：本文为议论文。文章的第一句话作者进行了立论，即尽管在美国青少年法庭上女性案例持续上扬，专家们仍然共同持有一个观点，即男性青少年犯罪仍然占据了青少年犯罪行为的主导。那么接下来作者一定会围绕着其提出的观点加以论证。文章的第二句话便是一个很好的证明。作者提出了有两个原因能够支持主题，以下再对这两个原因进行分别叙述。

有时文章的主题也可以通过一个问题来提出。而文章的展开就围绕着对这个问题的回答来进行。

例5：

(1) What are we? To the biologist we are members of a sub-species called Homo sapiens, which represents a division of the species known as Homo sapiens. Every species is unique and distinct: that is part of the definition of a species. But what is particularly interesting about our species? For a start, we walk upright on our hind legs at all times, which is an extremely unusual way of getting around for a mammal. There are also several unusual features about our head, not the least of which is the very large brain it contains. A second unusual feature is our strangely flattened face with its prominent, down-turned nose. Apes and monkeys have faces that protrude forwards as a muzzle and have "squashed" noses on top of this muzzle. There are many mysteries about human evolution, and the reason for our unusually shaped nose is one of them. Another mystery is our nakedness, or rather apparent nakedness. Unlike the apes, we are not covered by a coat of thick hair. Human body hair is very plentiful, but it is extremely fine and short so that for all practical purposes, we are naked. Very probably this has something to do with the second

interesting feature of our body: the skin is richly covered with millions of microscopic sweat glands. The human ability to sweat is unmatched in the primate world.

(2) So much for our appearance: what about our behavior? Our forelimbs, being freed from helping us to get about, possess a very high degree of manipulative skill. Part of this skill lies in the anatomical structure of the hands, but the crucial element is, of course, the power of the brain. No matter how suitable the limbs are for detailed manipulation, they are useless in the absence of finely tuned instructions delivered through nerve fibres. The most obvious product of our hands and brains is technology. No other animal manipulates the world in the extensive and arbitrary way that humans do. The termites are capable of constructing intricately structured mounds which create their own "air-conditioned" environment inside. But the termites cannot choose to build a cathedral instead. Humans are unique because they have the capacity to choose what they do.

Q: Which of the following can be the best title of the passage?

(A) What are Human Beings: Appearance and Behavior

(B) What are Primates: the Ability to Sweat

(C) What are Termites: Architects of the Animal World

(D) What are Human Hands Capable of: the Ability to Choose

正解: (A)

解析: 本文为说明文。文章伊始,作者提出了一个问题:我们是什么?这无疑是文章接下来要讨论的重点。接着作者开始针对这个问题做出了回答,由此引出了下文。人类的定性包括纯科学的定性(第二句话),同时也有区别于其他各种物种的特征(uniqueness)(第三句话以下)。而接下来第二小节的首句清楚地提示了人类的两个最明显的特征:外表和行为。

二、引导式

引导式指的是作者在文章的开始先做出一番铺垫,然后由此引导出主要的观点。这种形式在中口阅读理解的文章中出现的频率很高。 在这里要特别提出的是,考生们辨识作者运用铺垫的能力也是确定主题的一个关键,尤其在一个阅读时间受到严格控制的环境里,这就显得更为重要。如果在阅读文章的时候不能迅速地辨识铺垫,确定主题,考生会因此而延误了有效的阅读时间。如果在阅读时受到了铺垫中某些叙述的干扰,甚至会错误地判断主题。对于铺垫的阅读,需要注意以下两个方面:

1. 铺垫的方式:运用铺垫的方式一般可以有以下几种:(1) 一段介绍主题的陈述(introduction);(2)一个与主题相关的小故事、典故或俗语(anecdote);(3) 与主题有着逻辑关联的类比(analogy);(4)与主题相对立的观点(contrast);(5)主题的原因或结果(cause/effect)。无论以哪种形式做出铺垫,作者的目的都是能够更生动地或更有说服力地引导出主题。

2. 铺垫的篇幅：阅读时另一个值得注意的问题是，铺垫在一篇文章中所覆盖的篇幅。有时可以是寥寥几句话，但在有些文章中可能会横跨几个小节。较长的铺垫无疑会给考生带来阅读上的负担以及主题确定上的困惑。在这样的情况下，考生首先需要正确地判断哪些段落属于文章的铺垫，不要轻易地对文章的主题下结论。其次要学会分辨文章从次到主的过渡，尤论铺垫多长，作者总是要对主题做出陈述的。细节的描写，例如对人物、事物和场景的具体描写，对一个故事的叙述，对一种社会形态的展现等等，总是要上升到一段观点性、总结性的论述。这往往就是主题的出现。当然，确有少数文章的主题并不清晰，这我们也会在以下的章节中进行说明。下面我们来通过几个实例加以说明。

例1：陈述（Introduction）I

According to airline industry statistics, almost 90% of airline accidents are survivable or partially survivable. But passengers can increase their chances of survival by learning and following certain tips. Experts say that you should read and listen to safety instructions before takeoff and ask questions if you have uncertainties. You should fasten your seat belt low on your hips and as tightly as possible. Of course, you should also know how the release mechanism of your belt operates. During takeoffs and landings, you are advised to keep you feet flat on the floor. Before takeoff you should locate the nearest exit and an alternative exit and count the rows of seats between you and the exits so that you can find them in the dark if necessary.

解析：文章开始用了一句话交代了一个航空企业的调查数据，并用它做了主题的铺垫。调查的结论是，百分之九十的航空事故不是致命的。但是这个数据并不能说明问题。作者真正写作的目的，是给乘坐飞机的旅客提供一些提高他们在空难事故中生存率的建议。接下来文章就会沿着各条建议展开。这篇文章的首句属于一种基本介绍，在转折词"but"之后方才引出主题。

例2：陈述（Introduction）II

In some rural agricultural societies, the collection of available fuel such as firewood, dung cake, and agricultural waste can take 200 or 300 person-days per year. As well as being time consuming, the typical patterns of collection lead to deforestation, soil erosion, and ecological imbalances. In the future, experts predict that even if food supplies are adequate for rural populations, fuel supplies for domestic use may not be.

In the light of such considerations, a team in India has developed a solar oven for home use. The oven is cheaply constructed, easily operated, and extremely energy efficient. The device consists of an inner and outer metal box, a top cover, and two panes of plain glass. The inner box is painted black to absorb maximum solar radiation. The space between the two boxes is filled with an insulating material, such as rice husks, which are easily available and which, because of their high silicon content, neither attract insects nor rot easily. Other easily available materials for insulation are ground nutshells or coconut shells. An adjustable mirror mounted on one side of the oven box reflects the sunlight into the interior, boosting the temperature by 15-30 degrees Celsius. This is most useful during the winter when the sun is lower. Inside the oven, a temperature between 80 and 120 degrees Celsius above ambient temperature can be maintained. This is sufficient to cook food gradually but surely. Trials have shown that all typical food dishes can be prepared in this solar device without loss of taste or nutrition.

Q1: This passage is mainly about _____ .

    (A) deforestation in the rural agricultural societies

    (B) use of rice husks as an insulation material

    (C) design and use of a solar oven

    (D) maintenance of temperature in a solar oven

Q2: All of the following are mentioned as sources of energy of rural agricultural societies except _____ .

    (A) firewood   (B) dung cake

    (C) solar power   (D) agricultural waste

Q3: According to the passage, the use of an adjustable mirror increases the oven temperature by _____ .

    (A) 80 ~ 120 degrees Celsius   (B) at least 80 degrees Celsius

    (C) up to 30 degrees Celsius   (D) up to 15 degrees Celsius

解析：本文的第一小节都是主题的铺垫。作为一篇说明文，作者的主旨是为了介绍一种在印度使用的新型家用太阳能烤炉。而在文章的第一小节，作者先描述了在一些农业社会中收集燃料在人力付出上的耗费，又进一步地提到了这种收集燃料的方法不仅存在着耗时的弊病，还会导致地质和环境上的不良后果。最后作者提到了将来的家庭即便不会遇到粮食储备的危机，也会受到日益减少的燃料危机的威胁。这番铺垫充分体现了新型家用燃料用具在人们生活中的必要性和迫切性。由此太阳能烤炉的使用在第二小节被提出，也就奠定了文章的主题（划双线部分）。以下的文章必然会围绕这种烤炉的原理、特性、使用等各方面展开。本文中的铺垫也是一种叙述性的 introduction，但是篇幅明显要长于前一篇文章。如果仅仅依据第一小节的内容，盲目地推测作者写作的目的与燃料问题、环境问题、落后国家对于燃料的收集方法等相关，就会被误导。

Q1：根据以上的分析，作者最主要的写作目的是为了介绍太阳能烤炉。所以选 (C)。

Q2：能量的来源显然属于铺垫部分的内容，答案应该在第一小节。而文章在第一小节中不可能提到太阳能源，因为在第二小节作者把它当作新能源来看待。所以选 (C)。

Q3：题目显然在询问烤炉工作原理和效果方面的问题，所以一定在第二小节。再根据 "adjustable mirror" 一词我们找到答案出自 "boosting the temperatures by 15 ~ 30 degrees Celsius"，最高可以把温度提到 30 度。选 (C)。

例3：故事/事件 (Anecdote)

Outside Johnny & Gino Hairstyling on Hanover Street, the late September morning moved from soggy clouds to brilliantly clear, with a fresh breeze off the harbor and sun glinting from the golden domes of Boston's colonial buildings. Inside, Johnny "Shoes" Cammarata was putting the finishing touches on Rico Federico's trim, while assorted customers waited their turn. "I was born here," Johnny is saying in his broad Boston accent, "but I had to speak Sicilian at home if I wanted to eat." This would be an important point: His silhouette is clear evidence that his enthusiasm for talking is matched only by his passion for home cooking, not surprising for a man who was born on the kitchen table, "And I'll die on the table," he says cheerfully, "with my face in a plate of lasagna. With two meat balls, one on each side."

The North Ender is a complex breed composed of Mediterranean emotion, Yankee drive, and a seemingly limitless passion for their own. To be able to say you're a North Ender, I soon discovered, would put you several notches higher than Phi Beta Kappa, a 32nd degree Mason, and five Nobel Prize winners picked at random.

解析：本文为记叙文。在第一小节作者用了很长的篇幅叙述了一段理发店老板理发的场景和与这位老板的一番对话：在某个理发店里，一个外号叫"鞋子"的理发师正在完成他的理发工作。他操着一口波士顿口音，告诉作者他出生在美国，但在家里他要想吃到饭的话，就一定要说西西里话。接着又热情洋溢地赞美着家里的意大利菜，诙谐地说他是出生在厨房的台子上的,他也要在厨房的美食里离开这个世界。作者在文章的开头安排这段对话的真正目的体现在第二小节的首句：介绍一个特殊的人群：波士顿北区人——意大利的血统，美国的精神，自己的骄傲。文章成功地用了一个人的背景,对话和意识,提炼出了一群人的特点和精神,也就是文章的主题。不难推测以下的段落都将围绕着这群人的特点和精神展开。

例4：类比（Analogy）I

（1）In the mid-1980's no thrusting executive was complete without his/her personal organizer—a leather binder containing everything from address-book and diary to a career-planning chart. Then came the portable telephone, whispered into with ostentatious discretion. Now the electronic organizer has arrived. Psion, a British firm which created the first such digital diarycum-calculator, sells about 200,000 a year. Competitors are piling into the market.

（2）When Psion launched its hand-held computer in 1982, it foresaw two markets. One was in the salerooms and warehouses of large companies. Here, stocktakers and salesmen needed a portable way to talk to the big computers back at head office. About half of Psion's sales now come from companies—as well as many lucrative contracts to write software specially tailored to link its little machines into a firm's computer network.

（3）The other half of Psion's sales come from individuals keen to organize themselves electronically. Most use the machine as a "personal data base" (i. e., address book and diary) or to crunch numbers too tough for their calculators to handle. It takes several times longer to tap a name or a date into the tiny keyboard of a hand-held computer than it does to write it down on an Asprey pad. But hundreds of thousands of people seem to think it worthwhile—maybe because the computer can search speedily through electronically stored names—or because it impresses their friends.

Q1: The advantage of the Psion product over earlier personal organizers is _____ .

(A) that information can be retrieved more quickly

(B) the ability to provide a quicker input of information

(C) improved electronics

(D) its processing of numbers

Q2: Compared to traditional calculators, the Psion product _____ .

(A) is cheaper　　　　　　　　　(B) is more durable

(C) has greater capacity　　　　　(D) has a longer quality guarantee

解析：本文为说明文。作者所要说明的事物是市场上流行的电子记事簿。但是为了说明时代的进步以及电子记事簿的优点，作者在文章的开始进行了类比，从80年代商界人士所用的记事本，发展到后来的手机，直到现在电子记事簿的问世。这几样事物的共同点都是用来记录个人信息的，但随着科技的进步，电子记事簿一定会提高个人信息管理的效率。文章以下的内容便会按照电子记事簿的功能和特点，以及与同类产品的比较来展开。

Q1: 根据以上的分析我们可以看出，本题正是在考查电子记事簿与传统记事本的区别。同样作为记事工具，电子记事簿可以很快地搜索信息，所以选(A)，出处为"But hundreds of thousands of people seem to think it worthwhile—maybe because the computer can search speedily through electronically stored names"。

Q2: 本题考查的是电子记事簿与普通计算器的区别。具有运算功能的电子记事簿优于计算器的地方就是储存量大，可以操作更复杂的运算，所以选(C)，出处为"or to crunch numbers too tough for their calculators to handle."

例5：类比(Analogy)II

(1) Natural selection is the way nature chooses which organisms survive. Chance mutation occurs in response to chemicals of certain energy in the electromagnetic spectrum. If the mutant is better adapted to the environment, it thrives. If not, it dies out or becomes rare.

(2) Humans have used artificial selection to reproduce plants and animals with desirable characteristics. Many of these domesticated plants and animals can no longer survive in the wild. Their survival depends on the maintenance of an artificial environment and the desires of people.

(3) People select certain desired traits such as color, beauty, or scent (as in roses). Other traits which are bred artificially include uniqueness (as in the neck plumage of the prized Jacobin pigeon), size (as in miniature horses), meat quality or milk yield (as in cattle), or resistance to disease(as in fungus-resistant tomatoes). The traits usually are selected for convenience, pleasure, or financial gain of individuals. In this way, humans act as agents of evolution through artificial selection.

(4) Individual specimens with the desired traits are crossbred. The hybrid offspring are

then inbred to preserve and fix the desirable characteristics and eliminate unfavorable characteristics from the stock.

(5) A pure breed is formed when there is not any mixture of other genes over many generations. The American Kennel Club recognizes 121 breeds of purebred dogs. When ancestors of a pure breed are known and registered by a breed club, the dog is said to have a pedigree.

Q1: Which of the following is not mentioned as the result of artificial selection by humanity?

(A) Many new kinds of plants and animals are produced.

(B) Financial gain is increased considerably by producing better plants and animals.

(C) Humans are able to control plant and animal reproduction for humans' pleasure.

(D) It is necessary for humans to maintain the artificial environments.

Q2: Breeding the hybrid offspring to fix desirable traits is called _____ .

(A) naturally selecting   (B) inbreeding

(C) pedigree breeding   (D) pure-breeding

Q3: A farmer imported several fine long wool Tomney sheep from Australia to breed with his Debouittet sheep in hopes of increasing the value of the flock's wool. This is an example of _____ .

(A) pure-breeding   (B) crossbreeding

(C) reproducing   (D) cloning

解析：本文是一篇讲述人类使用人工基因合成来繁殖动植物的行为的文章。第一小节首先以自然选择作为类比，提出了观点：自然选择是自然力量决定生物生长和消亡的方式。而基因变异则是一种特例，变种如果能适应环境则能生存，相反则会消亡。由此我们已经理解了所谓"选择—— selection"的含义，而第二段再提出作者的主题，我们就更容易理解：人类选择就是用人类力量代替自然力量来对生物的生存做出人为的选择或修改。接下来文章将围绕着人类做出这类选择的标准和方式展开。

Q1: 根据以上的分析我们可以判断，人工选择的结果是紧接着中心段的第三小节：人们会按照一定的愿望和标准进行，从而在新的物种上得到一些预期的特征或效果。选项(A)、(B)、(C)在原文中皆有反映，只有(D)是出现在中心段中，作为人工选择的产物成活的必要条件，而非结果。所以正解是(D)。

Q2: 本题考查的就是人工选择的方式：混血繁殖在第四小节中被称之为 inbreeding，近亲交配。选(B)。

Q3: 和上题一样，题目描写了两种不同类型的羊进行交配，同样属于人工选择中的杂交(crossbreeding)，出自于第三小节，选(B)。

例6：对照(Contrast)

Most people picture sharks as huge, powerful, frightening predators, ready at any moment to use their sharp teeth to attack unwary swimmers without provocation. There are numerous fallacies, however, in this conception of sharks. First, there are about 350 species of shark, and not all of them are large. They range in size from the dwarf shark, which can be only 6 inches (0.5 feet) long and can be held in the palm of the hand, to the whale shark, which can be more than 55 feet long.

Q: The author's main purpose in the passage is to _____ .

(A) categorize the different kinds of sharks throughout the world

(B) warn humans of the dangers posed by sharks

(C) describe the characteristics of shark teeth

(D) clear up misconceptions about sharks

正解：(D)

解析：本文为一篇议论文。作者在立论之前先举出了一个相对照的观点（contrast），即大多数人都普遍认为鲨鱼是体积庞大、力大无穷、凶狠无比的食肉动物，随时随地都有可能对游泳者发起攻击。随即作者又对这个观点提出了质疑，认为它存在着许多谬论，从而树立了自己的观点（划双线部分）。所以作者真正的写作意图是为了澄清一些人们一贯以来对鲨鱼存在的偏见。接下来文章一定会针对三方面的错误观点（huge, powerful, frightening）展开叙述。

例 7：因果（Cause/Effect）

Psychologists have found that privately made confidential resolutions are rarely followed, whereas a public commitment to achieve some goal, such as losing weight or giving up smoking, is likely to be much more effective. This is because the approval of others for doing something desirable is valued. In contrast, disapproval or failure can lead to feelings of shame.

Q: It can be inferred that all of the following help motivate a person to achieve a goal EXCEPT _____ .

(A) a desire for approval　　　　(B) a fear of disapproval

(C) a fear of failure　　　　(D) a sense of noncommitment

正解：(D)

解析：作者在文章伊始提出了心理学家的一个发现：凡是人们私下里做出的决定都很难实现，但是如果是在公开场合做出的决定，比如说要减肥或戒烟，实行的效果就相对来说比较好。这个现象并不是作者所要讨论的主题，而仅仅是一种结果（effect），作者的意图是讨论造成这种结果的原因：（与完成一个决定相比，）人们更在乎其他人对自己的看法。我们希望别人认为我们很好地完成了一项工作，同样别人眼里的失败会让我们感到羞愧。从中心句中我们可以看出能帮助人们成功的因素应该包括：(A)希望得到他人的认可；(B)害怕受到他人的否定；(C)害怕失败。接下来文章便会由此接着论证人们这种心理的具体表现。

值得注意的是在运用因果关系的铺垫时，在主题或中心思想句中通常会出现表示原因（because/because of, reason, cause, source, ground, etc.）或表示结果（result, effect, product, etc.)的词汇。这也是帮助我们快速辨识这类主题句的好方法。

三、总结式

一篇文章的主题还可以出现在文章的中段,乃至末尾,作为对全文叙述的总结而出现,我们称之为总结式。这类文章的行文特点是作者对一个观点先进行分段论述,或一个事件进行详细记叙,最后再对文章的主题或中心思想进行总结。这样的总结其实就成了中心思想句。这样的行文方式多见于一些驳论文(反驳一种观点的文章)和记叙义(记叙一段历史事件或历程的文章)中。虽然这类文章并不多见,考生们仍然需要把握相应的阅读技巧。这类文章要求考生除了能够在随着文章的进程准确地判断文章的中心思想,同时也需要理顺文章中细节的推进,以及各个段落之间相互的关联。以下我们通过几个例子来说明:

例1:

(1) More than a hundred years ago, before the Civil War, a crew of bronc-busting cowboys stood outside a large horse corral. With them was their boss Bradford Grimes, a cattleman who owned a large South Texas ranch near the Gulf of Mexico.

(2) Inside the corral was a herd of wild mustangs, horses that had never been ridden. They milled around, snorting and rearing.

(3) One of the bronc busters roped a strong stallion and held him to be saddled. Then another cowboy climbed up and tried to ride. At first the animal trotted nervously, humping a little and shying from side to side. Then it went off in high jumps, spinning and shaking and jolting its rider. Finally it put its head between its front legs, bucked high in the air, and threw the cowboy off into the dust.

(4) Just then Mrs. Grimes, the cattleman's wife, came to the ranch house door and cried out. "Bradford! Bradford! Those Blacks are worth a thousand dollars apiece. One might get killed."

(5) The cowboys laughed, but they knew she was telling the truth. For they were all Black slaves. Bradford Grimes was their owner.

(6) Most of the first Black cowboys were slaves, brought by their masters from the old South. On the plantations in the South, the slaves cut cotton. On the ranches in Texas they had to learn a new trade—breaking horses and handling cattle. Some were taught by Mexican cowboys, some by Indians who knew the ways of horses and cattle.

(7) Grimes was only one of hundreds of slave-owning ranchers who ran cattle in Texas. The ranchers had brought their families and slaves from Mississippi, Georgia, and other southern states. They came on horseback, on foot, and in buggies and wagons. They drove hogs, oxen, and stock.

(8) Some ranchers settled near the Mexican border, but there they found that it was too

easy for their slaves to escape. Even slaves as far north as Austin, the capital of Texas, came to think of Mexico as the promised land. As early as 1845, the year that Texas became a state, a Texas newspaper reported the escape of twenty-five Blacks. "They were mounted on some of the best horses that could be found," the story said, "and several of them were armed." Thousands of other Black slaves escaped in the same way.

（9）East of the Nueces River, farther from the Mexican border, most slaves found it hard to escape. So there they stayed, learning to become cowboys in bleak, rough country and learning to chase wild cattle through heavy coastal brush.

（10）All-Black cattle crews were common throughout central and eastern Texas. There were even a few free blacks who owned ranches before the Civil War. Aaron Ashorth was one of them, and he owned 2,500 cattle, as well as some slaves of his own. He employed a white school-master to tutor his children.

（11）Black cowboys helped to tame and settle a wild country.

Q: According to the passage, Blacks helped to _____.

　　(A) tame the animals in Texas 　　　(B) solve living problems in Texas
　　(C) conquer the US 　　　　　　　　(D) settle the new territory

正解：(D)

解析：这篇文章开始用了整整五个小节的内容勾勒了一个牛仔在马场里力图驯服一匹野马的场景。同时也为考生勾勒出了生活在美国西部的牛仔典型的生活场景。考生在阅读过程中应该敏锐地注意到作者在叙述中的场景描写，包括牛仔的行为、他们主人的身份、马场里马匹的表情和动作、驯马的具体场景、场主夫妇之间的对话。这些都是细节描写，而作者所使用的也正是我们在前面一段中提到的一种铺垫的手法，运用小故事（anecdote）。那么作者真正的写作目的是什么呢？在这个小故事末尾（第五小节），我们借着农场主妻子的一番话得知这群牛仔都有一个共同的特点：他们都是黑奴。而在第六小节作者主要的写作目的才刚刚浮现出来，即描述在美国开发西部初期的过程：南部的庄园主迁徙到西部成为了当地的牧场主，从在南部庄园种植棉花过渡到了放牛养马的西部畜牧生活。而在西部这片荒凉的大地上，为农场主提供劳力的生力军便是他们从南部庄园带来的黑奴。第八小节进一步介绍了当时在靠近墨西哥边境的牧场里经常发生黑奴逃亡的事件，反映了黑奴对生活的不满和对自由的追求。当然，可以成功逃跑的黑奴毕竟占少数。大多数的黑奴追随他们的主人定居下来，成了黑人牛仔，开始了艰辛的牧场生活。第九和第十小节介绍了这种生活的大致状态。通过对黑人牛仔的迁徙和在西部生活的介绍，作者在最后一节推出了全文的中心思想——黑人牛仔不仅帮助他们的主人驯服了西部的野马，也帮助美国征服了一片荒蛮的土地，而这也是黑人牛仔最大的贡献。

例2：

（1）Another dropped stitch in life's rich tapestry: that 15-year-old schoolboy who was caught in the Stock Market crash after a £100,000 shares gamble. Peeved stockbrokers to whom he owes £20,000 now say in injured tones: "He has been very naughty. We thought he was 19."

(2) I must say that small fry finances have come on a bit since the era of Billy Bunter's non-arriving five bob postal order. While not in the same league as Britain's youngest yuppie, I see from a Health Education Authority survey that school teenagers are now spending £10 a week or more on records, clothes and booze. The good news is that nearly one in two of the big spenders holds down a part-time job, the boys financing their considerable commitments mainly from paper rounds, the girls either babysitting or working in shops and cafes.

(3) I call this a very welcome trend. For a very long time, going right back to the golden age of the Welfare State, there was a real social stigma attached to the idea of school kids working. Local authorities frowned on it, teachers disapproved of it, parents felt guilty about it, and children themselves came to believe that having to earn their own pocket money was a great imposition.

(4) To be sure, there is still opposition in some quarters. But by and large the pendulum seems to be swinging the right way again. The other day I heard of a gang of lads who station themselves outside a car wash every Saturday offering, much to the rage of the manager, to do the job half-price. Now that's enterprise. Back in the days of the Saturday penny. I was something of an entrepreneur myself. I had five paper rounds, a firewood business, a golf-caddying concession and a contract to carry groceries back to the convent for a bunch of local nuns. I was working a good twenty-four hours a week out of school, and as the saying goes, it never did me any harm. Indeed I'm sure it did me a good deal of good.

(5) Ten pounds a week does seem an awful lot to be squandering on fripperies, but at least it's as often as not their own hard earned cash. More to the point, they learn at a tender age that while it may or may not be true that money cannot buy happiness, at least happiness—in the form of satisfaction at a job well done, that is—can buy money.

(6) But don't sink it all in futures, kids.

Q: Which of the following can be inferred from the passage?

(A) Children may get satisfaction from working part-time.

(B) School teenagers usually spend 10 a week on records.

(C) A good 24 hours a week out of school is the right amount of time for kids.

(D) School girls often work in shops and cafes.

正解:(A)

解析:作者在文章的开始运用了一个小故事(anecdote)。一个 15 岁的少年骗取了股票经纪人的信任炒股,结果在股市暴跌(crash)中全军覆没。这段故事可以有很多展开的方向,所以考生们必须耐心地往下阅读,找出作者真正想要表达的观点。在第二小节,作者根据一项调查得知,青少年每周要在娱乐消费上花去 10 英镑之多,但是幸好大部分青少年都在勤工俭学,这样保证了他们开销的正常来源。由此我们关注的重点落到了青少年打工的问题上。但作者的态度仍然不是非常的明朗。在第三小节,作者首先提出了青少年打工是个受欢迎的趋势,我们由此可以感到作者在这个问题上所持的支持观点。接下来作者回顾了旧时代英国青少年打工受到了社会上普遍的反对。在第四小节,作者引用了自己上学时打工的往事来说明青少年打工是有益无害的。在文章的最后一小节,作者终于提出了自己最核心的观点(划双线部分):虽然我们不知道金钱是否能带来幸福,但是青少年打工不仅可以享受到顺利完成一项工作之后所得到的满足感,同时又可以得到应有的报酬,一举两得。值得注意的是,在全文的最后一句,出现了这样的引导词"More to the point"。这里的"point"一词本身就有"观点,立场"的意思,在阅读中应该对这个词格外注意。在这里它无疑指的就是文章的中心思想,这也给了我们一个最好的提示,表明"point"以下的话就是文章的中心所在。

四、省略式

一篇文章的主题或中心思想有时在全文中没有得到具体的体现。也就是说,我们不能在文章中找到主题或中心思想句。遇到这样的文章就更加需要考生在阅读时抓住作者在文章的每个段落中所要表达的观点或叙述的事件,以及这些观点和事件之间相互的关联和主次的区别,从而合理地推断主题。这样的文章经常出现在一些人物传记和讲述历史事件的记叙文以及一些说明文中。

例1:

(1) Every year about two million people visit Mount Rushmore, where the faces of four U. S. presidents were carved in granite by sculptor Gutzon Borglum and his son, the late Lincoln Borglum. (2) The creation of the mount Rushmore monument took 14 years — from 1927 to 1941—and nearly a million dollars. (3) These were times when money was difficult to come by and many people were jobless. (4) To move the more than 400,000 tons of rock, Borgium hired laid-off workers from the closed-down mines in the Black Hills area. (5) He taught these men to dynamie, drill, carve, and finish the granite as they were hanging in midair in his specially devised chairs, which had many safety features. (6) Borglum was proud of the fact that no workers were killed or severely injured during the years of blasting and carving.

Q. According to the passage, the men Borglum hired were _____.

(A) trained sculptors   (B) laid-off stone masons

(C) Black Hills volunteers   (D) visitors to Mount Rushmore

正解:(B)

解析:文章的首句讲了美国为数众多的游客前往著名的总统山观光旅游,也提到四座总统的雕像是由雕刻家 Gutzon Borglum 和他已故的儿子雕刻的。至此我们的阅读虽然有了大致的方向,但是作者所要表达的观点或描述的对象并不能马上得到确定,主题并不非常明确。第二句说到了建造时间和耗费,转入了细节描写。第三句提到了人力资源渠道,即当地失业的矿工。而雕刻家 Borglum 教会了这些工人施工所要具备的重要技能,例如爆破、挖掘、雕塑等等。最后一句提到了 Borglum 本人在整个施工过程中最为自豪的一点：没有发生一个施工人员的伤亡事故。虽然主题句并没有得到鲜明的体现，但是不难看出文章整体围绕了雕塑的全过程进行了叙述。而全文的主要内容无疑是完成雕塑所涉及的各种要素（factors），其中可能包括了时间、金钱、人力、技术方面的困难等等。而以上的题目恰恰考查的工程人力资源方面的知识，我们很快定位在本段的第四句话，选项中只有 (B) 出现了关键词"laid-off"。

例 2:

(1) WITNESSES may pick out from an identification parade the person who most resembles their idea of what the criminal would look like, a conference organized by the British Psychological Society was told on Saturday. Mr. Ray Bull, a senior lecturer at the North East London Polytechnic, said research had shown that the public tended to link abnormal appearance with abnormalities of behavior. The public and police do agree about what face fits what crime, he said. One apparently widely held belief is the "what is beautiful is good" stereotype. An individual's facial attractiveness has an effect on how threatening other people judge that person to be. "I have found that the addition of one or two small scars to a face leads to that face being judged more dishonest."

(2) Those beliefs also influence length of sentence and verdict, he said. Research in mock-trial settings had shown that the **(Q1)** → more unattractive defendant was more heavily sentenced than one of attractive character and appearance. Mr. Bull, an expert on identification by witnesses, was addressing psychologists and lawyers at a conference in London held by Sir Brian MacKenna, a retired high court judge, on the role of psychology in the legal system.

(3) **(Q2)** →For decades it has been known that people often do not see or hear things presented to their senses, but do "see" and "hear" things that have not occurred. But none of those factors meant that identification evidence was of little value. Laboratory research based on photographs had shown recognition rates were high, about 80 percent, even after delays of 35 days. But rates were lower when identification was tested in mock criminal episodes in the streets because of stress and the inability of the witness to concentrate simultaneously on self-preservation and remembering details to the culprit. **(Q3)** →Law enforcement authorities should be more aware of the factors that influence memory and identification, Mr. Bull said, apart from people's prejudices about the "look" of a criminal, the factors included the way questions were asked.

Q1: According to Mr. Ray Bull's research, which of the following defendants would be more heavily sentenced?

(A) The defendant with normal behavior.

(B) The defendant with attractive character.

(C) The defendant with unattractive appearance.

(D) The defendant with psychological problems.

Q2: According to the passage, people often _____ .

(A) have sensory problems

(B) foretell what have not yet happened

(C) distort what they have seen or heard

(D) neglect what they see or hear

Q3: According to the passage, which of the following statements is not true?

(A) Mr. Ray Bull pointed out that the criminal with abnormal appearance would be sentenced more heavily than the one with attractive appearance.

(B) Mr. Ray Bull delivered a speech at a conference to psychologists and lawyers on the role of psychology in the legal system.

(C) Mr. Ray Bull has found out that the addition of one or two small scars to a face leads to that face being judged more dishonest.

(D) Mr. Ray Bull argued that law enforcement authorities should be less aware of the factors that influence memory and identification.

Q4: What is the main idea expressed in the passage?

(A) Witnesses' memory and identification are unreliable.

(B) British Psychological Society has studied the role of psychology in legal system.

(C) Both the appearance and character of a person would influence peoples, judgment on him.

(D) What is beautiful is good.

解析：本文是一篇说明文。在第一小节，作者首先陈述了很多证人在指认嫌疑犯时往往是通过他们的感觉来辨认，依据是看谁的长相最符合他们想像中罪犯的模样。而犯罪心理学家也指出，人们通常把异样的长相和异常的行为结合起来（link abnormal appearance with abnormalities of behavior）。接下来作者把话题引向了"美丽的外表意味着美丽的心灵"（"what is beautiful is good" stereotype）这个成见。同样，在对罪犯的审判中有缺陷的外表也会给嫌疑犯带来不公正的判断。在第二小节作者指出，以上提到的一系列观点同时也影响着法官在量刑上的轻重。作者进一步提出外貌和性格是影响人们判断的两个重要因素。在第三小节作者又指出，人们一直以来在主观判断上都存在忽视事实的毛病（but do "see" and "hear" things that have not occurred），而这也应该引起执法人员的注意。

虽然全文没有一个明显的中心句，但是一条主线一直贯穿着全文，这就是人们以貌取人的主观臆断往往使得他们在判断上造成失误，而这种人为的失误在对罪犯的评判上的体现应该引起各方的注意。在确定了这个主题之后，再回顾文章的三个段落，全文的结构便一目了然了：第一小节是陈述基本事实，指出了人们在评判罪犯上具有的一些普遍的以貌取人的心理和具体的体现；第二小节指出了这些错误判断可能造成的实际后果；最后一节作者分析了这些心理的根源和影响它们的因素，并提醒法律工作者注意这些因素的存在。

Q1: 本题考查的是以貌取人在量刑上导致的后果——长相欠缺的人会受到更加严厉

的判罚，选 **(C)**，出处是第二小节的 "more unattractive defendant was more heavily sentenced than one of attractive character and appearance."

Q2: 本题考查的是这种心理的根源——人们经常对现有的事实置之不理，选 **(D)**，出处是第三小节的首句 "For decades it has been known that people often do not see or hear things presented to their senses, but do "see" and "hear" things that have not occurred."

Q3: 本题考查的是全文所覆盖的各个观点和要素。其中 **(D)** 中 "less" 是明显的错误，与文章最后的建议正好相互抵触，所以是我们要的选项，出处是 "Law enforcement authorities should be more aware of the factors that influence memory and identification."

Q4: 在完成了对全文各个观点的考查之后，我们完全可以透过细节了解作者的主要观点，即人们通常犯以貌取人的错误，选 **(C)**。

例 3：

（1）It took policeman John Pooley only an hour or two to solve the Case of the Thorpeness Burglary. It must be said, however, that the crime was not difficult. The description, though slight, narrowed the number of persons likely to commit such a crime... to one. Pooley, of course, knows everyone in the three villages in his care, and their children. But after he had made the arrest—something he has to do more rarely than once a month—he felt troubled because he not only knew the man, but also knew that he had family problems.

（2）Like most village policemen, John Pooley is in charge of a very large area by police standards, which includes the three villages of Middleton, Dunwich and Westleton, where he lives. **(Q1)**→With a total population of 1,219, he has more than twice as many people to look after as the average policeman has. Moreover, he is attached to the Halesworth subdivision and is frequently given duties outside his home area. After 15 years as a policeman, he accepts these duties without question, **(Q2)**→but his villages are clearly where his heart and interest really lie. When he was first sent to Westleton, he lived in the police house which was both his home and the police station; when the system was changed, he bought the house where he now lives with his wife, Ann, and his two daughters.

（3）He could hardly be better qualified for the job of village policeman. Before he joined the police, he was an agricultural worker for five years and a male nurse in a mental hospital for six years. **(Q3)**→He says: "If you haven't had another job before you join the police, you tend to think nothing but police."

（4）**(Q4)**→Crime in the country, of course, is somewhat different from city crime. Who was ever attacked while walking along the village street in Middleton? The things which John Pooley has to watch for are people stealing tools and equipment from farm vehicles, or wood from the surrounding forests. There are natural dangers too: he is so worried about the fire risk in forests that he has turned his bedroom window into a look-post.

Q1: From the passage it appears that nowadays a village policeman, like John

Pooley, has to _____ .

(A) live in a village police house

(B) put out forest fires

(C) go through a long period of training

(D) look after more people than policemen elsewhere

Q2: According to the passage, we learn that he _____ .

(A) is unpopular with the people in the villages

(B) objects when he is given work outside his own area

(C) prefers working in the villages of Middleton, Dunwich and Westleton

(D) feels unhappy when he arrests anybody

Q3: Crime in this area is different from crime in a big city because _____ .

(A) it is hardly ever violent   (B) people here have more family problems

(C) the victim is easily attacked   (D) it is connected with natural disasters

解析：本文属于一篇人物传记类型的记叙文。文章介绍的是一位乡村警察的工作和生活。第一小节用这位警察破案的一个事件引出了他的身份。第二小节叙述了他工作上的特性,这里包括他的职能范围,与城市警察的对比,以及他对待工作的心态等。后半部分还提到了他的生活状况。第三小节提到了他是一个非常称职的警察,这和他以前丰富的工作经历是分不开的。最后一段比较了一下乡村犯罪和城市犯罪行为的区别和乡村面临的自然灾害的威胁,同时也再次体现了一名乡村警察工作职能的特点。各段的叙述都围绕着一个乡村警察的工作和生活展开。

Q1: 考查的是 John Pooley 作为一个乡村警察的工作特征:比其他警察的工作量要大,选 **(D)**,出处是 "he has more than twice as many people to look after as the average policeman has..."

Q2: 考查的是 John Pooley 对待工作的态度,而他本人显然是热爱他的工作的,尤其热衷与自己的辖区,选 **(C)**,出处是 "... but his villages are clearly where his heart and interest really lie."

Q3: 考查的是乡村和城市犯罪的区别:乡村很少有暴力犯罪现象,选 **(A)**,出处是 "Crime in the country, of course, is somewhat different from city crime. Who was ever attacked while walking along the village street in Middleton? "

> 提示:许多叙述文的题目在排序上也顺承了文章叙述的顺序,循序渐进地展开。这证明了对文章框架的分析和掌握可以切实有效地帮助考生解答问题。

第二节 理清结构

文章的主题一旦得到了确定，接下来我们需要整理文章的结构。文章的主题是作者写作的主要目的，而结构则指的是作者如何组织文章的层次，安排叙述的顺序，从而更合理有效地阐述自己的观点。阅读理解部分的考试时间限制，不允许考生在阅读的过程中参透文章所有的内容，而需要考生在最短的时间内最实际有效地掌握文章的基本框架和主要内容，以便在解题时做到心理有数。和确定主题一样，整理一篇文章的结构也属于一种宏观技能。

中级口译考试阅读理解文章的结构大致遵循以下几种方式：

一、叙述型

这是一种最普通的行文方式。作者提出一个观点或一个要叙述或描写的对象，然后循序渐进，围绕着这个主题平铺直叙，最后完成对这个观点或对象的阐述或描述。大部分的记叙文和一些说明文采取的都是这样的形式。在这种类型的，文章结构中段落的推进一般存在以下几种方式：(1)时间的推移；(2)故事发展的顺序；(3)事件或理论演变的过程；(4)事件的前因后果；(5)事物的各项特性。

例1：时间推移

(1) On 27 January 1950 I was due at the Albert Hall, London, where Sir Adrian Boult was to conduct a programme including the Elgar and the Mendelssoh Violin Concerti.（第一时间段）[Diana and I left New York on the evening of the twenty-fifth, with ample time, as we presumed, to keep our appointment. With everyone secure in his safety belt, the plane shot down the runway, then halted with a tremendous screeching of brakes just short of takeoff. This was twice repeated before the shaken passengers were unloaded and told to return to the airport in the morning.]

(2)（第二时间段）[Next day we set off for England again. To begin with, so thick was New

York traffic that we almost missed the plane, which might have saved everyone a great deal of trouble. Disaster avoided, we took off at eleven-thirty, and shortly afterwards the pilot made his rounds. (Q2) → Wanting to reassure Diana, I stopped him and suggested that the untoward incidents of the day before hadn't been too serious. In that wonderful calm bluff English way, he answered, 'Airplane engines, you see, are made up of thousands of individual parts, and it is quite impossible to tell when any one of them may cease to function', with which job's comfort he passed on. A short while later one of those many parts did indeed cease to function; oil began blowing over the wings, and back we went to Idlewild Airport,](第三时间段)[as it then was at the third try, later that afternoon, we succeeded in crossing the Atlantic, making one stop to refuel in Newfoundland and another at Shannon in the Irish Republic, for one flew from landfall to landfall in those days。

(3) Here the English weather blocked further progress: fog had closed London Airport. It was about 6: 30 a.m. local time when we arrived at Sannon, (Q3) → too early to despair of reaching our destination. We telephoned my agent, Harold Holt, and (Q3) → I borrowed an airport office to practise in. However, as the hours passed and the London fog failed to lift, I grew anxious enough to try to charter from Aer Lingus a plane small enough to land in conditions which our big Stratocrusier could not cope with.](第四时间段)[For some reason Aer Lingus was not allowed to rescue us, so after more endless hours, we took off in the transatlantic plane, first at three forty-five—when the radio was found to be out of order and we had turn back, then, finally, at four-fifteen. (Q4) → All hopes of rehearsing had long been abandoned, but the concert itself still seemed safe. The fog had yet a couple of tricks up its sleeve, however. After circling over Heathrow a few times in a vain attempt to find a break in the blanket below him, the pilot landed at Manston on the east coast.](第五时间段)[Diana and I were delivered to the earth through the luggage shaft in the plane's belly, hustled through customs at a trot and thrust into a waiting car, which roared off the airfield with most gratifying drama. One mile farther on, the gentle fog of the countryside rolled toward us in thick. Soft, totally opaque clouds, and we crawled the rest of the way at hardly more than walking speed, Diana shivering in the unheated car.]

(4) We were of course late.

Q1: After the plane's first attempts to take off, the author and his wife were asked to come back on _____ .

   (A) 25th January   (B) 26th January

   (C) 27th January   (D) 28th January

Q2: The pilot's remarks, shortly after taking off from New York, _____ .

   (A) proved quite inaccurate

   (B) lead to their returning to Idlewild

   (C) referred to their previous disastrous flight

(D) were not helpful to ease Diana's distress

Q3: When they arrived in Ireland at 6: 30, the author and his wife _____ .

(A) were still hoping to reach London in time to rehearse

(B) chartered a small plane which could land in fog

(C) were late for their connecting flight

(D) were feeling absolutely desperate

Q4: What happened when they finally landed at Manston?

(A) They were held up going through Customs.

(B) The fog immediately came down thicker.

(C) They were given special treatment.

(D) Their car crawled because of an engine fault.

Q5: It can be concluded from the passage that the author was _____ .

(A) a rich man taking his wife to see a special concert

(B) a conductor who had to be in London to give a concert

(C) a violinist going to play in a concert in London

(D) an American musical agent who had an appointment with Sir Adrian Boult

解析：本文是一篇记叙文。主题在文章起始时提出：作者要在 1950 年 1 月 27 日去参加一个小提琴演奏会。故事接下来就从作者出发开始随着时间的推进和故事的发展而展开。段落结构如下：

主题	目的地和规定的到达时间（首句——双线）	1 月 27 日到达伦敦参加演出。
第一时间段	作者偕同他的妻子于 1 月 25 日出发。	乘坐的飞机两次起飞均告失败。
第二时间段	作者 1 月 26 日再次出发。	成功起飞，但是因为飞机故障又回到了机场。
第三时间段	作者当日下午再次出发。	成功飞越大西洋，但是由于天气原因(雾)没能到达伦敦，于早晨 6:30 迫降在爱尔兰。
第四时间段	作者再次乘坐飞机分两次起飞。	首次于下午 3:45，再于 4:15，最后仍由于天气原因迫降在东海岸的 Manston。
第五时间段	作者下飞机后改用陆路进发。	浓雾大大阻碍了他们的进程。
结局：	作者没能准时到达目的地。	以迟到告终。

Q1：第一到第二时间段。根据时间的推移，第二次出发是在 1 月 26 日，选(B)。

Q2：属于第二个时间段中的细节描写。回到文章中定位在第二小节。飞行员的一番话是用来回答作者的询问，而作者的询问则是为了安慰他的妻子，显然这番话没有起到预期的效果。选 (D)，出处是 "Wanting to reassure Diana, I stopped him and suggested that the untoward incidents of the day before hadn't been too serious."

Q3：属于第三时间段——迫降在爱尔兰。作者还很乐观，还借了一间房间来练习，所以选(A)。出处是 "too early to despair of reaching our destination." 和 "I borrowed an airport office to practise in...."注意文章中的"practise"和选项中的"rehearse"正好对应。

Q4: 属于第四时间段——迫降在东海岸的 Manston。作者下了飞机很快通过了海关，又有了一辆车等待他们，说明事先已经有人做了安排——选**(C)**。

Q5: 覆盖全文。在对文章全面了解的基础上，我们不难看出作者要赶去参加小提琴演奏会，同时沿途还抓紧时间练习，所以他一定是个要参加演出的小提琴手，选**(C)**，出处是"All hopes of rehearsing had long been abandoned, but the concert itself still seemed safe."

> 提示：值得注意的是，文章的结构和层次并不一定由文章给出的自然段落来决定。如果我们能够从一开始阅读时就意识到是按照时间和行程的推进来展开的话，便以照以上的结构图找出更为详尽的文章结构，从而为解题做好更充分的准备。

例2：故事的发展

(1) I think it was De Mandeville who suggested a river party for the staffs of the various embassies. Nor, on the face of it, was the idea a bad one. All winter long the logs come down the River Sava until the frost locks them in. Now with the spring thaw the east bank of the river has a pontoon of tree-trunks some forty feet wide lining the bank under the willows so that you can walk out over the river, avoiding the muddy margins, and swim in the deep water.

(2) These logs had been made into a raft about a hundred feet by sixty—big enough even to dance on. While everyone was dancing the rumba and while the buffet was plying a heavy trade, it was noticed that the distance between the raft and the shore had noticeably increased. The gang-plank subsided in the ooze. It was not a great distance—perhaps ten feet. But owing to the solid resistance such a large raft set up in the main current the pull was definitely outward. But as yet nobody was alarmed; indeed most of the party thought it was part of a planned entertainment.

(3) As we approached the next bend of the river it looked as if the whole thing would run around on the bank, and a few of us made preparations to grab hold of the overhanging willows and halt our progress. But by ill luck a change in the current carried us just too far into the center of the river and we were carried past the spit of land, vainly groping at the tips of bushes.

(4) It was about another five minutes before the full significance of our position began to dawn upon us. By this time we were moving in stately fashion down the center of the river, all lit up like a Christmas tree. Exclamations, suggestions, counter-suggestions poured from the lips of the diplomats and their spouses in a dozen tongues.

(5) Unknown to us, too, other factors were being introduced which were to make this a memorable night for us all. Spy-mania was at its height and the Yugoslav forces lived in a permanent state of alertness. There were frequent rumors of armed raids from Czechoslovakia.

(6) It was in this context that some Yugoslav infantryman at an observation post along the river saw what he took to be a large armed man-on-war full of Czech paratroops in dinner jackets

and ball-dresses sailing upon Belgrade. He did not wait to verify this first impression. He galloped into Belgrade Castle a quarter of an hour later on a foam-flecked mule with the news that the city was about to be invaded.

解析：本文记叙了一群使馆官员在一个木筏上举行派对时的一番历险的故事。全文完全是按照故事发展的顺序展开的。文章的结构如下：

事件：派对	一群各国使馆的人员在河岸边的木筏上举行一个河上派对。（1 小节）	
发展：被困	众人无意中把木筏推离了河岸，漂向了河中心。众人被困在了木筏上。（2 小节）	
经过：漂流	众人试图回到岸边，但却事与愿违，木筏越漂越远。（3～4 小节）	
结果：恐慌	南斯拉夫边境守卫误把这群人当作了入侵的军队，引起了不必要的军事恐慌。（5-6 小节）	

例 3：理论演变的过程

(1) Aside from the many political and social problems that would have to be solved, the engineering risk envisaged is monumental. (2) The initial stage requires the building of a circular dam 18 miles in diameter attached to the seabed in a relatively shallow place in international waters. (3) Then, several hundred pumps, operating for more than a year, would suck out the seawater from within the dam. (4) When empty and dry, the area would have a city constructed on it. (5) The actual land would be about 300 feet below sea level.

Q: According to the passage, the problems of Marinnation focused on here are mainly _____ .

(A) human   (B) engineering

(C) political   (D) social

正解：(B)

解析：本文是一个关于建造海底城市的计划。在计划中城市的建设必须严格按照一系列的程序进行。而段落的内容也顺延这个建造的程序和面临的挑战展开：

理论：建造一个海底城市	要建造一个海中城市问题重重，其中技术上的问题最为重要（第 1 句）
程序(1)：奠基	首先要在海底建造一个巨大的水坝（第 2 句）
程序(2)：准备工作	然后抽干海水，腾出建筑的空间（第 3 句）
程序(3)：建筑	城市将被建筑在抽干后的空间上（第 4 句）
程序(4)：落成	建成后城市延伸到水下 300 英尺（第 5 句）

而题目考查的是理论本身，所以定位在第一句话。

例 4：事件的前因后果 I

(1) (Q1) → Before Felix arrived in Baghdad, Miss Bohun had arranged for him to have lessons with a Mr. Posthorn of the Education Office. Mr. Posthorn was a busy man. He not only had his government job but also taught some Arab boys from a wealthy family who hoped eventually to go to an English university. He had agreed to fit Felix in his spare time, which meant

that sometimes Felix went to Mr. Posthorn's office and was told to study this or that, and occasionally Mr. Posthorn managed to find a spare hour when he dropped in to Miss Bohun's and gave Felix some instruction. (Effect 1) → Most of Felix's day was spent in study in his bedroom. He knew he would not get far in this way and he knew also that (Cause 1) → Mr. Posthom would have been willing to give him more attention had he, like Miss Bohun, not been disappointed in him. Miss Bohun did not say or do anything that gave Felix any clue as to how he had failed her, but Mr. Posthorn, after testing his knowledge, said without hesitation, (Effect 2) →'What on earth have you been doing with yourself since you left England?'

(2) Felix explained that in Cairo he had taken lessons with an old English lady, an ex-governess to a royal family, who had taught him English composition, French, drawing, geography and history. (Cause 2) → Unfortunately she had known less Greek, Latin and mathematics than he had. His mother had treated lessons there as a joke, and said: "Never mind, darling, when we return to England we'll make up for lost time."

(3) (Effect 3) → "Your parents ought to have been ashamed of themselves, keeping you away from school during the most important years of your life. I can't understand it," said Mr. Postthorn. "Your father was an educated man, wasn't he?" (Cause 3) → Felix explained: it wasn't my father's fault. Mother wouldn't let me go back to England when the war started. Father was angry, but Mother said: "If he goes I may not see him again."

(4) (Effect 4) → Mr. Posthorn said: "you'll never make up for it," but Felix, although he knew it to be a serious matter, could not really care.

Q1: Miss Bohun had arranged for Felix _____ before he arrived.

   (A) to go to school in the Education Office

   (B) to have lessons with some Arab boys

   (C) to study at home every morning

   (D) to received private tuition

Q2: Felix did not feel the arrangements Miss Bohun had made were satisfactory because _____.

   (A) he knew Miss Bohun was disappointed in him

   (B) he could not have regular lessons

   (C) he had not like Mr. Posthorn

   (D) he didn't like studying at Miss Bohun's

Q3: Before he came to stay with Miss Bohun, Felix's lessons _____.

   (A) were shared with some children from a royal family

   (B) were not suitable in his father's eye

   (C) had not been adequate in some subjects

   (D) had frequently been interrupted by his mother

Q4: Why didn't Felix go back to England when the war started?

  (A) His parents wanted him to be with them.

  (B) His mother would not agree to his going.

  (C) His father intended to teach Felix himself.

  (D) He himself did not really want to go.

解析：本文为记叙文，描述了 Felix 接受教育的情况。文章展开的方式是按照 Felix 受教育的状态和原因来叙述整件事情的，同时也伴随着时间和地点的转移。段落结构如下：

事件	Felix 接受教育的情况。
结果 1(Effect 1)(第 1 小节)	Felix 不能得到正常的课时。
原因 1(Cause 1)(第 1 小节)	Felix 的私人辅导老师对他的学习状况很不满，所以不热心。
结果 2(Effect 2)(第 1 小节)	Felix 的私人辅导老师对他的学习现状很失望，认为离开英国后没有接受到良好的教育。(1 小节末句)
原因 2(Cause 2)(第 2 小节)	在开罗的一段学习时间里由于老师知识面的不足，造成了有一些课程没有得到充分的学习。(2 小节第 2 句话—Unfortunately...)
结果 3(Effect 3)(第 3 小节)	Felix 没有及时回到英国去补习，结果浪费了宝贵的光阴，再也无法弥补了。
原因 3(Cause 3)(第 3 小节)	妈妈不舍得让他回到英国去接受更好的教育。(3 小节的最后两句)
结果 4(Effect 4)	Felix 知道自己的教育状况很糟糕，但是他无所谓。(全文末句)

文章结构和段落之间的关系一旦清晰，解题就变得很轻松了。

Q1: 文章开始提出了事件，也就是 Felix 接受了一个私人老师的辅导，选(D)。

Q2: 第一个因果关系：Felix 得不到正常的课时，选(B)。

Q3: 第二个因果关系：Felix 在开罗没能得到充分的学习，选(C)。

Q4: 第三个因果关系：造成 Felix 丧失了最佳学习时间的人是他的母亲，选(B)。

例 5：事件的前因后果 II

(1) FIRST the hamburger connection; now the songbird connection. The first link goes like this. Citizens of the United States are hungry for beef, especially in the form of fast foods such as hamburgers, frankfurters and the like. Yet beef has been one of the most inflationary items in the consumer's weekly shopping basket.

(2) So the US government has authorized import of so-called cheap beef from central America—beef raised on pasturelands established almost entirely at the cost of tropical forests. By trying to trim a nickel off the price of a hamburger, the US has contributed, albeit unwittingly but effectively and increasingly, to the massive loss of forests from southern Mexico to Panama.

(3) Now the second link. A vast throng of North American songbirds spend their winters in Central America and the Caribbean—about two thirds of all woodland and forest species, totaling around half of all land birds breeding in North America.

(4) But the migrants have been running into trouble, according to Dr Eugene S. Morton and his

colleagues at the Smithsonian Institution in Washington DC. When several billion birds leave North America each autumn, they find, on arriving in their wintering grounds of central America and the Caribbean, that their forest habitats have been succumbing to the machete and the match.

(5) As a result, fewer birds are heading back each spring north of the border. Smithsonian scientists notice that species numbers are declining at rates between one and four per cent a year. The prospect is that there will be major reductions in throngs of forest-dwelling migrants.

(6) Ironically, it is precisely at the time of the songbirds' return that number of insect species are likewise putting in a reappearance in North America. They tend to be at key phases of their life cycles, as larvae, etc., which leave them unusually vulnerable to insect-eating birds. The Smithsonian scientists speculate that the insect populations have thus far been held below levels at which they prove harmful to agricultural crops, through the predation pressures of huge numbers of songbirds returning over the horizon at just about the right time. If, however, the songbirds continue to decline, the insects could, within the foreseeable future, start to enjoy a population explosion every spring—which could mean bad news for US farmers.

Q1: According to the article, the US government has _____ .

(A) arranged for forest land in Central America to be cleared

(B) seen a massive fall in the consumption of hamburgers

(C) bought up grazing land for cattle in Central America

(D) made it possible for Americans to buy meat at reduced prices

Q2: Why are the numbers of birds returning north declining annually?

(A) There are fewer forests in the US for them to return to.

(B) A huge experiment is being conducted on bird populations.

(C) Tropical forests can support greater number now.

(D) Their southern habitat is being drastically reduced.

Q3: The bad news for farmers in spring might be an increase in _____ .

(A) the number of songbirds   (B) the number of insects

(C) the size of larvae   (D) the price of beef

解析：本文并没有明显的主题或中心思想句。文章按照四个因果关系展开，结构如下：

主题	没有直接提出
因果关系 1	美国人从中美洲进口廉价的牛肉→中美洲和加勒比海沿岸的热带雨林逐渐消失
因果关系 2	雨林消逝→从北美到中美洲过冬的鸟的栖息地遭到了破坏→回到北美的鸟的数量在不断减少
因果关系 3	鸟的数量减少→北美昆虫的数量急剧增加
因果关系 4	昆虫数量持续增长→美国的农作物要遭殃，农民要遭受损失
推论	人类要为破坏生态平衡的行为付出代价

Q1: 第一个因果关系: 美国通过进口为本国消费者提供了廉价的牛肉, 选 (D)。

Q2: 第二个因果关系: 鸟的数量减少是由栖息地受到破坏而造成的, 选 (D)。

Q3: 第三个因果关系: 鸟的数量减少导致昆虫滋长, 危害到农民的利益, 选 (B)。

例 6: 事物特性 I——产品

(1) The Poco body warmer measures about three by five inches and is one-quarter inch thick. (2) It consists of a cloth bag containing a mixture of iron powder, moisturized wood powder, activated carbon and salt. (3) To get it going, the user simply opens the outer vinyl bag in which the unit is vacuum-packed and shakes the cloth bag. (4) The unit then absorbs oxygen from the air, which in conjunction with the moisture from the wood powder oxidizes the iron, giving off heat. (5) The packet maintains an average temperature of 140 degrees Fahrenheit for 24 hours, according to the manufacturer. (6) Aoi Co. officials say that the product contains no toxic chemicals. (7) The only precaution users need to follow is to avoid direct contact between the skin and the body warmer because burns can occur. (8) The unit sells for about $ 1.

Q: Which of the following is LEAST likely to be characteristic of a Poco body warmer?

(A) It makes use of electric power to generate heat.

(B) It measures about three by five inches and is one quarter inch thick.

(C) It contains iron powder, wood powder, carbon and salt.

(D) It maintains an average temperature of 140 degrees Fahrenheit.

正解: (A)

解析: 本文是段说明文。文章的主题是介绍一种小型的取暖器。作者在这个段落中的行文方式完全是按照说明一个事物的特征来展开的。在很多描写事物的说明文中都用到了类似的结构。结构图如下:

特征 1 外观	取暖器的体积。(第 1 句) 提示词: measures...
特征 2 内部构造	各种原材料。(第 2 句) 提示词: consists of...
特征 3 工作原理	通过原材料的一些化学反应, 最终取暖器将释放出热量。(第 3-4 句) 提示词: To get it going...
特征 4 功效	取暖器所能达到的温度是华氏 140 度。(第 5 句)
特征 5 使用须知	取暖器本身没有有害的化学成分。只要在使用取暖器时不要太靠近身体。(第 6-7 句) 提示词: The only precaution...
特征 6 售价	取暖器售价为一元。(第 8 句) 提示词: sells for...

根据以上分析, 我们不难发现 **(A)** 选项在考查工作原理, 而其原理是化学反应发热, 而非电力, 所以 (A) 不是取暖器的特征之一。

例 7：事物特性 II——城市建设

(1) Seoul, once a city for kings, can now claim to be a city for commuters. (a) The third nation in the Orient to develop an underground rapid-transit system, Korea opened its first line in 1974. (b) After 12 years of continuing construction, Seoul had finally completed the rest of its extensive subway system, (c) capable of serving 5 million commuters a day.

(2) The 73-mile-long system, the world's seventh largest, is expected to alleviate the acute daily traffic congestion downtown.

(3) (a) For an estimated $2.7 billion, the city has built one of the most modern subways in the world, replete with air-conditioning, high-tech ticket machines and escalators to deep-level stations. (b) The subway stops, bucking an international tradition of dull concrete walls, are attractions themselves: many are lined with shopping arcades, others sponsor art exhibits and several have been blasted out of granite and left in their natural state, creating an eerie, cavelike effect.

(4) (a) The subway is a long-term solution to transit problems in a city that is bursting at the seams with 9.5 million people. (b) It is designed to encourage the growth of satellite cities along the lines that run outside the city proper. Efficiency, safety and economy are the catchwords of the Seoul Metropolitan Subway Corporation, which handled construction and now manages the four lines. (c) But traditional concern for cleanliness adds to the popularity of this rapid mode of underground transportation.

(5) Recently 20 young couples chose the subway as the site for their wedding ceremonies, proof that the system is heralding a new age of modern living for the inhabitants of the nation's capital.

Q1: According to the passage, how many cities in the world have subway systems larger than that in Seoul, Korea?

(A) None.   (B) Three.

(C) Six.   (D) Seven.

Q2: Which of the following is LEAST likely to be seen in the subway in Seoul?

(A) Commuters.   (B) Shopping arcades and art exhibits.

(C) Natural caves.   (D) Wedding couples.

Q3: Which of the following is NOT the reason for constructing the underground transit system?

(A) The growth of population in the city.

(B) The traffic congestion downtown.

(C) The traditional concern for a better environment.

(D) The lack of wedding ceremony sites.

解析：本文的结构与上文相似，也是介绍说明一个事物——汉城的地铁。而本文的结构也是按照事物的特征来展开的：

主题（第 1 小节）	汉城地铁	(1)建筑周期——74 年开始,12 年工期。(a~b 句) (2)容量(capacity)——一天 500 万人。(c 句)
特征 1：外观 （第 2 小节）	长度排名世界第七	提示词：long
特征 2：内部构造（第 3 小节）	各种硬件和软件的设施 提示词：Replete with...	(1)造价,空调,高科技的售票机,手扶梯。(a 句) (2)各个站点有商铺、艺术展览等,还有一些站点形状酷似阴森的山洞。(bq 句)
特征 3：用途 （第 4 小节）	三大用途 提示词：a long term solution to...	(1)缓解人口增长带来的城市交通问题。(a 句) (2)促进地铁沿线卫星城市的兴起。(b 句) (3)净化城市环境。(c 句)
特征 4：社会影响（第 5 小节）	地铁成了年轻人结婚的场所——引领时代的潮流	提示词：...modern living...

Q1：本题考外观,长度为世界第七,所以前面有六名,选 **(C)**。

Q2：本题考内部构造,地铁里没有天然山洞,选 **(C)**。

Q3：本题考用途,前面三个均符合,选项(D)明显有误,所以选 **(D)**。

例 8：事物特性 III——旅游建筑

（1）In a bay near Almeria in Southern Spain will be built the world's first underwater residence for tourists. The hotel will be 40 feet down in the Mediterranean. As all the world opened to tour operators, there was still a frontier behind which lay three quarters of the globe's surface, the sea; in whose cool depths light fades; no winds blow; there are no stars. There even the most bored travelers could recapture their sense of romance, terror or beauty. For a submerged hotel is such a beautiful idea.

（2）The hotel will cost \$170,000 and will be able to accommodate up to ten people a night. Up until now only scientists and professional divers have lived under the sea, but soon, for the first time, the public will be able to go down into the darkness. They will have to swim down in diving suits, but at 40 feet there would be no problem about decompression.

（3）Design of the hotel was crucial. Most of the underwater structures used before had been in the shape of a diving bell or submarine. Professional divers could cope with such things but ordinary people would run the risk of violent claustrophobia. (a) Then an Austrian architect had the idea of making three interconnecting circular structures, 18 feet in diameter, and looking much like flying saucers. (b) They would be cast in concrete and launched from the shore. Towed into position they would then be sunk. (c) A foundation of cast concrete would already be in place on the sea-bed. Pylons would attach the structures to this. Once in position the structures would be pumped dry. (d) The pylons made to withstand an uplift pressure of 350 tons, would then take the strain.

（4）Cables linking the underwater structures to the hotel on shore would connect it with electricity, fresh water, television, and an air pump, and also dispose of sewage. Entry would be from underneath, up a ladder; because of the pressure inside there would be no need of airlocks or doors.

(5) The first structure would include a changing room and a shower area, where the divers would get out of their gear. There would also be a kitchen and a lavatory. The second structure would contain a dining room/lecture theatre, and sleeping accommodation for eight people. The third structure would contain two suites. A steward would come down with the ten customers to cook and look after them. Television monitors would relay all that went on to the shore so that discussions on the sea bed could be transmitted to all the world.

Q1: From the passage we understand that tour operators and travelers will be interested in the submerged hotel as _____ .

(A) it is a quiet place for research work   (B) it is an ideal sea-food restaurant

(C) it will offer new possibilities   (D) it will have unchanging weather

Q2: What design was finally considered most suitable for the new hotel?

(A) Three separated circles.   (B) Three linked discs.

(C) three connected globes.   (D) Three interlocked cylinders.

Q3: The hotel would be able to float under water because it would be _____ .

(A) made of light material   (B) 350 tons in weight

(C) filled with air   (D) attached to pylons

Q4: It is planned that sleeping quarters will be provided for the guests in the _____ .

(A) second structure   (B) second and third structures

(C) first and third structures   (D) third structure

Q5: The purpose of television monitors under the sea would be to relay _____ .

(A) instructions from the sea bed to the shore

(B) news from the shore to the sea bed

(C) information from the world to the sea bed

(D) information to the world from the sea bed

解析：本文旨在介绍一个建造海底旅店的大胆设想。文章在首段提出了这个设想之后，接下来按照这个旅店的各个特性展开：

主题	计划建造一个海底酒店供游客参观和居住(首句)
特性1：感受	在远离陆地的海里,旅客将体验到一系列全新的感受(第1小节末句)
特性2：造价	$170,000。提示词：cost...(第2小节首句)
特性3：容量	最多10人。提示词：accommodate up to...(第2小节首句)
特性4：设计	(a)外形;(b)建造工程;(c)地基;(d)固定(第3小节)
	提示词：Design...
特性5：供给	通过输送线给酒店补给。(第4小节)

特性 6：内部构造	酒店分为三层,各有不同的房间和软硬件设施。(第 5 小节)
	提示词：The first struoture, second, third...
特性 7：通讯	酒店的生活状况皆由许多监控器传回到岸上,并向全世界转播。(第 5 小节末句)

Q1: 本题考查感受——水下世界将带给游人全新的感受,选(C)。

Q2: 本题考查设计——三个相连的碟状建筑,选(B)。

Q3: 本题考查固定——被拴在了塔柱上,选(D)。

Q4: 本题考查内部——第二和第三个建筑里都有住房 (sleeping accommodation & suites),选(B)。

Q5: 本题考查与外界的联系——摄像头可以让岸上了解到海底的情形,选(D)。

例 9：事物特性 IV ——自然现象

(1) Quite different from storm surges are giant sea waves called tsunamis, which derive their name from the Japanese expression for "high water in a harbor." These waves are also referred to by the general public as tidal waves, although they have relatively little to do with tides. Scientists often refer to them as seismic sea waves, far more appropriate in that they do result from undersea seismic activity.

(2) (a) Tsunamis are caused when the sea bottoms suddenly moves, during an underwater earthquake or volcano for example, and the water above the moving earth is suddenly displaced. (b) This sudden shift of water sets off a series of waves. These waves can travel great distances at speeds close to 700 kilometers per hour. (c) In the open ocean, tsunamis have little noticeable amplitude, often no more than one or two meters. (d) It is when they hit the shallow waters near the coast that they increase in height, possibly up to 40 meters.

(3) (a) Tsunamis often occur in the Pacific because the Pacific is an area of heavy seismic activity. (b) Two areas of the Pacific well accustomed to the threat of tsunamis are Japan and Hawaii. (c) Because the seismic activity that causes tsunamis in Japan often occurs on the ocean bottom quite close to the islands, the tsunamis that hit Japan often come with little warning and can therefore prove disastrous. (d) Most of the tsunamis that hit the Hawaiian Islands, however, originate thousands of miles away near the coast of Alaska, so these tsunamis have a much greater distance to travel and the inhabitants of Hawaii generally have time for warning of their imminent arrival.

(4) (a) Tsunamis are certainly not limited to Japan and Hawaii. In 1755, Europe experienced a calamitous tsunami, when movement along the fault lines near the Azores caused a massive tsunami to sweep onto the Portuguese coast and flood the heavily populated area around Lisbon. (b) The greatest tsunami on record occurred on the other side of the world in 1883 when the Krakatoa volcano underwent a massive explosion, sending waves more than 30 meters high onto nearby Indonesian islands; the tsunami from this volcano actually traveled around the world

and was witnessed as far away as the English Channel.

Q1: According to the passage, all of the following are true about tidal waves EX-CEPT that _____ .

(A) they are the same as tsunamis

(B) they are caused by sudden changes in high and low tides

(C) this terminology is not used by the scientific community

(D) they refer to the same phenomenon as seismic sea waves

Q2: It can be inferred from the passage that tsunamis _____ .

(A) cause severe damage in the middle of the ocean

(B) generally reach heights greater than 40 meters

(C) are far more dangerous on the coast than in the open ocean

(D) are often identified by ships on the ocean

Q3: A main difference between tsunamis in Japan and in Hawaii is that tsunamis in Japan are more likely to _____ .

(A) arrive without warning   (B) come from greater distances

(C) be less of a problem   (D) originate in Alaska

解析：本文属于自然科学方面的说明文，介绍的是一种自然现象海啸。全文的结构如下：

主题	海啸有三种名称：(1)日语：tsunamis；(2)民间：tidal waves；(3)学术界：seismic sea waves(第 1 小节)
	提示词：called...；referred to...；refer to...
特性 1：成因	由海底的地壳运动引起。(第 2 小节 a～b 句)
	提示词：cause...
特性 2：威力	在宽海域海浪低，浅海域海浪高。(第 2 小节 c～d 句)
特性 3：发生(1)	日本：特点是离海岸近，所以会突如其来(arrive with little warning)。
	(第 3 小节)
	提示词：occur...
特性 4：发生(2)	夏威夷：起源较远，所以可以得到及时的预警(have time for warning)。
特性 5：发生(3)	欧洲也经历过同样的海啸。
	提示词：not limited to Pacific...
特性 6：回顾历史	历史上最大的一次海啸。
	提示词：The greatest... on record...

Q1: 本题考查海啸的各项特征，其中成因是由于海底的地壳运动，而非潮汐，选**(B)**。

Q2: 本题考查海啸的威力——在浅海域威力最大，所以也就更加危险，选**(C)**。

Q3: 本题考查海啸在日本的发生——得不到预警，选**(A)**。

二、主题—举例—总结型

这种写作方式是在文章的开始提出主题，或是一个要描写的事物，或是一个要阐述的观点；接着作者用举例的方式在文章的各个段落中对主题加以介绍或阐述，每个例子是主题的一个组成部分；然后在文章的末尾对文章的主题加以总结。

阅读提示：用举例来进一步阐述一个观点是一种常用的写作手法。识别和归纳这种行文方式的最佳方法是注意用来引导各个分例的引导词，通常它们有以下一些组合：

one... another... third; one... another; half... the other half; first... second... third; some... other...; first... then... finally/at last...; if... if... if, etc.

这些引导词不仅罗列出了各个事例，同时也帮助我们勾划出了整个文章的结构，无论在理解文章还是解题定位方面都是需要注意的阅读重点。

例1：

(1) Some kinds of animals that are still around today were in existence millions of years ago during the time of the dinosaur.

(2) One of these survivors is the crocodile, which has been around for about 100 million years. Today's crocodiles can grow to a length of 20 feet and weigh about a ton. Their prehistoric ancestors were about two-and-a-half times the size of today's animals.

(3) Another survivor from the past is the Galapagos tortoise, whose history goes back around 200 million years. The tortoise of today has not evolved much over the last 200 million years; it looks about the same now as it did way back then.

(4) The oldest survivor from prehistoric times is, can you believe it, the cockroach. Cockroaches have been able to stick around for more than 250 million years. The main reason for their incredible endurance is their ability to live in all kinds of conditions and survive on all kinds of food.

Q1: This passage is mainly about _____ .

　　(A) the dinosaur

　　(B) how the crocodile has survived

　　(C) animals that live to be very old

　　(D) types of animals that have existed for a long time

Q2: According to the passage, the crocodile _____ .

　　(A) survived an attack by dinosaurs　　(B) first appeared 100,000 years ago

　　(C) has increased in size over time　　(D) has existed for millions of years

Q3: Which of the animals mentioned in the passage has been around for the longest time?

　　(A) The dinosaur.　　(B) The crocodile.

　　(C) The Galapagos tortoise.　　(D) The cockroach.

解析：本文为说明文。首段提出了文章的主题是要介绍几种现有的与远古时代的恐龙同时代的动物。文章以下分段举例说明：

主题	有几种现有的动物早在恐龙时代就存在了。(第 1 小节)
例子 1	鳄鱼(crocodile)：存活了 1 亿年左右。(第 2 小节)
例子 2	象龟(Galapagos tortoise)：2 亿年左右。(第 3 小节)
例子 3	蟑螂(Cockroaches)：2.5 亿年左右——生存最长久的动物。(第 4 小节)
结论	省略

Q1: 考查主题，选(D)。注意：选项中的"types"和原文中的"kinds"相对应

Q2: 考查第一个例子，选(B)。

Q3: 考查三个例子的比较，选(B)。

例 2：

（1）There must be few questions on which responsible opinion is so utterly divided as on that of how much sleep we ought to have. There are some who think we can leave the body to regulate these matters for itself. "The answer is easy," says Dr. A. Burto. "With the right amount of sleep you should wake up fresh and alert five minutes before the alarm rings." If he is right many people must be under sleeping, including myself. But we must remember that some people have a greater inertia than others. This is not meant rudely. They switch on slowly, and they are reluctant to switch off. They are alert at bedtime and sleepy when it is time to get up, and this may have nothing to do with how fatigued their bodies are, or how much sleep they must take to lose their fatigue.

（2）Other people feel sure that the present trend is towards too little sleep. To quote one medical opinion, "Thousands of people drift through life suffering from the effects of too little sleep; the reason is not that they can't sleep. Like advancing colonists, we do seem to be grasping ever more of the land of sleep for our waking needs, pushing the boundary back and reaching, apparently, for a point in our evolution where we will sleep no more. This in itself, of course, need not be a bad thing. What could be disastrous, however, is that we should press too quickly towards this goal, sacrificing sleep only to gain more time in which to jeopardize our civilization by actions and decisions made weak by fatigue.

（3）Then, to complete the picture, these are those who believe that more people are persuaded to sleep too much. Dr. H. Roberts, writing in Every Man in Health, asserts: "It may safely be stated that, just as the majority eat too much, so the majority sleep too much. "One can see the point of this also. It would be a pity to retard our development by holding back those people who are gifted enough to work and play well with less than the average amount of sleep, if indeed it does them no harm. If one of the trends of evolution is that more of the life span is to be spent in gainful waking activity, then surely these people are in the van of this advance.

Q1: The author seems to indicate that _____ .

(A) there are many controversial issues like the right amount of sleep

(B) among many issues the right amount of sleep is the least controversial

(C) the right amount of sleep is a topic of much controversy among doctors

(D) people are now moving towards solving many controversial issues concerning sleep

Q2: According to the author, sleeping habits _____ .

(A) are related to the amount of sleep　　(B) are inherited from the parents

(C) vary from person to person　　(D) would not change in one's lifetime

Q3: In the last paragraph the author points out that _____ .

(A) sleeping less is good for human health

(B) people ought to be persuaded to sleep less than before

(C) it is incorrect to say that people sleep too little

(D) those who can sleep less should be encouraged

Q4: We learn from the passage that the author _____ .

(A) revises someone else's opinion　　(B) explains an opinion of his own

(C) favors one of the three opinions　　(D) comments on three different opinions

解析: 本文为议论文。作者在文章开始提出了专家们在一个人的合理睡眠时间的问题上众说纷纭, 并没有统一的意见。接下来文章并没有去试图建立一个自己的观点, 争论合理的睡眠时间到底应该是多少。相反, 作者仅仅列举了所有不同的观点, 并一一做出评述。文章的结构如下:

主题	合理的睡眠时间是个众说纷纭的话题。(第1小节)
专家观点1	专家: 合理的睡眠完全靠身体的自我调节。
作者观点1	作者: 人们在睡眠上的惯性可能会影响自我调节的意义。(第1小节)
专家观点2 作者观点2	专家: 现代人睡眠不足。 作者: 睡的少不是一件坏事, 但不能让睡眠不足影响了我们的判断, 以至做出错误的决定。(第2小节)
专家观点3 作者观点3	专家: 现代人睡眠过剩。 作者: 在没有负面影响的前提下能够少睡就等于争取到了工作的时间, 不失为一件好事。(第3小节)
结论	省略

Q1: 考查主题:关于合理睡眠的问题众说纷纭,选**(C)**。

Q2: 考查作者整个的观点,可以看出只有(C)选项符合作者的观点一,选**(C)**。

Q3: 考查作者的第三个观点,根据结构图选**(D)**。

Q4: 考查的写作方式,根据结构图我们知道,作者只是列举三种观点以及相应的个人观点,选**(D)**。

例3:

(1) According to airline industry statistics, almost 90% of airline accidents are survivable

or partially survivable. <u>But passengers can increase their chances of survival by learning and following certain tips.</u> Experts say that (a) <u>you should read and listen to safety instructions before takeoff</u> and ask questions if you have uncertainties. (b) <u>You should fasten your seat belt low on your hips and as tightly as possible.</u> Of course, (c) <u>you should also know how the release mechanism of your belt operates.</u> (d) During takeoffs and landings, you are advised to keep your feet flat on the floor. (e) Before takeoff you should <u>locate the nearest exit and an alternative exit and count the rows of seats between you and the exits</u> so that you can find them in the dark if necessary.

(2) <u>In the event that you are forewarned of a possible accident,</u> you should put your hands on your ankles and keep your head down until the plane comes to a complete stop.

(3) <u>If smoke is present in the cabin,</u> (a) you should <u>keep your head low and cover your face with napkins, towels, or clothing.</u> (b) If possible, wet these for added protection against smoke inhalation. (c) To evacuate as quickly as possible, follow crew commands and do not take personal belongings with you. (d) Do not jump on escape slides before they are fully inflated, and when you jump, do so with your arms and legs extended in front of you. (e) When you get to the ground, you should move away from the plane as quickly as possible, and never smoke near the wreckage.

解析： 本文介绍在航空旅行中的一些基本安全措施以及在事故发生时的一些紧急措施。作者在全文的第二句话提出了主题，以下就按照各种情况一一列举。结构图如下：

主题	航空旅行中的生存技巧
	措施1：起飞前理解安全须知，不懂要问。(a句)
	措施2：系紧安全带。(b句)
基本措施(第1小节)	措施3：了解安全带的操作方式。(c句)
	措施4：把脚平放在地上。(d句)
	措施5：起飞前找到离座位最近的应急出口和另外一个出口，必要时数出座位到另一个出口的间距，以便能在黑暗中找到。(e句)
预警(第2小节)	措施：手放在脚踝上，低头，直到飞机成功降落
火警(烟)(第3小节)	措施1：低头，用纸巾等捂住嘴。(a句)
	措施2：最好弄湿捂嘴的工具。(b句)
	措施1：尽快撤离飞机，不要携带个人物品。(c句)
紧急迫降(第3小节)	措施2：在滑梯充满气之后再跳上去，跳时必须手脚向前。(d句)
	措施3：尽量远离飞机，不要在残骸附近吸烟。
结论	省略

例4：

Five Steps to Living Longer

Watch Your Temper

Scientists have long believed that Type A's -those people driven by ambition, hard work and tight deadlines—were most prone to heart attacks. But it's not striving for goals that leads to disease; rather, it's being hostile, angry and cynical.

Suggests Mittleman: if stress mounts so high that you begin snapping at people, "Ask yourself, 'Is it worth having a heart attack over this?'"

Lighten Your Dark Moods

For years, evidence linking depression to an increased risk of heart attack has been growing. Johns Hopking researchers interviewed 1551 people who were free of heart disease in the early 1980s and again 14 years later. Those who reported having experienced major depression were four times as likely to have a heart attack as those who had not been depressed.

Exercise is an often overlooked antidepressant. In a study at Duke University, 60 percent of clinically depressed people who took a brisk 30-minute walk or jog at least three times a week were no longer depressed after 16 weeks.

Flatten That Belly

More than 50 years ago French scientist Jean Vague noted that people with a lot of upper-body fat(those who looked like apples rather than pears) often developed heart disease, diabetes and other ailments. But it wasn't until the introduction of CT and MRI scans that doctors discovered that a special kind of fat, visceral fat, located within the abdomen, was strongly linked to these diseases.

According to the National Institutes of Health, there's trouble brewing when your waist measures 35 inches or more if you're a woman, and 40 inches or more if you're a man. And that's regardless of height.

Limit Your Bad Habits

Heavy drinking. Moderate drinker may be the least likely to develop Metabloic syndrome, while alcoholics are the most likely. In part that's because, pound for pound, they carry more abdominal fat. In one Swedish study, researchers found that male alcoholics carried 48 percent of their body fat within the abdomen, compared with 38 percent for teetotaler.

Cigarette smoking. Smoking is dangerous for reasons besides lung cancer or emphysema. Some 60 minutes after smoking a cigarette, one study revealed, smokers still showed elevated levels of cortisol, which promotes abdominal fat storage.

Over-caffeinating. Moderate caffeine consumption doesn't seem to be harmful for most people. But recent studies suggest that when men who have both high blood pressure and a family history of hypertension drink a lot of caffeinated coffee while under job stress, they may experience a dangerous rise in blood pressure.

Rev Up Your Metabolism

A new understanding of how disease sets up shop in your body focuses on metabolism—the sum of physical and chemical reactions necessary to maintain life. This approach reveals that a healthy metabolic profile counts for more than cardiovascular fitness or weight alone.

As Glenn A. Gaesser, professor of exercise physiology at the University of Virginia, notes, "metabolic fitness is one of the best safeguards against heart disease, stroke and diabetes."

Q1: According to the passage, which of the following people are liable to incur and suffer from heart attacks?

(A) Those whose waists measure 35 inches or less.

(B) those who take a brisk 20-minute walk twice a week.

(C) Those who have experienced major depression.

(D) Those who have been striving for goals.

Q2: Stress may lead to all of the following EXCEPT _____.

(A) hostile disposition   (B) cynical behaviour

(C) over-caffeinating   (D) great ambition

Q3: According to the passage, what kind of people are teetotalers (Step 4: Limit Your Bad Habits)?

(A) Non-alcoholics.   (B) Heavy drinkers.

(C) Chain smokers.   (D) Non-smokers.

Q4: Which of the following statements is TRUE according to the passage?

(A) There is trouble brewing when your waist measures 35 inches or less.

(B) Metabolic fitness might prevent people from having heart disease.

(C) Moderate drinkers may be the most likely to develop Metabolic Syndrome.

(D) Moderate caffeine consumption seems to be harmful for most people.

解析：本文是一篇健康方面的说明文，介绍的是 5 种抵御心脏病、延长生命的方法。本文的主题以一个总标题的形式出现，而段落大意则由 5 个小标题给出，文章分 5 段举例说明主题，结构一目了然。读完标题后便可直接读题。文章结构：

主题	5 种延年益寿的方法	
方法 1	注意脾气	敌意、愤怒、厌世导致疾病。
方法 2	改善心情	沮丧的人心脏病的发病率高； 运动可以帮助调节心情。
方法 3	减少腹部脂肪	腹部脂肪与心脏类疾病关系密切。
方法 4	改掉(有害健康的)坏习惯	坏习惯 1：酗酒 坏习惯 2：抽烟 坏习惯 3：过量摄取咖啡因
方法 5	促进新陈代谢	最佳方法——比其他健身方法都有效。
结论	省略	

Q1: 本题考查的是所有方法，其中可以看出导致心脏病的原因是精神沮丧，选 (C)，出处是"For years, evidence linking depression to an increased risk of heart attack..."

Q2: 本题考查的是第一种方法，选 (D)。

Q3: 本题考查的是方法 4 中的第一个习惯，既然和饮酒相对立，那就是指不喝酒的，选（A）。

Q4: 本题考查面又是覆盖所有的方法，经过一一核对，发现除（B）之外，其他所有的选项都和原文正好相反，选（B）。

三、观点—例证—结论型

这类文章的结构特征是作者首先提出观点，然后围绕观点展开论证，通过几个支持观点（supporting arguments）或事例（supporting factors）来进一步阐明自己的观点，最后在文章末尾做出总结。这种结构与前一种类型在段落的分布上很相似，皆为主题——举例——总结的形式，但是这种类型的例子更为突出地服务于证明作者的观点，而不是简单地列举主题包括的要素。此类文章结构在议论文中多见。

阅读提示：在这类文章结构中，用于例证的具体对象和内容在阅读时是次要的，有时甚至可以直接略过。这是因为例证在文章中所起到的最主要的作用是为了证明观点，所以无论作者用什么对象如何加以证明，最后的结论一定是符合文章的主题（thesis）或作者的主论点（main argument）。同时在阅读时要注意段落展开的引导词，这样不仅可以方便阅读，也可以更清晰地理解文章的结构。

如果在考题中出现了关于（1）作者采用某个例子的目的（The author mentioned... to...?）；（2）某个例子在文章中起到了什么作用（The use of... is to...?）的题型，那么这些问题考查的对象其实是作者在例证之前所提出的观点。解题的关键也在于理解作者的论点，而不是例证中细节的内容。

如果考题中出现了针对某个例证的细节内容的问题，那么只需根据题干或选项中的提示定位到对应的例证中，再通过重点阅读来解题。考生在阅读这类文章时只要对例证做基本了解，便于解题时定位即可。

下面我们通过几个例子来说明。

例 1：

（1）The bath was invented before the bath plug. The bath plug could not have been invented before the bath, except as a small object with which to play ice hockey. <u>The order in which inventions are made is very important, much more important than has ever been realized, because we tend automatically to think that later inventions are better than earlier ones. A moment's thought will show this is not so.</u> If, for example, a solution to today's urban traffic problems was proposed in the shape of a small man-powered two-wheeled vehicle which would make the motor car look like a cumbersome over-powered device, a space rocket trying to tackle suburban problems, we would greet it as a great technological breakthrough. "Bicycle makes car obsolete", we would cry. Unfortunately, the bike came first, so we shall always unconsciously see it as a cruder version of the car.

（2）<u>Other things, which may have been invented too early,</u> are the airship, the radio, the railway train, the piano-roll player and the cuff-link.

(3) Consider also the zip. Zips represent a technological advance on buttons, being faster and more complete. They are also more liable to come adrift, break, jam, malfunction, stick and catch. Buttons can only go wrong if the thread is faulty. Even then, buttons can be mended by the user. Zips rarely can.

Q1: If the bicycle were to be invented now the car would appear _____.

(A) unsuitable for its purpose   (B) in advance of its time

(C) unnecessarily expensive   (D) too fast for safety

Q2: The airship and the radio are examples of things which _____.

(A) were not fully appreciated at the time of their invention

(B) are more suitable for use now than when they were invented

(C) have been neglected in favor of more recent inventions

(D) are less suited to their purpose than earlier inventions

Q3: According to the writer, buttons are preferable to zips because they _____.

(A) are more convenient   (B) are more reliable

(C) cost less to replace   (D) are safer to use

解析：本文为一篇议论文。作者在首段用一个类比引出了一个人们通常持有的观点，即事物发明的顺序很重要，因为人们通常认为新发明一定要比以前的发明先进。接着作者通过对这个观点的否定提出了自己的观点，那就是事实并非如此。这种通过对立观点（contrast）提出主题的方式我们在前面已经学习过了。在主题或论点确立了以后，作者接下来分段进行了例证：

主题	事物发明的先后顺序并不一定能代表它们的先进程度。（第1小节）	
例证1	自行车 vs. 机动车（第1小节） 结构引导词：If, for example...	如果自行车是新发明，我们会认为它是解决城市交通和环境问题的好办法，但仅仅因为它不是，所以我们认为自行车很原始。
例证2	其他一些过早地被新发明所代替的事物（第2小节） 结构引导词：Other things...	
例证3	拉链 vs. 纽扣（第3小节） 结构引导词：Consider also...	拉链是超越纽扣的一个替代品。但是拉链极不牢靠，纽扣却非常牢靠且容易修补。
总结	省略	

Q1：本题考查的是第一个例证：很多考生误选了（B），犯了不尊重原文的错误。错误的思路是：机动车总要比自行车先进，如果机动车是先被发明的，那么它就会显得超越了时代。正确的思路应该是作者的假设，人们通常认为后发明的一定比先发明的先进，所以如果自行车和机动车的发明顺序一经颠倒，人们就会认为机动车落后，所以选（A）。

Q2: 本题考查的是第二组例证,根据结构图我们知道,这些事物过早地被新发明代替了,选(C)。

Q3: 本题考查的是第三个例证,作者旨在证明先发明的不一定比后发明的落后,所以我们要找纽扣的优势,选(B)。

例2:

(1) <u>Most people picture sharks as huge, powerful, frightening predators, ready at any moment to use their sharp teeth to attack unwary swimmers without provocation. There are numerous fallacies, however, in this conception of sharks.</u> <u>First,</u> there are about 350 species of shark, and not all of them are large. They range in size from the dwarf shark, which can be only 6 inches (0.5 feet) long and can be held in the palm of the hand, to the whale shark, which can be more than 55 feet long.

(2) <u>A second fallacy</u> concerns the number and type of teeth, which can vary tremendously among the different species of shark. A shark can have from one to seven sets of teeth at the same time, and some types of shark can have several hundred teeth in each jaw. It is true that the fierce and predatory species do possess extremely sharp and brutal teeth used to rip their prey apart; many other types of shark, however, have teeth more adapted to garbing and holding than to cutting and slashing.

(3) <u>Finally,</u> not all sharks are predatory animals ready to strike out at humans on the least whim. In fact, only 12 of the 350 species of shark have been known to attack humans, and a shark needs to be provoked in order to attack. The types of shark that have the worst record with humans are the tiger shark, the bull shark, and the great white shark. However, for most species of shark, even some of the largest types, there are no known instances of attacks on humans.

Q: The passage indicates that a shark attacks a person _____ .

  (A) for no reason   (B) every time it sees one

  (C) only if it is bothered   (D) only at night

解析:在确定主题的篇章里我们用过这篇文章。作者用了对立观点的方法来树立自己的观点,即人们对鲨鱼的一些看法是存在错误的。接下来作者分段进行了例证:

主题	人们认为鲨鱼是庞大、强壮、凶狠的掠食动物。这些看法存在偏差。(第1小节)
例证1	不是所有的鲨鱼都庞大。(第1小节)
	结构引导词:First...
例证2	鲨鱼的牙齿不一定被用来撕咬食物。(第2小节)
	结构引导词:Second...
例证3	不是所有的鲨鱼都有攻击人类的前科,而且它们一定是在被骚扰的情况下才会攻击。(第3小节)
	结构引导词:Finally...
总结	省略

Q: 根据"attacks"一词我们可以看出,本题考查第三个例证。关于鲨鱼攻击人这种说法,作者的观点是,鲨鱼只有在受到骚扰的情况下才会发起攻击,所以选(**C**)。

> 提示:选项中的"bother"和原文中的"provoke"正好对应。

例 3:

(1) Psychologists have found that privately made confidential resolutions are rarely followed, whereas a public commitment to achieve some goal, such as losing weight or giving up smoking, is likely to be much more effective. <u>This is because the approval of others for doing something desirable is valued. In contrast, disapproval for failure can lead to feelings of shame.</u>

(2) Advertising agencies have designed studies bearing out the truth of this observation. <u>In this research,</u> a group of strangers was bombarded with information about the qualities of a particular product. They were then asked to either announce out loud or write down privately whether they intended to buy the product. It was later discovered that those who publicly declared their intention to buy were considerably more likely to do so than those who affirmed their intentions in private.

(3) <u>In another study,</u> an experimenter claiming to represent a local utility company interviewed house owners telling them he was investigating ways in which energy consumption could be reduced. Half the subjects, randomly selected, were told that if they agreed to conserve energy their names would be mentioned in an article newspaper; the remaining half were told their names would not be used. All those interviewed agreed to cooperate and signed a form either giving consent for their names to be used or stating that their names would not be used. Later in the year, the amount of gas consumed in each house was recorded. The owners who had agreed to their names being published had used significantly less gas than those who remained anonymous.

解析:本文议论的重点是心理学上的一个现象及其背后的理论:现象——人们在私下里做出的决定往往得不到实现,而在公共场合做出的决定则相对完成得要好;理论——人们往往更在乎在别人眼里的形象。他们珍惜别人的赞许,同时也为别人的冷视感到羞愧。在讲主题的章节我们提到过,这是一种因果方式。接下来作者用了两段进行例证:

主题	人们在乎别人的赞许,羞于他人的鄙视。(第1小节)	
例证 1	广告公司做了一个调研,证明了这一观点(第 2 小节) 结构引导词:In this research...	口头声明要购买产品的客户比书面声明要购买的客户更容易实现消费。
例证 2	广告公司的另一个调研也说明了这个问题。(第 3 小节) 结构引导词:In another study...	名字将被刊登的家庭用户比不会被刊登的用户节省了更多的能源。
结论	省略	

例4：

(1) <u>Many folk cures which have been around for centuries may be more therapeutic than previously suspected.</u> A case in point is that of penicillin. Alexander Fleming did not just randomly choose cheese molds to study when he discovered its very important bacteria-killing substance. Moldy cheese was frequently given to patients as a remedy for illness at one time. Fleming just isolated what it was about the cheese which cured the patients.

(2) <u>In parts of South America, a powder obtained from grinding sugar cane is used for healing infections in wounds and ulcers.</u> This usage may date back to pre-Colombian times. Experiments carried out on several hundred patients indicate that ordinary sugar in high concentrations is lethal to bacteria. Its suction effect eliminates dead cells, and it generats a glasslike layer, which protects the wound and ensures healing.

(3) <u>Another example</u> of folk medicine which scientists are investigating is that of Arab fishermen who rub their wounds with a venomous catfish to quicken healing. This catfish excretes a gellike slime which scientists have found to contain antibiotics, a coagulant that helps close injured blood vessels, anti-inflammatory agents, and a chemical that directs production of a gluelike material that aids healing.

(4) It is hoped that by documenting these folk remedies and experimenting to see if results are indeed beneficial, an analysis of the substances can be made, and synthetic substances can be developed for human consumption.

Q1: It can be inferred from the passage that Alexander Fleming _____ .

   (A) discovered moldy cheese

   (B) isolated infectious patients

   (C) suspected medicinal properties of molds

   (D) enjoyed eating different kinds of cheese

Q2: We can learn from the passage that _____ .

   (A) bacteria feed on sugar   (B) sugar kills unhealthy cells

   (C) glass is formed from sugar   (D) sugar promotes healing

解析：本文的观点是一些民间疗方的确有治疗的效果。作者分三段举例来证明其观点，最后在证实的基础上做出了总结。结构如下：

主题	许多民间疗方对疾病的治疗能力要比我们想像的好。（第1小节）
例证1	发霉的奶酪能治病。（第1小节）
	结构引导词：A case in point…
例证2	普通的糖也能疗伤。（第2小节）
例证3	有毒的鲶鱼涂抹伤口，有助于伤口愈合。（第3小节）
	结构引导词：Another example…
结论	对民间疗方的疗效加以记录，研究其效果，提炼可治疗的成分，最终制成人工合成药物供大众使用。

Q1: 本题考查的对象是第一个例证，可以看出 Alexander Fleming 发明青霉素的过程中，显然受到了发霉的奶酪能治病的启发，所以选(**C**)。

Q2: 本题考查的对象是第二个例证，无论其具体内容是什么，都是为了说明民间疗方的疗效，所以选 (**D**)。

例 5:

(1) Experiments have shown that in selecting personnel for a job, interviewing is at best a hindrance, and may even cause harm. These studies have disclosed that the judgments of interviewers differ markedly and bear little or no relationship to the adequacy of job applicants. Of the many reasons why this should be the case, three in particular stand out. The first reason is related to an error of judgment known as the halo effect. If a person has one noticeable good trait, their other characteristics will be judged as better than they really are. Thus, an individual who dresses smartly and shows self-confidence is likely to be judged capable of doing a job well regardless of his or her real ability.

(2) Interviewers are also prejudiced by an effect called the primacy effect. This error occurs when interpretation of later information is distorted by earlier connected information. Hence, in an interview situation, the interviewer spends most of the interview trying to confirm the impression given by the candidate in the first few moments. Studies have repeatedly demonstrated that such an impression is unrelated to the aptitude of the applicant.

(3) The phenomenon known as the contrast effect also skews the judgment of interviewers. A suitable candidate may be underestimated because he or she contrasts with a previous one who appears exceptionally intelligent. Likewise, an average candidate who is preceded by one who gives a weak showing may be judged as more suitable than he or she really is.

(4) Since interviews as a form of personnel selection have been shown to be inadequate, other selection procedures have been devised which more accurately predict candidate suitability. Of the various tests devised, the predictor which appears to do this most successfully is cognitive ability as measured by a variety of verbal and spatial tests.

Q1: According to the passage, the halo effect _____ .

　　(A) stands out as the worst judgmental error

　　(B) works only when a candidate is well dressed and self confident

　　(C) exemplifies how one good characteristic colors perceptions

　　(D) helps the interviewer's capability to judge real ability

Q2: According to the passage, the impression given in the first few moments _____ .

　　(A) can easily be altered

　　(B) is the one that stays with the interviewer

　　(C) is unrelated to the interviewer's prejudices

　　(D) has never been reinforced throughout the interview

Q3: The author mentions all of the following reasons why interviewing is not an accurate way to predict candidate suitability EXCEPT _____ .

(A) the halo effect   (B) the primacy effect

(C) the contrast effect   (D) the cognitive effect

Q4: This passage mainly discusses _____ .

(A) the effects of interviewing on job applicants

(B) the inadequacy of interviewing job applicants

(C) the judgments of interviewers concerning job applicants

(D) the tactics and techniques for judging job applicants

解析：本文在首句提出了一个观点：面试常常会成为选择人才时的障碍，甚至会导致不良后果。接着作者提供了三个导致这个后果的原因作为支持其观点的例证。最后作者提出了更好的选择人才的方法。结构如下：

主题	专家证明在选择人才时，面试充其量是个障碍，更不用说有时还有不良的后果。其原因有三(第1小节)
例证(原因)1	Halo effect——观察人时以偏盖全，一个优点遮盖了其他的缺点。(第1小节) 结构引导词：The first reason...
例证(原因)2	Primacy effect——对个人信息的解读受到之前相关信息的影响。(第2小节) 结构引导词：Interviews are also prejudiced...
例证(原因)3	Contrast effect——对一个人的评判受到竞争者的表现的影响。(第3小节) 结构引导词：The phenomenon... also skews...
结论	其他测试，例如认识力的测试，可以更加有效地帮助挑选人才。

Q1: 本题考查的是第一个例证 Halo effect，根据结构图的解释选(**C**)。

Q2: 本题考查的是第二个例证 Primacy effect，根据结构图的解释选(**B**)。

Q3: 本题考查的是所有的例证，根据结构图我们可以发现，惟一没有出现的是 (D) cognitive effect，选(**D**)。

Q4: 本题考查的是全文的主题，根据结构图我们可以了解到，主题围绕着面试的诸多不足之处来展开，选(**B**)。

四、观点—叙述—驳论型

这种结构与前两种的相似之处是，作者首先提出一种观点，并且也对其进行叙述。但最明显的区别在于作者接着会树立一个对立的观点，反驳前文中的某个或整个观点，从而让考生更全面地了解论题的多面性。

例1：

(1)One of the most difficult questions to answer is how much a job is worth. We naturally expect that a doctor's salary will be higher than a bus conductor's wages. But the question becomes much more difficult to answer when we compare, say, a miner with an engineer, or an unskilled man working on an oil-rig in the North Sea with a teacher in a secondary school. (1st factor) [What the doctor, the engineer and the teacher have in common is that they have devoted several years of their lives to studying in order to obtain the necessary qualifications for their professions. We feel instinctively that these skills and these years, when they were studying instead of earning money, should be rewarded.] (2nd factor) [At the same time we recognise that the work of the miner and the oil-rig laborer is both hard and dangerous, and that they must be highly paid for the risks they take.]

(2) (3rd factor) [Another factor we must take into consideration is how socially useful a man's work is, regardless of the talents he may bring to it.] Most people would agree that looking after the sick or teaching children is more important than, say selling second-hand cars or improving the taste of toothpaste by adding a red stripe to it. Yet it is almost certain that the used-car salesman earns more than the nurse and the research chemist earns more than the schoolteacher.

(3) (Contradicting factor) Indeed, this whole question of just rewards can be turned on its head. You can argue that a man who does a job which brings him personal satisfaction is already receiving part of his reward in the form of a so-called "psychic wage", and that it is the man with the boring, repetitive job who needs more money to make up for the soul-destroying monotony of his work. It is significant that those jobs which are traditionally regarded as "vocations" — nursing, teaching and the Church, for example—continue to be poorly paid, while others, such as those in the world of sport or entertainment carry financial rewards out of all proportion to their social worth.

解析：本文讨论的主题是如何比较不同职位的价值以及相应的报酬。作者在前两段提出，有几个决定性的因素决定了不同劳动的报酬。作者在最后一节又提出了一个对立观点，对前面的例证进行了反驳，从而最终呼应了主题：要想比较一个工作的真正价值的确很难。全文结构如下：

主题	要确定一个工作的价值是很困难的。(第1小节)
因素(factor)1	学习知识和接受培训的过程的长短可以决定一种劳动的价值。(第1小节)
因素(factor)2	工作中的难度和危险程度也可以用来衡量劳动价值。(第1小节)
因素(factor)3	工作本身的社会有益性也可以用来衡量一种劳动的价值。(第2小节)
对立因素 (contradicting factor)：针对第3个因素	工作的社会有益性在现实中并没有带来高薪。热爱自己工作的劳动者已经得到了一种精神报酬("psychic wage")，所以经济酬劳反而少了。而无聊的重复劳动应该得到高薪,以弥补对精神的摧残。(第3小节)
总结	社会上存在着很多薪水和劳动比例失调的问题,足见确定一种劳动的价值是个不能面面俱到的问题。(第3小节)

例2：

(1) "It's not what you know but who you know that counts." People who get on in life may be successful not because they deserve it, but because of influential friends or the right

background. We say "Ah yes, he must have gone to the right school", or "She must come from a good family." We may suspect that some people in positions of authority are there because they belong to the right group or party. To get something done—a signature on a document, or a quick decision—it helps to know someone "on the inside". At least, this is the widespread belief.

(2) It is a comforting belief too. If your boss strikes you as incompetent, it is tempting to believe that he only got the job because his father pulled some strings. If someone else gets the job which you should have had, well, the "old boy network" must be operating. And yet, if we can get what we want by "having a word" with so-and-so, or by getting so-and-so to put in a good word for us, which of us would not take advantage of the opportunity?

(3) Often it is quite harmless. For instance, when Miguel went with Julia to visit Michelle in hospital, he bumped into someone he knew, a doctor who had been at medical school with his father. As a result of this chance meeting, Miguel was able to find out a great deal about Michelle's condition. Julia was not only grateful to him for making use of his connection, but delighted that she was able to learn so much by this means which she might never have found out otherwise.

(4) At the other extreme it can be very destructive. I once met a brilliant young engineer who worked in a chemical plant. Because of her knowledge and experience, she should have been promoted to Production Manager. Instead, the job went to a man who was totally unsuited for the post. Everyone knew that he only got it because he was politically acceptable to his superiors. This injustice demoralized the young engineer and many of her colleagues. It also meant that the factory was much less efficient than it could have been.

(5) All the same, we should not be pessimistic. More and more, the modern world depends on having people who are in the job because they are good enough, not just because their face fits. There is a story of a factory owner who sent for an engineer to see to a machine which would not go. He examined it, then took out a hammer and tapped it, once. The machine started up immediately. When he presented his bill, the owner protested, "This can't be right! 100 pounds just for tapping a machine with a hammer?" The engineer wrote out a new bill: "For tapping a machine, 1 pound; for knowing where to tap it, 99 pounds."

(6) Maybe it is what you know that really counts, after all.

解析：作者在文章开始时引用了人们常说的话："人际关系远比真才实学要重要。"文章的主题便围绕着这个论题展开。作者接下来叙述了这种观点的几个表现，并做了相应的例证。但是作者在文章的后半部又提出了相反的论调，从而奠定了文章的尾处的自己的观点。文章结构如下：

主题	人们相信人际关系胜过真才实学。（第1小节）
表现1	这种观点可以帮助人们自我安慰——例证。（第2小节）
表现2	这种观点有时是无害的——例证。（第3小节）
表现3	这种观点有时会导致严重的祸害——例证。（第4小节）
驳论	其实真才实学越来越受到人们的重视——例证。（第5小节）
结论	也许还是真才实学更重要(第6小节)

例3：

(1) Many researchers believe that apes can communicate with human beings. Investigations made at several laboratories in the United States and elsewhere indicate that chimpanzees and gorillas are capable of understanding language and using linguistic responses at the level of a four-year-old child. Washoe, an adult chimpanzee who was raised as if she were a deaf child, can translate words she hears into American Sign Language. Koko, a 400-pound lowland gorilla, is claimed to have understood a poem written about her. Tests of Koko's auditory comprehension show that she is able to make discriminations between such words as "funny", "money" and "bunny".

(2) The scientists at the forefront of this research admit that their work has been severely criticized. The skeptics in general claim apes' language behavior is merely imitative. For this behavior to be called "language", it must also be communicative. The proponents of ape language counter that those who deny the validity of this research have never worked with apes. They point out that new fields of investigation always create controversy. They add that subhuman primates have not been taught to speak, however, because the outer layer of their brain hemispheres is not sufficiently refined.

Q1: According to the passage, ape-human communication is _____.

(A) observed readily by most scientists　(B) rejected by all researchers

(C) treated skeptically by some scientists (D) not questioned by linguists

Q2: Which of the following is the main topic of the passage?

(A) Research into apes' imitative behavior.

(B) Studies of language abilities of humans.

(C) Communicative behavior of subhuman primates.

(D) Uses of American Sign Language in research.

解析：本文是一篇介绍动物对话交流能力的说明文。文章在第一段提出了支持的观点，即猿类是可以和人对话的，并给出了例证；但是在第二段又提出了相悖的观点，即猿类的交流仅仅是一种模仿，而非对话，也给出了例证。最后文章做了相应的总结。结构如下：

主题	类人猿的语言交流能力。
观点	许多研究者发现猿类具备与人类对话的能力。(第 1 小节首句)
反驳观点	以上的观点受到了强烈的批判——猿类所谓的对话能力仅仅是模仿,不成其为实质上的交流。(第 2 小节首句)
结论	没有教类人猿对话的原因是它们的脑部没有完全发育。(末句)

Q1: 本题考查的正是第二小节的主要思想。根据结构图得出正确选项为 **(C)**,出处是第二小节的首句。

Q2: 本题考查的是文章的主题,根据结构图也可以清晰地找到答案 **(C)**。

章 节 小 结

在前面两个章节中,我们学习了对文章进行快速分析的两个关键技能:确定主题和理清结构。对这两种技能的熟练掌握和结合运用可以帮助我们高效地理解文章,既抓住了文章的精华,又理顺了文章的层次。更重要的是,这种阅读技巧能够使得解题事半功倍。无论是考查整体篇章或是局部细节的题目,我们都可以通过以上的阅读分析在文章中精确地定位,从而找到相对应的正确答案。

第三节 捕捉重点

在阅读过程中,除了掌握文章的整体结构,考生们还应该培养对文章局部一些重点内容的认识。这些内容不仅可以帮助考生更有效地理解局部段落的大意,同时也可以起到推测题目出处和类型的功效。

一、重点句型

在分析文章结构时,我们已经注意到,每个自然段的首句 (leading sentence) 和末句 (concluding sentence) 对概括个别段落的大意很有帮助。同时,因为这类句子在文章中也充当着过渡句(transitional sentence),引导文章的结构,所以它们也能帮助我们理顺文章的层次。除此之外,在段落中可能还有一些重要的句型能够对我们阅读以及解题起到很好的帮助。

1. 概括、总结性的句型

由表示主要的、重点的、关键的词汇群和表示观点、原因、要点、因素的词汇群结合成的句型:

表示主要的、重点的、关键的词汇群:"main", "major", "crucial", "vital", "basic", "fundamental", "chief", "most significant", "most important", "key", etc.

表示观点、原因、要点、因素的词汇群:"fact", "factor", "element", "ingredient", "reason", "concept", "idea", "notion", "thought", etc.

这些句型通常对一个段落或局部的篇章做出总结，不仅可以帮助我们更有效地理解文章，也可以给解题带来不少的帮助。下面我们参考几个例子：

例1：

The oldest survivor from prehistoric times is, can you believe it, the cockroach. Cockroaches have been able to stick around for more than 250 million years. The main reason for their incredible endurance is their ability to live in all kinds of conditions and survive on all kinds of food.

Q: The expression "stick around" in the last paragraph is closest in meaning to _____ .

(A) endure   (B) attack

(C) travel around   (D) look around

解析：本段的一个重点句型就是解释蟑螂具有持久生命力的原因在于，它能够在任何环境下靠任何食物生存，从"endurance"一词中我们已经可以得到"stick around"的意思，即坚持，选(A)。

例2：

Lincoln's now famous Gettysburg Address was not, on the occasion of its delivery, recognized as the masterpiece that it is today. Lincoln was not even the primary speaker at the ceremonies, held at the height of the Civil War in 1863, to dedicate the battlefield at Geetysburg. The main speaker was orator Edward Everest, whose two-hour speech was followed by Lincoln's shorter remarks. Lincoln began his small portion of the program with the words that today are immediately recognized by most Americans: "Four score and seven years ago our father brought forth on this continent a new nation, conceived in liberty and dedicated to the proposition that all men are created equal."

Q: Which of the following is true about the ceremonies at Gettysburg during the Civil War?

(A) Lincoln was the main speaker.   (B) Lincoln gave a two-hour speech.

(C) Everest was the closing speaker. (D) Everest's speech was longer than Lincoln's.

解析：从关键句中"main"一词我们已经得知 Everest 是主要发言人，由此自然可以知道他的演讲一定比 Lincoln 的时间长。另外，他的演讲还在 Lincoln 发言之前。由此我们可以轻松地排除前三个选项。答案选(D)。

2. 定性句型（常伴随绝对性词汇出现）

It seems to be only when the picnic has to be staged in one particular spot, as the center-piece of a day's outing that it starts to become an elaborate endurance test. I have rarely met a child who did not enjoy the idea—and almost never a father who did not detest it. The worst place for a picnic is the beach. Sand is a great infiltrator. It furs the children's hands like gloves of grit. You cannot stand up or sit down, reach over or cross your legs, without sending up a volcanic cloud of its tiny, glittering, rock-sharp fragment. The only advantage that can be claimed for sand as a picnic surface is that it is good to spill things on. One of the joys of family tea at our local seaside, inside the deck-chair corral formed by dozing aunts and uncles, was pouring the last of your lemonade on to the bleached-white dust and watching how the bubbles foamed like glass beads over the dark-brown, molten-snake patterns.

Q: The writer considers the only advantage of the beach as a picnic place to be that _____ .

    (A) deck-chairs are available   (B) there is plenty of room

    (C) food and drink can be spilled   (D) children enjoy it

解析：本段落中最关键的两句话就是我们标出的两句，确定了海滩作为野营场所的优劣之处，其他都是细节描写。考查这段内容的题目直接指向了关键句，根据关键句的内容，海滩惟一的优势就是可以随意地泼洒东西，选（C）。

3. 列举句型

表示列举的表达有："consist of..."，"contain..."，"include..."，"have..."，"enclose"，"comprise"，etc.。这类表达引导的句型往往是列举一系列的事实或一个事物以及观点的组成部分。在考题中针对这样的列举经常用一些是非题，即"三对一错"或"三错一对"的题型来考查考生对局部知识的理解和掌握。在讨论文章结构的篇幅里，我们提到的许多讨论事物特性的文章都运用这样的句型。

二、转折词的阅读

转折词汇在文章中，尤其是议论文的立论过程中出现的频率很高。这其中有表示强转折的词汇，例如："but"，"on the contrary"，"however"，"yet"，"nevertheless"，"nonetheless"，"on the other hand"，"still"，"conversely"，"then again"，"in spite of"；表示委婉转折的词汇，例如："although"，"though"，"even though"，"while"；有转折意境的词汇，例如："unfortunately"，"sadly"，"unluckily"。

在文章结构的章节中我们提到，在许多议论文中作者提出主题的方式往往是先提供一个对立观点（Contradiction），然后通过对其否定来阐明自己的观点。在这种情况下，转折词对主题的确定能够起到很好的提示作用。除此之外，转折词汇通常还出现在文章对一些重要观点或事实的表述上，而这些观点常常成为题目考查的对象。由此我们可以看出，转折词的出现和作用也是一个值得注意的阅读重点，因为它不仅是帮助理解一篇文章的工具，更是解答题目时定位的法宝。

三、引用

在文章的叙述中，作者为了更有力地说明一个观点或现象，经常引用一些他人的原话作为旁证。而在考题中我们往往会遇到一些考查文章中某个人物的观点及态度的题型，我们称之为人物观点题。这时我们对引用要特别留意，因为人物的原话是体现观点的最佳途径。

例1:

He could hardly be better qualified for the job of village policeman. Before he joined the police, he was an agricultural worker for five years and a male nurse in a mental hospital for six years. 引用→ He says："If you haven't had another job before you join the police, you tend to think nothing but police."

Q3: John Pooley thinks he is well qualified for his job because _____ .

（A）he had other jobs before he became a policeman

（B）he has been a policeman for fifteen years

（C）he has lived in Westleton all his life

（D）he is a countryman at heart

解析：题目询问的是为何 John Pooley 本人认为他能够胜任这个工作,而文中的一句引用恰好说明了一切,其他工作背景能帮助他更好地完成警察的工作。选 (A)。

例2:

（1）Before Felix arrived in Baghdad, Miss Bohun had arranged for him to have lessons with a Mr. Posthorn of the Education Office. Mr. Posthorn was a busy man. He not only had his government job but also taught some Arab boys from a wealthy family who hoped eventually to go to an English university. He had agreed to fit Felix in his spare time, which meant that sometimes Felix went to Mr. Posthorn's office and was told to study this or that, and occasionally Mr. Posthorn managed to find a spare hour when he dropped in to Miss Bohun's and gave Felix some instruction. Most of Felix's day was spent in study in his bedroom. He knew he would not get far in this way and he knew also that Mr. Posthorn would have been willing to give him more attention had he, like Miss Bohun, not been disappointed in him. Miss Bohun did not say or do anything that gave Felix any clue as to how he had failed her, but Mr. Posthorn, after testing his knowledge, said without hesitation, 引用 1→"What on earth have you been doing with yourself since you left England?"

（2）Felix explained that in Cairo he had taken lessons with an old English lady, an ex-governess to a royal family, who had taught him English composition, French, drawing, geography and history. Unfortunately she had known less Greek, Latin and mathematics than he had. His mother had treated lessons there as a joke, and said: "Never mind, darling, when we return to England we'll make up for lost time."

（3）引用 2→"Your parents ought to have been ashamed of themselves, keeping you away from school during the most important years of your life. I can't understand it," said Mr. Posthorn. "Your father was an educated man, wasn't he?" Felix explained: it wasn't my father's fault. Mother wouldn't let me go back to England when the war started. Father was angry, but Mother said: "If he goes I may not see him again."

(4) 引用 3→Mr. Posthorn said: "you'll never make up for it," but Felix, although he knew it to be a serious matter, could not really care.

Q: What did Mr. Posthorn think of Felix's education?

(A) He thought his father had not encouraged him enough.

(B) He was surprised that Felix had managed to learn anything at all.

(C) He thought Felix had wasted a great deal of valuable time.

(D) He believed that Felix could catch up with the other boys later.

解析：题目询问 Mr. Posthorn 对 Felix 的教育现况的态度。文中引用的 Mr. Posthorn 的三句话无不体现出 Mr. Posthorn 的不满。综合后两句我们可以确定，他认为 Felix 浪费了很多宝贵的、无法弥补的学习时间，所以答案选 **(C)**。

第四节 省略细节

在时间受到严格限制的阅读理解考试中，考生不仅要培养抓住文章重点信息的能力，也要训练对细节，尤其是对无足轻重的文章内容的判断和省略的技能，力求避免阅读精力的分散。这样才能真正从整体上完成对一篇文章的高效阅读。

一、人名、地名、公司名、数字、年代、尺寸、职位等

例1：

(1) A fledgling British firm has launched an electronic "Agenda" with a new, faster way of entering "lunch with Desdemona". It uses the Microwriter keyboard, which was invented some years ago by Mr. Cy Endfield, a film director whose other words include "Zulu". His idea soon gained the support of Sir Mark Weinberg, chairman of an insurance group. Allied Dunbar. He is a 30% shareholder in Microwriter and has written its notably undaunting instruction book.

(2) In addition to the standard letter keys, the Microwriter has a second keyboard consisting of five unmarked keys, one for each finger. By pressing the keys in various combinations, one can learn quickly to "type" almost as fast as on a full keyboard. The Microwriter was first peddled as a sort of hand-held word-processor, but only about 7,000 were sold. Now the firm is hoping that the boom in electronic organizers will revive its fortunes.

Q: We can learn from the passage that one novel feature of the Microwriter is _____.

(A) its instruction book　　(B) the fact that it was invented by a film director

(C) its dual keyboard　　(D) the fact that it is a word-processor

解析：本题询问的是关于 Microwriter 的一个新颖的特征。第一小节提出了 Microwriter 可以更快地输入，但是接着文章却开始介绍它发明者的身份、职业、其他的作品、他的支持者以及另一个的身份、职业......阅读时应该注意到，这些细节内容毫无意义，而问题的

答案要跳跃到第二小节的首句，Microwriter 之所以可以更快地输入是因为有双重键盘，所以选（C）。

二、人物心态、外貌、思维的具体描写

例2：

（1）She looked in the pockets of the black leather jacket he had reluctantly worn the night before. Three of his suits, a pair of blue twill work pants, an old gray sweater with a hood and pockets lay thrown across the bed. The jacket leather was sleazy and damply clinging to her hands. She had bought it for him, as well as the three suits: one light blue with side vents, one gold with green specks. And one reddish that had a silver imitation-silk vest. The pockets of the jacket came softly outward from the lining like skinny milktoast rats. Empty. Slowly she sank down on the bed and began to knead, with blunt anxious fingers, all the pockets in all the clothes piled around her. First the blue suit, then the gold with green, then the reddish one that he said he didn't like most of all, but which he would sometimes wear if she agreed to stay home, or if she promised not to touch him anywhere at all while he was getting dressed.

（2）She was a big awkward woman, with big bones and hard rubbery flesh. Her short arms ended in ham hands, and her neck was a squat roll of fat that protruded behind her head as a big bump. Her skin was rough and puffy, with plump molelike freckle down her cheeks. Her eyes glowered from under the mountain of her brow and were circled with expensive mauve shadow. They were nervous and quick when she was flustered and darted about at nothing in particular while she was dressing hair or talking to people.

（3）Her troubles started noticeably when she fell in love with a studiously quiet schoolteacher, Mr. Jerome Franklin Washington III, who was ten years younger than her. She told herself that she shouldn't want him, he was so little and cute and young, but when she took into account that he was a schoolteacher, well, she just couldn't seem to get any rest until. As she put it, "I were Mr. and Mrs. Jerome Franklin Washington the third, and that's the truth!"

Q1: Jerome's taste in clothing is probably _____ .

（A）worse than the woman's   （B）very loud and flashy

（C）different from the woman's   （D）in agreement with the woman's

Q2: Apparently Jerome will occasionally wear the reddish suit if _____ .

（A）she is very good to him   （B）she will leave him alone

（C）she buys him more clothes   （D）she gets a better education

Q3: According to the passage, which of the following is not true about the woman?

（A）She is married to a school teacher.   （B）Her eyes move around a lot at times.

（C）She is ten years older than Jerome.   （D）She has found what she is looking for.

Q4: According to the passage, which of the following can be concluded from the

passage about this couple?

  (A) They will live happily ever after. (B) Their marriage is not harmonious.

  (C) The couple will adopt children. (D) They will become schoolteachers.

  解析：本文第一小节对一位妇女在家里整理她丈夫的衣服的场景做了具体描写，在阅读时应该一带而过，因为从里面我们得不出任何有价值的观点，直到最后一句文章的重点才浮现出来，即她的丈夫很讨厌她买的衣服，也不喜欢她亲近他，充分体现了他们之间的不和。值得注意的是，在介绍问题时同时也出现了强转折词"but"。第二小节对这位妇女的外表又做了更为细致的描写，同样可以略过。第三小节文章交代了这位妇女在一段不幸福的婚姻中感到很困惑。文章阅读的重点就是第一节的末句以及第三小节。对细节的省略既提高了阅读效率，又不影响解题。

  Q1：Jerome 对衣服的品味正好体现在第一小节的末句：Jerome 不喜欢这位妇女买的衣服，证明他们品味不同，选**（C）**。

  Q2：Jerome 穿红色西装的条件也在第一小节的末句：只要这位妇女不碰他，或不和他一起出门，所以选**（B）**。

  Q3：本题的 (D) 选项明显和文章第三小节中反映出来的问题不符，这位妇女并没有找到她理想的对象，选**（D）**。

  Q4：本题要求对全文做出推断，第三小节可以看出这对夫妻的婚后生活并不美满。

三、例子 (for example, for instance, such as, like, a case in point, etc.)

  (1) "It's not what you know but who you know that counts." People who get on in life may be successful not because they deserve it, but because of influential friends or the right background. We say "Ah yes, he must have gone to the right school", or "She must come from a good family." We may suspect that some people in positions of authority are there because they belong to the right group or party. To get something done—a signature on a document, or a quick decision—it helps to know someone "on the inside". At least, this is the widespread belief.

  (2) It is a comforting belief too. If your boss strikes you as incompetent, it is tempting to believe that he only got the job because his father pulled some strings. If someone else gets the job which you should have had, well, the "old boy network" must be operating. And yet, if we can get what we want by "having a word" with so-and-so, or by getting so-and-so to put in a good word for us, which of us would not take advantage of the opportunity?

  (3) Often it is quite harmless. For instance, when Miguel went with Julia to visit Michelle in hospital, he bumped into someone he knew, a doctor who had been at medical school with his father. As a result of this chance meeting, Miguel was able to find out a great deal about Michelle's condition. Julia was not only grateful to him for making use of his connection, but delighted that she was able to learn so much by this means which she might never have found out otherwise.

  (4) At the other extreme it can be very destructive. I once met a brilliant young engineer

who worked in a chemical plant. Because of her knowledge and experience, she should have been promoted to Production Manager. Instead, the job went to a man who was totally unsuited for the post. Everyone knew that he only got it because he was politically acceptable to his superiors. This injustice demoralized the young engineer and many of her colleagues. It also meant that the factory was much less efficient than it could have been.

(5) All the same, we should not be pessimistic. More and more, the modern world depends on having people who are in the job because they are good enough, not just because their face fits. There is a story of a factory owner who sent for an engineer to see to a machine which would not go. He examined it, then took out a hammer and tapped it, once. The machine started up immediately. When he presented his bill, the owner protested, "This can't be right! 100 pounds just for tapping a machine with a hammer?" The engineer wrote out a new bill: "For tapping a machine, 1 pound; for knowing where to tap it, 99 pounds."

(6) Maybe it is what you know that really counts, after all.

Q1: Miguel took advantage of the fact that he knew the doctor in order to get more information about Michelle's condition. According to the writer, Migule's action is _____.

(A) an example of how badly everybody behaves in using such opportunities

(B) an example of how some people have an unfair advantage over others

(C) an example of the way we can use such opportunities without hurting anyone else

(D) a good example of how to get something done by knowing someone "on the inside"

Q2: The engineer at the chemical plant was not promoted because _____.

(A) it is very difficult for a woman to get a promotion to a managerial position

(B) her bosses did not think she had the right qualifications for the job

(C) the man who got the promotion was more experienced than she was

(D) her bosses did not approve of her political opinions

Q3: The engineer who repaired the machine was right to charge 100 pounds because _____.

(A) he was the only person who could find out what was wrong with it

(B) he was charging for his knowledge and expertise

(C) the factory owner could not have repaired it himself

(D) he hit the machine to get it started again

解析：本文的主题是讨论知识和人际关系的重要性。其中文章的第三、四、五小节的论证方式皆为提出观点，然后举出具体的事例来说明。对事例本身无须重点阅读，只要做到在解题时能够定位就可以了。而即便题目涉及到具体的事例，其考查的重点仍然是围绕着观点展开的。在前面的章节中，我们已经提到过在例证类型的文章中对例子的处理。

Q1: 这个事例是为了说明靠人际关系解决问题有时是不会伤害到他人利益的，所以选(C)，出处是第三自然段的首句。

Q2：这个事例是为了说明靠人际关系解决问题有时会造成恶劣的后果，所以与当事人的性别(A)，她的工作能力(B)，以及得到工作的人的能力(C)都没有关系，所以选(D)，答题的关键是第四自然段的首句。

Q3：这个事例是为了说明知识终究还是要胜于人际关系，所以选(B)，出处是第五自然段的首句。

章 节 小 结

　　能够在阅读考试中敏锐地确定主题、理清结构、抓住重点、省略细节，不仅需要大量的总结和练习，做到无论对什么体裁或类型的文章都心中有数，同时也需要一个良好阅读习惯的配合。通常考生采取的逐字逐句的阅读势必要给阅读造成阻碍。所以在阅读时考生们仍需充分运用扫读(scanning)和略读 (skimming)的阅读方法来帮助自己提高速度。至于这些方法的运用，考生们可参考各类阅读理解的书籍资料，在这里就不一一做出详尽的解说了。

第三章 解题技巧

高效的阅读能力必须辅以完善的解题技巧，才是攻克中口阅读理解的完备技能组合。阅读理解部分的试题分为不同的种类，每种试题类型都具有相对应的考查重点，其中包括对一篇文章宏观布局的理解、局部细节的把握、词句含义的揣测、写作目的的推断等等。考查的对象和方式的不同决定了在解答思路和方法上的差异，所以如果我们想要完备解题技巧，必须要对各种题型做到充分的了解。在掌握了基本的考题类型和解答规律的基础上，我们再接着讨论一些更加行之有效的实战技巧。

第一节 辨识题型

中口阅读理解部分的考题大致可分为四大类：(1)主旨题，(2)细节题，(3)推断题，(4)指代题。除此之外还有一些特殊的变形。每种题型的特点各有不同，对考生的阅读和解题要求也不尽相同。考生们在解题时最基本的技巧就是辨识题型，从而有的放矢地确定解题思路，并找到适合于不同题型的行之有效的解题方法。

一、主旨题

主旨题旨在测试考生对文章整体的理解能力，即在阅读文章之后能够抓住作者写作的主要意图，归纳文章的主题或中心思想。

阅读要求： 这种题型对考生的阅读要求是贯穿全文，在通读文章的同时理解作者的主题或中心思想，以及文章在表达或阐述的过程中对信息的组织，即文章的结构和段落层次。

题型特征： 这类题型的最大特征在于表示"主要的"一组词汇与表示"观点、题目、中心以及目的"的另一组词汇的结合。

表示"主要的"词汇群："main"，"major"，"chief"，"principal"，"prime"，"primary"，"basic"，"fundamental"，"central"，"crucial"，etc.

表示"观点，题目，中心，以及目的"的词汇群："point"，"idea"，"topic"，"issue"，"concern"，"focus"，"subject"，"theme"，"aim"，"goal"，"purpose"，"argument" etc.

以上两组词汇任意组合，便形成我们常见的主旨题：

What's the main idea of the passage?

What's the main concern of the passage?

What's the main idea expressed in the passage?

What is the passage mainly about?

What does the passage primarily discuss?

What's the main argument of the passage?

The author's main purpose in this passage is?

The principal idea of the passage is?

The prime topic of the passage is?

解题技巧：在阅读技巧篇中，我们首先提出的阅读技巧就是确定文章的主题句（Topic Sentence）或中心句（Thesis Sentence）。这恰恰是解答主旨题的一个简明快捷的方法。大多数作者都习惯于通过这类句型来点明其写作的主要意图。当考生遇到主旨题时，可以直接与在阅读过程中确定的主题句或中心句对应起来解答。

例 1：

(1) A Japanese construction company plans to **build a huge independent city-state**, akin to the legendary Atlantis, in the middle of the Pacific Ocean. The city, dubbed "Marinnation", would have about one million inhabitants, two airports, and possibly even a spaceport. Marinnation, if built, would be a separate country but could serve as a home for international organizations such as the United Nations and the World Bank.

(2) Aside from the many political and social problems that would have to be solved, the engineering risk envisaged is monumental. The initial stage requires the building of a circular dam 18 miles in diameter attached to the seabed in a relatively shallow place in international waters. Then, several hundred pumps, operating for more than a year, would suck out the seawater from within the dam. When empty and dry, the area would have a city constructed on it. The actual land would be about 300 feet below sea level.

(3) According to designers, the hardest task from an engineering point of view would be to ensure that the dam is leak proof and earthquake proof.

If all goes well, it is hoped that Marinnation could be ready for habitation at the end of the second decade of the twenty-first century. Whether anyone would want to live in such an isolated and artificial community, however, will remain an open question until that time.

Q: What is the main idea expressed in the passage?

(A) The uses of a city like Marinnation

(B) The inhabitants of a city built in the ocean

(C) The construction of an independent city-state

(D) The engineering feats needed for building an oceanic city.

正解:(C)

解析:本文旨在介绍一个在海中建造城市的构想。在文章的首句,我们能够找到文章的主题(划双线部分)。根据主题句和选项的对比,不难看出(C)是正解。

例 2:

Even if the saying "cold hands, warm heart" were really true, the warmhearted probably would prefer to forgo frozen fingers during the winter. <u>In Japan, where central heating is still something of a luxury, Aoi Co., Ltd. has been distributing a small, disposable hand-and-body **warmer** that makes use of a harmless chemical reaction in order to generate heat.</u> This winter the Poco body warmer is making its debut in Canada, the United States and parts of Europe. In addition to chasing away winter chills, the body warmer can be used to help relieve pain that results from muscle sprains and arthritis.

The Poco body warmer measures about three by five inches and is one-quarter inch thick. It consists of a cloth bag containing a mixture of iron powder, moisturized wood powder, activated carbon and salt. To get it going, the user simply opens the outer vinyl bag in which the unit is vacuum-packed and shakes the cloth bag. The unit then absorbs oxygen from the air, which in conjunction with the moisture from the wood powder oxidizes the iron, giving off heat. The packet maintains an average temperature of 140 degrees Fahrenheit for 24 hours, according to the manufacturer. Aoi Co. officials say that the product contains no toxic chemicals. The only precaution users need to follow is to avoid direct contact between the skin and the body warmer because burns can occur. The unit sells for about $1.

Q: **What is the author's main purpose in the passage?**

(A) To explain a chemical reaction.

(B) To recommend a cure for arthritis.

(C) To introduce a new product.

(D) To compare central heating with the body warmer.

正解:(C)

解析:作者根据一个俗语"手冷没关系,心好就可以"推出即便好心人也不想冻僵自己的手,然后再引出在严冬里取暖的工具——"body warmer"。主题的出现是引导式,接下来文章对取暖器各项特征做了详细的介绍。由此我们可以确定作者写作的主要目的是介绍一种产品,选(C)。

例 3:

(1) Napoleon famously described the British as a nation of shopkeepers. These days it would be equally true to describe them as a nation of shoppers. <u>Either way, London is the UK's shopping mecca; if you can't find it here you probably can't find it at all.</u>

(2) <u>Some London shops are more or less tourist attractions in their own right.</u> Few visitors come away without popping into Harrods, even if only to gawp. This famous store is a real one-off. The toilets are fab, the food hall enough to make you swoon, and if they haven't got what you want, it probably doesn't exist. No other store has such a sense of sheer, outrageous abundance. Since Absolutely Fabulous brought Edina and Patsy steaming onto our screens, Harvey Nichols ('Harvey Nicks') has become another must-see attraction. It boasts a great food hall, an extravagant perfume department and jeweler to save up for. But with all the big names from Miyake to Lauren, Hammett to Calvin Klein and a whole floor of up-to-the-minute menswear, it's fashion that Harvey Nichols does better than the rest. The selection is unrivalled and the prices high, although the sales offer some great bargains, and the store's won clothing line is reasonable.

(3) <u>Carnaby Street</u> still reeks of the 60s although it's had something of a revival since the 'Cool Britannia' kick brought Union Jack dresses back into fashion. The last punks have long since slunk away from Chelsea's King's Rd but there are still plenty of interesting shops slotted in amid the high-street chains.

(4) <u>The shops and stalls inside the old Covent Garden market building</u> tend to be pricey and tourist-oriented, while the streets running off it remain a happy hunting ground for shoppers, with Neal St and Neal's Yard in particular offering a range of interesting one-off shops.

(5) <u>Oxford St and classier Regent St</u> come into their own in the six weeks running up to Christmas when they're festooned with lights. At other times of the year Oxford St can be a great disappointment. Selfridge's is up there with Harrods as a place to visit and the flagship Marks & Spencer at the marble Arch end has its fans, but the farther east you go the tackier and less interesting it becomes.

(6) <u>Although most things can be bought in most parts of town, there are also streets with their own specialties;</u> tottenham Court R & for example, is one long electrical goods shop (watch out for tip-offs though), while Charing Cross Rd is still the place to come for offbeat books.

(7) <u>Many tourist attractions have excellent shops, selling good-quality souvenirs</u> like mugs, pens, pencils, stationery and T-shirts, often with themes to match their content (war books and videos at the Imperial War Museum). By buying from these shops you help contribute towards the building's maintenance, especially important in the cases of those without entry charges.

Q: The overall purpose of the passage is to_____ .

(A) describe the British as shoppers

(B) introduce shopping places in London

(C) show how the British have changed from shopkeepers to shoppers

(D) indicate the British are better at doing business than other people

正解：（B）

解析：首段先从当年拿破仑对英国商店的评价，过渡到今日英国购物者的概述，最后推出文章的主题句（划双线部分），即 London 是英国的购物中心（shopping mecca），商品应有尽有。但仅依赖这句话很多考生在分析选项时仍然不能确定答案。那么只要在阅读时注意了各段的首句（划单线部分），发现全文的展开是以列举的方式分段介绍 London 各种不同的购物去处，自然会发现答案是（B）。

（A）选项：片面，仅为文章首段的第二句内容。

（C）选项：没有提及。若要做过去和现在的对比，则必须提到以前和现在的不同和变化。文章中没有反映。

（D）选项：片面，仅为文章首段的第一句内容。

> 提示：鉴于不同文章的结构和展开皆有所不同，有时单单依靠主题句或中心句并不能理想地解答主旨题。这就需要在阅读时进一步了解文章的结构以及段落大意来帮助解答。便捷的途径是，找到我们在阅读技巧时提到过的段落引导句（leading sentence）或过渡句（transitional sentence）。这些句型能够进一步帮助考生了解文章的结构、作者的观点以及阐述观点的方法。

例4：

(1) Great emotional and intellectual resources are demanded in quarrels; stamina helps, as does a capacity for obsession. But no one is born a good quarreler; the **craft** must be learned.

(2) There are two generally recognized apprenticeships. First, and universally preferred, is a long childhood spent in the company of fractious siblings. After several years of rainy afternoons, brothers and sisters develop a sure feel for the tactics of attrition and the niceties of strategy so necessary in first-rate quarrelling.

(3) The only child, or the child of peaceful or repressed households, is likely to grow up failing to understand that quarrels, unlike arguments, are not about anything, least of all the pursuit of truth. The apparent subject of a quarrel is a mere pretext; the real business is the quarrel itself.

(4) Essentially, adversaries in a quarrel are out to establish or rescue their dignity. Hence the elementary principle: anything may be said. The unschooled, probably no less quarrelsome by inclination that anyone else, may spend an hour with knocking heart, sifting the consequences of calling this old acquaintance a lying fraud. Too late! With a cheerful wave the old acquaintance has left the room.

(5) Those who miss their first apprenticeship may care to enroll in the second, the bad marriage. This can be perilous for the neophyte; the mutual intimacy of spouses makes them at once more vulnerable and more dangerous in attack. Once sex is involved, the stakes are higher

all round. And there is an unspoken rule that those who love, or have loved, one another are granted a license for unlimited beastliness such as is denied to mere sworn enemies. For all that, some of our most tenacious black belt quarrelers have come to it late in life and mastered every throw, from the Crushing Silence to the Gloating Apology, in less than ten years of marriage.

(6) A quarrel may last years among brooding types with time on their hands, like writers, half a lifetime is not uncommon. In its most refined form, a quarrel may consist of the participants not talking to each other. They will need to scheme laboriously to appear in public together to register their silence.

(7) Brief, violent quarrels are also known as rows. In all cases the essential ingredient remains the same; the original cause must be forgotten as soon as possible. From here on, dignity, pride, self-esteem, honour are the crucial issues, which is why quarrelling, like jealousy, is an all-consuming business, virtually a profession. For the quarreler's very self-hood is on the line. To lose an argument is a brief disappointment, much like losing a game of tennis, but to be crushed in a quarrel... rather bite off your tongue and spread it at your opponent's feet.

Q: In the passage as a whole, the writer treats quarreling as if it were _____ .

    (A) a military campaign   (B) a social skill

    (C) a moral evil   (D) a natural gift

正解：(B)

解析：从文章的首段可以看出，作者写作的主要目的是为了阐明关于争吵的一些道理。首句提出争吵要投入很多精力，借转折词"but"引出了本文的主题，争吵并非与生俱来，而是需要磨练的一种技能。文章接下来便围绕这个主题展开，提到了争吵的两个学习期和不同的类型，在文章的末段又把争吵上升到了近乎一种职业。所以主旨题选(B)。

> 提示：(B)选项中的"skill"和文章主题句中的"craft"正好相对应。

题型变换： 除以上的基本题型之外，主旨题还有一种变换形式，我们称之为"最佳标题"(Best Title)题。众所周知，一篇文章的标题可以被看作文章的灵魂，其作用是完整且又精确地勾勒出文章的主题和作者的观点和态度。字数虽少，但可以起到画龙点睛的效果。所以这也属于主旨题的一种。这种题型要求考生在抓住和理解作者的主题或中心思想的基础上，对其进行归纳、总结和提炼，从而得出一个准确、精练的标题。

题型特征：

Which of the following is the best title for the passage?

The best title for the passage would be _____.

What's the best title for the passage?

解答技巧： 在解答过程中考生应依据主旨题的基本解答方法——锁定文章主题句，比较选项，找出最佳答案。但值得注意的是，和一般的主旨题不同，一个文章的标题不一定对文章内容进行直接概括，而是会以某些特殊的方法精练地点题，例如用一个成语、一个反问的方式引出文章的一个主题，所以乍看之下标题和主题句的关联不一定非常紧密。这要求考生在理解主题的前提下更仔细地推敲选项，做出合理的推断。

例1：

(1) While earthquake remains as one of the most formidable forces of nature, studies are carried out worldwide in attempt to effectively prevent catastrophic destructions it causes. Most earthquakes occur within the upper 15 miles of the earth's surface. But earthquakes can and do occur at all depths to about 460 miles. Their number decreases as the depth increases. At about 460 miles one earthquake occurs only every few years. Near the surface earthquakes may run as high as 100 in a month, but the yearly average does not vary much. In comparison with the total number of earthquakes each year, the number of disastrous earthquakes is very small.

(2) The extent of the disaster in an earthquake depends on many factors. If you carefully build a toy house with an Erector set, it will still stand no matter how much you shake the table. But if you build a toy house with a pack of cards, a slight shake of the table will make it fall. An earthquake in Agadir, Morocco, was not strong enough to be recorded on distant instruments, but it completely destroyed the city. Many stronger earthquakes have done comparatively little damage. If a building is well constructed and built on solid ground, it will resist an earthquake. Most deaths in earthquakes have been due to faulty building construction or poor building sites. A third and very serious factor is panic. When people rush out into narrow streets, more deaths will result.

(3) The United Nations has played an important part in reducing the damage done by earthquakes. It has sent a team of experts to all countries known to be affected by earthquakes. Working with local geologists and engineers, the experts have studied the nature of the ground and the type of most practical building code for the local area. If followed, these suggestions will make disastrous earthquakes almost a thing of the past.

(4) There is one type of earthquake disaster that little can be done about. This is the disaster caused by seismic sea waves, or tsunamis. In certain areas, earthquakes take place beneath the sea. These submarine earthquakes sometimes give rise to seismic sea waves. The waves are not noticeable out at sea because of their long wave length. But when they roll into harbors, they pile up into walls of water 6 to 60 feet high. The Japanese call them "tsunamis", meaning "harbor waves", because they reach a sizable height only in harbors.

Q: Which of the following is the best title for the passage?

(A) Earthquake—a formidable force of nature

(B) The destruction of Agadir

(C) Earthquake and tsunamis

(D) Earthquake—No longer feared

正解：(D)

解析：本文是说明文。主题出现在第一句话(画双线部分)，"地震仍然是一种令人敬畏的自然力量，尽管世界各地都在对其进行研究，力图找出措施来有效地预防地震带来的毁灭性灾难"。以下文章在第一节中分析了地震产生的特点和频率；在第二节中阐述了影响地震的灾难程度的要素；在第三节提到了联合国在减轻地震灾难上的贡献，并举例说明了可行性；最后一节提醒大家在海底发生的地震及其引起的海啸是无法避免的。从主题句中我们不难看出，文章旨在探讨降低地震所造成的损害的办法，再和选项比较，只有(D)最接近文章的大意，因为如果我们能成功减少地震带给人类的危害，我们对其就无所畏惧了。

(A)选项：走题。文章的第一句，也就是主题句的确提到了这句话，但是"while"的使用其实是一种转折，而作者真正要说的要点在后半句，即如何减少地震的危害。考生在阅读时对句式中的各种转折词的使用一定要格外注意，分清作者的观点或主题究竟是什么。

(B)选项：片面。只是第二小节的一个例子。

(C)选项：片面。地震和海啸的关系只能说明文章最后一小节的大意，而非全文大意。

例2：

(1) The bath was invented before the bath plug. The bath plug could not have been invented before the bath, except as a small object with which to play ice hockey. The order in which inventions are made is very important, much more important than has ever been realized, because we tend automatically to think that later inventions are better than earlier ones. A moment's thought will show this is not so. If, for example, a solution to today's urban traffic problems was proposed in the shape of a small man-powered two-wheeled vehicle which would make the motor car look like a cumbersome over-powered device, a space rocket trying to tackle suburban problems, we would greet it as a great technological breakthrough. "Bicycle makes car obsolete" we would cry. Unfortunately, the bike came first, so we shall always unconsciously see it as a cruder version of the car.

(2) Other things, which may have been invented too early, are the airship, the radio, the railway train, the piano-roll player and the cuff-link.

(3) Consider also the zip. Zips represent a technological advance on buttons, being faster and more complete. They are also more liable to come adrift, break, jam, malfunction, stick and catch. Buttons can only go wrong if the thread is faulty. Even then, buttons can be mended by the user. Zips rarely can.

Q: **Which of the following is the best title for the passage?**

(A) A Cumbersome Over-Powered Device

(B) A Great Technological Breakthrough

(C) Do Zips Represent A Technological Advance?

(D) Does Technological Progress Work Backwards?

正解：(D)

解析：本文对人们的习惯性思维提出了质疑和反驳：后发明的事物不一定就比先发明的事物要先进。作者运了树立观点——驳倒观点的立论手法：首先给出了一个常人毋庸质疑的观点——后发明的事物都比先发明的先进，然后否定了这个观点。一旦抓住了这个主题(划双线部分)，剩下来的就一目了然了。作者在三段中分别举出了例证来阐明观点。但在"best title"中的四个选项并没有对这个主题进行直接概括，比如"Later inventions don't necessarily outdo their former versions..."之类的表达。但是人们之所以会认为事物发明的顺序决定了它们的优劣，是由于大家相信科技总是在进步的，而如作者所说科技也有倒退的时候。**(D)**选项中的反问句，"科技进步可能会成为倒退吗？"恰好符合这个推论。所以答案选**(D)**。

(A)选项：片面，仅仅是第一小节的一个例证；

(B)选项：体裁偏差——文章是个议论文，而不是说明一个伟大科技进步的说明文；

(C)选项：片面，仅仅是第三小节的一个例证。

例3：

(1) An unexpectedly bitter dispute between the Royal Mail and the union of postal workers has kept Britain's postal service closed for two weeks.

(2) Street-corner mailboxes are sealed and international mail suspended until the Union of Communication Workers and post-office management settle their differences over special pay for new recruits.

(3) The strike began as a spotty, 24-hour work stoppage Aug. 31 but was extended last week to include most of the 1,500 Royal Mail offices and more than 100,000 union members. It is the first major disruption of service since 1981, and has prompted discussion of further privatizing postal deliveries. British Prime Minister has said the Royal Mail is one public service that should remain in government hands. But some businessmen have pressed British Prime Minister to expand the market for private courier services to include carrying large volumes of mail. The pay dispute concerns special bonuses of between £15 and £35 a week for workers in the London area where the cost of living is high and it is difficult to attract new recruits. The Royal Mail is offering the premiums to help alleviate an acute shortage of workers in London but union leaders want the bonuses distributed equally across the country.

(4) The post office has asked other countries to hold all mail deliveries for Britain until the strike is settled, because it is difficult to guarantee security for mail bags piling up at air and seaports.

Q: What would be the best title for this passage?

　　(A) Britain's postal strike　　　　　(B) Britain's post-office management

　　(C) Britain's private courier services　　(D) Britain's Royal Mail offices

正解：(A)

解析：本文的主题在第一自然段很清晰地出现——英国皇家邮政和工会的矛盾导致

了一场至今已持续了两周的罢工。接下来文章介绍了罢工的原因和罢工举行之后的邮政状况。所以最佳标题应该反映这个主题,选(A)。

例4:

(1) One hundred and thirteen million Americans have at least one bank-issued credit card. They give their owners automatic credit in stores, restaurants, and hotels, at home, across the country, and even abroad, and they make many banking services available as well. More and more of these credit cards can be read automatically, making it possible to withdraw or deposit money in scattered locations, whether or not the local branch bank is open. For many of us the "cashless society" is not on the horizon—it's already here.

(2) While computers offer these conveniences to consumers, they have many advantages for sellers too. Electronic cash registers can do much more than simply ring up sales. They can keep a wide range of records, including who sold what, when, and to whom. This information allows businessmen to keep track of their list of goods by showing which items are being sold and how fast they are moving. Decisions to record or return goods to suppliers can then be made. At the same time these computers record which hours are busiest and which employees are the most efficient, allowing personnel and staffing assignments to be made accordingly. And they also identify preferred customers for promotional campaigns. Computers are relied on by manufactures for similar reasons. Computer-analyzed marketing reports can help to decide which products to emphasize now, which to develop for the future, and which to drop. Computers keep track of goods in stock, of raw materials on hand, and even of the production process itself.

(3) Numerous other commercial enterprises, from theaters to magazine publishers, from gas and electric utilities to milk processors, bring better and more efficient services to consumers through the use of computers.

Q: Which of the following would be the best title for this passage?

(A) The wide use of electronic banking card

(B) Advantages of computer service for corporations

(C) Mutual benefits through computerized services

(D) Corporate decision-making made easier

正解:(C)

解析:本文是说明文。作者首先用一个庞大的数学统计引出,使用信用卡的人数正在与日俱增,而信用卡也为它的使用者带来了很大的便利。随着我们对信用卡的广泛使用,一个无需现金的社会已经诞生了。电子服务不仅给消费者带来了便利,对商家也是如此。所以文章的主题确定为第二小节的首句。根据这个中心,我们可以确定文章介绍了消费者和商家的共同收益,选(C)。

二、细节题

细节题旨在考查考生对文章某个局部的定位和理解能力。

阅读要求：这类考题要求考生对一篇文章局部知识的把握能力。在阅读部分我们提到了，在通读文章时我们的主要目的是确定文章的主题和结构，而对局部的细节只需略读。所以解答细节题的关键在于根据题干或选项中的提示在原文中迅速准确地定位，再就对应的知识点与题目的选项进行比较，最后找到最佳答案。

题型特征：最基本的细节题具体地指向文章的某个局部，考查与之相关的知识。同时这种题型也可以覆盖文章多个局部的细节。另外还有一种很常见的细节题，也被称为是非题，要求考生区分出在给出的四个关于某个或多个局部的知识点中惟一正确的或错误的是哪个。

细节题最明显的特征是出现一些反映文章具体内容的表达，例如："According to passage..."；"In the passage..."；"From the passage..."；"Described in the passage..."；"Discovered in the passage..."；"The passage says..."；"The passage holds..."；etc.。

以上的这类表达与文章中的具体事物联系起来就构成了细节题的基本题型，例如：

According to the passage, what can we learn about_____?

What does the passage say about_____?

What is the author's opinion of _____?

如果题干覆盖全文，则属于考查多个局部的题目。例：

What can we learn according to the article?

Which of the following is mentioned in the passage?

The passage holds...?

Which of the following is discussed in the passage?

Which of the following points is given in the passage?

是非题：

According to the passage, what is true about _____?

According to the article which of the following statement is not true?

All of the following statements are true about_____ EXCEPT_____?

Which of the following is not mentioned in the article?

In the passage, the author recommends all of the following EXCEPT_____?

解题技巧：由于细节题直接指向文章局部的细节内容，所以这类题型的最大特点是总可以在文章中找到正确答案。所以解题的关键便是能找到题目以及各个选项在文章中的定位。然后再通过文章内容与选项的比较来确定正确的答案。

定位技巧：通常定位的方式是通过题干和选项中的关键词在文章中找到其相对应的位置，从而确定考点和正确选项，这种方法我们称之为文字再现法。值得注意的是，用于定位的词汇在文章中不一定可以找到完全的再现，同样原文中的内容也不一定在正确的选项中全文再现。许多情况下题目会对文字稍加处理，例如在关键词的词性、词义或是整句内容上。这就要求考生不仅要准确定位，还要做到更细致地辨析选项。

以下我们通过几个实例来说明：

例1：

(1) According to airline industry statistics, almost 90% of airline accidents are survivable or partially survivable. But passengers can increase their chances of survival by learning and following certain tips. Experts say that you should read and listen to safety instructions before takeoff and ask questions if you have uncertainties. You should fasten your seat belt low on your hips and as tightly as possible. Of course, you should also know how the release mechanism of your belt operates. Q1 → During takeoffs and landings, you are advised to keep your feet flat on the floor. Q2 → Before takeoff you should locate the nearest exit and an alternative exit and count the rows of seats between you and the exits so that you can find them in the dark if necessary.

(2) In the event that you are forewarned of a possible accident, you should put your hands on your ankles and keep your head down until the plane comes to a complete stop.

(3) Q3 → If smoke is present in the cabin, you should keep your head low and cover your face with napkins, towels, or clothing. If possible, wet these for added protection against smoke inhalation. To evacuate as quickly as possible, follow crew commands and do not take personal belongings with you. Do not jump on escape slides before they are fully inflated, and when you jump, do so with your arms and legs extended in front of you. When you get to the ground, you should move away from the plane as quickly as possible, and never smoke near the wreckage.

Q1: According to the passage, airline travelers should keep their feet flat on the floor _____.

(A) throughout the flight　　(B) during takeoffs and landings
(C) especially during landings　　(D) in case of an accident

Q2: According to the passage, which exits should an airline passenger locate before takeoff?

(A) The front one and the back one.

(B) The two closest to the pilot seat.

(C) The ones that can be found in the dark.

(D) The ones with counted rows of seats between them.

Q3: People are more likely to survive fires in the aircraft if they _____.

(A) keep their heads low　　(B) wear a safety belt
(C) don't smoke in or near a plane　　(D) read airline safety statistics

Q4: In an emergency airline passengers are advised to do all of the following except

_____　.

(A) follow crew commands　　(B) jump on fully inflated escape slides

(C) run away as soon as possible　　(D) carry personal belongings

解析：文章介绍的是在航空旅行中的一些求生技能。由于是给考生列举各种技能，所以文章较多地考查细节方面的内容。

Q1: 考查的是基本细节。定位词："keep their feet flat on the floor"。在第一小节我们可以准确地找到答案是**(B)**。

Q2: 考查的是基本细节。定位："exits... locate before takeoff"。同样在第一小节我们可以找到：一个是最近的出口，一个是备用出口，必要的话要数出座位到那个备用出口的间距，答案是**(D)**。

Q3: 考查的是覆盖第三自然段的各个细节。定位词：各个选项。我们可以很容易地找到"keep your head low"，所以答案是**(A)**。

Q4: 考查的是覆盖第三自然段的各个细节。定位词：各个选项。我们可以看出选项(D)与原文中"do not take personal belongings with you"不符，所以选**(D)**。

例2：

(1) For most people, boasting about oneself does not come naturally. It is not easy or comfortable to tell someone all the wonderful things you have accomplished. But that is exactly what you need to do if you are seeking a new job, or trying to hold on to the one you have.

(2) Of course, there is a fine line between self-confidence and arrogance, so to be successful in winning over the interviewer you must learn to maximize your accomplishments and attributes without antagonizing the interviewer.

(3) The natural tendency for most job seekers is to behave modestly in a job interview.

(4) To do the best job of selling yourself in an interview, you have to be prepared in advance. As part of your job-hunting check list, write down on a piece of paper your major job-related accomplishments. Commit them to memory. You will probably be pleasantly surprised to see in writing all that you have done.

(5) By developing this list, you will have accomplished two things: the first is you will impress the interviewer by being able to talk confidently and succinctly about your accomplishments. You will not have to sit uncomfortably while you think of your successes.

(6) They will be at the tip of your tongue. Secondly, rather than dwell on your own personality characteristics, such as how hardworking or creative you are, you can discuss hard facts, such as how you saved your employer money or an idea you developed that helped a customer make more money. When chronicling your accomplishments for the interviewer, take as much credit as you honestly can. If you were a key part behind a major group project, tell the interviewer. If you developed a specific idea without help from your supervisor, it is acceptable to say that. Remember, you are at that interview to sell yourself, not your former co-workers.

(7) **Q1** → However, never criticize your former employer. Sharing your negative thoughts with the interviewer is an immediate turn-off and will only brand you as a complainer and gossip whom no one likes or will hire.

(8) Keep in mind that the most important part of a job interview is making the employer like you and presenting yourself as the person he or she wants you to be. Consciously or not most employers tend to hire people who reflect their own values and standards.

(9) Once you get the job you want, boasting about your accomplishments does not stop. Although you may think all your successes and achievements are highly visible, remember that you are only one of many people in a company. Lack of recognition is cited by a majority of discharged managers as the most frequent complaint against the former employer.

(10) To help make yourself more visible in the company, volunteer for additional assignment—both job-related and **Q2**→non-business-related. These could include community relations or charitable activities in which your company is involved. These types of activities may enable you to have more time and access to top executives of the company to whom you may endear yourself. You might even have the opportunity to tell them what you are doing for the company, which can never hurt.

Q1: The author states that the one thing you should never do during an interview is__

_____.

(A) list your successes in previous jobs

(B) promote your qualifications for the job

(C) tell your potential boss about the projects you've worked on

(D) make negative comments about your former employer

Q2: In the passage, the author recommends all of the following EXCEPT _____.

(A) making a point of telling your supervisor what you have done

(B) taking part in non-business-related activities

(C) going on boasting about your successes and achievements

(D) giving the employer an idea on how to run his other business

解析：本文讨论的问题是一个人如何突出自己的优势。在文章的首段作者提出了一个中心，即这样做能够帮助一个人找到一个新的工作，或者保住现有的工作。文章接下来分为两个板块：(1)如何通过突出个人优势来找到一份新工作(2~7小节)；(2)如何通过突出个人优势来留住一份工作(9~10小节)。

Q1: 考查第7小节中的基本信息。定位词："one thing you should never do during an interview"。文中告诫切忌批评原来的上司，选(D)。

Q2: 考查全文的信息，是非题，三对一错题。所谓"对"，就是在文章中得到体现的，"错"则相反。如果可以确定惟一的一个在文章中没有得到反映的选项，它就是答案。如果不能，则验证其他三个可以在文章中确定的选项，剩下的就是答案。

(A)：主题

(B)：第 10 小节

(C)：主题

(D)：正确答案

例 3：

(1) Today one in every ten of us has difficulty getting to sleep and, according to Dr. Ian Oswald of Edinburgh University, the reason is simple. Most people who can't sleep are their own worst enemies. **Q1** → They go to bed too early.

(2) For every person who works most efficiently on the usual eight hours of sleep a night, two work best on five or six, and two on nine or ten. Voltaire made do with three hours **Q2** → but Sir Winston Churchill would happily sleep for 12-14 hours at a stretch if he could.

(3) So how much sleep does a person really need? **Q3** →It seems that the national average for men is seven hours and ten minutes, and for women ten minutes less, but everyone's needs are different. Find out what you need and, according to Dr. Ernest Hartmann, one of America's leading sleep scientists, you're well on your way to allowing your body to work at its greatest efficiency.

(4) After studying the sleep habits of nearly 1000 people, Dr. Hartmann believes it's the amount of deep sleep we get that really matters. We all need roughly the same amount—about 75 minutes a night. The rest, a shallower type of sleep, varies greatly from person to person.

(5) How much of the second type of sleep you need seems to depend on what sort of person you are. According to Dr. Hartmann short sleepers—those sleeping less than six hours a night— were busy, active people, employed in demanding jobs, and often worked a 60 or 70-hour week. Most of them had started sleeping shorter hours to deal with the pressure of schoolwork or business and found that a few hours sleep a night was quite enough. Their defense against worry and stress was usually "to keep so busy that I don't have time to think about these things. . . . "

(6) Most of the long sleepers—those needing at least nine hours—were self-employed. Almost all of them had slept for nine hours a night since late childhood, long before their work pattern became fixed. They tended to complain more than the short sleepers and several admitted that sleeping was an escape from life.

(7) In the past it was believed that too much sleep could be just as disturbing as too little, but now a study in America has shown that many people can enjoy ten hours or more and still be able to sleep through the following night.

(8) A sleep researcher says: "No one should worry about not sleeping unless they are not feeling well or cannot do their work properly. Lack of sleep doesn't matter greatly if we are resting—the body can still get on with its repair work. **Q4** → But worrying about not sleeping can sometimes do you harm. There would be far less sleeplessness if we planned our sleeping

lives as carefully as we plan our waking ones. "

Q1: According to the passage, people have difficulty getting to sleep because _____ .

(A) they work more than sixty hours a week   (B) they have too many enemies

(C) they do not sleep happily   (D) they are not tired enough

Q2: In comparison with Voltaire, Sir Winston Churchill _____ .

(A) was happier with three hours of sleep (B) would sleep more when stretched out

(C) would enjoy a longer sleep if possible (D) was less happy when he was asleep

Q3: Studies show that the average woman _____ .

(A) sleeps less than the average man   (B) sleeps longer when she goes out to work

(C) has difficulty in getting to sleep   (D) sleeps over eight hours a night

Q4: Not being able to sleep can be dangerous if we _____ .

(A) are feeling well   (B) worry about it too much

(C) repair our bodies by resting   (D) plan our sleeping lives carefully

解析:本文围绕着人类的睡眠问题展开:很多失眠的人其实是因为担心不能入睡或没有足够的睡眠而早早入睡导致的。

Q1: 考查的是第一小节的信息,定位词: "have difficulty getting to sleep because"。 根据第一小节的末句我们得知通常人们睡不着是因为睡得太早,也就是还不够疲劳,选**(D)**。

Q2: 考查的是第二小节的信息,定位词: "Sir Winston Churchill"。选**(C)**。

Q3: 考查的是第二小节的信息,定位词: "average woman"。从文中我们可以看出妇女的平均睡眠要比男子少 10 分钟,选**(A)**。

Q4: 考查的是最后一小节的信息,定位词: "Not being able to sleep can be dangerous"。选**(B)**。

提示:Q4 中文章并没有直接出现 "dangerous" 一词,但是却有相近的表达——"do you harm"。在定位时对这些词汇表达上的互换要十分注意。

小 结

有效地解答细节题的关键是能从题干和选项中找出关键词句,并在文章中找到相应的定位。但是从宏观角度来说,阅读时对文章结构和层次的理解对迅速定位起着至关重要的作用,因为只有了解文章的结构才能做到有的放矢地搜索,而不是仅仅带着几个词在文章中盲目地寻找。

三、推断题

推断题要求考生在理解了文章内容和作者观点的基础上做出合理的推断，从而获得一个符合逻辑的结论。

阅读要求：比较细节题，推断题的难度在于：（1）既要在文章中准确地找到与题目相对应的知识点，（2）又不能单单依靠原文知识解题，而是要在其基础上做出合乎逻辑的推断。注意段落之间、词句之间的逻辑联系，从而在推断时可以有据可寻。

题型特征：推断题可以分为局部型和篇章型：前者推断的基础是文章的一个或多个局部的细节内容，后者则覆盖全文，要求考生推断出文章的写作手法、出处、作者的语气等等。一般常见的题型有：

推断一般事实

It can be inferred from the passage that _____.

What can we conclude from the passage_____?

What does the passage imply?

What does the author suggest in the last passage?

Which of the following can be inferred from the passage?

推断人物观点、态度以及人物、事物背景

What is the author's opinion about_____?

What is_____'s attitude towards the issue?

The mentioning of_____ is to _____.

推断文章行文方式、出处

The author is most likely a_____.

What's the passage most probably taken from?

The way author expresses himself is by _____.

推断文章的前文或后文

What does the paragraph preceding this passage most probably discuss?

What does the following paragraph most likely talk about?

解题技巧：

推断一般事实：技巧类似于解细节题的技巧，在原文中定位，找到与题目相对应的文章内容，运用个人的逻辑分析和判断，找出合理的推断。

推断人物观点、态度和背景：留意观点性词句和与人物态度相关的表达，人物原话的引用和人物在文章中所起到的作用。

推断文章行文方式、出处：应该留意文章行文措辞的风格和方式，作者写作的语气，文章的体裁以及人称的使用。

推断文章的前文或后文：包括两种题型：前文题，即要求考生通过对文章的阅读推断出在首段之前的段落的主要内容；下文题，即要求推断文章后一段的主要内容，或续写题，即在文章的最后做出省略，要求考生接着续写下去。解题的技巧有两方面：一，抓住关键词汇，辩清题型。前文题：表示"之前"的词汇群："preceding"，"previous to"，"prior to"，"ahead of"，"former"，"before"，etc.；下文题：表示"之后"的词汇群："following"，"next"，"subsequent"，"succeeding"，etc.。二，详读承上启下，合理推断。解题的关键句是"承上启下句"（transitional sentence），即衔接两个段落的句子。这是因为这类过渡句型通常会起到总结上文引出下文的作用，是猜测前文或下文的最佳工具。对于前文题来说"承上启下句"即是全义或衔接段落的首句，而下文题则为全义或衔接段落的末句。

例1：推断一般事实

Seoul, once a city for kings, can now claim to be a city for commuters. <u>The third nation in the Orient to develop an underground rapid-transit system, Korea opened its first line in 1974.</u> After 12 years of continuing construction, Seoul had finally completed the rest of its extensive subway system, capable of serving 5 million commuters a day.

Q: Which of the following can be concluded from the passage?

(A) The subway system was completed in 1986.

(B) Everyday more than nine million people travel by subway.

(C) The subway was built in a huge cave.

(D) The subway corporation is making a huge profit.

解析：本题要求对文章多个局部的知识点进行推断。(A)选项要求推断竣工时间，1974年开工，历经12年，简单相加，是1986年竣工，选(A)。

例2：推断一般事实

(1) Most towns up to Elizabethan times were smaller than a modern village and each of them was built around its weekly market where local produce was brought for sale and the townsfolk sold their work to the people from the countryside and provided them with refreshment for the day. Trade was virtually confined to that one day even in a town of a thousand or so people. On market days craftsmen put up their stalls in the open air whilst <u>on one or two other days during the week the townsman would pack up his loaves, or nails, or cloth, and set out early to do a day's trade in the market of an adjoining town where,</u> **Q1→** <u>however, he would be charged a heavy toll for the privilege and get a less favorable spot for his stand than the local craftsmen.</u> Another chance for him to make a sale was to the congregation gathered for Sunday mooring worship. Although no trade was allowed anywhere during the hours of the service (except at annual fair times), after church there would be some trade at the church door with departing country fold.

(2) **Q2→** <u>The trade of markets was almost wholly concerned with exchanging the products of the nearby countryside and the goods made by local craftsmen with the result that the genuine retail dealer had very little place.</u> In all goods sold in the market but particularly in food retail dealing was distrusted as a kind of profiteering. Even when there was

enough trade being done to afford a livelihood to an enterprising man ready to buy wholesale and sell retail, town authorities were reluctant to allow it.

(3) Yet there were plainly people who were tempted to "forestall the market" by buying goods outside it, and to "regrate" them, that is to resell them, at a higher price. The constantly repeated rules against these practices and the endlessly recurring prosecutions mentioned in the records of all the larger towns prove that some well-informed and sharp-witted people did these things.

(4) Every town made its own laws and if it was big enough to have craft guilds, these associations would regulate the business of their members and tried to enforce a strict monopoly of their own trades. Yet while the guild leaders, as craftsmen, followed fiercely protectionist policies, at the same time, as leading townsmen, they wanted to see a big, busy market yielding a handsome revenue in various dues and tolls. Conflicts of interest led to endless, minute regulations, changeable, **Q3→** often inconsistent, and frequently absurd. There was a time in the fourteenth century, for example, when London fishmongers were not allowed to handle any fish that had not already been exposed for sale for three days by the men who caught it.

Q1: Craftsmen might prefer to trade in their own town because there they could _____ .

(A) easily find good refreshment　　(B) work in the open air

(C) start work very early　　(D) have the well-placed stalls

Q2: In medieval markets there was little retail trade because _____ .

(A) money was never used in sales　　(B) producers sold directly to consumers

(C) there were no fixed positions for shops (D) authorities were unwilling to make a profit

Q3: It can be concluded from the passage that the regulations enforced by craft guilds were often _____ .

(A) unfair and unreasonable　　(B) in the interest of the customers

(C) too complicated to comply with　　(D) disapproved by the local authorities

解析:本文介绍的是中世纪时代英国乡镇的商品交换和雏形中的零售业状况。题目要求推断文章中具体现象的原因。

Q1: 推断的基础是第一小节的内容。定位词是:"trade in their own town",是商品交易方面的内容。文章开始提到了在商业不发达的过去,一个城镇的商品交换只有等到每周一次的集市,限制了一个生产者出售自己的劳动成果,换取生活必需品。除此之外,生产者还可以到邻近城镇的集市日进行交换,但是文章提到"however, he would be charged a heavy toll for the privilege and get a less favorable spot for his stand than the local craftsmen.",表明了两种在他镇所受到的限制——交纳额外的赋税和没有理想的摊位。由此可以推断,如果在自己所在的镇交易,其益处便是不再受以上两个限制的约束,选(D)。

Q2: 要求推断的是当时缺乏零售的原因:根据"retail trade"定位,发现推断的基础出现在第二段。从首句我们可以看出,当时的商品交换仅限于物品生产者之间简单的物品交换,所以作为一种中间渠道的零售是没有需求的,选**(B)**。

Q3: 推断的对象是当时的行业协会所提出的规定:定位在文章的最后一段,根据"Conflicts of interest led to endless, minute regulations, changeable, often inconsistent, and frequently absurd."我们可以看出由于利益冲突,作者对当时行业协会的一些规定使用的形容词是易变的、不一致的、荒谬的。与之相比,**(A)**选项所表述的"不公平的和不合理的"最为接近。

例3:推断人物背景

(1) So how much sleep does a person really need? It seems that the national average for men is seven hours and ten minutes, and for women ten minutes less, but everyone's needs are different. Find out what you need and, according to Dr. Ernest Hartmann, one of America's leading sleep scientists, you're well on your way to allowing your body to work at its greatest efficiency.

(2) After studying the sleep habits of nearly 1000 people, Dr. Hartmann believes it's the amount of deep sleep we get that really matters. We all need roughly the same amount—about 75 minutes a night. The rest, a shallower type of sleep, varies greatly from person to person.

(3) How much of the second type of sleep you need seems to depend on what sort of person you are. According to Dr. Hartmann short sleepers—those sleeping less than six hours a night—were busy, active people, employed in demanding jobs, and often worked a 60 or 70-hour week. Most of them had started sleeping shorter hours to deal with the pressure of schoolwork or business and found that a few hours sleep a night was quite enough. Their defense against worry and stress was usually "to keep so busy that I don't have time to think about these things...."

Q: Dr. Hartmann is mentioned in the passage _____ .

(A) as the opponent of Dr. Ian Oswald

(B) because he has strange sleeping habits

(C) as the pioneering sleep scientist

(D) because of his observation and analysis of sleep habits

解析: Dr. Hartmann 以一名睡眠专家的身份出现在文中。在每段中都出现了"According to..."以及"Dr. Hartmann believes..."句型结构,说明作者提出 Dr. Hartmann 是为了以他的专家意见作为理论依据,选**(D)**。

例4:推断文章行文方式、出处

(1) For most people, boasting about oneself does not come naturally. It is not easy or comfortable to tell someone all the wonderful things you have accomplished. But that is exactly what you need to do if you are seeking a new job, or trying to hold on to the one you have.

(2) Of course, there is a fine line between self-confidence and arrogance, so to be successful in winning over the interviewer you must learn to maximize your accomplishments and

attributes without antagonizing the interviewer.

(3) The natural tendency for most job seekers is to behave modestly in a job interview.

(4) To do the best job of selling yourself in an interview, you have to be prepared in advance. As part of your job-hunting checklist, write down on a piece of paper your major job-related accomplishments. Commit them to memory. You will probably be pleasantly surprised to see in writing all that you have done.

(5) By developing this list, you will have accomplished two things: the first is you will impress the interviewer by being able to talk confidently and succinctly about your accomplishments. You will not have to sit uncomfortably while you think of your successes.

(6) They will be at the tip of your tongue. Secondly, rather than dwell on your own personality characteristics, such as how hardworking or creative you are, you can discuss hard facts, such as how you saved your employer money or an idea you developed that helped a customer make more money. When chronicling your accomplishments for the interviewer, take as much credit as you honestly can. If you were a key part behind a major group project, tell the interviewer. If you developed a specific idea without help from your supervisor, it is acceptable to say that. Remember, you are at that interview to sell yourself, not your former co-workers.

(7) However, never criticize your former employer. Sharing your negative thoughts with the interviewer is an immediate turn-off and will only brand you as a complainer and gossip whom no one likes or will hire.

(8) Keep in mind that the most important part of a job interview is making the employer like you and presenting yourself as the person he or she wants you to be. Consciously or not most employers tend to hire people who reflect their own values and standards.

(9) Once you get the job you want, boasting about your accomplishments does not stop. Although you may think all your successes and achievements are highly visible, remember that you are only one of many people in a company. Lack of recognition is cited by a majority of discharged managers as the most frequent complaint against the former employer.

(10) To help make yourself more visible in the company, volunteer for additional assignment—both job-related and non-business-related. These could include community relations or charitable activities in which your company is involved. These types of activities may enable you to have more time and access to top executives of the company to whom you may endear yourself. You might even have the opportunity to tell them what you are doing for the company, which can never hurt.

Q: The author provides his views on winning and holding a new job by _____ .

    (A) offering suggestions   (B) presenting facts and statistics

    (C) describing extreme situations   (D) telling stories

解析：通过对文章的阅读，我们不难发现作者的写作方式为在首段立论（尽量突出个人的优势和长处），再分两种不同的情形（求职和留职）提出了相应的建议，旨在帮助考生在每种情况下更好地发挥个人优势，写作方式属于提供建议，选(A)。

例5：推断上下文内容：前文题

Quite different from storm surges are giant sea waves called tsunamis, which derive their name from the Japanese expression for "high water in a harbor". These waves are also referred to by the general public as tidal waves, although they have relatively little to do with tides. Scientists often refer to them as seismic sea waves, far more appropriate in that they do result from undersea seismic activity.

Q: The paragraph preceding this passage most probably discusses _____ .

  (A) tidal waves   (B) tides

  (C) storm surges   (D) underwater earthquakes

解析：此题的基本结构和主旨题非常相像，粗心的考生错把这题当作了主旨题。根据文章的主题句（划双线部分）推断出本文的主题是一种被称之为"tsunamis"的自然现象，再从第二句（划单线部分）得知这种自然现象在民间又被称之为"tidal waves"，从而错误地选择了(A)。在课堂练习中这题的错误率很高，其原因就在此。题干中的关键词汇"preceding"的意思为"在前的"，相当于"before"，所以题目问的是如果在这篇文章之前还有一段的话，那么这一段最有可能讨论什么问题。全文的首句中"Quite different from storm surges are giant sea waves called tsunamis"，划线部分为解题的关键。既然作者通过"与storm surges 不同的是...tsunamis"这样的句型来引出"tsunamis"这个主题，那么前文内容最合理的推断就应该是"storm surges"，选(C)。

例6：推断上下文内容：下文题

(1) According to airline industry statistics, almost 90% of airline accidents are survivable or partially survivable. But passengers can increase their chances of survival by learning and following certain tips. Experts say that you should read and listen to safety instructions before takeoff and ask questions if you have uncertainties. You should fasten your seat belt low on your hips and as tightly as possible. Of course, you should also know how the release mechanism of your belt operates. During takeoffs and landings, you are advised to keep your feet flat on the floor. Before takeoff you should locate the nearest exit and an alternative exit and count the rows of seats between you and the exits so that you can find them in the dark if necessary.

(2) In the event that you are forewarned of a possible accident, you should put your hands on your ankles and keep your head down until the plane comes to a complete stop.

(3) If smoke is present in the cabin, you should keep your head low and cover your face with napkins, towels, or clothing. If possible, wet these for added protection against smoke inhalation. To evacuate as quickly as possible, follow crew commands and do not take [personal belongings—(A)选项] with you. Do not jump on escape slides before they are fully inflated, and when you jump, do so with your arms and legs extended in front of you. When you get to the

ground, you should [move away from the plane as quickly as possible— (C) 选项], and never smoke near the wreckage.

Q: **What does the paragraph** <u>following</u> **the passage most probably discuss?**

(A) How to recover your luggage?

(B) Where to go to continue your trip?

(C) When to return to the aircraft?

(D) How to proceed once you are away from the aircraft?

解析：本文的主题句（划双线部分）指出了本文旨在介绍在航空旅行时遇到紧急事件的各种应对和自救措施。但这对解决本题并无直接的帮助。因为作为下文题，解题的关键应在紧接下文的过渡句上（划单线部分），也就是全文的最后一句。最后一句的定语"when you get to the ground"已经明确地指出这时你已离开飞机来到地面，那么对下文最合理的推断应是乘客在离开飞机之后接下来该做的事情，选(D)。

(A) 选项：文中最后一段指出在发生紧急情况离开飞机时不要带"personal belonging"，即私人物品。这和选项中的"luggage"行李吻合。

(B) 选项：最后一段提供的是紧急情况下飞机迫降后乘客应采取的措施，所以继续旅行不是首要目的，而是要先安顿好自己。

(C) 选项：文中最后一句要求乘客尽量地远离飞机，所以回到飞机上肯定不对。

四、指代题

这类题型要求考生理解文章中某个个别的词汇或句子的含义和用法，考查的是对基本词汇和句型的掌握能力。

指代题分为两大类题型：代词指代题和词句解释题。

代词指代题要求考生了解文章局部的某个特定的代词所指代的对象；而词句解释题则要求考生对文章局部的某个词句做出解释，找出最可以取而代之的选项。

阅读要求：指代题与其他题型最大的区别在于无需费力在原文中定位。这是因为题目中已经清晰地给出了所考查的知识点在文章的出处。但解题时切忌根据自己的主观想法对词句进行臆测，而是要回到文章给出的范围内仔细阅读，推测其在文章中的意思，再与选项相比较，选出最为接近的答案。

题型特征：

代词指代题：询问文中的某个词汇指代的对象。此类题型在考试中出现的频率很低。一般形式有：

What does the word "it" refer to in the last paragraph?

Who does the word "them" refer to in the first paragraph?

词句解释题：询问文中某个词汇或表达的解释。此类题型在每年的考试（30题）中出现2-6题，频率相对来说要高很多。一般形式有：

The word "_____" in the last paragraph is closest in meaning to _____.

What does the word "_____" in the first paragraph probably mean?

In paragraph 2, the word "_____" means to_____.

The word "_____" (paragraph 2) is used to describe_____.

解题技巧：

代词指代题：解答这类题型要根据题目给出的提示认真阅读代词所在的句子,仔细推敲其所指代的对象,尤其注意在句子中的其他结构是否可以找出提示。比方说如果考查的代词所指代的是句子的主语,则找到句子的宾语看其是否能够提供答案线索。

词句解释题：此类题型的一个基本目的是考查考生对许多一词多义现象的掌握。而考生们在平时对词汇的学习中可能存在学习比较片面、一知半解的情况,所以解题时阅读原文是关键。这不仅是因为我们要确定文章对某个词汇的具体使用,同时也可以参照上下文帮助我们揣测其含义。下面通过几个实例来说明：

1. 代词指代题

例1：

Sixty percent of all ethnic minorities in Britain live in London. Ethnic minorities only make up a small fraction of Britain's population as a whole, Q→ but coming to London you could quite easily be mistaken for thinking there were many more. I have taken this for granted having grown up with this fantastic diversity of culture, background and influence. I have people all around me, who talk with varying accents, speak different languages, share distinct foods and celebrate special festivals. However, London is far from being without its racial problems.

Q: The word "this" in "I have taken this for granted" (para. 1) refers to which of the following?

(A) Sixty percent of all ethnic minorities in UK live in London.

(B) minorities only constitute a small part of UK's population.

(C) There are more minority people in Britain than it appears.

(D) It is unwise for many more to come to London.

解析：通过对上下文的分析,原文中提到的"it"只可能指向在这句话出现之前作者所描述的情景,其中关键是由转折"but"引导的"but coming to London you could quite easily be mistaken for thinking there were many more.",在伦敦人们会误以为英国少数民族的人口很多(因为他们都聚居在大城市),所以选(C)。

例2：

At the time of the speech, little notice was given to what Lincoln had said, and Lincoln considered his appearance at the ceremonies rather unsuccessful. After his Q→**speech** appeared in print, appreciation for his words began to grow, and today it is recognized as one of the all-time greatest Q→ **speeches.**

Q: The pronoun "it" in the last sentence refers to which of the following?

(A) His speech. (B) Print.

(C) Appreciation.　　　　　　　　　　(D) His appearance.

解析：最后一句话中的"it"所指的对象可以从两个地方看出：这段话是两个并列句组成，所以"it"作为后句的主语，应该和前句的主语是并列关系，同指"speech"，演讲；第二句话的宾语也是一个很好的提示。

例3：

Q→The Poco body warmer measures about three by five inches and is one-quarter inch thick. It consists of a cloth bag containing a mixture of iron powder, moisturized wood powder, activated carbon and salt. Q→To get it going, the user simply opens the outer vinyl bag in which the unit is vacuum-packed and shakes the cloth bag. The unit then absorbs oxygen from the air, which in conjunction with the moisture from the wood powder oxidizes the iron, giving off heat. The packet maintains an average temperature of 140 degree Fahrenheit for 24 hours, according to the manufacturer. Aoi Co. officials say that the product contains no toxic chemicals. The only precaution users need to follow is to avoid direct contact between the skin and the body warmer because burns can occur. The unit sells for about $ 1.

Q: In the second paragraph, the word "it" in "To get it going" refers to _____ .

(A) arthritis　　　　　　　　　　(B) muscle sprain

(C) the body warmer　　　　　　　(D) moisturized wood powder

解析：从文章的结构上我们很容易看出，文章是围绕着取暖器的各项特征展开的。以下第二句和第三句中的"it"必定是指取暖器的，选(C)。

例4：

For those present, many sources of information become accessible and many carriers (or "sign-vehicles") become available for conveying this information. If unacquainted with the individual, Q→observers can glean clues from his conduct and appearance which allow them to apply their previous experience with individuals roughly similar to the one before them or, more important, to apply untested stereotypes to him. They can also assume from past experience that only individuals of a particular kind are likely to be found in a given social setting. They can rely on what the individual says about himself or on documentary evidence he provides as to who and what he is. If prior to the interaction, they can rely on assumptions as to the persistence and generality of psychological traits as a means of predicting his present and future behaviour.

Q: In paragraph 2, what does the underlined word "them" in "... which allow them to apply their previous experience with individuals..." refer to?

(A) beliefs　　　　　　　　　　(B) emotions

(C) individuals　　　　　　　　(D) observers

解析：从句"which allow them to..."中的"them"显然指代了主句中的主语部分，选(D)。

2. 词句解释题

解题的关键在于根据对文章的阅读和上下文的推理来猜测被考查词汇的含义。其中推理的方法和依据有很多,以下我们借实例来一一介绍:

例1:阅文辨义

(1) A Japanese construction company Q→plans to build a huge independent city-state, akin to the legendary Atlantis, in the middle of the Pacific Ocean. The city, dubbed "Marinnation," would have about one million inhabitants, two airports, and possibly even a spaceport. Marinnation, if built, would be a separate country but could serve as a home for international organizations such as the United Nations and the World Bank.

(2) Aside from the many political and social problems that would have to be solved, the engineering risk envisaged is monumental. The initial stage requires the building of a circular dam 18 miles in diameter attached to the seabed in a relatively shallow place in international waters. Then, several hundred pumps, operating for more than a year, would suck out the seawater from within the dam. When empty and dry, the area would have a city constructed on it. The actual land would be about 300 feet below sea level.

Q: In paragraph 2, the underlined word "envisaged" is closest in meaning to _____ .

(A) undertaken   (B) conceived

(C) completed   (D) implicated

解析:整篇文章讨论的是一个构想,并没有具体实现。在中心句"A Japanese construction company plans to build a huge independent city-state, akin to the legendary Atlantis, in the middle of the Pacific Ocean."中的"plan"就说明了这个工程是在构思之中。所以相关的一切风险都是在设想中的,所以答案选(B)。

例2:释文定义

The trade of markets was almost wholly concerned with exchanging the products of the nearby countryside and the goods made by local craftsmen with the result that the genuine retail dealer had very little place. In all goods sold in the market but particularly in food retail dealing was distrusted as a kind of profiteering. Even when there was enough trade being done to afford a livelihood to an enterprising man ready to buy wholesale and sell retail, town authorities were reluctant to allow it.

Yet there were plainly people who were tempted to "forestall the market" Q→ by buying goods outside it, and to "regrate" them, that is to resell them, at a higher price. The constantly repeated rules against these practices and the endlessly recurring prosecutions mentioned in the records of all the larger towns prove that some well-informed and sharp-witted people did these things.

Q: The expression "forestall the market"(Paragraph 3) means _____ .

(A) buy from a stall outside the market place

(B) acquire goods in quantity before the market

(C) have the best and the first stall in the market

(D) sell at a higher price than competitors.

解析：文章在提出一个专业名词或术语时，用一些特定的词汇来形容和描述事物或场景时，常常会附有一定的通俗易懂的解释，帮助考生理解。这种解释也就成了理解词汇含义的关键。

在本文中作者已经解释了，"forestall the market"是通过在集市之外购买商品完成的，所以一定和购买有关。这样(C)和(D)选项就排除了。同时通过前一个小节的末句我们知道，本段其实是在讨论囤货零售受到限制的问题，所以该词就是指在集市开始之前购买物品。

例3：总结获义

Refuse gimmicks

As competition heats up and pushes prices down, businesses scramble to boost their profits by heaping on extras: Q→ rust proofing your car, service contracts on your appliances, prepaid gasoline for your rental car. These gimmicks are devised to make you pay more at the last minute and probably aren't a good deal.

Q: The word "gimmicks" in this passage is closest in meaning to _____ .

(A) services (B) extras

(C) tricks (D) games

解析：如果一个词汇或表达对文章中的某段描述起到了概括的作用，那么就可以通过对相应描述的总结获取词汇的含义。

"gimmicks"一词是本段的标题，也就起到了概括整段的作用。而细看之下这一段都在讨论商家在竞争激烈的市场中往往采用一些手段来提高盈利，其中一种方法就是用各种附加的服务收费。这里最易混淆的选项便是(B)——extras(附加服务)。但是附加服务只是表面性质，而真正的性质是商家玩的营销手段，所以最接近的选项是(C)。

例4：顺理成义

(1) For most people, Q→ boasting about oneself does not come naturally. It is not easy or comfortable Q→ to tell someone all the wonderful things you have accomplished. But Q→ that is exactly what you need to do if you are seeking a new job, or trying to hold on to the one you have.

(2) Of course, there is a fine line between self-confidence and arrogance, so to be successful in winning over the interviewer you must learn to maximize your accomplishments and attributes without antagonizing the interviewer.

Q: In paragraph 2, the word "maximize" means to _____ .

(A) talk about (B) make the most of

(C) be modest about (D) play down

解析：考查的词汇或表达往往在文章中承接了上下文的内容。这时通过对具有承接关系的段落的阅读可以帮助我们更准确地理解被考查词句的意思。

本文的主题讨论的是如何"boasting about oneself"，而对这句话的解释则在第二句话"to tell someone all the wonderful things you have accomplished"，即尽量地夸耀自己的优点和成绩，而这么做的作用体现在"that is exactly what you need to do if you are seeking a new job"，找工作上。那么第二段中所谓"maximize your accomplishments and attributes"也就承接了上文的观点，顺理成章地理解为尽可能地炫耀自己的成就和优势，选(B)。

(A) 选项：仅仅说，程度不够。

(C) 选项：谦虚，与文章的观点相悖。

(D) 选项：低调，和上个选项一样，意义相悖。

例5：借词猜义 I

Many folk **Q→**cures which have been around for centuries may be more therapeutic than previously suspected. A case in point is that of penicillin. Alexander Fleming did not just randomly choose cheese molds to study when he discovered its very important bacteria-killing substance. Moldy cheese was frequently given to patients as a remedy for illness at one time. Fleming just isolated what it was about the cheese which cured the patients.

Q: The word "therapeutic" in paragraph 1 is closest in meaning to _____ .

  (A) physiological   (B) medicinal

  (C) traditional   (D) psychological

解析：通过文章中相关的词汇来揣测被考查词的意思也是一种很有效的方法。

文中"therapeutic"一词是用来形容名词"cure"的，而后者的意思大家很清楚，是疗方。既然是疗方，其体现出来的效果便是疗效，所以选(B)，有益，有帮助的。

例6：借词猜义 II

More than a hundred years age, before the Civil War, a crew of bronc-busting **Q→** cowboys stood outside a large horse corral. With them was their boss Bradford Grimes, a cattleman who owned a large South Texas ranch near the Gulf of Mexico.

Q: The word "bronc-busting" in the beginning sentence of the passage can be paraphrased as _____ .

  (A) driving hogs   (B) cutting cotton

  (C) breaking horses   (D) handling cattle

解析：与上文相似，考查的词汇"bronc-busting"是一个形容词短语修饰名词"cowboys"，即牛仔。牛仔驯服野马的形象大家早就很熟悉了，所以"bronc-busting"也就是驯马的意思，选(C)。注意(C)中的动词"breaking"在这里不是分开、分断的意思，而是驯服的意思，平时并不多用，这对考生同样也是一个知识上的考验。

例7：并列生义

In some rural agricultural societies, the collection of available fuel such as firewood, dung cake, and agricultural waste can take 200 or 300 person-days per year. As well as being time consuming, the typical patterns of collection lead to deforestation, soil erosion, and ecological imbalances. In the future, experts predict that even if food supplies are adequate for **Q→** rural populations, fuel supplies for domestic use may not be.

Q: The word "domestic"(paragraph 1) is closest in meaning to _____ .

(A) industrial   (B) agricultural

(C) natural   (D) household

解析：在文章中经常出现一些并列的句型结构。我们可以由此推断并列部分的意思是相近的,从而猜出被考查词的含义。

本文的并列结构是 food supplies 食物的储存 ↔ fuel supplies 燃料的储存；rural populations 农村人口（使用）↔ domestic use→家庭使用,由此我们可以推断是**(D)**。

例8：转折取义

Other people feel sure that the present trend is towards too little sleep. To quote one medical opinion, "Thousands of people drift through life suffering from the effects of too little sleep; the reason in not that they can't sleep. Like advancing colonists, we do seem to be grasping ever more of the land of sleep for our waking needs, pushing the boundary back and reaching, apparently, **Q→** for a point in our evolution where we will sleep no more. This in itself, of course, **Q→** need not be a bad thing. What could be disastrous, **Q→** however, is that we should press too quickly towards this goal, sacrificing sleep only to gain more time in which to jeopardize our civilization by actions and decisions made weak by fatigue.

Q: The word "jeopardize"(Paragraph 2) is closest in meaning to _____ .

(A) endeavor   (B) endanger

(C) endorse   (D) endow

解析：如果一个被考查的词汇在文章中的转折结构中出现,那么形成转折的词汇或概念也可以帮助我们获取被考查词的信息。

本文中先交代了人们现在睡眠的特点趋于少睡,作者认为这不一定是件坏事。接下来用了一个"however"转折,提出了如果因缺乏睡眠而做出了一些不明智的决定,其所导致的后果是"jeopardize our civilization",也就证明了"jeopardize"一定是个负面的、带来不好后果的词汇,所以选**(B)**,带来危险。

例9：因果立意

Extraordinary creative activity has been characterized as revolutionary. **Q→** According to established formulation, highly creative activity transcends the limits of an existing form and **Q→** establishes a new principle of organization. However, the idea that extraordinary creativity transcends established limits is misleading when it is applied to the arts, even though it may be valid for the sciences.

Q: The word "transcends"(para. 1) in the sentence "highly creative activity tran-

scends the limits of an existing form" is closest in meaning to which of the following?

(A) go beyond   (B) fit into

(C) subject to   (D) set up

解析：如果在文章中确定了被考查词和其他的一些内容形成了因果关系，即被考查词造成了或引起了某种后果，那么我们可以从因果关系上确立被考查词的含义。

本文中提到高度创造性的行为"transcends the limits of an existing from"，… 现有状态的极限，从而创造了一种新的组合的法则。既然结果是推陈出新，那么对于现有的极限就只有超越才能实现这样的后果，所以选项是(A)。

例 10: 代词测义

In parts of South America, a powder obtained from grinding sugar cane is used for haling infections in wounds and ulcers. This usage may date back to pre-Colombian times. Experiments carried out on several hundred patients indicate that ordinary sugar in high concentrations is lethal to bacteria. Its suction effect eliminates Q→ dead cells, ant it generated a glasslike layer, which protects the wound and ensures healing.

Q: The word "eliminates" in Paragraph 2 can be replaced by which of the following?

(A) cleanses   (B) excretes

(C) disposes of   (D) kills off

正解：(C)

解析：有时一个词汇的多种意义在选项中同时出现，这会使我们把握不准，而有时文章本身的提示也不充分。这时不妨用各个选项——代替被考查词在原文中加以验证，反而可以事半功倍。

被考查词"eliminate"做动词可表示：(1) 消灭，消除；(2) 排除，忽略；(3) 淘汰；(4) 排泄等意思，每个选项都有相似性。这时解题的捷径是将四个选项分别在文章的原句中使用，测试一下哪个是最佳答案。原句的大致意思是糖能够帮助消毒疗伤，因为它的某种效果可以"eliminate dead cells"，"… 已死的细胞"。

(A)选项：表示纯净，清洗。我们可以说去清洗皮肤或伤口，但不能清洗已死的细胞，谓语和宾语搭配有误。

(B)选项：表示排泄。人体排泄要通过排泄系统，而在伤口的局部是无法完成排泄的，谓宾搭配有误。

(C)选项：表示排除，除去，搭配无误，正确选项。

(D)选项：表示"杀死"，细胞既然已死，那么再杀它们一次就未免太荒唐和"残忍"了，所以也不对，谓语和宾语搭配仍然有误。

例 11:

（1）By 2008, drivers should be able to steer around tie-ups with a personalized virtual traffic reporter, giving directions to the clearest roads from the passenger seat. Some time beyond that, people won't even steer, brake, or accelerate as they're swept along the clearest roads to work.

(2) That's the vision of the Intelligent Transportation Society, which had its annual meeting here in Boston earlier this month.

(3) Many parts of this technology are already here. What isn't should flood into the most congested cities by the end of the year.

(4) So far the global positioning satellite navigation systems offered in many upscale cars are helpful mostly to traveling salespeople, travelers renting cars in strange cities, and people who otherwise don't know where they're going. They're nearly useless most of the time.

(5) **Q1→**Moving from novelty to necessity depends on a convergence of technologies known as ITS, or Intelligent Transportation Systems. Today, smart roads use signs and lane markers to direct drivers around delays or into reversible commuter lanes. Systems in many cities allow tourists to call for traffic reports on specific roads from their cell phones. Others use cameras along roads to distribute pictures via the Internet of television traffic reports.

(6) The goal is to build a giant database of real-time congestion on virtually every road in the US. And then send that data to cars in a format that doesn't distract drivers.

(7) **Q2→**The problem so far is that few of the systems talk to each other.

(8) Different cities monitor traffic speed and density using electronic roadway sensors, video cameras, or simply by extrapolating data from how many people are talking on local cellphone networks. Many cities feed this information into computers that can adjust the timing of traffic lights, for instance, and display maps on the Internet.

(9) Others simply use the data to run videotapes of road congestion on evening newscasts, or leave human operators to interpret it and control traffic patterns. Even the electronic maps used in GPS systems and on the Internet **Q2→**don't match.

(10) It's an open secret, obscured by optimistic business bluster. But, behind the scenes, the companies are all trying to link into one seamless traffic-information network. It's nothing short of merging the signal network of the industrial age—the interstate highway system—with the defining network of the Information Age, says Gerald Conover, Manager of product and technology at Ford Motor Company.

(11) Nevertheless, it's happening—slowly. The first systems that integrate traffic data on in-car GPS screen should appear in 18 months, says John Sickler, a project manager at Iteris, which builds a system to collect traffic data.

(12) **Q3→** That should make everyone's driving on the road less onerous.

Q1: The expression "from novelty to necessity" means _____ .

   (A) from fiction to report   (B) from investigation to conclusion

   (C) from invention to application   (D) from military use to civic application

Q2: According to the passage, the problem that "few of the systems talk to each other"

   (Paragraph 7) means that _____ .

(A) human operators have different ways to control traffic patterns

(B) the timing of traffic lights is more difficult than expected

(C) traffic monitoring systems developed in many cities do not match smoothly

(D) Transport navigation systems interpret data in different ways

Q3: The word "onerous" in the last sentence of the passage can be paraphrased as_____ .

(A) optimistic   (B) difficult

(C) confident   (B) pessimistic

解析：本文叙述的是关于汽车里的电子导航系统，用于指示行驶方向和路况。这种技术现在已经有所应用，但普及有限，因为其中还有很大的技术难题。但是在人们的共同努力下，这种科技产品最终将造福于我们。

Q1: 类比推义："novelty"指的是新颖的事物，而"necessity"则是必需的事物。根据文章所叙，电子导航系统已经产生，但是不实用。用以上的类比，我们可以得知所谓新颖的事物就是一项科技新发明，所谓必需的事物就是投入日常使用，所以(C)选项中的一对类比"invention—application"。应该最符合全文。

Q2: 在第七自然段作者提出了问题，即系统之间不能交流。以下就开始举例说明不能相互交流的具体体现，直到第九小节做了总结，"Even the electronic maps used in GPS systems and on the Internet don't match。""Even"表示程度的递进，也就是说前面的系统都不相配，甚至连以下的也不相配。那么例子说明了问题所在，即系统不相配，选(C)。

Q3: 通过阅读得知，作者在文章的末句展望了电子导航系统可能会给我们带来的美好未来，所以结果应该是积极的。接下来我们注意到"onerous"前面的修饰词是"less"，表示不如以前如何。所以"onerous"一定是在形容现在缺乏电子导航的困难驾驶状态，选(B)。

章 节 小 结

词句解释题中所考查的词汇往往都具有一词多义的特性。所以靠我们对词汇的一知半解是无法准确地区分出正确选项的。被考查的词汇并不是孤立地呈现在我们的面前，而是在原文中扮演着一个角色。所以除了对词汇基本知识的了解之外，我们解答的关键是阅读原文，根据上下文进行合理地逻辑推断。以上推荐的推断技巧都有很强的实战性。

第二节　综合练习精解

一、

(1) Winding through the dense Philippine rainforest, my guide slows to a halt. He leans over and carefully plucks a leaf from a bright green plant. Holding it to his arm as if it is covering

a wound, he says simply "medicine". My guide is definitely no doctor, but he knows what he is talking about. He is a native Negrito tribesman who once taught American soldiers about his people's ancient ways in the jungle.

(2) Jungle survival tours are a popular attraction in Subic Bay, the former US naval base that has been transformed into a special economic zone and tourist area. Starting at the time of the Vietnam War, American soldiers used the area's lush jungles and the knowledge of the local tribesmen to train for the harsh conditions of jungle warfare. After the Americans pulled out of the Philippines in 1992, tribesmen started guiding tourists.

(3) Throughout Asia, former military sites have been transformed into unusual and fascinating tourist attractions. Not far from Subic, on the windblown island of Corregidor at the mouth of Manila Bay, visitors can huddle in the same tunnels where American general Douglas MacArthur made his last stand before the Philippines fell to Japan in World War II. A light-and-sound show recreates the nerve-wracking bombing soldiers endured.

(4) On Singapore's Sentosa Island, Fort Siloso, a beautifully restored gun site, was one of the 12 coastal artillery batteries that tried to defend Singapore during its brutal downfall to the Japanese in 1942.

(5) On Penang, Malaysia, Fort Cornwallis is a reminder of the island's former strategic importance. Built by British naval officer Captain Francis Light in 1786, it was later rebuilt by prisoners. Today it offers a great view of the ocean.

(6) US military personnel are now back in Subic Bay. Many come on joint military exercises; others are simply tourists. And many echo the sentiment of one US soldier who recently marveled at Subic's pristine jungle and deep water port. "Why did we give this place up?" he asked military Manoeuvres.

(7) For more information on Subic Bay, check out the Philippine Department of Tourism website (www. wowphilippines. com. ph) and look for Subic in the Where To Go section. To learn more about sites on Corregidor Island, check out www. corregidorphilippines. com for tour and hotel information. Sentosa Island maintains an impressive website at www. sentosa. com. sg. More deails on modern-day Penang can be found at www. exoticpenang. com. my.

Q1: Subic Bay is famous for _____ .

    (A) lush jungles   (B) knowledgeable local tribesmen

    (C) jungle survival tours   (D) joint military exercises

Q2: What can a tourist experience on Conegidor Island ?

    (A) The atmosphere of World War II.   (B) Life of Dougles MacArthur.

    (C) Nerve-wracking bombing.   (D) The war against Japan.

Q3: Fort Cornwallis was finally built by _____ .

    (A) the Francis Light   (B) the British navy

(C) the Malaysian navy   (D) the prisoners

Q4：More information about <u>Fort Siloso</u> is available at website _____ .

    (A) www.wowphilippines.com.ph   (B) www.corregidorphilippines.com

    (C) www.exoticpenang.com.my   (D) www.sentosa.com.sg

Q5：Which of the following statement is NOT true, according to the passage?

    (A) Visitors can gather together in the same tunnels where American general D. MacArthur made his last stand in World War II.

    (B) Many military personnel are now back on joint military exercises in Subic Bay.

    (C) Jungle survival tours are a popular attraction in Manila Bay.

    (D) Fort Cornwallis, built by a British naval officer in 1786 and rebuilt by prisoners, offers a great view of the ocean.

阅读方法：

定主题：第一小节有具体人物、动作、场景的描写，属于细节描写，考生应马上意识到，作者在运用一个"anecdote"，即小故事来引出土著居民曾经传授驻扎在当地的美军士兵丛林生存技巧。第二小节首句指出了，Subic Bay 从原先的一个美军基地变成了现今的一个旅游胜地，而当地的土著居民则由原先的部队向导变成了今日的导游。本篇主题句并不明确，第三小节的首句可以算是一个中心思想句，即介绍分布在亚洲的各个由原先的军事基地变成了现如今各具特色的旅游胜地的地方。文章中心的体现属于引导式。

理结构：一旦中心确定，以下的阅读就简单了。根据各段的首句我们不难看出，作者在第二、三、四、五小节一一列举了四个类似的景点，第六小节提到了美国的军事人员以不同的身份又回到了 Subic Bay，并对今天的它大为赞叹。最后一段中的几个并列句给出了各个旅游景点的网站，同时说明了本文很有可能来源于介绍旅游的杂志。结构为举例型。至此文章框架明确，剩下的细节内容考生可根据问题提示推敲解答。

解析：

Q1：细节题。Subic 海湾以什么而出名？定位的词汇是"Subic Bay"，第一次出现在第二小节，首句提示"Jungle survival tours are a popular attraction in Subic Bay"，和选项对比锁定在(C)选项。

正解：**(C)**

Q2：细节题。在 Conegidor 岛上游客们会有什么样的感受？与上题一样通过"Conegidor Island"定位在第三小节，详读一下得知游客们可以体验到当年美军忍受的隆隆炮火，比较选项锁定在(C)选项。

正解：**(C)**

Q3：细节题。Cornwallis 堡垒最后是由谁建造的？依旧通过题干中的"Fort Cornwallis"定位在第四小节，通过阅读得知这个堡垒先由一名英国海军的船长建造，然后又由战俘重修。题干中的第二个关键词为"finally"，所以最后一次建造是由战俘完成的，选(D)。

正解：**(D)**

Q4: 细节题。在哪个网站上可以找到更多关于 Siloso 堡垒的信息？根据"Fort Siloso"定位在第四节的首句,确定是属于"Sentosa Island",再由"website"一词定位在最后一节,找到与"Sentosa Island"相对应的网站是 www. sentosa. com. sg,选(D).

正解: (D)

Q5: 细节——是非题(三对一错)。 (A) 通过美国将军"American general D. MacArthur"来定位,比较一下第三小节,正确。(B) 通过美国军事人员"Many military personnel"和"Subic Bay"共同定位在第六节,正确。 (C) 通过"Jungle survival tours"定位在第二节,发现对应的是"Subic Bay";再通过 "Manila Bay" 定位在第三节,发现没有丛林生存旅行的说明,错误。(D) 根据"Fort Cornwallis"定位在第五小节,选项里的内容是文章的全文再现,正确。

正解: (C)

二、

(1) It was the American consumer who saved the country from becoming mired in recession last year. But some corporations have a strange way of expressing their appreciation: hiking fees and cutting services, sometimes in the wake of corporate missteps.

(2) Massive economic and political changes—including the waves of corporate layoffs, the airline bankruptcies and the Republican sweep last November—have created both opportunities and hurdles for consumers. Moving forward, the trick is knowing where you can expect to find them.

(3) To help you navigate, here are our best recommendations for saving money in 2003.

(4) Throughout the year, you make down payments on your coming tax bill either through withholding from you paycheck or estimated quarterly payments. If you happen to get a refund check, you are thrilled, right? Just remember: you are paying too much upfront, you are giving Uncle Sam a free loan-money that should be earning interest for you, not the government. Most taxpayers make this mistake, and the number grows every year.

(5) Some people pay as much as $150 a year to be in rewards programs, but a growing number of cards give you the same benefits for free. If it is miles you want, there are at least two good options. The Amtrak Guest Reward MasterCard gives users one point in the Amtrak frequent-traveler program for every dollar they spend. Points can be cashed in for train tickets or air miles on United, Continental or Midwest Express.

(6) American Express offers the Delta Sky Miles Options credit card, which gives cardholders a mile for every two dollars spent. However, people who charge a lot will probably want to pony up the $85 annual fee for a regular delta card, which offers more than twice the miles.

(7) Don't buy the latest cell phone immediately. The newest models—the ones with color screens and high-speed Web access—are finally hitting the United States. If you buy now, you'll pay a premium. Analysts expect the phones to catch on quickly, which will probably mean a

major price drop later in the year.

（8）Don't assume Treasury bonds are safe. Uncle Sam may not default on his interest payments, but if interest rates rise, T-bonds can still suffer severe short-term losses. It's happened before: Longer-term government bonds have lost money for 9 of past 30 years, even after figuring in the interest that investors earned.

（9）Don't hang on to rotten stocks, hoping to get back to even. The market may recover, but many individual stocks will never bounce back. What to do? Consider selling your losers, which will give you a handsome tax loss if the stocks are held in a taxable account. Then reinvest the money in well-diversified, low-cost stock funds.

Q1: The word "hurdles" in Paragraph 2 is closest in meaning to "_____".

    （A）chances   （B）challenges

    （C）tricks   （D）obstacles

Q2: "Uncle Sam" (Paragraph. 4) refers to the _____ .

    （A）American government   （B）American people in general

    （C）American taxpayers   （D）American bankers

Q3: Which of the following is NOT true about the latest cell phone?

    （A）Its price may drop dramatically in the next few months.

    （B）It has screens of different colors.

    （C）It is expected to become popular soon.

    （D）You have to pay for an insurance policy if you buy now.

Q4: A wise way of reinvestment is to _____ .

    （A）buy long-term government bonds

    （B）buy more rotten stocks until they get back to even

    （C）sell rotten stocks and buy various low-cost stock funds

    （D）deposit it in the bank because interest rates may rise

Q5: Which of the following is TRUE, according to the passage?

    （A）The American economy was in recession last year.

    （B）You should cut back on the amount of your withholding from your paycheck.

    （C）A regular Delta card saves you more money than other credit cards.

    （D）The chances for long-term T-bonds to suffer losses are slim.

阅读方法：

定主题：主题的推出方式是引导式。文章的前两个小节为主题做了铺垫，说出了作者在下面给大家提出的知识的重要性和必要性：第一节叙述了消费者的购买使得美国从萧条中走出来，接下来在转折之后提到了商家仍然在提高价格，减少服务，谋取暴利；第二节提到巨大的政治和经济变化同时带来了机会和挑战。注意第二节首句的第一个破折号是用来列举各种政治和经济变化的具体事例，所以可以忽略。主题句出现在第三小节：基于上述情况，作者给出了考生一系列的措施来节省不必要的开支。

理结构：主题句已经确立在第三小节，而且作者旨在给考生提供"recommendations"。所以下面的内容就该罗列出这些建议分别是什么。从结构上来说，根据每段的首句可以找出内容上的变换。第一个内容在第四节，个人缴税方面；第二个内容横跨第五和第六小节，说的是里程积分卡；第三个内容在第七节，手机的购买欲；第四个内容在第八节，提到了政府发放的国库券；第五个内容在最后一节，提醒考生要合理地理财。结构和上文一样属于列举型。考生在阅读时应该通过主题的提示，搜集和整理出这五个方面的建议。更重要的是，考生应该意识到题目也将围绕着这五个方面展开，通常有细节题和是非题。这样解题时就可以做到胸有成竹了。

抓重点：虽然我们已经理清了文章的结构，但这五大方向中的重点是什么，具体的建议又是什么，在阅读时仍有待确定。

建议一（第4节）：重点句型是"Just remember"（划单线部分），提出了问题的本质，即人们预支给政府的税金太多了，而这笔钱本可以用来再投资，获得利息。其引申的建议便是推迟缴纳的时间，让现金为己所用。

建议二（第5~6节）：作者在第五节的首句便提出了自己的建议，其中后半句的强转折"but..."（划单线部分）就是作者提出观点的一个明显的信号，也是考生门阅读的重点。这里作者建议大家使用不用交费的积分卡，这样既能享受积分，又省下了现金。后面显然作者举出了两种类似的提供免费里程累积的积分卡，属于举例，略读。这里判断的重点是第五节第三行的"two good options"。

建议三（第7节）：首句给出了建议，即不要马上购买最新款式的手机。

建议四（第8节）：首句提出了不要轻信国库券。而第二句的转折"but..."又指出了其真正的原因：利率的调整会影响到债券的价值，从而可能会给投资者带来损失。

建议五（第9节）：同样在首句提出了建议：不要被深度套牢的股票束缚了手脚。早点割舍，可以重组自己的投资。在这个小节中还有一个重点就是一个反问句——"what to do?"对这个问题的回答自然就是作者对其建议的再次阐述。

解析：

Q1：指代—词汇题。本题的题干已经指明了在文中的定位，在第二小节。（这是指代题的一个特征）详读原文"Massive economic and political changes... have created both opportunities and hurdles for consumers"，我们发现这里"and"连接的是两个意思相互对立的词汇，"opportunities"和"hurdles"。分析选项不难看出与"机遇"相对立的最佳选项是"challenge"（挑战），选(B)。

(A)选项：是"机会"的一个近义词；

(C)选项："tricks"是"把戏，诡计"等意思，和"机会"没有直接联系；

(D)选项：是与答案最接近的混淆选项。"obstacles"表示"障碍"。文章的原句指出政治和经济变化将给人们带来某些一般性的的后果，而"obstacles"则特指在完成某个目标的过程中遇到的阻挠，所以无法在这里和"机遇"并列使用。

正解：(B)

Q2: 指代—词汇题。定位在第四小节。原句"you are paying too much upfront, you are giving Uncle Sam a free loan-money that should be earning interest for you, not the government."中提出了纳税人把钱给了"Uncle Sam"，而在破折号后面的另一个宾语是"government"。按照句型的上下承接，我们不难发现两者所指为同一物。当然知识背景全面的同学应该从很多关于美国的读物中了解到"Uncle Sam"就是美国的一个别称。

正解：(A)

Q3: 细节—是非题(三对一错)。定位词是"latest cell phone"。锁定在原文中的第七小节。有三个选项一定和原文的内容相符，所以一旦能够确定三个相符合的选项，余留的选项一定就是我们要找的答案。

(A)选项：价格将在未来几个月中大幅下调。定位词是"drop dramatically"，符合原文的最后半句。这里文中的"major"和选项当中的"dramatically"相互印证，都表示价格将大幅下降；

(B)选项：(最新的手机)有不同颜色的屏幕。定位词是"screens of different colors"，与原文中的第二句符合。

(C)选项：(最新的手机)不久将变得非常抢手。定位词是"become popular soon"，也体现在原文的第二句话。这里要注意原文中有个很好的词汇："The newest models—the ones with color screens and high-speed Web access—are finally hitting the United States."。"hit"在这里不是我们通常所说的"打、打击"的意思，而是表示新款的手机即将上市，也就是说会变得越来越受欢迎。

(D)选项：现在买手机的同时必须买保险。前三个选项都符合原文，本选项自然就是答案。文中根本没有提到买手机的同时要买保险。这里出题者考查的一个混淆词汇是第三句"If you buy now, you'll pay a premium."里的"premium"一词。这个词的一种意思是买保险时所要支付的"保费"。但作者在文中使用这个词是代表"额外的、超出正常的支出和费用"的意思，即如果消费者在新款的手机刚上市就购买，他们将会支付更昂贵的价格。

正解：(D)

Q4: 细节题。再投资的好方法是什么？定位词是"reinvestment"，在文中最后一小节的最后一句。作者的叙述是末句：买分布均匀的、价格低廉的股票基金。即便考生们没有金融产品方面的知识，仍然可以依据"文字再现法"确定(C)选项就是正确选项，因为原文中词汇只有在这个选项中得到了再现。

(A)选项：没有提及。在最后一小节根本没有出现"购买长期债券"的字样。况且前一个小节已经提到买债券有风险。错误点："buy...bonds"。

(B)选项：与原意相悖。文章提到要卖掉业绩不好的股票，而不是买。错误点："buy rotten stocks"。

(D)选项：指代不清。"it"的指代物不明确，是股票，现金，还是股票套现之后获得的现金，不得而知。而且把钱存银行也不是作者的建议。错误点："deposit it in the bank"。

正解：（C）

Q5：细节—是非题（三错一对）。问题覆盖全文，依据选项中的关键词来定位。

（A）选项：定位词是"recession last year"，在第一小节。文中提到美国的消费者帮助美国走出了去年经济萧条的泥潭。由此可以看出美国去年的确经历了经济萧条。正确。

（B）选项：定位词是"withholding from your paycheck"，在第四小节第一句。这句话的意思是减少在工资上的预扣税。预扣税（withholding）是单位在付薪之前就提前扣除的，所以是无法减少的。错误点："cut back on withholding"。

（C）选项：定位词是"regular Delta card"，在第六小节的末句。文章中提到要得到一张"regular Delta card"需要每年交纳85美金的费用，而与免费就能得到的积分卡相比，这种卡显然不省钱。错误点："saves more money than any other credit card"。

（D）选项：定位词是"T-bonds"，在文章的第八小节。文中提到国库券是会贬值的，并且给出了数据作为例证。而选项中的"slim"却错误地表示国库券贬值是很少见的事。错误点："slim"。

正解：（A）

三、

(1) It's easy to tell people to make exercise part of their daily routine. It's not so easy to tell them what to do. Some folks like to run marathons or climb mountains. But if you would rather care for your body without risking life or limb or increasingly creaky joints, you might consider Tai Chi Chuan, the ancient martial art that looks like a cross between shadow boxing and slow-motion ballet. Tai Chi combines intense mental focus with deliberate, graceful movements that improve strength, agility and—particularly important for the elderly-balance.

(2) Practitioners praise Tai Chi's spiritual and psychological benefits, but what has attracted the attention of western scientists lately is what Tai Chi does for the body. In many ways, researchers are just catching up to what tens of millions of people in China and Chinatowns around the rest of the world already know about Tai Chi. Scientists at the Oregon Research Institute in Eugene reported that Tai Chi offers the greatest benefit to older men and women who are healthy but relatively inactive. Previous studies have shown that Tai Chi practiced regularly helps reduce falls among healthy seniors. The next step, from a scientific point of view, is to determine whether Tai Chi can help those who are already frail.

(3) There are several styles of Tai Chi, but most of them start with a series of controlled movements, or forms, with names like Grasping the Sparrow's Tail and Repulsing the Monkey. There are any good how-to books to get you started, or you can choose from among the growing number of classes offered at rec centers and health clubs in the U. S., and around the world. (There have the added benefit of combining instruction with a chance to meet new people.) Either way, the goal is to move at your own pace. As Tai Chi Cultural Center in Lost Altos,

California, puts it, "Pain is no gain."

(4) Any form of exercise, of course, can do only so much. "For older individuals, Tai Chi will not be the end-all," says William Haskell, an expert in chronic-disease prevention at Stanford University. "But Tai Chi plus walking would be a very good mixture." Younger people probably need more of an aerobic challenge, but they can benefit from Tai Chi's capacity to reduce stress. "

(5) The best thing about Tai Chi is that people enjoy it, so they are more likely to stick with it long enough to get some benefit. It helps when something that's good for you is also fun.

Q1: Tai Chi movements can improve all the following EXCEPT _____ .

(A) strength   (B) balance

(C) nimbleness   (D) integrity

Q2: According to some scientists, what kind of people can benefit most from Tai Chi?

(A) Healthy but relatively inactive old people.

(B) Active but relatively unhealthy old people.

(C) Frail old people, just released from hospital.

(D) Energetic young people.

Q3: The author mentions "Pain is no gain" (Paragragh. 3) in order to advise you _____ .

(A) move as slowly as possible   (B) act elegantly

(C) meet new people   (D) follow your own pace

Q4: Tai Chi can help young people _____ .

(A) keep slim   (B) reduce stress

(C) grow taller   (D) meet challenges

Q5: The author's main purpose of writing this article is _____ .

(A) to challenge the idea that Tai Chi is the best exercise

(B) to introduce Tai Chi to North Americans as a good exercise

(C) to invite people to take part in a training course on Tai Chi

(D) to differentiate Tai Chi with other physical exercises

阅读方法:

定主题: 主题属于引导式。作者在文章开头提出了健身在于每日的运动,但是许多运动方式都有可能导致意想不到的伤害。文章从而引导出了一种健身的佳法——太极拳。接着在第一小节的末句,作者提出了太极拳是结合意志和体力的一种运动,旨在加强锻炼者的力量和敏捷度,尤其对中老年人的平衡力帮助尤佳。

理结构: 文章的中心思想句出现在第一小节。接下来各段围绕中心展开叙述,结构属于叙述型。值得注意的是文章分析了老年人和年轻人的不同收益程度,突出了太极拳老少

主题	提出太极拳这种运动方式
益处(benefits)	(首句)除了精神和心理上的益处之外,对人体(保健)也很有帮助,对老年人尤佳。
样式(styles)	有多种样式,因人而异。
局限	老年人可以辅以走路,年轻人可以用它来缓解压力。
总结	最大的益处是人们喜欢这种锻炼方式,相比之下更可以持之以恒。

皆宜的特点。结构图如下:

抓重点: 重点句型

第一小节: ... particularly important for the elderly-balance.

第二小节: Tai Chi offers the greatest benefit to older men and women who are healthy but relatively inactive.

第三小节: ... The goal is to move at your own pace. ... "Pain is no gain."

第四小节: Any form of exercise... can do only so much.

第五小节: The best thing about Tai Chi is that people enjoy it...

解析:

Q1: 细节题。分析选项可以发现,(D)中的"integrity"不是描绘身体机能的词汇,孤立于其他三个选项之外。

正解: (D)。

Q2: 细节题。根据"... benefit most from Tai Chi"定位在第二小节的重点句型—Tai Chi offers the greatest benefit to older men and women who are healthy but relatively inactive。

正解: (A)。

Q3: 推断题。"Pain is no gain"在第三节中属于一种举例,其目的是为了表述前面的观点—The goal is to move at your own pace。

正解: (D)。

Q4: 细节题。根据"对年轻人的帮助"定位在第四小节。

正解: (B)。

Q5: 主旨(推断)。根据对主题句的分析,作者目的在于介绍太极拳这种运动,并且全文也是围绕它的各种特点展开。

正解: (B)。

四、

(1) The strange fact is that the last hundred years have seen not only the dehumanizing of manual work with the introduction of mass-production methods and scientific management, and a consequent reduction in the satisfaction which an individual can derive from the performance of a skilled craft, but also universal acceptance of the idea that everyone ought to work, even though

they may have no absolute economic necessity to do so. Even those fortunate enough to inherit great wealth have been unable to resist the prevailing climate of opinion and a large proportion of those who suddenly find that they no longer have to work, after winning a lottery or the football pools, now choose to continue working finding it too difficult to sustain a lifestyle which is not built around some form of work.

(2) I don't think that we should be unduly impressed by surveys which claim to show that the vast majority of workers, even in what appear to be the most soul-destroying jobs, actually enjoy their work: the workers' response may just indicate that they are happy to be doing any job at all, rather than a positive feeling about their particular work. But we do seem to have reached a position where people prefer to work rather than not to work, and the reasons for this are complicated by the fact that different people look for different sorts of rewards, while different people look for different types of satisfaction in their work. A basic tenet of the scientific management pioneered by Frederick Winslow Taylor at the end of the 19th century was that man the worker was a rational, economic creature, motivated only by his pay-packet. As the original Henry ford put it, the average worker wants a job into which he does not have to put much physical effort. Above all, he wants a job in which he does to have to think, what Ford thought the average worker did want can be deduced from the fact that he paid his workers a minimum wage which was more than twice the national average.

(3) Money is certainly an effective motivator, but it is not the only reason why we work. There is no doubt that the economic motive can be overridden by other considerations: for example, even when they are being paid according to individual productivity, people tend to work at the same pace as those around them, and a number of studies have shown that the output of a team may actually fall when it gains a new member who refuses to accept the group norm and works at a faster rate. Being accepted as a member of a stable working group brings its own social reward, which may explain why many workers have mixed feelings about technological advances that remove them from the noise and dirt of the shop floor and leave them in splendid isolation, in charge of a machine which can carry out the tedious work they formerly did. It may also account for the behavior of people who choose to work even though there is no economic necessity for them to do so—after all, it is not easy to be a playboy when there are so few people to play with!

Q1: Which of the following statements is NOT true, according to the passage?

(A) Scientific management has made it necessary for everyone to work.

(B) Mass production methods offer less job satisfaction for skilled workers.

(C) What the average worker wants to get from his job is the pay-packet.

(D) Wealthy people choose to work because they feel uneasy about not working.

Q2: Men like Taylor and Ford believed that the vast majority of workers _____ .

（A）enjoy their work

    （B）work only for money

    （C）enjoy the companionship of those around them

    （D）work for different purposes

Q3. All of the following are reasons why people work EXCEPT _____.

    （A）economic benefits   （B）a sense of belonging to a group

    （C）technological development   （D）social rewards

Q4. In the last paragraph, the phrase "shop floor" is best interpreted as the _____.

    （A）board for placing a machine   （B）management in a factory

    （C）factory area where products are made（D）store where products are sold

Q5. The purpose of the article is _____.

    （A）to criticize the invention of machines which make workers jobless

    （B）to explain why people want to work irrespective of their economic status

    （C）to question the necessity for people who can afford not to work to do so

    （D）to compare the motivations of the poor workers with those of the rich people

    阅读方法：文章在首段提出了一些奇怪的社会现象，其中包括由于规模生产代替了手工劳动改变了人们对从事手工技术劳动的看法，以及人们对是否应该工作产生的疑问。接着在第二段的中间确立了个人的观点（提示词 proposition）：人们希望工作的愿望是一致的，不同的是他们从工作中索取的回报。作者接下来在第二、三段中进一步阐述了不同的回报形式，同时也说明了人们希望从事劳动的原因：（1）经济回报——现金；（2）社会回报——从属感。

    解析：

    Q1：细节——是非题。（A）选项中出现了绝对化词汇——科学管理不可能造成每个人都必须工作。

    正解：**（A）**。

    Q2：细节题。根据题干中的人物名称定位在第二小节——他们的观点是，普遍大众的工作目的是为了经济收入。

    正解：**（B）**。

    Q3：细节——是非题。根据阅读分析。

    正解：**（C）**。

    Q4：指代——词汇题。通过阅读"... many workers have mixed feelings about technological advances that remove them from the noise and dirt of the shop floor and leave them in splendid isolation, in charge of a machine which can carry out the tedious work they formerly did."我们可以了解到"floor"一词指的是场所，而非地板，关键是"shop"一词的含义，这里我们可以从两个角度推测词义：（1）"Shop"有商店、生产车间等意思，但是与"worker"一起相关联地使用时多指工人们生产工作的场所；（2）"worker"在这个场所从事的工作是管理

一些用以代替他们生产劳动的机器，这样也可以推断出这个场所是一个工厂的车间。

正解：**(C)**。

Q5：主旨——推断题。阅读分析已经表明文章的主题是为了阐述人们都有工作的需要，行文方式是立论——分段说明原因。

正解：**(B)**。

五、

(1) The invention of the snow house by the Eskimo was one of the greatest triumphs over environment that man has ever accomplished.

(2) In the Arctic Circle, it is not that people lack ability or industry, but the surroundings restrict constructive effort to the barest necessities of existence.

(3) Agriculture is impossible all along the thousands miles of the north shore. The only wood is such as drifts in. Other than this driftwood, the only available building materials are snow, ice, stone and bones of animals. All of these have been used for dwellings and storage paces, differing in various tribes according to the requirements and skill of the workers.

(4) The lack of necessary timbers to build walls and span wide spaces is probably one reason why these tribes construct their houses at least partly beneath the surface of the ground. This device also makes the houses more impervious to the cold. Most of us are inclined to think that the Eskimo lives always in an igloo or snow house. This is not entirely true. After the long cold winter, the family is very apt to move, when the weather permits, into a tent of sealskin. The actual construction of such tents is similar to that used by other, more southerly tribes.

(5) The snow house, however, is an interesting and unique habitation. Out summer campers will not build with snow, but the ingeniousness of the art is worth recoding, and some of our winter camps in the mountains might try to make snow houses.

(6) It is essential that the snow itself be of the right kind. It must be taken from a bank formed by a single storm, or the blocks will break when cut. The snow must be very fine-grained but not too hard to be cut with a snow knife.

(7) At Point Barrow, Alaska, houses of snow are used only temporarily; for example, at the hunting grounds on the rivers, and occasionally by visitors at the village who prefer having their own quarters. These houses are not built in the dome or beehive shape. The walls are made of blocks of snow, high enough so that a person can stand up inside the rooms.

(8) Outside at the south end a low, narrow, covered passage of snow leads to a low door. Above this is a window made of seal entrails. The door of the house is protected by a curtain of canvas. At the other end, the floor is raised into a kind of settee on which are laid boards and skins.

Q1: According to the author, the building of the snow house was necessary because __ of _____ .

(A) the inhabitants' lack of ability and industry

(B) the extreme cold temperatures

(C) the large expense involved in shipping raw materials to the Arctic Circle

(D) the surroundings, which restrict any building to what is essential

Q2: Which of the following is NOT commonly available for building houses in the Arctic Circle?

(A) Stone   (B) Animal bones

(C) Timber   (D) Snow and ice

Q3: After the long winter, an Eskimo family is likely to _____ .

(A) move into a sealskin tent   (B) build an underground dwelling

(C) continue living in the snow house (D) move to town and live in a regular house

Q4: Which of the following statements is NOT true according to the passage?

(A) The construction of a sealskin tent is similar to that used by other tribes who live in more southern region.

(B) The snow house is an interesting, unique and ingenious habitation.

(C) Snow houses are built partly below the surface of the ground to make the house warmer.

(D) The window of a snow house is made of thin sealskin.

Q5: The author's attitude toward the invention of snow houses by Eskimos is _____ .

(A) impartial   (B) admiring

(C) sympathetic   (D) critical

阅读方法: 文章直接提出了主题——Eskimo 的 snow house，接着围绕 snow house 展开叙述: (需要建造这种房子的)原因——建筑特点——用途——内、外部结构。

解析:

Q1: 细节题。文章的 2~4 段着重分析了建造"snow house"的原因是受恶劣环境所限。

正解: **(D)**。

Q2: 细节题。文章的第 3 小节介绍了在北极农业极不发达，木料匮乏。

正解: **(C)**。

Q3: 细节题。根据第 4 小节的"After the long cold winter, the family is very apt to move, when the weather permits, into a tent of sealskin..."，我们可以了解长冬过后，Eskimo 会迁入海豹皮制成的帐篷。

正解: **(A)**。

Q4: 细节——是非题。根据"window"可定位在第 8 小节，通过阅读"Above this is a window made of seal entrails"，我们得知窗户的材料是海豹内脏。

正解: **(D)**。

Q5: 推断题。作者在文中几次直接提到了"snow house"，出处分别是"The invention of the snow house by the Eskimo was one of the greatest triumphs over environment..."（全文首句）；"The snow house, however, is an interesting and unique habitation."（第 5 小节首句）。根据作者的叙述，我们可以看出，作者对"snow house"充满了赞誉。

正解：**(B)**。

六、

（1）Men have walked on the moon, transplanted hearts and invented machines to think for them. But they cannot cure the common cold. A spokesman at the world-famous cold research center in Salisbury sounded understandably bad-tempered when I spoke to him about it. They have been working on the problem for years but the most optimistic he could be was to hope that they would find a cure within the next 10 years. So what was their advice on coping with a cold meanwhile? "Ignore it, "he sniffed.

（2）In urban areas we average about three colds a year and they are caused not by wet feet or sitting in a draught, but by a virus, or rather many viruses which are always changing, so that a vaccine prepared for one is useless against the next. But every year the pharmaceutical companies spend millions of pounds trying to persuade us that their products will banish the miseries of sneezing, running noses, sore throats, headaches and coughs. They admit they can't cure the cold, but they do promise to relieve the symptoms.

（3）We looked at 10 well-known brands of cold remedies and asked a doctor to explain, in laymen's terms, exactly what they contain （each ingredient is for） and his opinion on the effectiveness. Although none of the preparations had exactly the same ingredients, they fell into certain categories.

（4）Nearly all contained a painkiller, either aspirin or paracetamol. These help to reduce temperature and relieve general aches and pains. Aspirin can irritate the stomach, so paracetamol is generally preferred. Many also contain decongestants, which constrict the blood vessels in the nose and relieve congestion. But they can raise blood pressure and should be avoided by people with hypertension or any heart complaint. The decongestant in Vicks Medinite is known to cause wakefulness, so it is strange to find it in a night-time remedy. But maybe it is counterbalanced by the antihistamine which it also contains, like the other nighttime preparations. Antihistamines are used to treat hay fever and other complaints caused by allergies. But for a common cold all they will provide is sedation. They shouldn't be mixed with alcohol.

（5）None of the preparations was harmful as long as you observed the warnings on the packets and didn't take them if you were suffering from certain conditions, were under other medication or were pregnant. But the worst thing about them was the cost. The pharmaceutical industry's advertising and packaging efforts had grossly inflated the price of relatively cheap ingredients, and in many cases you could get the same relief from straightforward paracetamol taken with a soothing warm drink of lemon and honey.

(6) Maybe the old wives had it right all along with their remedy of "hanging your hat on the bed-post, drinking from a bottle of whisky until two hats appear, then going to bed and staying there." That's probably what the researchers will come up with in 10 years' time.

Q1: In talking about the treatment of cold a spokesman at the cold research center in Salisbury made a comment "Ignore it", because he thought that _____ .

(A) the pharmaceutical companies change too much for the remedies

(B) optimism is the best medicine for the common cold

(C) it would be impossible to find a cold cure in ten years' time

(D) remedies for cold are harmful to health

Q2: Paracetamol is preferable to aspirin because it _____ .

(A) does not affect your stomach

(B) kills pain

(C) reduces temperature

(D) does not raise your blood pressure for the treatment of a cold

Q3: If you suffer from heart trouble it is unwise to take _____ .

(A) aspirin   (B) antihistamines

(C) decongestants   (D) paracetamol

Q4: Antihistamines are dangerous for people who _____ .

(A) are allergic to pollen   (B) suffer from hypertension

(C) suffer from sleeplessness   (D) take them with the 'old wives' remedy

Q5: The writer's main criticism of the pharmaceutical industry is that it _____ .

(A) charges too much for its products

(B) claims its products cure cold

(C) claims its products relieve cold symptoms

(D) does not warn people of the medical risks involved

阅读方法： 本文的中心是对（治疗感冒的）药物的成分及作用/副作用做比较（第三小节）。文章的铺垫集中在前两个小节：作者先提出了人类目前无法根治感冒的无奈，接着提出了众多的感冒药物不能根治感冒，但是可以消减感冒的症状，由此引出了对药物的比较。在四、五小节里作者具体比较了药物里的各种成分，最后作者作了总结：10年之后我们仍然对感冒毫无对策。

解析：

Q1: 推断题。人物观点可以参照文章中对其言论的引用——发言人对感冒的态度反映在"but the most optimistic he could be was to hope that they would find a cure within the next 10 years"，说明他本人对 10 年内能否根治感冒也不乐观。

正解：(C)。

Q2：细节题。两者的比较定位在第 4 小节，根据"Aspirin can irritate the stomach, so paracetamol is generally preferred"，我们得知前者会对胃产生副作用。

正解：(A)。

Q3：推断题。根据"But they can raise blood pressure and should be avoided by people with hypertension or any heart complaint"，我们发现心脏病患者不宜服用"decongestants"。

正解：(C)。

Q4：推断题。根据"Antihistamines... They shouldn't be mixed with alcohol"，我们可以了解 Antihistamines 不能和酒精合用（第 4 小节），同时根据"hanging your hat on the bed-post, drinking from a bottle of whisky until two hats appear, then going to bed and staying there"（第 6 小节），我们了解到所谓"old wives" remedy 就是在上床之后喝酒，然后入睡。那么两者合用是不适宜的。

正解：(D)。

Q5：推断题。在第 5 小节出现了一个重点句型，"But the worst thing about them was the cost"，说明作者认为各种药物最糟糕的地方是价格昂贵，也就是说制药产业把价格定得太高了。

正解：(A)。

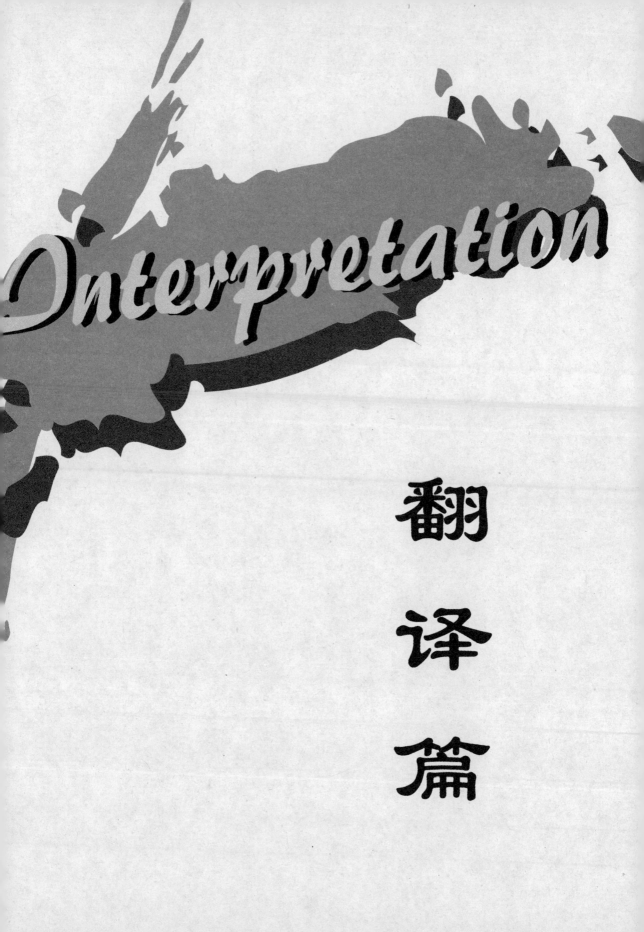

Interpretation

翻译篇

序　言

一、中口翻译部分指导理论

1. "信"、"达"、"雅"

清代翻译家严复提出的"信"、"达"、"雅"奠定了我国早期翻译文学作品的理论基石。"信"即 faithfulness，简单的说即忠于原著，表述无误；"达"即 expressiveness，做到笔译流畅，符合目标语习惯；"雅"即 gracefulness，在以上基础上更上一层楼，做到文字典雅，言简意赅。可以说，我国后来的翻译学理论都得益于这一理论，并在此基础上进一步发展而成。

2. "传神"

1951 年傅雷先生提出的更高标准，主要倡导"形似"和"神似"。翻译就像描摹绘画，简单的临摹重复只是最低的标准，如果能根据画中的主旨和意境做到"神形兼备"，则是大匠之作。因此翻译形式只是形式，而翻译效果才是真正的目的。这点对我们中级翻译的启示是很大的。

3. "化境"

1964 年，钱钟书先生提出翻译的最高标准是"化"，即翻译作品其实是原著的"投胎转世"，从内容、思想、风格、感情色彩甚至修辞手法上都要继承原著的特色，因此，翻译作品也是一部不朽的著作。

4. 字母理论

其实上述理论对于我们中级口译的考生来说，起到了一个总纲的作用。鉴于中级翻译考试毕竟不是翻译文学作品，总体上来说是个应试考试，且难度与文学作品相距甚远，因此在"信"、"达"、"雅"及上述理论的基础上，字母理论是广大考生值得参考的实用翻译标准。

A——Appropriateness

B——Briefness

C——Coherency

D——Diversification

A 指"合适原则"，即在正确通顺的基础上考虑译文在目标语中是否适合。

初学翻译者，虽然能够较快克服"形式拘泥症"，摆脱翻译位置感的束缚，但由于受到语汇的限制，有时候处理词汇、短语或句型翻译时，会就词论词，就事论事。比如说在处理"老年人"的翻译上，人们大都会翻译成"the old man/people"。这个说法从英文表达上来说是正确的，而且理解上也不存在障碍，符合"信"和"达"的标准，但不一定符合"合适原则"。根据情况或许应说成 the senior, the elderly 等。这个原则可以说是中级翻译最重要的原则，如未达到连基本分都不能保证。

B 指"简洁原则"，即在正确通顺合适的基础上尽量使译义言简意赅。

这点在英译汉的练习中特别重要。众所周知，汉语因其文化底蕴的博大精深和历史的源远流长，孕育出内涵极其丰富的字汇和语汇，大量的成语、俗语能够把通过直译难以表达或根本不能表达的意思表达得淋漓尽致。原文与目标语的比例也是衡量翻译质量的一个标准，能够在保证意思正确的基础上，尽量使比例接近于 1:0.9，这是个较高的标准。请看下面两个实例：

Russia is a huge-geographical country, with well-educated people, and will eventually recover. （摘自 2001 年 9 月考题 英译汉部分）

1) 俄罗斯是一个地域广阔的国家，人民受到良好的教育，最终将彻底地复苏。

2) 俄罗斯国土面积广大，人民受到良好的教育，全面复苏只是时间问题。

3) 俄罗斯幅员辽阔，国民素质良好，最终将东山再起。

4) 俄罗斯人杰地广，东山再起指日可待。

我们发现以上四句话都是正确无误的，且在翻译中都能拿到前面的基本语汇分，但是在后面的 wording nativeness 中，前两句不可避免地要损失一些分数。显然，后两句表达简洁，语言干练，特别是最后一句创意性地借鉴了成语"人杰地灵"，恰到好处地展现了词境和句境。

A short girl in a black straw hat appeared in the doorway.

1) 一位头戴扁平的黑草帽的矮个儿姑娘，出现在门口。

2) 一位头戴黑色扁平草帽的小个儿姑娘，出现在门口。

3) 一位姑娘出现在门口，只见她个头不高，头戴一顶浅浅的黑草帽。

4) 门口闪出了一位个头不高的女孩子，头上戴着一顶平平的黑草帽。

5) 门口出现一矮妞，头戴扁平黑草帽。

第 1、2 句看似简洁，其实存在定语偏长、头重脚轻的问题，而 3、4、5 句采取了长句短译的方法，最后一句生动地展示了动态的效果，而且运用了较高级的对仗修辞手法。

C 指"连贯原则"，即为了保持译文能够最大限度地使读者理解，对译文做出增词、换序、换形、转态等一系列的处理方式。

对于有一定翻译基础的考生来说，困扰他们的问题是怎样使句与句之间建立起超级链接，而不是简单的单句翻译。常见的方法是根据句群之间的关系，增加一些关系连词，使理解更加通顺。而这种连词的添加，对于翻译初学者来说，显得很不习惯。此外，句子翻译的顺序也不是千篇一律的先从后主——先从句后主句，有时必须根据语境做出调整，甚至是相当大的调整。后面的具体翻译技能将对此详细阐述。先见下例：

In this way, they may devote their time to the study of policy alternatives <u>free from</u> the teaching and departmental duties <u>that</u> are part of the daily routine for most members of the academic community.

译文：正因为如此，这些专家就可以从大多数学术人士习以为常的日常教学和课系公务中脱离出来，全身心地投入到政治决策的研究中去。

从句由 free from 后的补语和 that 引导的定语从句构成，由于此定语不算太长，不建议采用断句法，因此可以前置做修饰语先翻译。倘若先讲"致力于……"，后讲"脱离……"，句子侧重点就有所不同，因为"脱离课系公务"在前，且是手段，而"致力于政策研究"在后，且是目的。这个例子说明中级笔译要求考生能够对句子的翻译顺序有一定的调整能力，详见评分标准。

D 指"多样性原则"，即在翻译中有意识地丰富表达方式，体会不同译法的精确性和合理性，同时增加回译练习。

翻译无定式，好的译本用词各有千秋，拘泥于一种标准化的翻译方法只能算"得其形忘其神"。翻译教学不应提倡标准答案的概念，也不应随意否定与标准答案有差异的译文，相反，在翻译技能落实的情况下，鼓励考生用自己的话语诠释原文。其实，在很多情况下，学生局部的翻译版本要胜于一些标准译文，足以证明翻译是一个智者见智的工作。

回译练习对于翻译水平到一个瓶颈期的考生来说十分有用。以英译汉为例，当你把英文翻译成中文后，不妨再把之翻回到英文，把回译好的译文与原来的英文做一个比较，初期你会觉得相差甚远，特别是形式。这就给我们一个启发：在单项翻译的过程中应注意逆向的语汇整理。如 short-range thinking，你可能会得意地把它翻译成"鼠目寸光"，但过后，你是不是还应该留意一下，以后碰到"鼠目寸光"，你可以翻译成 short-range thinking。前面的顺向思维没什么稀奇，后面的逆向思维就是你的本事了。因此以后做一个练习，做完以后决不意味着此练习价值的中止，应多注意逆向的借鉴。

二、翻译部分考试大纲

第三部分（英译汉）

考试要求

英译汉考试要求考生在 30 分钟内，凭自己的英语和汉语能力（不能使用任何词典、参考资料或其他媒介），运用所学到的翻译知识和技巧，将一篇长度为 180 个词左右的英语文章段落译成汉语。译文须忠实原文的意思，且语言通顺，符合汉语规范。

考试题型

所给文章段落是原汁原味的英文，选自近年国外英语书报杂志，内容涉及国际、美国和英国的政治、经济、社会、文化或历史。句子有长有短，结构简繁不一，语言难度适中。

考试目的

英译汉的考试目的，旨在考核考生经过正规培训或系统自学后所具备的英译汉的实际能力，检查考生是否达到《上海市中级口译资格证书考试大纲》所规定的要求，是否具有继续进入高级阶段培训所需要的水平。

第四部分(汉译英)

考试要求

汉译英考试要求考生在 30 分钟内,凭自己的英语写作能力(不能使用任何词典、参考资料或其他媒介),运用所学到的翻译知识和技巧,将一篇长度为 180 个字左右的汉语文章段落译成英语。译文须忠实原文的意思,且语言通顺,符合英语规范。

考试题型

所给文章段落选自近年国内书报杂志,内容涉及我国的内政外交、改革开放、社会文化、历史大事或上海在各个方面的发展。句子有长有短,结构简繁不一,语言难度适中。

考试目的

汉译英的考试目的,旨在考核考生经过正规培训或系统自学后所具备的英语水平和汉译英的实际能力,检查考生是否达到《上海市中级口译资格证书考试大纲》所规定的要求,是否具有继续进入高级阶段培训所需要的水平。

三、翻译部分评分标准

虽然翻译讲究整体效果,其好坏很难用分数来量化,但是中级笔译毕竟是一个标准化考试,也就存在着相应的阅卷尺度和评分标准。经过中级笔译考试多年的不断完善和发展,现行的评分标准大致如下:

1. 分数分配

   1) 英译汉 50 分

   2) 汉译英 50 分

2. 时间分配

   1) 英译汉 30 分钟

   2) 汉译英 30 分钟

3. 单词数量

   180 个词左右

4. 句子数量(以句号为准)

   1) 英译汉 5~8 句

   2) 汉译英 4~6 句

5. 句群数量(不以句号为准)

无论英译汉还是汉译英都是五个句群,每句群 10 分。

考虑到以句号为准的话,每句的长度参差不齐,为了阅卷的方便,翻译文章按照所考查的翻译技能点被均匀的分成五个句群,每个句群包含相关数量的小分句。因此中级笔译考评小组会把每篇翻译文章进行"断章",使每个句群大致包括相同数量的单词、短语、句型、翻译技能及综合技能。

6. 评分标准

1) Wording Accuracy——翻译词汇正确度 　　占 40%

在每个句群中占到 4 分，即这个句群中每翻错一个单词，扣一分，直至 4 分全部扣完，超过部分不累计扣分或倒扣分，因此每个句群这部分最多扣 4 分。

例: a corps of <u>technicians</u>, <u>aides</u>, <u>speechwriters</u>, <u>symbol manufacturers</u>, <u>investigators</u>, and <u>policy proposers</u>（摘自 2003 年 9 月考题 英译汉部分）

译: 大批的技术人员、助手、演讲稿撰写人、徽章生产商、调查人员和政策研究员

评: 这是一个局部句群，划线单词都是采分点。除却表达方式的微小差异，如把"调查人员"说成"调研人员"，"演讲稿撰写人"说成"撰稿人"，错误的表达将导致每处扣去 1 分，如考生划线处全部错误，并不会被扣去 6 分，最多 4 分。

例: 我们希望各国人民都能享有不被人压迫、歧视和欺凌的自由。（摘自 2000 年 3 月考题 汉译英部分）

译: We hope that people of all nations will enjoy freedom immune to <u>oppression</u>, <u>discrimination</u> and <u>humiliation</u>.

评: 由于英语中的同义词较中文的要相对多一点，因此一般在意思上能够成为同义词的单词基本在这一部分都给分。根据外文出版社出版的《企鹅英语同义词反义词词典》（ *the PENGUIN Dictionary of English Synonyms and Antonyms* ）,**oppression** 共收录了 11 个同义词: tyranny, despotism, subjection, persecution, cruelty, severity, harshness, injustice, suffering, misery, hardship, 但大多数学生的词汇量还不能适应前 4 个单词的难度，使用者不多也就不足为奇。

humiliation 共收录了 9 个同义词: shame, disgrace, degradation, lowering, mortification, chagrin, embarrassment, abashment, indignity, 其中除 shame, disgrace, embarrassment, indignity 还有人问津，其余的单词使用者也是寥寥无几。

因此，我们可以得出这样的结论，中级笔译的考官还是比较"仁慈"的。除却一些专有名词、数字、地点等无法 paraphrase 的词汇，考官都会在每个考查词汇处储备大量学生可能会用到的单词，如考生所用单词在所选词范围之内，当然在这一部分是得分的，如所选词汇不属所选词范围，如果是一看便知错的词汇，当然就被"枪毙"；如果是属于考官在收集时的编外词汇（当然可能性不大），一般考官内部会商量研究一下，做出及时的判断，这种情况在中级笔译的考试中很少出现。如果你的用词有幸能够胜过考官的储备词的话，说不定还会把你的这个"经典词"加入到储备词中呢。

需要特别指出的是，在中级笔译练习到一定阶段以后，学员会发现其实真正的难词绝不是那些看上去属于生词的单词，而是一些看上去不能再简单的多义词及怪异词。如 1997 年 3 月的第一篇英译汉的文章中，有一句为:

We all have a stake in building peace and prosperity, and in <u>confronting</u> threats that <u>respects</u> no borders.

划线字 confronting 和 respects 是两个基本意思十分明确的单词。confront 一般解释为"（使）……面对……"，但在原文中翻译为"面对威胁"，其感情色彩搭配不合适，应翻译成

confront 的另外一个意思"抵御"。许多学生看到 respect 不假思索地翻译成"尊敬",但自觉不妥,又不知如何搭配。 这里 respect 居然匪夷所思地解释为"具有",即"不分国界的威胁",让考生大跌眼镜。

这种例子在每次考试中比比皆是,因此广大考生在准备一些基本词时,切忌只掌握基本意思,应打下一个良好的词汇基础。

2) **Phrase Accuracy**——翻译短语正确度   占 30%

刚才讲过词汇正确度,短语也是中级笔译考查的一个重点项目,其难度要胜于一般的词汇翻译。每次中级笔译考试中会有一两处较难的短语,即所谓"翘尾巴"题。如上文提到的例子:

We all <u>have a stake in</u> building peace and prosperity, and in confronting threats that respects no borders.

译 1: 我们<u>致力于</u>缔造和平与繁荣,抵御不分国界的诸多威胁。

译 2: 缔造和平与繁荣,抵御不分国界的诸多威胁,这些与我们大家<u>有着利害关系</u>。

译 3: 缔造和平与繁荣,抵御不分国界的诸多威胁,与我们<u>息息相关</u>。

例: 中国政府在宣布实行和平统一的方针时,是<u>基于</u>一个前提,即当时的台湾当局坚持世界上只有一个中国,台湾是中国的一部分。(摘自 2000 年 9 月考题 汉译英部分)

译 1: The Chinese government proclaimed to implement the policy of peaceful reunification <u>on the premise</u> that the then Taiwan authorities maintained that there is only one China in the world and Taiwan is only a part of China.

译 2: The declaration by the Chinese government to implement the policy of peaceful reunification was based <u>on the prerequisite that</u> the then Taiwan authorities insisted that there is only one China in the world and Taiwan is only a part of China.

3) **Paraphrasing Nativeness**——翻译自然度和专业度   10%

毕竟翻译不是一个简单的数学运算和公式,词汇和句型的选择可以说是千变万化,各有所长。但是不可否认的是其中一些翻译从正确的角度来说没有问题,但是总是差一点"火候",不是通顺度差一点,就是不符合一些特定场合的术语或专业讲法,因此在每个句群中有 1 分属于对翻译中小到语汇、大到句子自然度和专业度的考查。

例: valid information(摘自 2000 年 3 月考题 英译汉部分)

译 1: 正确的信息

译 2: 无误的信息

评: 译 2 好于译 1,这牵涉到后面所讲的正反译法。

例: the upkeep of exotic gardens and old mansions(摘自 2002 年 3 月考题 英译汉部分)

译 1: 奇异园林和古老大厦的保养

译 2: 古色古香的园林和古老建筑的维护

译 3: 奇园古宅的维护

评: 译 1 根本翻错,词汇部分就会扣分;译 2 尚可,只不过前面"古色古香"和后面的

"古"字义重复,有所累赘,翻译自然度有些小问题;译3简洁明了,通顺自然,实为上乘之作。

例: 中国改革开放以来,国民经济平均增长速度达到9.7%。(摘自2003年3月考题汉译英部分)

译1: China's **annual** growth of national economy reaches 9.7 percent since the adoption of opening and reform policy.

译2: China's national economy reaches 9.7% **every year** since the adoption of opening and reform policy.

评: 孰优孰劣,十分明显。在经济中诸如翻译"人均"时,一定要讲成 per capita,如表达成 for every person,理论上并不能算错,在第一条评分标准下不扣分,但是难逃扣1分的命运,因为其专业度可想而知。

4) Sequence Coherency——翻译句序连贯度 10%

这主要是针对一些长句。在翻译一些长句时,句子基本架构的判断以及分句翻译顺序的选择,有时直接影响翻译后读者的理解。这一部分在后面的断句译法中会详细总结。如果按照不合理的句序翻译,每个句群也会被扣掉1分。

例: ③ There is probably no better way ① for a foreigner (or an Englishman!) ② to appreciate the richness and variety of the English language than by studying the various ways in which Shakespeare used it.

译1: 外国人欣赏丰富多彩的英语可能没有比学习莎士比亚使用英语的各种方法更好的方法了。

译2: ①对于外国人(甚至还有英国人!)来说,②要欣赏丰富多彩的英语,③学习莎士比亚使用英语的各种方法可能是最好的方法。

评: 译2进行了断句和重组,使之成为汉语小分句,脉络清楚,符合汉语表达习惯,译1冗长繁琐,关键是没有进行句群的分割。

例: 这所大学的任务是培养德智体全面发展,能熟练运用外语从事外事和文化交流工作的合格人才。(摘1998年3月考题 汉译英部分)

分析: 这句句子较长,在长句翻译时对基本主谓宾的把握是十分关键的。

> 主:这所大学的任务
>
> 谓:培养
>
> 宾:合格人才
>
> 定:德智体全面发展,能熟练运用外语从事外事和文化交流工作

明确这些以后,就掌握了句子大致的采分点,即使"德智体"都不会翻,大不了定语的分数全部失掉,而把句子的主干部分翻译出来,则不会导致大规模的失分。因此考生切忌犯"翻译晕眩症",即看到句子开始部分有大量不会翻译的所谓"术语",就好像一片天黑,轻则放弃全句,重则失去对全文的信心,这种 trans-phobia(称为翻译晕眩症)完全是因为不了解分数的分布而致。因此考生应当明确在翻译中有个把单词或短语不会翻译是很正常

的,这是出题的难度要求,大可不必恐慌绝望。

译: The task of the university is to cultivate qualified personnel for foreign affairs and cultural exchange who are morally, intellectually and physically qualified with proficient use of English.

5) Spelling & Tense——拼写和时态   10%

并不严重的拼写错误和时态错误,在每个句群中会扣去 1 分。因此考生在翻译完后至少要预留 2 分钟对整篇文章进行检查,防止一些低级错误的发生。

第一章 语义翻译

第一节 一词多义

无论是在英语还是汉语中，一词多义的现象是十分普遍的，而且越是形式上简单的单词，其搭配越是丰富，词义引申现象越是频繁。中级笔译考试中自然也会对一词多义现象进行考查，考查学生在遇到较陌生词汇或短语时的语境推测能力。不过考生在准备复习时，不可寄希望于临场的判断预测，应在考前重视一些基本词汇的开拓，对于一些常用基本动词要尽可能了解字典中前3个以后的较复杂含义。

在中级笔译中，**come** 一词数次被测试到，我们不妨来了解一下关于 **come** 的一些较常用搭配，以此明确中级笔译中一词多义的重要性。考生不妨自己先来一个自测 warm-up，翻译出每个例句中斜体短语的含义。做完以后比较题后提供的参考答案，了解自己目前对于"一词多义"的掌握。

1) **come about**

　　eg. Could you tell me how the accident *came about*?

2) **come across**

　　eg1. He made such a monotonous lecture that his meaning didn't really *come across*.

　　eg2. It's indispensable to *come across* well in interviews, which will enhance your chance of success.

　　eg3. I *came across* an old friend of mine on my way to school yesterday.

3) **come after**

　　eg. The investigator paid me £100 per hour to *come after* the suspect.

4) **come along**

　　eg1. When the fight opportunity *comes along*, she will take it.

　　eg2. His French has *come along* a lot since he joined the conversation class.

　　eg3. Her baby is *coming along* well out of her expectation.

5) **come at**

eg. The truth is often difficult to *come at*.

6) **come back**

eg1. The colour is *coming back* to her cheeks.

eg2. Miniskirts are starting to *come back*.

eg3. She can't bear the teacher's arrogance so she *came back* at the teacher with some sharp questions.

eg4. The dribs and drabs of the past memory are all *coming back* to me on Valentine's Day when I am alone.

7) **come before**

eg. Fighting poverty and unemployment should *come before* all other political considerations.

8) **come between sb. and sb.**

eg. It's quite insensible to *come between* a man *and* his wife.

9) **come between sb. and sth.**

eg. Franklin never lets anything *come between* him *and* his playing play station 2 every night.

10) **come by**

eg. I was on tenterhooks in that I had *come by* a wallet on my way home.

11) **come down on sb.**

eg1. Don't *come down* too bad *on* her, for she is still childlike after all.

eg2. The courts are *coming down* heavily *on* juvenile delinquency.

12) **come down with**

eg. I *came down with* flu and was unable to go to work that day.

13) **come from**

eg1. Much of the butter eaten in England *comes from* New Zealand.

eg2. She *comes from* a long line of actresses.

14) **come in**

eg1. Long hair for men *came in* in the sixties.

eg2. She has £1000 a month *coming in* from her stocks and futures.

15) **come into**

eg. She *came into* a fortune when her uncle died.

16) **come off**

eg. The wedding didn't *come off* successfully because the bride suddenly ran off.

17) **come on**

eg1. The actor is nervous to *come on* because he is always forgetting his lines.

eg2. There is a new play *coming on* at the local theatre next week.

18) **come out**

eg1. The workers have *come out* because of the low pay and unfavourable working environment.

eg2. When will her new novel *come out*?

eg3. It *came out* that he had been telling a pack of lies.

eg4. Our photo didn't *come out* because the film was faulty.

eg5. She *came out* first in the oral presentation test.

19) **come round**

eg1. Pour some water on his face—he will soon *come round*.

eg2. Why don't you *come round* to my flat this evening for a further discussion?

eg3. It took her months to *come round* to writing me back.

20) **come to**

eg1. A fancy idea *came to* him in his bath.

eg2. Having a glimpse of the bill *coming to* 300 dollars, I wished I hadn't promised to entertain all the guests.

21) **come under**

eg. During the meeting, we *came under* severe criticism and sarcasm, leading to disappointment.

22) **come up**

eg1. We will let you know if any vacancies *come up*.

eg2. The issue is bound to *come up* at the meeting.

23) We have **come** fifty miles since lunch.

24) His family **came** first in his mind.

25) This company has **come** a long way in the last five years.

26) The dress **comes** in three sizes.

27) She had **come** to see the problem in a new light.

28) She tried to **come** the innocent with me.

29) I am as good as a cook as she is except when it **comes** to making pastry.

30) If she spent five years in Paris, how **come** she can't speak a word of French?

答案:

1) 发生

2) eg1 被理解

　eg2 表现;给人以(特定的)印象

　eg3 偶然遇见

3) 跟踪;追踪

4) eg1 到达;出现

　eg2 进步

　eg3 发育

5) 发现,获知(事实、真相)

6) eg1 返回

eg2 再度流行

eg3 反驳;顶嘴;回击

eg4 想起;记起

7) 比……更重要

8) 干预;离间

9) 妨碍;阻挠

10) 偶然得到

11) eg1 严厉批评

　　 eg2 惩罚

12) 病倒

13) eg1 产于;来自

　　 eg2 出生于

14) eg1 流行;时髦

　　 eg2 作为收入;收到

15) 继承

16) 举行;发生

17) eg1 上场;出场

　　 eg2 (指电影、戏剧)上演

18) eg1 罢工

　　 eg2 出版

　　 eg3 (指新闻、实情)传出;真相大白

eg4 (指照片)冲洗

eg5 考试获得名次

19) eg1 苏醒;恢复知觉

　　 eg2 来访;来……坐一坐

　　 eg3 拖延很久后才做……

20) eg1 (指主意)想起;认识到

　　 eg2 共计;总共

21) 成为……的目标

22) eg1 出现

　　 eg2 被提出、讨论

23) 我们饭后已经走了50英里了。

24) 他把家庭放在第一位。

25) 这家公司在最近的五年里取得了很大的进展。

26) 这种衣裙有三种型号。

27) 她终于对这个问题有了新的认识。

28) 她尽量对我装出无辜的表情。

29) 除制作糕点外,我的烹饪技术与她不相上下。

30) 如果她在巴黎度过了5个春秋,怎么竟连一句法语也不会说呢?

同样,在汉译英练习中,一字多义的现象也是极其普遍的,下面请看"投"的实例。

1) 投保 insure

2) 投标 submit a tender; enter a bid

3) 投产 go into operation; put into production

4) 投诚 surrender; cross over

5) 投递 deliver

6) 投稿 contribute

7) 投合 get along; cater to

8) 投机 agreeable; speculate

9) 投考 sign up for an examination

10) 投篮 shoot; shot

11) 投票 vote

12) 投其所好 cater to another's pleasure

13) 投射 throw; cast

14) 投身 throw oneself into

15) 投石问路 throw a stone to clear the road

16) 投手 pitcher

17) 投鼠忌器 spare the rat to save the dishes; burn not your horses to rid it of the mouse

18) 投宿 seek temporary lodging; put up for the night

19) 投诉 complain

21) 投降 surrender; capitulate

21) 投影 projection　　　　　22) 投资 invest

如果把字和词语比作砖头，字和词语赖以生存的上下文就是框架结构。如果没有上下文这个框架结构，字和词语这些砖头就无法建立起高楼大厦。翻译中对字和词语的理解就是要从上下文入手。接下来，我们来看第一组例句中 hand 和第二组例句中"手"在不同上下文里的不同选义。

hand

1) He was badly wounded in the **hand**.

他手受了重伤。

2) Please give me a **hand** with the washing-up.

请帮我刷锅洗碗。

3) The second **hand** of a watch is moving faster than the minute **hand**.

手表的秒针比分针走的要快。

4) Since our department is short of **hands**, I hope everyone should work on your best.

既然我们部门缺少人手，大家就应该全力以赴。

5) He has a light **hand** with hamburger.

他很会做汉堡包。

6) My ill luck came, let's play one more **hand**.

刚才我运气太差，咱们再玩一局吧！

7) What impresses me most is her legible **hand**.

给我印象最深刻的是她的一手好字。

8) After 5 years of living together merrily, she gave him her **hand**.

共同幸福地生活了 5 年之后，她答应了他的求婚。

9) Take it easy! Your big moment is at **hand**.

别当真！你就要时来运转了。

10) The suits made by **hand** are more expensive than those by machine.

手工做的西装比机器做的要贵。

11) The affair is no longer in my **hands**.

这件事我不再管了。

12) On the one **hand**, it's indispensable to have a through review before the exam; on the other **hand**, a good night's sleep is necessary for sitting up for the test.

一方面，考前全面复习必不可少；另一方面，考前晚上充足的睡眠很有必要。

手

1) 这孩子手真软，适合弹钢琴。

The kid has soft **hands** for playing piano.

2) 人手一册。

Everyone has a copy.

3) 她是讨价还价的能手。

She is really an **expert** in bargaining.

4) 他真有两手。

He really knows the **stuff**.

5) 原则是一手交钱，一手交货。

The principle is cash **on** delivery.

6) 他总是手忙脚乱，给他老板造成一种无能的印象。

He is always in such a **muddle** that he strikes his boss as incompetent.

7) 他想试试他的手气。

He is trying to figure out his **luck** at gambling.

8) 这徒弟手脚快。

This apprentice is keen and quick **in his work**.

9) 你这个人关键时候总是手软，这样是不能当老板的。

You are always **irresolute** when firmness is needed, which prevents you from being a boss.

10) 在年终的时候，有些人手头松，而有些人手头则紧。

When it comes to the end of the year, some are quite **well off** while others are **hard up** at the moment.

第二节 一句多义

相比单词的多义，句子中也存在着多义。虽然句子的多义归根结底是词汇上的理解，但是这些单词往往是引导从句时的连接词，对其不同的理解直接导致对句义的不同理解。请看下面的实例：

1) You had better tell me **if** you can help us.

★如果你能帮助我，最好请告诉我。

▲请告诉我你是否能帮助我。

评：★句的弦外之音就是"如果你不能帮助我，就不要跟我说话了"。而▲的意思是"不管你能不能帮助我，都请告诉我一下"。

2) She moved to London last May **since** she got a job on a newspaper.

★自从她在一家报社任职，她去年5月就搬到伦敦去住了。

▲既然她在一家报社任职，她去年5月就搬到伦敦去住了。

评：两句话差别不大，因果也十分明确。★句强调时间关系，而▲句表明了"任职"与"伦敦"的关系，暗示在伦敦对报社工作有利，伦敦可能会有多一些的新闻渠道等。

3) **While** locked up in prison, she managed to write her first novel.

★ 当她坐牢时，写出了自己第一部小说。

▲ 尽管她在坐牢，但还是成功地写出了自己第一部小说。

评：▲ 句体现了她百折不挠的气概，有丰富的感情色彩。

第三节　直译与意译

直译与意译是翻译中最常见的问题，也是最主要的两个翻译方法。所谓**直译**，就是既**保持原文内容、又保持原文形式的翻译方法或翻译文字**。译文的语言（或始发语）与原文的语言（或目的语）常常拥有相同的表达形式来体现同样的内容，并能产生同样的效果。在这种情况下，我们就采用直译。所谓**意译**，就是指**保持原文内容、不保持原文形式的翻译方法或翻译文字**。译文的语言（或始发语）与原文的语言（或目的语）在许多的情况下并没有同样的表达形式来体现同样的内容，更谈不上产生同样的效果。在这种情况下，一般采用意译为好。

对于中级笔译的考生，考试中大多数场合下只需要译出词的基本意思即可，这样的话可以确保翻译基本分的落实。但不可否认的是，在每次考试中，一定会有一些场合下需要使用到意译，往往这种情况是此篇翻译中的难点。因此只满足直译，是不可能拿到高分的，在一些场合下也必须使用意译。

但是一些考生在基本功不扎实的情况下，容易盲目地对一些直译可以讲清楚的短语或句型进行莫名其妙的意译，结果反而弄巧成拙，这种现象称为"意译幻想症"。因此学员需要明确一点，意译是在直译不能清晰表达或根本不能表达原文意思的时候，才"不得已"运用的。对于中级口译考试来说，考生首先必须考虑直译的可能性，其次才是意译。考生如要彻底掌握意译，也必须掌握一些常用字词的引申意思。下面我们就来分析直译与意译在中级口译考试翻译部分中的运用。

1) There is **no way of** proving this point. （摘自 1997 年 9 月考题 英译汉部分）

   直译：现在**没有办法**证明这一点。

   意译：这一点尚无定论。

2) An organization that has **open lines of communication** with **valid, honest** information going **up, down, and throughout** the organization will be much more **effective** and **a much better place to work** in than the organization that attempts to restrict the flow of information or distort and deceive. （摘自 2000 年 3 月考题 英译汉部分）

   直译：一个企业如果具备公开的传播渠道，公司上级、下级、同级之间传递真实、可信的信息，比起那些试图限制信息流通、歪曲甚至欺骗的企业来说，将会有更高的效率，并是一个更适宜于工作的地方。

   意译：如果一个企业具备公开的传播渠道，企业内部信息传播流畅、内容真实可信，比起那些试图封闭信息，歪曲甚至欺骗的企业来说，将会有更高的工作效率，更好的工作环境。

3) Restricting communication and distorting information are **symptoms of short-range thinking**. (摘自 2000 年 3 月考题 英译汉部分)

直译 1: 限制沟通和曲解信息是企业缺乏远见的前兆。

直译 2: 限制沟通和曲解信息是企业目光短浅的前兆。

意译 1: 限制沟通和曲解信息使企业逐渐变得鼠目寸光。

意译 2: 限制沟通和曲解信息使企业逐渐成为井底之蛙。

4) Think tanks and university research institutes are nonprofit organizations that have been developed to provide **settings** for experts in various academic disciplines. (摘自 2002 年 3 月考题 英译汉部分)

直译: 智囊团和大学中的研究机构是非赢利性组织，为不同学术领域的专家提供了环境。

意译: 智囊团和大学中的研究机构是非赢利性组织，为不同学术领域的专家提供了舞台。

5) Their expanding appetite for imports would have **bolstered** the United States and so-called emerging market countries from Brazil to South Korea. (摘自 2003 年 3 月考题 英译汉部分)

直译: 那些国家对进口需求很大，刺激了美国和一些所谓新兴市场国家诸如巴西、韩国。

意译: 那些国家热衷于进口，确实给美国和一些所谓新兴市场国家诸如巴西、韩国打了一针强心剂。

6) The project budget **sustains** both the existence of graduate students and the fiscal solvency of the university, which takes a percentage "overhead" out of every project budget. (摘自 2003 年 9 月考题 英译汉部分)

直译: 项目预算维持着研究生的存在和大学的资金偿还能力，大学的资金偿还在整个项目预算中占有重要比例。

意译: 研究生是否存在，大学是否存在资金偿还能力，这些都**取决于**项目预算。大学的资金偿还在整个项目预算中占有重要比例。

7) 本届会议将围绕"新世纪、新挑战：参与、合作、促进共同繁荣"的主题，审议 5 个方面的议题，以期促进亚太地区和全球经贸的发展。(摘自 2001 年 9 月考题 汉译英部分)

直译: This meeting will **discuss** the topic of "**new century, new challenge: participate, cooperate and promote common prosperity**" covering 5 **areas** with a view to enhancing the development of economy and trade in the Asian-Pacific region and the rest world.

意译: This meeting will, **centering round the theme of "Meeting new challenges in** the new century: achieving common prosperity through participation and cooperation", reviewing the agenda under 5 **heads** with a view to promoting the economic and trade development in the Asia-Pacific region and the world at large.

8) 因为从市民的衣、食、住、行消费来讲,住房是一个重要的因素,而且占了大头。(摘自 2002 年 9 月考题 汉译英部分)

直译: Among the basic necessities of life——food, clothing, shelter and transportation, housing is an important element, accounting for **a majority** in the money they spend.

意译: Among the basic necessities of life——food, clothing, shelter and transportation, housing is an important element, accounting for **a lion's share** in the money they spend.

第四节 望文生义

翻译之所以成为一项高深的艺术,很大程度上缘于译者在鳞次栉比的词群中具备的那种精确的"定位能力",即选择上下文语境相对应的字词含义。但中级考生由于受字词积累的限制,对词义选择的敏感度和灵活性还未达到收放自如的地步,因此造成考生在翻译中往往不由自主地考虑采纳自己较熟悉的释义,对一些较冷僻的词义则"不知"或"不察",造成望文生义。 历年翻译考题中都有大量字词句选用了非"常见义",致使考生犯下大量错误,导致大量失分。下面请看历年来考生在中级翻译考试中的一些误译。

1. 词语

1) shape (97/3)　　　误译: 形状　　　正译: 格局
2) dramatically (97/3)　　误译: 戏剧地　　正译: 剧烈地
3) skyline (97/3)　　误译: 空中线条　　正译: 空中轮廓;苍穹
4) respect (97/3)　　误译: 尊敬　　正译: 具有
5) backwards (97/3)　　误译: 向后　　正译: 相反
6) surface (97/9)　　误译: 表面　　正译: 游到表面
7) company (97/9)　　误译: 公司　　正译: 陪伴
8) invite (98/3)　　误译: 邀请　　正译: 征集
9) desire (98/3)　　误译: 想要;迷恋　　正译: 录用
10) panel (98/3)　　误译: 嵌板;金属块　　正译: 小组
11) review (98/3)　　误译: 复习　　正译: 审阅
12) specification (98/3)　　误译: 详细说明　　正译: 特长要求
13) reasonable (98/9)　　误译: 合理的　　正译: 不劣的
14) poor (00/3)　　误译: 可怜的　　正译: 不良的

15) trap (00/3)	误译：陷阱	正译：做法；禁锢
16) hangover (00/9)	误译：残留物	正译：痕迹
17) exhibit (00/9)	误译：展览；展示	正译：体现
18) collectively (01/9)	误译：总而言之	正译：整体
19) economic equality (01/9)	误译：经济平等	正译：经济均衡
20) foundations (02/3)	误译：基金	正译：基金会
21) upkeep (02/3)	误译：维持	正译：维护
22) alternative (02/3)	误译：方法	正译：决策
23) bad loan (03/3)	误译：坏贷款	正译：不良贷款
24) poised (03/3)	误译：犹豫不决	正译：信誓旦旦
25) produce (03/9)	误译：生产	正译：诞生
26) secure (03/9)	误译：使……安全	正译：得到
27) 红红的脸 (97/3)	误译：red face	正译：ruddy face

28) 过多过厚的衣服 (98/9)	误译：too warm and heavy clothes
	正译：overdressed clothes
29) 沧桑 (99/3)	误译：past memory of suffering
	正译：vicissitudes
30) 航空业务量 (99/9)	误译：aviation business
	正译：aviation services
31) 最终设计能力 (99/9)	误译：final design capacity
	正译：maximum design capacity
32) 绿化 (99/9)	误译：green land
	正译：green space; green belt
33) 住房面积 (02/9)	误译：house space
	正译：living space; dwelling area
34) 人均 (02/9)	误译：every person
	正译：per capita

2. 短语

1) push and go	误译：推着走	正译：精力
2) smile at	误译：对……微笑	正译：讥笑
3) come down to	误译：来到……	正译：归结为……
4) equal to be an engineer	误译：相当工程师的职务	正译：胜任工程师的工作
5) sick to death of	误译：病得要死	正译：腻得要命
6) bring to life (97/3)	误译：使……生动	正译：激发；促成
7) immune to (97/3)	误译：对……免疫	正译：免受……；免遭……
8) have a stake in (97/3)	误译：下赌金	

正译: 致力于……;与……息息相关

9) a number of criteria (98/3)   误译: 许多标准

正译: 若干标准

10) before lower adolescence (00/9)   误译: 在青少年早期之前

正译: 少年时期;十来岁

11) after upper adolescence (00/9)   误译: 晚于青少年后期

正译: 青年时期;十六、七岁

12) a large minority (01/9)   误译: 很多少数派   正译: 少数派为数不少
13) think tanks (02/3)   误译: 思想集中地   正译: 智囊团
14) sick man (03/3)   误译: 病人   正译: 病根
15) 与……一比长短 (97/9)   误译: compare with   正译: compete with
16) 第一件大事 (98/9)   误译: the first thing   正译: a top priority
17) 繁衍生息 (99/3)   误译: multiply   正译: live and work
18) 充分发挥 (03/9)   误译: develop fully   正译: give full play

第二章 词 法 翻 译

　　虽然中级口译的翻译考试还是一门相对较简单的考试，对考生的翻译技能要求还不是非常的严格，考生也没有时间、没有必要非常系统地掌握所有的翻译技巧（包括词法翻译和句法翻译）。但有些翻译技能在中级笔译中考查得特别频繁，甚至是每次考试中的"保留节目"。对于这些"重中之重"的翻译技能，考生务必要烂熟于心。本章讲述考生必须掌握的一些词法翻译，并且举出中级笔译已考的实例，供考生总结体会；在此基础上，我们还给出了一些将来考试中也必须掌握的一些同类现象，做到未雨绸缪。考生也应举一反三，融会贯通，切忌死盯实例，见木不见林。在每章后面，我们也配了一些练习题，供考生在看完该章后即可练习巩固，加深对此翻译现象的理解。书后提供了参考答案。

第一节 具体译法

　　这是词法中最基本的翻译方法，即对原文中比较抽象的单词、词组、成语或句子用比较具体的单词、词组、成语或句子翻译，使之符合相对应的语境，理解更加通顺自然。但是我们中国学生对此掌握得并不好。原因是我们从小学英语时，老师在教我们背单词的过程中，无意地使我们对单词产生了机械化的记忆，我们看到某个特定单词，也就产生了巴甫洛夫的"条件反射"，比如一看到 government，立马说出"政府"，忽视了"政府部长"、"政府部门"、"政府官员"等一切相关意群的表达。在这句话中 "She has resigned from the **Government**."，Government 解释为"政府部长职务"，在"The **government** is immune to taking bribery."这句话中，government 解释为"政府官员"。因此对于参加翻译考试的考生来说，即使再简单的单词切忌形成"条件反射"，不假思索地翻译其抽象意思，应首先考虑语境表达的需要，选择是否要使单词"具体化"。经验告诉我们，往往越是简单的单词越有可能使用到具体译法，越是复杂的单词，其选择面反而狭窄，具体译法的可能性和必要性也不大。请看具体译法的实例。

一、单词、词组和成语英译汉时具体译法的译例：（括号内为考题日期）

1. 加字法——在抽象名词前后添加名词构成具体名词

1) economy	经济→经济;体经济规模	（97/3）
2) risk	危险→危险性	（97/3）
3) importance	重要→重要性	（97/9）
4) language	语言→语言形式	（97/9）
5) organization	组织→企业组织	（98/3）
6) profile	材料→个人材料	（98/3）
7) job	工作→工作情况	（98/3）
8) individual	各人→有关人士	（98/3）
9) management	管理→管理部门;管理层	（98/3）
10) specifications	特长→特长要求	（98/3）
11) applications	应聘→应聘情况	（98/3）
12) broadcasting	广播→广播节目	（98/9）
13) on-line	在线→在线频道	（98/9）
14) victimization	受害→受害者	（99/3）
15) dimensions	特点→性格特点	（99/9）
16) sympathy	同情→同情心	（99/9）
17) vibrations	颤动→颤动的原因	（99/9）
18) grammar	语法→语法书	（00/9）
19) troubles	问题→经济问题	（03/3）
20) expansion	增长→不断增长	（03/9）
21) independence	独立→独立性	（03/9）
22) translation	翻译→翻译作品	
23) press	出版→出版物;报纸;杂志;出版社	

2. 集合名词法——把集合名词的整体概念转换成个体概念

24) government	政府→政府官员	
25) family	家庭→家庭成员	
26) class	班级→全班学生	
27) committee	委员会→委员会成员	
28) team	队伍→队员	
29) nation	国家→国家人口	（01/9）

3. 比喻法——形容词、副词修饰时形成比喻

30) short-range thinking	目光短浅的思考→鼠目寸光;井底之蛙	（00/3）
31) economic shift	经济转变→经济东风	（01/9）

32) very timid 非常胆小→胆小如鼠

33) very strong 非常强壮→壮得像头牛

4. 成语法——用成语概括抽象名词

34) act in concert 协力行动→齐心协力 （97/3）

35) keep workers in the dark 让员工不清楚→让员工蒙在鼓里 （00/3）

36) special organized programs of instruction 特定的程序和计划→繁文缛节 （00/9）

37) hangover of... is likely to persist... 的痕迹会遗留下来...→会根深蒂固 （00/9）

38) mass prosperity 普遍繁荣→欣欣向荣 （01/9）

39) a great and thorough-going change 巨大而彻底的变化→翻天覆地的变化

40) very important 很重要→举足轻重 （02/3）

41) very anxious to return home 回家心切→归心似箭

二、单词、词组和成语汉译英时具体译法的译例：

1) 同舟共济 in the same boat

2) 火上加油 pour oil on fire

3) 大器晚成 a late bloomer

4) 坐立不安 have ants in one's pants

5) 简言之 in a nutshell

6) 难言之隐 secret sorrow

7) 家丑 a skeleton in the cupboard; a family skeleton

8) 河东狮吼 under petticoat government

9) 老滑头 a soft soap

10) 别泼冷水 Don't be wet blanket!

11) 自食其言 eat the Bible

12) 飘飘欲仙 on cloud nine

三、句子英译汉时具体译法的译例：

1) Prices drop because there's too little global demand chasing too much global supply—everything from **steel** to **shoes**. （03/3）

从钢铁业到鞋业，全球需求急剧萎缩，而供给源源不断，从而导致商品价格下跌。

2) Japan's **ills** are **well known** its banks are **awash** in bad loans. （03/3）

众所周知的是，日本对不良贷款的冲击头疼不已。

3) Only 15 years ago, these countries seemed **poised** to assume **leadership** of the world economy. Now they are **dragging** it **down**. （03/3）

仅仅15年前，这些国家曾信誓旦旦地想要扛起全球经济的领导大旗，而现在却在拖后腿。

4) The project budget sustains both the existence of graduate students and the fiscal **solvency** of the university. （03/9）

研究生的存在，大学的资金偿还能力，这些都依靠项目预算。

5) The **evaporation** of alcohol will make the temperature lower.

酒精的蒸发作用能够降低温度。

6) We were disgusted by his **adulation** to his superior.

他对他上司阿谀奉承的行为，让我们感到恶心。

7) Since the 29th Olympic Games will be held in Beijing, the **necessity** of studying hospitality management and foreign languages has been fully realized.

由于北京将举办第29届奥运会，越来越多的人认识到学习酒店管理和外语的必要性。

8) Project management focuses on deliberating the **feasibility** of project budgeting.

项目管理将集中审议项目预算的可行性。

9) His **loftiness** sends him into **despair** when deprived of his job.

他的自命清高使他在下岗后陷入绝望的境地。

10) My **underestimation** of the test leads to the outcome which is lower than my expectation.

我对考试过于轻视，结果比预想的要差。

11) Many changes take place during the **transformation**.

转化过程中发生了许多变化。

12) **Tension** between Israel and Palestine can be eased through diplomatic negotiations, which will resume bilateral relations having been suspended for a long time.

以巴双方的紧张局势可以通过外交谈判得以缓解，从而恢复中断许久的双边关系。

13) The progression of **idolization** among the young is inevitable and undeniable. What is under controversy is whether it will set a positive **model** for the adolescents or lead to aftermath of degradation because of **conformism**.

年轻人中的偶像化是不可避免和不可否认的，现在引起争议的是偶像化是给青少年树立一个正面的楷模形象，还是导致他们因从众心理而堕落。

四、句子汉译英时具体译法的译例：

1) 他每天要与许多重要人物打交道。

He has many **big potatoes** to deal with every day.

2) 他真是一个无用而又累赘的东西，整二沉溺于打电子游戏和赌博。

He is such a **white elephant** that he is indulged in playing video games and gambling.

3) ——既然你已经错过良机了，振作起来吧！天涯何处无芳草，将来有的是机会。

——你这是放马后炮，岁月不饶人啊。

——Since you have **missed the bus**, **keep up your spirits! There is plenty of fish in the sea**.

——You are **a Monday morning quarterback. Time and tide wait for no man**.

4) 这件事你最好过问一下后台老板，毕竟项目预算他说了算。

You had better exchange ideas with **the power behind the throne**. After all he **has the floor** in the project budget.

第二节　抽象译法

与具体译法相反，**抽象译法是指把原文中较具体的单词、词组、成语或句子进行抽象化处理**。这种现象在英译汉或汉译英的翻译里都有。英译汉里主要是一些涉及成语、俗语的表达。由于中级翻译对考生掌握成语及俗语方面的要求并不高，基本上考生对付这类翻译现象时应无大碍，根据字面就比较容易理解原文的含义，如：

1) wall of bronze　　　　　　　　　→铜墙铁壁

2) tooth for tooth; eye for eye　　　→报复

3) get the green light　　　　　　　→得到允许

4) blow one's own trumpet　　　　　→自吹自擂

5) in weal or woe　　　　　　　　　→同甘共苦

6) pull the strings　　　　　　　　　→幕后操纵

7) armed to the teeth　　　　　　　→全副武装

8) apple of discord; Pandora's box　→祸根

9) show the white feather　　　　　→示弱

10) It doesn't hold water.　　　　　　→那是站不住脚的。

在考过的全真试题中，有两处的抽象译法现象较难，请考生注意总结。

The free flow of goods and ideas is **bringing to life** the concept of a global village. (97/3)

译文：商品和观念的自由流通激发/促成着地球村概念的形成。

We all **have a stake** in building peace and prosperity, and in confronting threats that respects no borders—terrorism and drug trafficking, disease and environmental destruction. (97/3)

译文：缔造和平与繁荣，抵御不分国界的诸多威胁——恐怖主义、贩毒、疾病和环境破坏，这些与我们大家都有着利害关系。

在汉译英时，抽象译法的使用就更为普遍了，不过考生可能在使用时自己还不知道。其实在许多场合下英语中一些常见的后缀即体现了抽象译法，如 -ness, -ment, -ty, -ity, -ability, -ence, -ency, -tion, -y, -ing, -ization。请看下面的实例：

1) 卑微态度　　　humbleness
2) 发展过程　　　development
3) 可塑性　　　　flexibility
4) 适应能力　　　adaptability
5) 杰出的表现　　prominence
6) 变态行为　　　abnormality
7) 同化作用　　　assimilation
8) 同情心理　　　sympathy
9) 青少年犯罪　　juvenile delinquency
10) 全球化　　　　globalization

第三节　增词译法

在中英互译中，由于英语重语法，而汉语重表达；前者强调结构，而后者更注重内容，因此两者之间有时会产生结构或内容不十分吻合的现象。这时就需要在原文的基础上添加润饰语，包括词语、词组、分句或主句，做到词法、语法、文化背景以及作者语气等多方面的统一。这种使译文更加通顺而添加润饰语的翻译方法称为增词译法。中口翻译中存在大量增词译法的现象，下面将详细展开论述，以真题为例：

一、增加时间状语

Dolphins, like whales, must surface to breathe air through a blowhole on top of their heads. (97/9)

译文：海豚与鲸一样，需要不时浮出水面以其头顶上的鼻孔进行呼吸。

Her main message was and is, "We're like everybody else. We're here to be able to live a life as full as any sighted person's. And it's O. K. to be ourselves." (99/9)

译文：她传递的信息过去是、今天依然是，"我们和别人一样。我们在这个世界上能够和视力正常的人一样过上充实的生活。我们成为盲人没有什么不好。"

二、增加定语

上海的优势在于科技实力。(97/9)

译文：The advantage of Shanghai lies in its **advanced** scientific and technological strength.

深圳作为全国最早的特区，与内地经济往来极为密切。(98/9)

译文：As the nation's earliest established special **economic** zone, Shenzhen has very close economic contacts with the innerland provinces.

早在 80 年代，世纪伟人邓小平就提出了"一国两制"的伟大构想。(99/3)

译文: Early in the 1980s, Mr. Deng Xiaoping, **one of** the great figures of the century, put forward the bold concept of "One Country, Two Systems".

社会保持稳定,市场经济体制正在逐步建立和完善,为西部经济持续快速增长创造了有利的市场环境。(03/9)

译文: With the society enjoying a **rather satisfactory** stability, and the market economy system being established and improved on a daily basis, there appears a favourable market environment for the western region to maintain the sustained and rapid economic growth.

三、增加主语

Less understood (at least in the United States) is the fact the Europe's Economic troubles stem significantly from Germany. (03/3)

译文: 但有一点全世界(至少美国)搞不太明白,即欧洲国家的经济问题主要由德国引起。

在采取每一行动之前,都必须向党员和群众讲明我们的政策。

译文: Before any action is taken, **we** must explain our policy to Party members and to the masses.

不坚持就会失败。

译文: **One** will fail unless **one/he** perseveres.

四、增加宾语

Usually, in Japan, when people discuss the war at all, they speak of victimization: their own victimization by the militarists who led the country into battle and by the Americans who bombed their cities. (99/3)

译文: 通常在日本,只要一提到战争,就会讲到受害,讲他们是军国主义的受害者,军国主义把国家引入战争;他们是美国的受害者,美国向他们的城市投掷了原子弹。

Collectively, the Asian Countries will have a larger economy than the rest of the world put together. (01/9)

译文: 亚洲国家的整体经济规模,将超过其他国家和地区经济规模的总和。

Germany is Europe's "sick man", just as Japan is Asia's. (03/3)

译文: 德国是欧洲的病根,就像日本是亚洲的病根一样。

通用语种的学生,在能熟练使用外语后,还要接受诸如外事翻译、语言学、文学、新闻、国际文化交流等方面的专业训练。(98/3)

译文: Students of commonly used foreign languages, after acquiring the **ability** to use language efficiently, receive special training in such fields as foreign affairs translation, linguistics, literature, journalism, intercultural communication.

五、增加谓语

That's why the stage appealed to her, why she learned to speak, to deliver speeches and to feel the vibrations of music, of the radio, of the movement of lips. (99/9)

译文: 这就是为什么讲坛对她有如此的吸引力,她为什么去学习说话,学习演说,学习去感受由音乐、收音机、人的嘴唇嚅动所发出的颤动的原因。

Inside these nations there will be mass prosperity, but with a large minority in serious poverty, and a small number who are very rich. (01/9)

译文: 这些国家呈现出欣欣向荣的态势,但是将出现**两极分化**,为数不少的弱势群体将极端贫穷,一小部分人则极端富有。

六、增加连接词

The inevitable collapse of America's speculative boom would not have been especially damaging if the world's other advanced economies were healthy. (03/3)

译文: 如果世界上其他发达经济体保持良好态势,**即使**美国投机热不可避免地覆灭,**也**不会带来特别的危害。

The trouble is that other advanced economies aren't healthy. (03/3)

译文: 不过问题在于其他发达经济体并不完善。

Deflation could emerge from simultaneous slumps in the world's three major economies. (03/3)

译文: 如果全球三大经济体同时下滑,通货紧缩就会产生。

七、增加介词

今年的亚太经济贸易合作组织会议将主要侧重两个方面:一是加强亚太经合组织成员之间的合作,共同应对可能出现的经济衰退,重树信心;二是继续推进亚太经合组织贸易投资自由化进程,推动世界贸易组织尽早开始新一轮谈判。(01/9)

译文: The APEC meeting in this year will focus mainly on two aspects: one is **on** strengthening the cooperation among all the APEC members in confronting the possibly occurring economic recession with rebuilt-up confidence; the other is **on** promoting the progression of liberalization of trade and investment among all APEC members for the start of a new round of negotiations for WTO.

2003 年的春天,中华大地面临 SARS 的考验。

译文: **In** the spring of 2003, China was confronted with the trial of SARS.

八、增加强调句式

我们解决台湾问题的原则是"和平统一祖国和一国两制"。

译文: **It is** based on the guideline of "peaceful reunification and the one country, two systems" **that** we solve the Taiwan issue.

一个中国原则是实现和平统一的基础和前提。

译文: **It is** the one-China principle **that** provides the basis and prerequisite for achieving peaceful reunification.

九、增加词语，使句意更准确

Internet radio does not only mean competition but also great opportunities. (98/9)

译文: 互联网广播的出现不仅意味着竞争,同时也提供了机遇。

She was complex. (99/9)

译文: 她的思想丰富而深邃。

The Chicago company's television-manufacturing division had been large and profitable in the 1960s. (01/3)

译文: 在20世纪60年代,其在芝加哥的电视机制造分公司规模大,利润高。

From a small beginning at the turn of the century they have become a very important factor in shaping developments in higher education and the arts. (02/3)

译文: 本世纪初, 基金会数量并不多/比较少, 而现在已在高等教育和艺术发展的格局中显得举足轻重了。

According to Dr. Zhang, the patient's life is still in danger. The first aid must be rendered as soon as possible.

译文: 根据张医师**的诊断**,这位患者的生命仍然处于危险之中, 必须尽快采取急救措施。

This is a passage quoted from William Shakespeare.

译文: 这是从莎士比亚著作中引用的一段话。

深圳机场为方便旅客,设置了4间更衣室。(98/9)

译文: For the convenience of the passengers, Shenzhen Airport **Administration** set up 4 changerooms.

十、增加背景知识

If there's a threat of dangerous deflation—a general fall in prices—the causes lie as much in Europe and Japan as in the United States. (03/3)

译文: 如果全球经济中出现通货紧缩的危险信号——即消费品价格普遍下跌的现象, 那么欧洲、日本以及美国都难辞其咎。

冰冻三尺,非一日之寒。

译文1: It takes more than one cold day for the **river** to freeze three feet deep.

译文2: Rome was not built in a day.

第四节 省词译法

翻译中也存在各式各样的省词译法，省词译法可以被看作增词译法的逆推，其翻译规律也可认为是增词译法规律的逆推，即把原文中需要而译文中不需要的单词、短语甚至句型省略不译的翻译方法。我在前面的评分标准中指出，Paraphrasing Nativeness 是一个获取翻译高分的重要条件，只满足于翻译的正确是远远不够的，这种小词小句的增减就像乒乓球中的"小球技术"，才是翻译高低的真正体现，考生要加以重视，并着重培养这些技能。下面是省词译法的一些实例。

一、省略名词

The rest of the world will have to react to this millennial economic shift to Asia, and to the rising power of China. **The rest of the world** will be divided between the Euro-American countries, and the two big peripheral powers, Japan and Russia. (01/9)

译文：其他国家将不得不面对新千年吹向亚洲的经济东风和中华民族的迅速崛起。它们被划分为欧美国家及两大边缘势力国家，日本和俄罗斯。

The expansion of the universities since the beginning of World War II and the great increase in number of college graduates and Ph. D. s have produced a corps of technicians, aides, speechwriters, symbol manufacturers, investigators, and policy proposers who are now employed by **practical men** in all institutions. (03/9)

译文：第二次世界大战以来，大学的数目不断增长，本科、甚至是博士毕业生也与日俱增，从而诞生了大批的技术人员、助手、演讲稿撰写人、徽章生产商、调查人员和政策研究员，他们效力于各类务实的机构中。

Between you and me and **the post**, Jack will take over his father's business.

译文：这是咱们私下说的话，杰克将接管他老爸的公司。

他承担了莎士比亚著作的翻译任务。

译文：He undertook the translation (task) of Shakespeare's works.

我们必须进行积极的宣传工作以提高市民公共卫生的意识。

译文：We must wage a publicizing campaign (task) to raise the citizens' awareness of public health.

通过强制和高压手段，迫使他们的对手让步。

译文：Their opponent was forced to make concessions through (means of) compulsion and coercion.

二、省略代词

Although its sound quality is far from perfect, it excels **that** of short-wave. (98/9)

译文：虽然互联网广播的音质远非完善,但却胜于短波(的音质)。

One shall pay for what **one** has said.

译文：言责自负。

Let's shake hands on **it**.

译文：咱们握手为定吧。

My schoolmates had a good time, but I was not in **it**.

译文：我的同学们玩得很高兴,但我并未参加。

Some books are to be tasted, **others** to be swallowed, and some few to be chewed and digested. (Francis Bacon: *Of Studies*)

译文：书有可浅尝者,有可吞食者,少数则须咀嚼消化。

三、省略连词

I went home, **and** found the babysitter dead.

译文：我回家,发现保姆死了。

If you cheat in the exam, you will be deprived of your Bachelor's degree.

译文：你考试作弊,就会被剥夺学士学位。

四、省略分词

他晚上没洗澡就上床睡觉了。

译文：He went to bed without (having) a bath.

她这次考试没犯任何错误,拿到了奖学金。

译文：She managed to be awarded scholarship without (making) any mistakes in the exam.

五、省略形容词、副词

The pooled wisdom is superior to the wisdom of a **single** individual.

译文：集体智慧胜于个人的智慧。

Each and **every** man has a duty to guard the public health.

译文：保持公共卫生,人人有责。

My friend, whose death was **so** untimely, intended to make an experiment on musical therapy.

译文：我朋友曾打算进行音乐疗法的实验,却不幸早逝。

家长会完全符合"廉政建议"的要求,与会的家长绝不会像参加行业、单位的一些会议,先看看会议地点是不是设在风景旅游区,会后发不发纪念品之类,然后方决定是否参

加。(02/3)

译文：The parents' meeting is in full conformity with the requirements for "building an honest and clean government". Before making a decision whether to attend the meeting or not, nobody will be interested in knowing whether the meeting place is located in a tourist area and whether gifts or souvenirs will be handed out after the meeting while these factors arc commonly considered in the case of attending meetings organized by a certain trade or unit.

人群渐渐静了下来。

译文：Silence (gradually) crept up on the crowds.

六、省略介词短语

这个数码相机真是**价廉物美**。

译文：This digital camera is really cheap (in price) and fine (in quality).

七、省略句子

From then until now, dolphins have been helping swimmers who are in trouble. **Swimmers**, however, **are not the only humans they help.** (97/9)

译文：至今为止，海豚一直在帮助遇到麻烦的游泳者。不仅如此，……(接下文)

第五节　转性译法

初学翻译者经常按照原文的原始词性进行翻译，不敢轻易变换词性。有时尽管考生有大量的词语或成语，但因受词性的局限，苦无用武之地。其实转性译法不仅十分普遍，几乎每篇已考英译汉或汉译英的文章中，都或多或少存在转性译法，而且转性译法历来是翻译中最重要的手法之一，考生应明确转性译法是所有词法翻译中最重要的翻译技能，是整个翻译技能复习的重点。转性译法说到底就是根据目标语境的需要，对原文中的词性进行调整，译成不同词性的过程。已考试题中转性译法的现象比比皆是，请看下面的实例。

一、名词转译为动词

Dolphins are social animals and love **company**. (97/9)

译文：海豚是群居动物，爱结伴。

Brain size is not an absolute **measure** of intelligence. (97/9)

译文：脑容量并不能绝对衡量聪明程度。

It is important that an application form sent to a prospective applicant should request clear information about such things as the applicant's age, qualifications and work experience as well as **references** from other individuals who know the applicant well. (98/3)

译文: 因此向待选的应聘者寄发申请表,询问包括诸如年龄、资历、工作经验等简明信息并向了解应聘者情况的有关人士征求参考意见是很重要的。

To help the panel in their **selection**, an interview assessment form is often used during the interview. (98/3)

译文: 面试中经常使用面试评定表来帮助面试小组做出选择。

It's a cheap way of getting a reasonable quality signal to places in the world that even our short-wave **transmitters** can't adequately reach. (98/9)

译文: 互联网广播可以将音质不劣的信号传送到短波都无法达到的地区,且耗资少。

The appealing image of Japan the victim has **no room** for the underside of Japan the aggressor. (99/3)

译文: 日本作为战争的受害者,其乞怜形象掩盖了其侵略者的一面。

Those people whose only **experience** of Helen Keller is *The Miracle Worker* will be surprised to discover her many dimensions. (99/9)

译文: 对于那些仅仅通过《奇迹创造者》了解海伦·凯勒的人们,她各方面的性格特点将令他们大吃一惊。

They wanted to get market **share**. (01/3)

译文: 他们想分享市场。

support for the poor and the **upkeep** of exotic gardens and old mansions (02/3)

译文: 扶贫和对奇园古宅进行养护。

Think tanks and university research institutes are nonprofit organizations that have been developed to provide **settings** for experts in various academic disciplines. (02/3)

译文: 智囊团和大学中的研究机构是不同学术领域专家展示才能的非赢利性组织。

The idea of a national ID, however, was locked out of earlier drafts of legislation by a **coalition** of civil rights and ethnic groups, who opposed a requirement that all non-citizens carry identifying documents. (02/9)

译文: 然而,公民权利维护团体和少数民族结成联盟共同反对要求非美国公民必须随身携带身份证的提案,因此,最初的几次立法草案都未收录关于实施全国统一身份证的主张。

The inevitable **collapse** of America's speculative boom need not have been especially damaging if the world's other advanced economies were healthy. (03/3)

译文: 如果世界上其他发达经济体保持良好态势,即使美国投机热不可避免地覆灭,也不会带来特别的危害。

Their expanding **appetite** for imports would have bolstered the United·States and so-called emerging market countries, from Brazil to South Korea. (03/3)

译文: 那些国家热衷于进口,确实给美国和一些所谓新兴市场国家如巴西、韩国打了一针强心剂。

Deflation could emerge from simultaneous **slumps** in the world's three major economies. (03/3)

译文：如果全球三大经济体同时**下滑**，通货紧缩就会产生。

The expansion of the universities since the beginning of World War II and the great **increase** in number of college graduates and Ph. D. s have produced a corps of **technicians**, aides, speechwriters, symbol manufacturers, investigators, and policy proposers. (03/9)

译文：第二次世界大战以来，大学的数目不断**增长**，本科、甚至是博士毕业生也与日俱增，从而诞生了大批的技术人员、助手、演讲稿撰写人、徽章生产商、调查人员和政策研究员。

The project budget sustains both the **existence** of graduate students and the fiscal solvency of the university. (03/9)

译文：研究生的**存在**，大学的资金偿还能力，这些都依靠项目预算。

二、名词转译为形容词、副词

Inside these nations there will be mass **prosperity**, but with a large minority in serious **poverty**, and a small number who are very rich. (01/9)

译文：这些国家呈现出**欣欣向荣**的态势，但是将出现两极分化，为数不少的弱势群体将极端**贫穷**，一小部分人则极端富有。

Supported by foundation grants and government contracts, they are a major **source** of the new ideas that are discussed in the policy-formation groups. (02/3)

译文：有了基金会的资助和政府的合约保护，这些专家就能够为政策的制定提供**源源不断**的新思维。

Unlike the engineer, however, these professional intellectuals are free from much of the routine **grind** of daily work: they carry light teaching load and enjoy government and foundation grants and subsidies for their research. (03/9)

译文：然而这些人员与工程师还有所不同——他们不需从事**繁重**的日常工作，仅承担少量教学工作，同时享受政府研究津贴或补贴。

走发展高科技贸易之路，是历史的**必然**，也是未来的**需要**。(97/9)

译文：It is not only **indispensable** in history, but also **necessary** in the future to develop by way of promoting high-tech trade.

这所大学的任务是培养**德智体**全面发展，能熟练运用外语从事外事和文化交流工作的合格人才。(98/3)

译文：The task of this university is to train qualified personnel for foreign affairs and cultural exchange, who are **morally**, **intellectually** and **physically** qualified and have a good command of foreign languages.

虽然有关人士声称调查具有**科学性**，我仍不敢相信。(01/3)

译文：I remain suspicious of the survey, though the people concerned claimed it to be **scientific**.

三、动词转译为名词

That's why the stage **appealed** to her. (99/9)

译文：这就是为什么讲坛对她有如此的吸引力。

From a small beginning at the turn of the century they have become a very important factor in **shaping** developments in higher education and the arts. (02/3)

译文：本世纪初，基金会数量并不多/比较少，而现在已在高等教育和艺术发展的格局中显得举足轻重了。

望着病中的妈妈，我想起了1981年夏天奶奶生病的情景。(97/3)

译文：The **sight** of sick Mom reminded me of the summer of 1981 when Granny was ill.

这样，毕业生在掌握一门外语之外还具备上述专业的基础知识。(98/3)

译文：Therefore, the graduates will have a basic knowledge in those fields in addition to their **mastery** of a foreign language.

香港回归祖国 (98/9)

译文：Hong Kong's **return** to the motherland

深圳机场为方便旅客，设置了4间更衣室。(98/9)

译文：For the **convenience** of the passengers, Shenzhen Airport Administration set up 4 changerooms.

本届会议将围绕"新世纪、新挑战：参与、合作、促进共同繁荣"的主题，审议5个方面的议题，以期促进亚太地区和全球经贸的发展。(01/9)

译文：This meeting will, centering round the theme of "Meeting new challenges in the new century: achieving common prosperity through **participation** and **cooperation**", reviewing the agenda under 5 heads with a view to promoting the economic and trade development in the Asia-Pacific region and the world at large.

中国加入世贸组织后，外商参与中国西部开发的机会越来越多。(03/3)

译文：With China's **entry** into the WTO, there are more and more opportunities for foreign businessmen to join in the development of the West.

中国政府坚持实行以扩大内需为主的发展方针，并把扩大内需与调整经济结构，推动科技进步，促进对外开放结合起来。(03/9)

译文：While focusing on its policy of raising domestic demand, the Chinese government also attaches rather great importance to the **restructuring** of the economy, the **promotion** of the scientific and technological development, the **deepening** of the opening-up policy as well.

四、动词转译为形容词、副词

孝敬父母是我们中华民族的美德。(97/3)

译文: Showing **filial** respect to parents is a virtue of our Chinese nation.

五、形容词、副词转译为动词

Today the cold war is **over**. (97/3)

译文: 当今,冷战已经结束。

I believe they have it exactly **backwards**. (97/3)

译文: 我认为这些人刚好说反了。

We are determined **anew** to work for world peace. (99/3)

译文: 我们决心为世界和平继续奋斗。

When leadership attempts to keep workers in the dark, workers tend to become **distrustful**. (00/3)

译文: 如果领导层让员工蒙在鼓里,员工很难信任领导。

Prices drop because there's too **little** global demand chasing too **much** global supply—everything from steel to shoes. (03/3)

译文: 从钢铁业到鞋业,全球需求急剧萎缩,而供给却源源不断,从而/这样就会导致商品价格下跌。

妈妈多少天没有好好吃饭 ,她明显瘦了。(97/3)

译文: Having had no good meal several days running, Mom **was** obviously **thinning**.

在家长会上,家长们个个个**全神贯注**地倾听、记录,生怕漏掉一点内容。(02/3)

译文: At the parents' meeting, every parent is **concentrating** on listening and taking notes lest he or she might miss anything.

六、形容词、副词转译为名词

An organization that has open lines of communication with valid, honest information going up, down, and throughout the organization will be much more **effective** and a much better place to work in than the organization that attempts to restrict the flow of information or distort and deceive. (00/3)

译文: 如果一个企业具备公开的传播渠道,企业内部信息传播流畅、内容真实可信,比起那些试图封闭信息,歪曲甚至欺骗的企业来说,将会有更高的工作效率,更好的工作环境。

support for the **poor** and the upkeep of exotic gardens and old mansions (02/3)

译文: 扶贫和对奇园古宅进行养护

They provide a means by which wealthy people and corporations can in effect decide **how** their tax payments will be spent. (02/3)

译文：通过基金会,有钱人和大公司能实际支配缴纳税款的用途。

We already **routinely** screen people. (02/9)

译文：对人们进行甄别,在我们这儿早就是**例行公事**。

The inevitable collapse of America's speculative boom need not have been especially **damaging** if the world's other advanced economies were healthy. (03/3)

译文：如果世界上其他发达经济体保持良好态势,即使美国投机热不可避免地覆灭,也不会带来特别的**危害**。

Japan's ills are well known its banks are **awash** in bad loans. (03/3)

译文：众所周知的是,日本的症结在于银行不良贷款的冲击。

The major feature of project money, whether its source is government or business, is that it is given on a **contractual** basis. (03/9)

译文：无论来自于政府或商界,项目资金的重要特点是其建立在**契约**上。

中国人民始终希望天下太平,希望各国人民**友好**相处。(00/3)

译文：The Chinese people always seek the global peace and **friendship** among all nations.

世界各国和地区不少有远见卓识的企业家,都将目光投向了中国,投向了西部,并从投资活动中获得了丰厚的回报。(03/3)

译文：A number of entrepreneurs of **foresight** around the world have cast their eye on China, especially the west China and gained abundant profit from investment.

七、副词转译为形容词

Collectively, the Asian Countries will have a larger economy than the rest of the world put together. (01/9)

译文：亚洲国家的**整体**经济规模,将超过其他国家和地区经济规模的总和。

八、形容词转译为副词

这一目标的实现,最直接的应该是老百姓住得更**宽敞**,更**舒服**了。(02/9)

译文：The goal's direct result is that common people will live more **spaciously** and **comfortably**.

九、介词转译为动词

Many of them, in fact, even enjoy being **around** humans. (97/9)

译文：事实上,不少海豚还以与人相处为乐。

One way an organization can find staff **for** job vacancies is to recruit outside the company. (98/3)

译文：企业组织找人补充职位空缺的办法之一是外部招聘。

BBC World Service is the world's biggest radio network, **with** 140 million listeners across the globe. (98/9)

译文: 英国广播公司国际广播电台是世界上最大的广播网,在全球**拥有**1.4亿听众。

She was a tireless activist **for** racial and sexual equality. (99/9)

译文: 她是一个孜孜不倦的活动家,**呼吁**种族和男女平等。

We must avoid these stupid, short-sighted traps and constantly strive for an open communications system **with** objective information. (00/3)

译文: 我们必须告别这些愚蠢、缺乏远见的做法,并致力于建立一个公开的沟通系统,**确保**信息客观公正。

The major feature of project money, whether its source is government or business, is that it is given on a contractual basis, a different contract **for** each project. (03/9)

译文: 无论来自于政府或商界,项目资金的重要特点是其建立在契约上,即不同的项目可以**争取**不同的项目资金。

十、动词转译为介词

中国政府在实行和平统一方针的同时始终表明,以任何方式解决台湾问题是中国的内政,并无义务承诺放弃使用武力。(00/9)

译文: Adopting the policy of peaceful reunification, the Chinese government always makes it clear that it is China's internal affair to solve the Taiwan issue by whatever means and China is **under no obligation** to undertake to give up military force.

十一、动词转译为连词

在家长会上,家长们个个全神贯注地倾听、记录,**生怕漏掉一点内容**。(02/3)

译文: At the parents' meeting, every parent is concentrating on listening and taking notes **lest** he or she might miss anything.

第六节　褒贬译法

词汇按照感情色彩可分成褒义、贬义和中性。除却一些带有明显褒贬色彩的词汇外,在翻译中有时需根据词汇的感情色彩选取相应感情色彩的词汇进行翻译,这种现象称为褒贬译法。在中口翻译中,这种翻译现象并不是十分常见,考生根据常规,应能做出褒贬的判断。下面是考过的三处褒贬译法的实例:

We have an **ambitious** plan for the brand new technology of Digital Broadcasting by Satellite, due to start next year. (98/9)

译文: 我们有一项**雄心勃勃**的计划,即明年起使用全新的卫星数码技术进行广播。

The **appealing** image of Japan the victim has no room for the underside of Japan the aggressor. (99/3)

译文：日本作为战争的受害者，其乞怜形象掩盖了其侵略者的一面。

The Japanese were very **aggressive**. (01/3)

译文：日本人非常嚣张。

在上文的例子中，第一个例子选择了 ambitious 的褒义用法，但是 ambitious 也可翻译成"野心勃勃的"，如：He is claimed to be one of the most **ambitious** emperors during the history of China. 这句中的 ambitious 就解释为"野心勃勃的"。在上文第二个和第三个例子中，分别选用了 appealing 和 aggressive 的贬义用法，不过考生也应注意它们的褒义和中性的用法：an **appealing** voice→有感染力的嗓音（褒义）；**appealing** eyes→哀求的眼神（中性）；an **aggressive** salesman→积极进取的销售人员（褒义）；an **aggressive** tumor→迅速蔓延的肿瘤（中性）。

除此之外，考生还应对以下一些常见的褒贬现象加以注意，做到融会贯通。

stubborn defence→ 顽强防守（褒义）

stubborn soil→坚硬的土壤（中性）

as **stubborn** as a mule→像骡子一样顽固；顽固不化（贬义）

an active imagination→丰富的想像力（褒义）

an active volcano→活火山（中性）

an active trouble-maker→调皮的捣乱者（贬义）

As luck would have it, he was not on the spot during the 911 event. →真幸运（褒义）

As luck would have it, he got 59 in the test, a bit from passing. → 倒霉的是（贬义）

你现在在教育界很有名啊。→famous（褒义）

这个总统在政治界臭名昭著。→notorious; infamous（贬义）

由于改革开放政策，农民们过上了幸福安逸的生活。→thanks to（褒义）

由于美国经济的下滑，全球经济受到波动。→in consequence of/as a consequence of /in the aftermath of（贬义）

关于 **something/anything/nothing** 和 **somebody/anybody/nobody** 的翻译：

这些代词在翻译中十分灵活，褒贬的转换十分频繁。一般来说，somebody 和 anybody 都可表示 a person of importance；a big potato 表示重要人物，nobody 表示"小人物；无足轻重的人"。与此相应的是 something, anything 表示"重要的事"，nothing 当然就是"不重要的

事情"。请看下面的实例:

Everybody who is **anybody** has showed up in the meeting.

重量级的人士都参加了这次会议。

Chinese are liable to say the polite **nothings** when meeting with the acquaintances, which is a tradition in the Chinese culture.

中国人见到熟人时总喜欢说些**客套话**,这是中国文化的传统。

It's **something** to have a job at all these days, not to speak of a satisfactory one.

现在能找到一份工作就**不错**了,更别提找到一份满意的工作了。

Your friends are all just a bunch of **nobodies**.

你的朋友都是一伙无足轻重的人。

第三章 句法翻译

第一节 换序译法

无论从语法或修辞学的角度来说，都必须重视翻译中词序和句序的顺序。英语和汉语的词序和句序各有其特点，必须知己知彼，充分掌握这些特点，翻译时才能得心应手。

汉语是分析性的语言，既无形态变化，又少关系词。词序在决定词与词之间的关系中起着举足轻重的作用，而且具有较大的固定性，不能轻易改动。如："我到夏威夷游泳"和"我游泳到夏威夷"意思截然不同。一般说来，汉语词序与英语词序相比，前者规律性较强，变动性较小；后者规律性较弱，变动性较大。

在中口翻译的评分标准中也有 Sequence Coherency 一项，因此对考生的句序调整能力也做出了一定的要求。特别是对于长句的翻译，考生首先不应盲目地开始翻译，而应首先对句子进行断句。建议考生在句子上标上项目符号，进行句子翻译顺序的甄别，通盘考虑后，再从容下笔，这样就不会产生因句意层次判断不明而随意插入箭头，导致卷面不美观的状况。

下面请看历年考过的实例，考题上作者已经标明可供参考的翻译顺序，考生应揣摩调整的必要性。

(1) Since the company would not desire applicants who do not have a good profile, (6) it is important (4) that an application form sent (2) to a prospective applicant should request (3) clear information about such things as the applicant's age, qualifications and work experience (5) as well as references from other individuals who know the applicant well. (98/3)

译文：由于公司不会录用个人材料不佳的申请者，因此向待选的应聘者寄发申请表，询问包括诸如年龄、资历、工作经验等简明信息并向了解应聘者情况的有关人士征求参考意见是很重要的。

(1) This information assists the company's management in (3) making a final decision on those applicants (2) they can short-list for an interview. (98/3)

译文：这些信息有助于公司管理部门缩小面试人员名单以最终做出录用决定。

(1) BBC World Service is the world's biggest radio network, (2) with 140 million listeners across the globe, (4) broadcasting in 44 languages, (3) heard on short-wave, medium-wave, FM and satellite. (98/9)

译文：英国广播公司国际广播电台是世界上最大的广播网，在全球拥有1.4亿听众，通过短波、中波、调频和卫星以44种语言广播节目。

(1) An organization that has open lines of communication with valid, honest information going up, down, and throughout the organization (3) will be much more effective and a much better place to work in (2) than the organization that attempts to restrict the flow of information or distort and deceive. (00/3)

译文：如果一个企业具备公开的传播渠道，企业内部信息传播流畅、内容真实可信，比起那些试图封闭信息，歪曲甚至欺骗的企业来说，将会有更高的工作效率，更好的工作环境。

(1) But this is equally true of cultural traits, (5) which indicate clearly a person's value system (3) when crucial decisions need to be made (2) before there is any time to think about alternatives, (4) for example, diving into a flooding stream to rescue a drowning child. (00/9)

译文：文化特征何尝不是如此？有时候，人们来不及思索就必须做出关键决定，比如说跳进湍急的水流中救一个溺水儿童，那么这种情况下一个人的文化特征就清晰地折射出他的价值体系。

(1) In this way, they (4) may devote their time to the study of policy alternatives (3) free from the teaching and departmental duties (2) that are part of the daily routine for most members of the academic community. (02/3)

译文：正因为如此，这些专家就可以从大多数学术人士习以为常的日常教学和科系公务中脱离出来，全身心地投入到政策的研究中去。

(2) Identification cards already are required here (1) for most persons to enter their workplace, take an airplane flight or go into a public building, including my campus library. (02/9)

译文：在美国，现在大多数人进入工作场所，乘飞机或进入公共大楼，包括我所在大学的图书馆，已经需要出示身份证。

(4) The idea of a national ID, however, (3) was locked out of earlier drafts of legislation by (1) a coalition of civil rights and ethnic groups, (2) who opposed a requirement that all non-citizens carry identifying documents. (02/9)

译文：然而，公民权利维护团体和少数民族结成联盟共同反对要求非美国公民必须随身携带身份证的提案，因此，最初的几次立法草案都未收录关于实施全国统一身份证的主张。

(3) Prices drop (2) because there's too little global demand chasing too much global supply—(1) everything from steel to shoes. (03/3)

译文：从钢铁业到鞋业，全球需求急剧萎缩，而供给却源源不断，从而/这样就会导致商品价格下跌。

(2) The expansion of the universities (1) since the beginning of World War II and (3) the great increase in number of college graduates and Ph. D. s have produced a corps of technicians, aides, speechwriters, symbol manufacturers, investigators, and policy proposers (4) who are now employed by practical men in all institutions. (03/9)

译文：第二次世界大战以来，大学的数目不断增长，本科、甚至是博士毕业生也与日俱增，从而诞生了大批的技术人员、助手、演讲稿撰写人、徽章生产商、调查人员和政策研究员，他们效力于各类务实的机构中。

(2) These people, called intellectuals in the sense that (1) they deal with symbols and ideas, (4) have become professionalized (3) in exactly the same sense as the engineer. (03/9)

译文：这些人员主要与符号和概念打交道，所以人们把他们称为知识分子，他们已经与工程师几乎一样高度专业化。

(3)从北方来的旅客，(5)为了适应深圳的气候，(2)走下飞机的(1)第一件大事就是(4)脱掉身上过多过厚的衣服。(98/9)

译文：So first thing after landing the passengers from the north take off their extra warm clothes in order to adapt themselves to the local temperature.

(2)这一目标的实现，(1)最直接的应该是(3)老百姓(4)住得更宽敞，更舒服了。(02/9)

译文：As a direct result of the achievement of the goal, common people will enjoy larger living space and greater comfort.

许多考生在翻译形容词时，往往对形容词之间的优先顺序头疼不已。根据冯庆华《英汉翻译教程》(上海外语教育出版社)中所述，英语和汉语在处理定语修饰的词序上有着较大的不同，请考生加以明确。

英语中出现多项定语修饰同一中心词时，一般采取下列词序：

1. 冠词、指示代词、不定代词、名词所有格、序量词等充当的定语
2. 表达主观判断的定语
3. 描述客观表象的定语
4. 国别定语
5. 原材质料定语
6. 用途定语
7. 中心词

汉语中出现多项定语修饰同一中心词时，常用的词序为：

1. 限定性定语
2. 国别定语
3. 时间、地点定语
4. 数量、种类、次第等定语
5. 判断性定语
6. 陈述性定语
7. 本质性定语
8. 中心词

汉语里没有后置定语。
英语多项状语的词序一般为：

1. 条件状语 2. 目的状语
3. 主语   4. 程度状语
5. 谓语   6. 方式状语
7. 频度状语 8. 时间状语
9. 宾语

汉语多项状语的词序一般为:

1. 主语   2. 目的状语
3. 时间状语 4. 条件状语
5. 方式状语 6. 频度状语
7. 程度状语 8. 谓语
9. 宾语

第二节 定语从句译法

英国语法家 Robert Valentine 有一句名言: "Attributives are to a sentence what feathers are to a peacock. As fine feathers make a fine bird, so graceful attributives make a graceful sentence." 其意如下: 定语之于句子, 犹羽毛之于孔雀。漂亮的羽毛才能装饰成美丽的孔雀;同样,优雅的定语才能修饰出美妙的句子。**由此可见,定语和定语从句在中口翻译考试中的重要性是显而易见的。** 从定语的位置来说,有前置定语,后置定语和分隔定语;从定语从句的性质来说,可分为限制性 (restrictive) 和非限制性 (non-restrictive) 两种;从定语从句的功能而言,可译成条件从句、原因从句、结果从句、目的从句或让步从句等;就译句的形式来讲,可以根据原句的结构及上下文关系译成独立句、并列句、对立句、复合句等。

对于中口翻译的考生来说,以下四种定语从句的翻译方法是最为常见和最为重要的,考生应熟练掌握,举一反三。

一、前置法(Preposition)

一般适用于限制性定语从句,但对于一些句子较短、句意较简单的非限制性定语从句也适用。**前置法即把定语从句的部分前移到先行代词指代名词的前面,成为前置的定语,做修饰成分。** 请看下面的考题。

We all have a stake in building peace and prosperity, and in confronting threats **that** respects no borders. (97/3)

译文: 我们要致力于缔造和平与繁荣,抵御**不分国界**的诸多威胁。

From then until now, dolphins have been helping swimmers **who** are in trouble. (97/9)

译文: 至今为止,海豚一直在帮助遇到麻烦的游泳者。

Very recently, we launched "BBC On-Line", **which** incorporates a 24-hour news service.

(98/9)

译文：最近，我们开通了一条包括 24 小时新闻联播服务在内的英国广播公司联网频道。

Since the company would not desire applicants **who** do not have a good profile, it is important that an application form sent to a prospective applicant should request clear information about such things as the applicant's age, qualifications and work experience as well as references from other individuals **who** know the applicant well. (98/3)

译文：由于公司不会录用**个人材料不佳的**申请者，因此向待选的应聘者寄发申请表，询问包括诸如年龄、资历、工作经验等简明信息并向**了解应聘者情况的有关人士**征求参考意见是很重要的。

It's a cheap way of getting a reasonable quality signal to places in the world **that** even our short-wave transmitters can't adequately reach. (98/9)

译文：互联网广播可以将音质不劣的信号传送到短波都无法达到的地区，且耗资少。

Those people **whose** only experience of Helen Keller is *The Miracle Worker* will be surprised to discover her many dimensions. (99/9)

译文：对于那些仅仅通过《奇迹创造者》了解海伦·凯勒的人们，她多方面的(性格)特点会令他们感到惊奇。

My sympathies are with all **who** struggle for justice. (99/9)

译文：我的同情心是向着所有为正义而斗争的人们的。

By the middle of this century, some two thirds of the world's nation, with at least five billion people, will enjoy a standard of living, **which** only the advanced economies now have. (01/9)

译文：到本世纪中叶，世界上约三分之二的国家，至少 50 亿人口，将会过上当今发达经济体所享有的生活。

In this way, they may devote their time to the study of policy alternatives free from the teaching and departmental duties **that** are part of the daily routine for most members of the academic community. (02/3)

译文：正因为如此，这些专家就可以从大多数学术人士习以为常的日常教学和科系公务中脱离出来，全身心地投入到政策的研究中去。

中国已经发展成为一个对全球极富吸引力的大市场。(03/3)

译文：China has developed into a big market, **which** is attractive to the rest of the world.

望着病中的妈妈，我想起了 1981 年夏天奶奶生病的情景。(97/3)

译文：The sight of sick Mom reminded me of the summer of 1981 **when** Granny was ill.

旅客可以在轻松愉快的环境中更换衣服，整理仪容，给前来迎接的亲朋好友留下良好的第一印象。(98/9)

译文：The passengers can change their clothes and tidy themselves up in the easy and pleasant surroundings so as to leave a good first impression on the relatives and friends **who** come to meet them at the airport.

二、省略法(Ellipsis)

省略法即省去先行代词的翻译,直接把定语从句承接上文的翻译方法。一般有介词加先行代词的定语从句使用省略法,如 most of which, in which, where 等。

It may opt to put an advertisement in a newspaper or magazine, **which** gives a short description of the job and invites introductory letters from applicants. (98/3)

译文: 它可以选择在报纸或杂志上登广告,简要地介绍工作情况并征集应聘者的自荐信。

Foundations are tax-free institutions that are created to give grants to both individuals and nonprofit organizations for activities **that** range from education, research, and the arts to support for the poor and the upkeep of exotic gardens and old mansions. (02/3)

译文: 基金会是免税组织,其设立的目的是赞助一系列个人或非赢利性组织的活动,包括教育、调研及艺术,以及扶贫和对奇园古宅进行养护。

They provide a means **by which** wealthy people and corporations can in effect decide how their tax payments will be spent, for they are based on money **that** otherwise would go to the government in taxes. (02/3)

译文: 通过基金会,有钱人和大公司能实际支配缴纳税款的用途,因为这些税款如果不用于基金会,就会划并到政府税收中去。

Think tanks and university research institutes are nonprofit organizations **that** have been developed to provide settings for experts in various academic disciplines. (02/3)

译文: 智囊团和大学中的研究机构是非赢利性组织,为不同学术领域的专家提供了舞台。

That means that practically all Americans already must have **what** in effect is a national ID card. (02/9)

译文: 这意味着,实际上所有美国人必定早就持有事实上的全国通用的身份证。

西部大开发一定能成为沟通世界各国和中国的一座桥梁,促进中国和世界经济共同发展,共同繁荣。(03/3)

译文: The Great Western Development is sure to be a bridge between China and the rest of the world, **which** promotes the common development and prosperity of China and the world.

三、重复法(Repetition)

如果主句的句意已表达明确,不需要后面的定语从句进行补充性的说明,换言之即缺了定语从句并不影响主句的含义,那么在这种情况下,大多要用到重复法。**重复法即把先行代词指代的名词重复译出,构成并列分句的主语。**

At any rate, they make whistling, clicking and buzzing sounds **which** seem to be at least a form of language. (97/9)

译文: 不管怎么说, 它们能发出哨音、咔嗒声和嗡嗡声, 这种声音至少是一种语言形式。

On August 6, 1991, when 55,000 people gathered in Hiroshima to commemorate the 46th anniversary of the devastating bombing **that** killed an estimated 140,000 people and brought World War II to a sudden halt. (99/3)

译文: 1991年8月6日, 55000人在广岛集会, 纪念原子弹轰炸事件46周年。毁灭性的原子弹爆炸致使约14万人丧生, 平息了第二次世界大战的战火。

Usually, in Japan, when people discuss the war at all, they speak of victimization: their own victimization by the militarists **who** led the country into battle and by the Americans **who** bombed their cities. (99/3)

译文: 通常在日本, 只要一提到战争, 就会讲到受害, 讲他们是军国主义的受害者, 军国主义把国家引入战争;他们是美国的受害者, 美国向他们的城市投掷了原子弹。

But this is equally true of cultural traits, **which** indicate clearly a person's value system when crucial decisions need to be made before there is any time to think about alternatives, for example, diving into a flooding stream to rescue a drowning child. (00/9)

译文: 文化特征何尝不是如此?有时候, 人们来不及思索就必须做出关键决定, 比如说跳进湍急的水流中救一个溺水儿童, 那么这种情况下, 一个人的文化特征就清晰地折射出他的价值体系。

Foundations are tax-free institutions **that** are created to give grants to both individuals and nonprofit organizations for activities. (02/3)

译文: 基金会是免税组织, 其设立的目的是赞助一系列个人或非赢利性组织的活动。

The expansion of the universities since the beginning of World War II and the great increase in number of college graduates and Ph. D. s have produced a corps of technicians, aides, speechwriters, symbol manufacturers, investigators, and policy proposers **who** are now employed by practical men in all institutions. (03/9)

译文: 第二次世界大战以来, 大学的数目不断增长, 本科、甚至是博士毕业生也与日俱增, 从而诞生了大批的技术人员、助手、演讲稿撰写人、徽章生产商、调查人员和政策研究员, 他们效力于各类务实的机构中。

The project budget sustains both the existence of graduate students and the fiscal solvency of the university, **which** takes a percentage "overhead" out of every project budget. (03/9)

译文: 研究生的存在, 大学的资金偿还能力, 这些都依靠项目预算。大学的资金偿还在每个项目预算中都占有重要比例。

今年, 澳门又将彻底结束外国管治, 回到祖国怀抱, 这是中华民族的又一件历史盛事。(99/3)

译文: This year, Macao will completely get rid of the foreign regime and return to motherland, **which** is another great historical event for the Chinese people.

据调查,我国有 40% 的青少年除了课本以外不看其他书籍。对此,我感到极为震惊。(01/3)

译文: According to a survey, (about) 40% of the youth in our country do not read any books other than their textbooks, **which** take me by great surprise.

四、综合法(Integration)

综合法指灵活运用句子相互之间的关系,调整定语从句的位置,译成单独的分句。

To help the panel in their selection, an interview assessment form is often used during the interview **when** each applicant is checked according to a number of criteria indicated on the form. (98/3)

译文: 为了帮助面试小组做出选择,在面试中经常使用面试评定表,以根据表上的若干标准对应聘者进行考评。

The suffering inflicted by the imperial army on the peoples of Asia is ignored, **as** is Japan's aggression in China and at Pearl Harbor. (99/3)

译文: 然而他们闭口不谈皇军给亚洲人民带来的灾难,也不谈对华侵略和偷袭珍珠港。

Supported by foundation grants and government contracts, they are a major source of the new ideas **that** are discussed in the policy-formation groups. (02/3)

译文: 有了基金会的资助和政府的合约保护,这些专家就能够为政策的制定提供源源不断的新思维。

第三节 转态译法

所谓**转态译法**,就是在翻译过程中把原文中的被动语态转换成译文中的主动语态,或把原文中的主动语态转换成译文中的被动语态。对于中口翻译的考生来说,转态译法的重要性,在句法翻译中也是仅次于定语从句译法。转态译法总的原则为: 英语中被动语态使用的频率十分高,因此在汉译英时经常把主动语态译成被动语态;汉语却恰恰相反,较少使用被动句,更多地偏重主动句,因此在英译汉时,经常把被动语态译成主动语态。以下是一些常见的转态译法的技能:

一、一般译法

一般译法即把被动语态翻译成"被"字的句子结构,是最常见的处理方式。

For example, as early as 400 B. C. the Greek poet Arion **was saved** from drowning **by** a dolphin. (97/9)

译文：例如，早在公元前 400 年希腊诗人艾里昂就在溺水时被一只海豚救起。

The rest of the world **will be divided** between the Euro-American countries, and the two big peripheral powers, Japan and Russia. (01/9)

译文：它们**被划分为**欧美国家及两大边缘势力国家，日本和俄罗斯。

二、采用多种被动词

除去"被……"外，根据句子感情色彩的褒贬，考生还可**选择其他的被动表达方式**，如"受……"、"遭……"、"由……"、"给……"、"使……"、"为……所……"、"予以……"、"加以……"等。这种方法称为"**采用多种被动词法**"。

The criminal **was dealt with** according to law.

译文：罪犯**受到**了法律制裁。

Americans prefer to discipline themselves rather than **be disciplined** by others.

译文：美国人宁愿自我约束，也不愿**受**人约束。

The Chinese Olympic delegation **was** enthusiastically **welcomed** home.

译文：中国奥运代表团回国**受到**了热烈欢迎。

He **was brought to** trial by jury.

译文：他**受**陪审团审讯。

The whole world **has been infected** with a great loss due to SARS.

译文：因为 SARS 的影响，全球**遭受**很大损失。

This matter **may be left** to his own discretion.

译文：此事**由**其本人斟酌处理。

I am quite confident that bicycles **will not be sifted out** by history.

译文：我深信自行车不会**为**历史**所**淘汰。

His mispronunciation **was pointed out** by the teacher.

译文：他发音上的错误**给**老师指出来了。

The newly promulgated Constitution **must be made known** to every household and every citizen.

译文：必须**使**新宪法家喻户晓，人人皆知。

The students **must be enabled** to develop morally, intellectually and physically in an all-round way.

译文：必须**使**学生能在德智体三方面得到全面的发展。

三、省略法

省略法也是转态译法常见的技能，即不改变主语的位置，把原本被动的句子形式译成主动形式。这种方法具体还包括两种：一种为及物动词译成不及物动词。在英语中有大量动词既可作及物动词，又可作不及物动词，如 reduce, increase 等，这些动词没有必要译成

"被……"的被动语态。另外一种为处理成汉语主动形式语汇的方法。请看下面的实例：

The risk of global nuclear conflict **has been** greatly **reduced**. (97/3)

译文：全球核冲突的危险性已经大大减小了。

In some parts of the world, they can **be counted on** to help men catch fish. (97/9)

译文：不仅如此，它们还能帮助人们捕鱼。

The staff conducting an interview together **are called** an "interview panel". (98/3)

译文：主持面试的工作人员称为"面试小组"。

Foundations are tax-free institutions that **are created** to give grants to both individuals and nonprofit organizations for activities. (01/9)

译文：基金会是免税组织，其设立的目的是赞助一系列个人或非赢利性组织的活动。

Identification cards already **are required** here for most persons to enter their workplace, take an airplane flight or go into a public building, including my campus library. (02/9)

译文：在美国，现在大多数人进入工作场所，乘飞机或进入公共大楼，包括我所在大学的图书馆，已经需要出示身份证。

社会保持稳定，市场经济体制正在逐步**建立和完善**，为西部经济持续快速增长创造了有利的市场环境。(03/9)

译文：With the society enjoying a rather satisfactory stability, and the market economy system being **established and improved** on a daily basis, there appears a favourable market environment for the western region to maintain the sustained and rapid economic growth.

随着西部大开发战略的稳步推进，西部地区的资源优势，经济优势将**得到充分发挥**，经济增长的质量和水平将进一步提高。(03/9)

译文：With the stable advance in the development of the western region, the advantages of the region in resources and economy will **be given full play**, thus further improving the quality and standard of the economic growth.

四、被主交换

1. 主状交换

主状交换就是把英文中的**主语＋谓语＋状语**结构，转化成中文中的**状语＋谓语＋宾语**(原主语)的结构。

下例中＿＿＿为主语，＿＿＿为谓语，＿＿＿为状语

To help the panel in their selection, an interview assessment form is often used during the interview when each applicant is checked according to a number of criteria indicated on the form. (98/3)

译文：为了帮助面试小组做出选择，在面试中经常使用面试评定表以根据表上的若干标准对应聘者进行考评。

Movies were first made in Hollywood before WWI.

译文：一战前好莱坞首次制作了电影。

经过二十多年的快速发展，<u>中国西部地区已奠定了一定的物质技术基础</u>。(03/9)

译文：Thanks to the rapid economic development in the past 20-plus years, a relatively solid foundation in terms of material wealth and technology was laid in the western region of China.

2. 受动使动交换

受动使动交换就是把英文中的**受动者＋谓语＋（by）施动者**结构，转化成中文中的**施动者＋谓语＋受动者**的结构。

The suffering inflicted by the imperial army on the peoples of Asia **is ignored**. (99/3)

译文：然而他们闭口不谈皇军给亚洲人民带来的灾难

Both language and culture **are learned by** children without special organized programs of instruction. (00/9)

译文：儿童学习语言和文化，无需专门编制的教学计划。

The idea of a national ID, however, **was locked** out of earlier drafts of legislation by a coalition of civil rights and ethnic groups, who opposed a requirement that all non-citizens carry identifying documents. (02/9)

译文：然而，公民权利维护团体和少数民族结成联盟共同反对要求非美国公民必须随身携带身份证的提案，因此，最初的几次立法草案都未收录关于实施全国统一身份证的主张。

学生毕业考试及格并且通过论文后，即可获得学士学位。(98/3)

译文：Those who have passed the graduation examination and have written an acceptable thesis **are awarded a Bachelor's degree**.

五、形式主语法

英语中 it 作形式主语的句子，在译文中一般处理成主动形式，一般不用增加主语，如：

It is said that...→据说……

It is reported that...→据报道……

It can he asserted that...→可以断言……

It may be safely said that...→可以有把握地说……

It can be said without exaggeration that...→可以毫不夸张地说……

有时必须加上不确定的主语，如"有人"、"大家"、"人们"、"我们"等。

It is believed that...→有人（我们、人们）相信（认为）……

It is well-known that...→众所周知……

It is not uncommon that...→……时有发生

It should also be recalled, he declared, that "Japan inflicted great suffering and despair on the peoples of Asia and the Pacific during its reign of colonial domination and war. For this we are truly sorry". (99/3)

译文: 他表示人们不应忘记"日本在对亚洲和太平洋地区实行侵略和殖民统治期间，给这些地区的人民带来了苦难和绝望，为此我们深感内疚"。

众所周知，书籍是人类智慧的结晶。(01/3)

译文: **It is well known** that books are a crystallization of human wisdom.

第四节 正反译法

在翻译过程中，有时一个极其简单的词语在翻译后显得十分不自然，或与上下文搭配发生一定的阻塞，原因之一可能是需要使用正反译法。在英语中表示否定的词缀如 un-, im-, -less 等以及否定词 not, never 等，在汉语中表示否定的一些成分如"不"、"无"、"未"、"别"、"休"、"莫"、"非"、"毋"、"勿"等，以上这些成分构成了否定语气，而不含这些成分的为肯定语气。简言之，**正反译法就是把原文的肯定语气翻译成否定语气，或把原文的否定语气翻译成肯定语气的翻译方法**。请看历年的考题：

一、原文用肯定语气，译文用否定语气

In the long run, **poor** communication will undermine the entire organization. (00/3)

译文: 不良沟通从长远上讲就会危害整个企业.

But if learned **after upper adolescence** some hangover of a mother-tongue feature is very likely to persist. (00/9)

译文: 但如果成年后还没有学语言，母语的一些习惯特征就会根深蒂固。

Unlike the engineer, however, these professional intellectuals are **free from** much of the routine grind of daily work. (03/9)

译文: 然而这些人员与工程师还有所不同——他们**不需**从事繁重的日常例行工作。

二、原文用否定语气，译文用肯定语气

It is **not uncommon** to hear of dolphins giving rides through the water to humans. (97/9)

译文: 它们在水中供人乘骑之事也是**常有所闻的**。

By the early 1970s, however, high costs and a rising tide of **inexpensive** Japanese TVs were taking a heavy toll. (01/3)

译文: 但在 70 年代初，生产成本上升，而日本廉价电视机数目日趋增多，其市场份额遭受重创。

No one can drive, or fly, or enter many private and public buildings **without** a picture ID, usually a driver's license or passport. (02/9)

译文: 任何人驾车、乘飞机或进入许多私人大楼或公共大楼，都必须出示有照片的身

份证,通常是驾驶执照或护照。

虽然有关人士声称调查具有科学性,我仍**不敢相信**。(01/3)

译文: I remain **suspicious** of the survey, though the people concerned claimed it to be scientific.

三、译文肯定否定语气都能使用

No nation is **immune** to its perils. (97/3)

正译: 祸害会降临每一个国家。

反译: 没有一个国家能免遭其祸害。

Many of them, in fact, even enjoy being around humans. (97/9)

正译: 事实上,很多海豚还以与人相处为乐。

反译: 事实上,不少海豚还以与人相处为乐。

It is **easy** to understand the value and importance of **open**, **honest** communications and **valid** information. (00/3)

正译: 开诚布公的沟通和可靠的信息,它们的价值和重要性是显而易见的。

反译: 公开真诚的交流和无误信息的价值和重要性是不难理解的。

Yet, **few** organizations are able to function in this manner. (00/3)

正译: 然而很少有企业能够这样做。

反译: 然而能够做到这点的企业并不多见。

We must avoid these stupid, **short-sighted** traps and constantly strive for an open communications system with objective information. (00/3)

正译: 我们必须摆脱这些愚蠢、短浅的思想羁绊,不断地努力营造一个客观信息公开交流的系统。

正译: 我们必须告别这些愚蠢、缺乏远见的做法,并致力于建立一个公开的沟通系统,确保信息客观公正。

from a **small** beginning at the turn of the century (02/3)

正译: 本世纪初,基金会数量比较少

反译: 本世纪初,基金会数量并不多

The trouble is that other advanced economies **aren't healthy**. (03/3)

正译: 不过问题在于其他发达经济体存在弊端。

反译: 不过问题在于其他发达经济体并不完善。

其他会议都难得准时,惟有家长会绝对正点召开。(02/3)

正译: While other meetings are rarely convened on time, the parents' meeting **absolutely** starts with punctuality.

反译: While other meetings are rarely convened on time, the parents' meeting **invariably** starts with punctuality.

第五节 比较级和最高级的译法

英语的比较结构是非常复杂的，其表现形式是多样性的。就其等级而言，有原级（positive degree）、比较级（comparative degree）、最高级（superlative degree）。就其性质而言，有强化性质的比较、递增和递减性质的比较、否定性质的比较、选择性质的比较、限制性质的比较、含蓄性质的比较等。不过对于中口翻译的考生来说，在历年真题出现的比较结构都十分简单，属于比较结构的一般翻译。请看下面的实例：

The shape of the world is changing almost **as** dramatically **as** this city's skyline. (97/3)

译文：世界的面貌/格局正在发生引人注目的变化，其变化之快几乎就像这座城市的空中轮廓。

A dolphin's brain resembles a human brain, but it is **larger**. (97/9)

译文：它的大脑与人类的相似，但容量更大。

Consequently, some people claim that dolphins are really **smarter than** men. (97/9)

译文：因而有人宣称，海豚真的比人更聪明。

We're here to be able to live a life **as** full **as** any sighted person's. (99/9)

译文：我们在这个世界上能够和视力正常的人一样过上充实的生活。

That means we have the freedom to be **as** extraordinary **as** the sighted. (99/9)

译文：这意味着我们拥有和视力正常者一样的成为非凡者的自由。

Collectively, the Asian Countries will have a **larger** economy **than** the rest of the world put together. (01/9)

译文：亚洲国家的整体经济规模，将超过其他国家和地区经济规模的总和。

If there's a threat of dangerous deflation—a general fall in prices—the causes lie **as much** in Europe and Japan **as** in the United States. (03/3)

译文：如果全球经济中出现通货紧缩的危险信号——即消费品价格普遍下跌的现象，那么欧洲、日本以及美国都难辞其咎。

Germany is Europe's "sick man", just **as** Japan is Asia's. (03/3)

译文：德国是欧洲的病根，就像日本是亚洲的病根一样。

These people, called intellectuals in the sense that they deal with symbols and ideas, have become professionalized in exactly **the same** sense **as** the engineer. (03/9)

译文：这些人员主要与符号和概念打交道，所以人们把他们称为知识分子，他们已经与工程师几乎一样高度专业化。

我总以为，在中国效率最高的会议要数学校召集的家长会。(02/3)

译文：I always believe that **the most efficient** meeting in China is the parents' meeting called by the school.

用一句话来说,那便是未来老百姓的生活会更好,那时的老百姓的生活将和中等发达国家的居民一样。(02/9)

译文: In a word, the citizens will live a better life, a life of **the same** standard **as** enjoyed by those in the middle-ranked developed countries.

由于中口翻译考试的难度逐年升温,下面请考生注意以下一些比较特殊的比较级用法,做到未雨绸缪。

一、强化语势的比较

1. more than + 原级: 表示强调

She is **more than** charming and lovely.

译文: 她分外多娇。

You do me **more than** pride.

译文: 你使我感到不胜荣幸。

2. as. . . as. . . : 不仅……而且……;既……又……

Your composition is **as** concise **as** potent.

译文: 你的文章短小精悍。

3. still less = much less: 更谈不上,何况,甚至……还

For the sake of scientific research, we spare no sacrifice of life, **much less** time and energy.

译文: 为了科学研究,我们甚至不惜牺牲生命,还舍不得付出实践与精力吗?

4. far/much/considerably/appreciably/a lot/a good deal/ + 比较级: 远胜于; 远比……多

In a sense, translation is **considerably more difficult than** composition. As an English proverb goes, "a genuine translator must necessarily be 'a man of common sense'."

译文: 从某种意义上说,翻译**比**写作难得多,正如英语谚语所说的那样,"一个真正的翻译家必定是有'常识的人'。"

5. no + 比较级: 并不;一点也没有

He is **no** better after taking the pills.

译文: 他吃完药后一点也没好。

6. second to none: 比……毫不逊色;最好的

China is a highly civilized nation. She cherishes a time-honored cultural tradition. Chinese architecture is **second to none** in artistic style.

译文: 中国是一个高度文明的国家,她有历史悠久的文化传统。其建筑在艺术风格方面,与其他国家相比毫不逊色。

二、递增级和递减级

1. the more. . . the more. . . : 越……越……;愈……愈……

The more developed is industry, **the more** serious is environmental pollution.

译文: 工业越发达,环境污染越严重。

2. more. . . , less. . . : 越……,反而更……

More haste, **less** speed.

译文: 欲速则不达。

3. 最高级……最高级: 越……越……;最……最……

He who smiles **last** smiles **best**.

译文: 谁笑到最后,笑得最好。

4. all the + 比较级: 反而更……

He is suffering from insomnia. Hence, he usually takes overdose of methaqualone, and that is **all the worse** for his health.

译文: 他患失眠症,因而时常服用过量的安眠酮,但这对他的健康,反而更加不利。

5. no less than: 不但……而且……

He is **no less** proficient in astronomy **than** in geography.

译文: 他不仅精通天文,而且精通地理。

6. more than: 很……;……有余

He is **more than** a gentleman, who will give his seat to the elderly on the bus.

译文: 他很绅士,在公交车上会给老年人让座。

三、否定性质的比较

1. 比较级 + than + 原级: ……有余而……不足;有……而无……

The commander is **more** brave **than** wise.

译文: 司令官有勇无谋。

You are **more** cautious **than** decisive.

译文: 你谨慎有余而果断不足。

2. 比较级 + of + 名词 + than + 被比较的名词: 与其说……不如说……

He is **more of** a strategist **than** a statesman.

译文: 与其说他是一个政治家,不如说他是个战略家。

3. more than + 名词: 非……

His feeling is **more than** words can describe.

译文: 他的感情非语言所能描绘。

4. more than + 动词: 毫不……

He **more than** hesitated to undertake this task and expressed his firm resolution to overfulfill it ahead of time.

译文：他毫不迟疑地承担了这项任务，而且表示决心，一定要提前超额完成。

5. 否定词 + than(prep.)：并不；并非

Due to his lack of experience, he is **no more** skillful **than** Alice in practical operation.

译文：由于缺乏经验，他在实际操作方面，并不比艾丽丝熟练。

四、选择性比较和限制性比较

1. had better：最好……；以……为妙

You'd **better** look before you leap.

译文：凡事要三思而后行。

2. prefer to... rather than...：宁可……不愿……；与其……不如……；宁……毋……

The hero **preferred to** die standing **rather than** live kneeling.

译文：这位英雄宁可站着死，不愿跪着生。

3. so/as far/long as：只要

So long as my lingering gasp lasts, I will never cease studying.

译文：只要我一息尚存，就要学习不止。

第四章 历年中级口译考题翻译
部分例句精解和考点整理

（注：建议考生先做完真题练习，然后再参考真题的分析，总结译法。）

第一节 1997 年 3 月考题

TRANSLATION TEST (1) (30 minutes)

Directions: Translate the following passage into Chinese and write your version in the corresponding space in your ANSWER BOOKLET.

The shape of the world is changing almost as dramatically as this city's skyline. Today the cold war is over. The risk of the global nuclear conflict has been greatly reduced and the free flow of goods and ideas is bringing to life the concept of a global village. But just as all nations can benefit from the promise of this new world, no nation is immune to its perils. We all have a stake in building peace and prosperity, and in confronting threats that respect no borders—terrorism and drug trafficking, disease and environmental destruction.

To meet these challenges most effectively, China and the United States must act in concert. Some argue that with the Cold War's end, the strategic importance of the US-China relationship has diminished. I believe they have it exactly backwards. As a new century begins, the importance of strengthening the ties between the United States and China will grow even greater.

分析:

一、The **shape** of the world is changing almost as **dramatically** as this city's **skyline**.

译文 1: 世界的面貌/格局正在发生引人注目的变化，其变化之快几乎就像这座城市的空中轮廓。

译文 2: 世界的面貌/格局就像这座城市的空中轮廓，发生了巨大的/翻天覆地的变化。

考点: 1. shape→面貌;格局　skyline→空中轮廓;苍穹

2. 比较级的一般用法: as...as 与……一样;正如;好像

二、Today the **cold war** is over.

译文: 当今/现在/今天,冷战已经结束。

考点: 1. today 在三个翻译中,前两个属于时间虚指,适用性较大,"今天"则更多偏向于实指,在翻译中较少使用。

2. 转性译法: 副词→动词 over→结束

三、The **risk** of the global nuclear **conflict** has been greatly reduced and the free flow of goods and **ideas** is bringing to life the concept of a global village.

译文: 全球核冲突的危险性已大大减小,商品和思想/观念的自由交流正在激发/促成地球村的概念。

考点: 1. 具体译法: risk→危险性

2. 转态译法: 省略法 has been greatly reduced→大大减小

3. 抽象译法: bring to life→促成;激发

四、But just as all nations can benefit from the **promise** of this new world, no nation is immune to its **perils**.

译文1: 但是,正如世界各国会受益于这个新世界的美好前景,没有一个国家能免遭其祸害。

译文2: 但是,正如世界各国会受益于这个新世界的美好前景,祸害也会降临到每一个国家。

考点: 1. 意译: peril→危险(直译)
　　　　　　　　　→祸害(意译)

2. 正反译法: no nation is immune to its perils

五、We all **have a stake in** building peace and prosperity, and in **confronting** threats（that **respect** no borders—**terrorism** and **drug trafficking**, disease and environmental destruction.）

译文1: 缔造和平与繁荣,抵御不分国界的诸多威胁——恐怖主义、贩毒、疾病和环境破坏,这些与我们大家都有着利害关系。

译文2: 我们要致力于缔造和平与繁荣,抵御不分国界的诸多威胁——恐怖主义、贩毒、疾病和环境破坏。

考点: 1. 抽象译法: have a stake in→致力于;与……息息相关

2. confront→抵御 respect→具有

3. 定语从句的一般译法: 前置法 that respect no borders

六、To meet these challenges most effectively, China and the United States must act **in concert**.

译文: 为了最有效地迎接这些挑战,中国和美国必须协力行动/齐心协力。

七、Some **argue** that **with** the Cold War's end, the **strategic** importance of the US-China relationship has **diminished**.

译文： 有些人说，随着冷战的结束，美中关系的战略意义已经减弱了。

考点： 1. "认为"的讲法：个人一般认为→believe　　个人严肃认为→argue

外交政府认为→maintain　　外交政府宣告认为→proclaim

2. 介词 with 的翻译：基本上在句首大都翻译成"随着"。

八、I believe they have it exactly **backwards**.

译文： 我认为这些人刚好说反了。

考点： 转性译法：副词→动词　　backwards→说反了

九、**As** a new century begins, the **importance** of strengthening the **ties** between the United States and China will grow even greater.

译文： 随着新世纪的开始，加强美国和中国的联系，将具有更重要的意义。

考点： 1. 介词 as 的翻译："随着"

2. 具体译法：importance→重要性

TRANSLATION TEST（2）（30 minutes）

Directions: Translate the following passage into English and write your version in the corresponding space in your ANSWER BOOKLET.

手术室的门开了，我和爸爸急忙走进去。啊，妈妈那双炯炯有神的大眼睛紧闭着，平时红红的脸现在苍白了。

望着病中的妈妈，我想起了1981年夏天奶奶生病的情景。

那年是上海少有的炎热天气。奶奶住院了，妈妈一天要去医院好几次，晚上还要去看护奶奶。妈妈多少天没有好好吃饭，她明显瘦了。

妈妈是音乐教师，她不仅用歌声教育学生什么是爱，也用实际行动告诉我孝敬父母是我们中华民族的美德。现在妈妈病了，我一定要好好照顾她，做一个孝敬妈妈的好女儿。

分析：

一、手术室的门开了，我和爸爸急忙走进去。

译文 1： The operating room opened, and Dad and I hurried in.

译文 2： The door to the operating room opened, and Dad and I hurried in.

二、啊，妈妈那双炯炯有神的大眼睛紧闭着，平时红红的脸现在苍白了。

译文： Oh, Mom's big, bright/shining eyes were closed tight, and her normally red/ruddy face looked pale.

考点： 1. 红红的脸→ruddy face

2. 转态译法：主被交换：紧闭着→were closed tight

三、望着病中的妈妈，我想起了1981年夏天（奶奶生病的情景）。

译文 1： Looking at sick Mom, I recalled the summer of 1981 (when Granny was ill).

译文2: The sight of sick Mom reminded me of the summer of 1981 (when Granny was ill).

考点: 1. 定语从句的翻译: 前置法

2. 分词短语的翻译

3. 转性译法: 动词→名词 望着→sight

四、那年是上海少有的炎热天气。

译文: That summer was unusually/extraordinarily hot in Shanghai.

五、奶奶住院了,妈妈一天要去医院好几次,晚上还要去看护奶奶。

译文1: Granny was hospitalized. Mom went to the hospital several times a day, and in the evening she was also there looking after Granny.

译文2: Granny was in hospital. Mom went to the hospital several times a day, and in the evening she also went there to look after Granny.

六、妈妈多少天没有好好吃饭,她明显瘦了。

译文1: Having had no good meal several days running, Mom was obviously thinning.

译文2: Without a good meal for (several) consecutive days, Mom was obviously thinning.

考点: 1. 转性译法: 形容词→动词 瘦→be thinning

2. 分词短语和介词短语的转换

七、妈妈是音乐教师,她不仅用歌声教育学生什么是爱,也用实际行动告诉我孝敬父母是我们中华民族的美德。

译文1: Mom is a music teacher. She not only teaches her students what love is all about with her songs but tells me by what she does that showing filial respect to parents is a virtue of our Chinese nation.

译文2: As a music teacher, Mom not only teaches her students what love means with her songs but tells me by what she does that being dutiful to parents is a virtue of our Chinese nation.

考点: 转性译法: 动词→形容词 孝敬→filial

八、现在妈妈病了,我一定要好好照顾她,做一个孝敬妈妈的好女儿。

译文: Now that Mom is sick, I must take good care of her and perform my filial duties as a fine daughter.

考点: 转性译法: 动词→形容词 孝敬→filial

第二节 1997 年 9 月考题

TRANSLATION TEST (1) (30 minutes)

Directions: Translate the following passage into Chinese and write your version in the corresponding space in your ANSWER BOOKLET.

Dolphins, like whales, must surface to breathe air through a blowhole on top of their heads. Dolphins are social animals and love company. Many of them, in fact, even enjoy being around humans. It is not uncommon to hear of dolphins giving rides through the water to humans.

In addition to being playful, dolphins are helpful to men. For example, as early as 400 B. C. the Greek poet Arion was saved from drowning by a dolphin. From then until now, dolphins have been helping swimmers who are in trouble. Swimmers, however, are not the only humans they help. In some parts of the world, they can be counted on to help men catch fish.

Moreover, dolphins are very intelligent. A dolphin's brain resembles a human brain, but it is larger. Consequently, some people claim that dolphins are really smarter than men. Of course, there is no way of proving this point. Brain size is not an absolute measure of intelligence. Furthermore, measuring dolphins' intelligence in other ways is not possible since men cannot fully communicate with them. Apparently, however, dolphins communicate with each other. At any rate, they make whistling, clicking and buzzing sounds which seem to be at least a form of language. So far, however, men have not been able to figure out the communication code the dolphins use.

分析:

一、Dolphins, **like** whales, must **surface** to breathe air through a **blowhole** (on top of their heads).

译文: 海豚与鲸一样,需要不时浮出水面以其头顶上的鼻孔进行呼吸。

考点: 1. 转性译法: 名词→动词 surface→浮出水面

2. 介词 like 的翻译: like 一般翻译成"像……";"与……一样",表示前者与后者是两个不同的事物,只是相像而已;而 as 大多翻译成"作为……",表示前者就是后者,两者是同一个身份。

3. 介词短语的前置翻译

4. 增词译法: 如整句译为"海豚与鲸一样,需要浮出水面以其头顶上的鼻孔进行呼吸",与原文相比少了"不时",就使句子产生误解,似乎海豚需要一直浮出水面呼吸,因此"不时"就是根据常识原则翻译时新加出的词。

二、Dolphins are **social** animals and love **company**.

译文: 海豚是群居动物,爱结伴。

考点: 转性译法: 名词→动词 company→结伴

三、**Many** of **them**, in fact, even enjoy being **around** humans.

译文: 事实上,不少海豚还以与人相处为乐。

考点: 1. 代词 them 的翻译: 重复法

2. 正反译法: many→不少

3. in fact 的翻译: in fact 一般在翻译中,无论其短语位置出现在哪里,都应当提前到句首翻译。

4. 转性译法: 介词→动词   around→相处

四、It is **not uncommon** to hear of dolphins giving **rides** through the water to humans.

译文 1: 它们在水中供人乘骑之事也是常有所闻的。

译文 2: 它们在水中供人乘骑之事也不稀罕。

考点: 正反译法: 反转正 not uncommon→常有所闻

五、**In addition to** being **playful**, dolphins are helpful to men.

译文: 除了可爱逗趣之外,海豚对于人类是极有帮助的。

考点: "除了"的翻译:

1) 主句意思包括"除了"的宾语,即所谓做"加法"。此类单词、短语包括 also, as well, too, besides, moreover, in addition to, additionally

eg. Everyone showed up in the meeting in addition to Sam.

所有人包括萨姆也出席了这次会议。

2) 主句意思排除"除了"的宾语,即所谓做"减法"。此类单词、短语包括 except, but, save(prep. /conj.), saving(prep. /conj.), other than, apart from, excluding, with the exception of。

eg. Everyone showed up in the meeting except Sam.

所有人都出席了这次会议,除了山姆。

eg. We know nothing about her save that her surname is Jones.

她姓琼斯,除此之外,我们对她一无所知。

3) except/except for/except that 的区别

except for 与 except 的区别主要在于: 1) except for 能用于句首,也能用于句中;而 except 不能用于句首,只能用于句中。如: Except for the first course, the meal was excellent. 除了第一道菜,这顿饭很好。2)except for 表示强调主句,弱化 except for 后部分的涵义,强调只是美中不足或稍显遗憾。上句例句中的涵义为"这顿饭非常好,只是第一道菜差一点",句子总体强调饭非常的好,流露出"如果第一道菜好就完美了"的意思。3)except that 和前两者都不同,后跟从句。如: She remembered nothing about him except that his hair was black.

六、For example, as early as 400 **B. C.** the Greek poet **Arion** was saved from **drowning** by a dolphin.

译文 1: 例如,早在公元前 400 年希腊诗人艾里昂就在溺水时被一头海豚救起。

译文 2: 例如,早在公元前 400 年一头海豚救起了溺水的希腊诗人艾里昂。

考点: 1. 公元前→B. C. 公元后→A. D. 史前的→prehistoric

2. 人名的译法: 1)一般人名译法→只需根据音译即可,只要音大致对就行,切忌不翻。如: Christina→克里斯蒂娜,Timothy→蒂莫西

2）特殊人名译法→必须音对字对。如 Shakespeare→莎士比亚，
Mark Twain→马克·吐温

3）英美人名构造: 如: John Davison Rockefeller
第一个名　　中间名　　姓(最后的名)
first name　　middle name　　surname
given name　　　　　　　　family name
Christian name　　　　　　　clan name

4）中文人名构造:
- 两字人名姓和名首字母大写 王刚→Wang Gang
- 三字人名姓和第一个名首字母大写 张驰新 Zhang Chixin

　　3. 转态译法: the Greek poet Arion was saved from drowning by a dolphin→希腊诗人艾里昂就在溺水时被一头海豚救起

七、**From then until now**, dolphins have been helping swimmers (who are in trouble).

译文: 至今为止,海豚一直在帮助遇到麻烦的游泳者。

考点: 定语从句的翻译: 前置法

八、Swimmers, **however**, are not the only humans they help.

译文: 不仅如此,

考点: 1. 省词译法: 如把这句话再次译为"海顿不仅帮助游泳者",就和上文的意思重复了,因此不必重复译出,只需翻译 however 即可。

　　　　2. 连词的语境翻译: however→不仅如此
许多考生看到 however,不假思索的翻译成"但是",其实这里 however 和后面的 only 提示我们是递进关系,而不是转折关系。因此在翻译连词时,一定要首先判断句义的关系,然后选择相关的连词来表达,且不能望文生义。有时语境中的连词涵义和其基本意思有很大的差别,考生应当注意。

九、In some parts of the world, they can be counted on to help men catch fish.

译文1: (不仅如此,)它们还能帮助人们捕鱼。

译文2: (不仅如此,)人们还能依靠海豚捕鱼。

考点: 转态译法: 省略被动词

十、Moreover, dolphins are very intelligent.

译文: 更有甚者/不仅如此,海豚智力发达/非常聪明。

十一、A dolphin's brain **resembles** a human brain, but it is larger.

译文: 它的大脑与人类的相似,但容量更大。

考点: 比较级的基本翻译

十二、Consequently, some people **claim** that dolphins are really **smarter** than men.

译文: 因而有人宣称,海豚真的比人更聪明。

考点: 比较级的基本翻译

十三、Of course, there is no way of proving this point.

译文 1：当然，现在没法证明这一点。

译文 2：当然，这一点尚无定论。

考点：具体译法：成语法

十四、Brain **size** is not an absolute **measure** of intelligence.

译文 1：脑容量并不是一个决定聪明程度的检测标准。

译文 2：脑容量并不能绝对衡量聪明程度。

考点：转性译法：名词→动词 measure→衡量

十五、Furthermore, measuring dolphins' intelligence in other ways is not possible **since** men cannot fully communicate with them.

译文：还有，由于人们无法完全同海豚进行交流，也就不可能用其他方法测定它们的智力。

十六、Apparently, **however**, dolphins communicate with each other.

译文 1：然而，海豚与海豚之间显然能进行交流。

译文 2：然而，海豚之间显然能相互进行交流。

十七、**At any rate**, they make **whistling, clicking** and **buzzing** sounds（which seem to be at least a form of language）.

译文：不管怎么说，它们能发出哨音、咔嗒声和嗡嗡声，这种声音至少是一种语言形式。

考点：1. 象声词的翻译：先明确动词主语，然后想像其发出声音，加上"……声"。先补充以下常考象声词：

tick→钟表→嘀嗒声 　　　　　　　boom→炮火；海浪→隆隆声

rustle→树叶；风→沙沙声；瑟瑟声　drone→飞机；蜜蜂→嗡嗡声

2. 定语从句的翻译：重复法

十八、**So far**, however, men have not been able to **figure out** the communication code the dolphins use.

译文：但是，迄今为止人们尚不能解译/破译海豚语言交流的密码。

考点：意译：figure out→解译；破译 如让考生在以下选项中选择 figure out 的涵义

a）解释 　　　　　　　　　b）理解

c）解译 　　　　　　　　　d）破译

其中 c 和 d 还是比较贴切的，因为"解释"、"理解"和"密码"的搭配都不是很通顺，因此短语的选择应满足宾语的搭配。

TRANSLATION TEST (2) (30 minutes)

Directions: Translate the following passage into English and write your version in the corresponding space in your ANSWER BOOKLET.

每年春季，数以万计的中外客商云集申城，参加一年一度的华东出口商品交易会。上海各类商品在这里与全国各地一比短长。上海的优势在于科技实力，因此高技术产品的出口应成为上海外贸出口增长的"排头兵"。

著名物理学家杨振宁教授曾说："高科技战场是中国超越发达国家的主战场，也是最后的战场。"走发展高科技贸易之路，是历史的必然，也是未来的需要。

分析：

一、每年春季，数以万计的中外客商云集申城，参加一年一度的华东出口商品交易会。

译文： Every spring tens of thousands of domestic and foreign businessmen swarm into Shanghai to attend the annual East China Export Commodity Trade Fair.

考点： 1. 数字的虚指：

数以万◎计→tens ★ of thousands ☆ of

翻译原则：★×☆＝◎ 以此类推

数以十万计→hundreds of thousands of　　数以百万计→millions of

数以千万计→tens of millions of　　数以亿计→hundreds of millions of

数以十亿计→billions of　　数以百亿计→tens of billions of

数以千亿计→hundreds of billions of　　数以兆计→trillions of

数以千兆计→quadrillions of　　数以百万兆→quintillions of

2. annual→每年一度；　　biannual→每年两次；

biennial→每两年一度　　triennial→每三年一度

quadrennial→每四年一次　　centennial→百年一度；

bicentennial→两百年一度

3. "会"的翻译：

交易会→ trade fair　　展览会→exhibition

博览会→exposition　　世博会→World Expo

拍卖会→auction　　欢迎会→welcome party

欢送会→bid-well/send-off party　　庆功会→celebration

表彰会→commendation meeting　　演唱会→vocal concert/musical show

音乐会→concert　　运动会→sports meet(ing)

家长会→parents' meeting　　推介会→promotion meeting

筹备会→preparatory meeting　　非正式会议→unofficial meeting

全体会议→plenary meeting　　小组会议→group meeting

秘密会议→secret/private session　　圆桌会议→round-table conference

最高级会议→summit meeting/conference

二、上海各类商品在这里与全国各地一比短长。

译文： Here, all kinds of/various goods/commodities from Shanghai compete with the goods from other places in China.

三、上海的优势在于科技实力，因此高技术产品的出口应成为上海外贸出口增长的"排头兵"。

译文 1: The export of high-tech products that demonstrate the city's advanced scientific and technological strength should take the lead in increasing Shanghai's foreign export volume.

译文 2: The export of high-tech products that demonstrate the city's advanced scientific and technological strength should be the avant-garde in increasing Shanghai's foreign export volume.

考点: 1. 转性译法: 名词→形容词　优势→advanced

　　　　2. 意译: 排头兵→take the lead/be the avant-garde

四、著名物理学家杨振宁教授曾说: "高科技战场是中国超越发达国家的主战场，也是最后的战场。"

译文 1: Professor Yang Zhenning, a famous physicist, once said, "The high-tech battlefield is the main and the last battlefield for China to overtake the developed countries."

译文 2: Professor Yang Zhenning, a famous physicist, once said, "The high-tech arena is the main and the last arena for China to catch up with and surpass the developed countries."

考点: 1. 头衔称号的排列顺序: 名姓之前为爵号,爵号之前为学衔,学衔之前为职称,其余部分作为主语同位语置于名字之后。如:

　　　Professor Doctor Sir Arthur Quiller-Conch, a well-known humanist

　　　　↓　　　↓　　　↓　　　　↓　　　　　　　　　↓

　　　职称　学衔　爵号　　名字　　　　　　　其余部分

　　　　2. 意译: 战场→arena

五、走发展高科技贸易之路,是历史的必然,也是未来的需要。

译文 1: It is not only indispensable in history, but also necessary in the future to develop by way of promoting high-tech trade.

译文 2: It is not only indispensable in history, but also necessary in the future to adopt the way of developing high-tech trade.

考点: 转性译法: 名词→形容词　必然→indispensable,需要→necessary

第三节　1998 年 3 月考题

TRANSLATION TEST (1) (30 minutes)

Directions: Translate the following passage into Chinese and write your version in the corresponding space in your ANSWER BOOKLET.

One way an organization can find staff for job vacancies is to recruit outside the company. It may opt to put an advertisement in a newspaper or magazine, which gives a short description of the job and invites introductory letters from applicants. Since the company would not desire applicants who do not have a good profile, it is important that an application form sent to a prospective applicant should request clear information about such things as the applicant's age, qualifications and work experience as well as references from other individuals who know the applicant well. This information assists the company's management in making a final decision on those applicants they can short-list for an interview.

The staff conducting an interview together are called an "interview panel", who, prior to the interview, carefully review the job descriptions, personnel specifications, and applications. To help the panel in their selection, an interview assessment form is often used during the interview when each applicant is checked according to a number of criteria indicated on the form.

分析:

一、**One way** an organization can find **staff for** job vacancies is to **recruit** outside the company.

译文 1: 企业组织找人补充职位空缺的办法之一是向公司以外招聘。

译文 2: 企业组织找人补充职位空缺的办法之一是外部招聘。

考点: 1. 转性译法: 介词→动词 for→补充

2. one way 的翻译: 通常先翻译后面的部分, 后加 "……办法之一"。

3. staff 原本解释 "员工", 但如翻译成 "找员工补充职位空缺", 就自相矛盾了, 既然已经是员工了, 怎么还会去补充职位空缺呢? 除非是内部举荐, 那么和后面的外部招聘就矛盾了。因此把 staff 翻译成 "人"。

二、It may opt to put an advertisement in a newspaper or magazine, (which gives a short description of the job and **invites** introductory letters from applicants).

译文: 它可以选择在报纸或杂志上登广告, 简要地介绍工作情况并征集应聘者的自荐信。

考点: 1. 定语从句的翻译: 省略法

2. 意译: invite→征集

3. introductory letter 解释为 "自荐信", 而不是 "介绍信", 后者翻译成 recommendation letter, 相当于 "推荐信"。

三、(1) Since the company would not **desire** applicants (who do not have a good **profile**), (6) it is important (4) that an application form (sent (2) to a **prospective** applicant) should request (3) clear information about such things as the applicant's age, **qualifications** and work experience (5) as well as **references** from **other individuals** (who know the applicant well).

译文: 由于公司不会录用个人材料不佳的申请者, 因此向待选的应聘者寄发申请表, 询问包括诸如年龄、资历、工作经验等简明信息并向了解应聘者情况的有关人士征求参考意见是很重要的。

考点： 1. 换序译法：这是句相当复杂的句子，明确主句是 It is important...，这个句式一般在翻译中最后翻，明确主语是 an application form，主动词为 request，宾语为 clear information。这样整个翻译句序应为(1)(2)(3)(4)(5)(6)。

2. 定语从句的翻译：其中有三句定语从句，第一句和第三句都使用了前置法，第二句处理成综合法。

3. desire→录用，other individuals→有关人士

4. 转性译法：名词→动词　references→向……征求意见

四、This information **assists** the company's **management** in making a final decision on those applicants (they can short-list) for an interview.

译文： 这些信息有助于公司管理部门缩小面试人员名单以最终做出录用决定。

考点： 1. 具体译法：management→管理层

2. 定语从句的翻译：综合法

3. 换序译法：按照英文句序应先翻译"做出最终决定"，后译"缩小面试人员"，这样的话其实逻辑顺序相反。"缩小面试人员"为手段，应先翻译，而"做出最终决定"为目的的，应后翻译。所以应调整翻译的句序。

五、The staff (conducting an interview) together are called an "interview panel", (who, **prior to** the interview, carefully **review** the **job descriptions, personnel specifications**, and **applications**).

译文： 主持面试的工作人员称为"面试小组"，他们在面试之前要仔细审阅职位描述、招聘条件和应聘简历。

考点： 1. 具体译法：job descriptions→职位描述

personnel specifications→招聘条件

applications→应聘简历

2. 定语从句的翻译：重复法

3. 转态译法：省略被动词：are called→称为

六、To help the panel in their **selection**, an interview **assessment form** is often used during the interview (when each applicant is checked according to **a number of criteria** indicated on the form).

译文： 为了帮助面试小组做出选择，在面试中经常使用面试评定表以根据表上的若干标准对应聘者进行考评。

考点： 1. 转性译法：名词→动词 selection→做出选择

2. 转态译法：被主交换 is often used→经常使用，is checked→进行考评

3. 定语从句的翻译：综合法 when each applicant...

4. a number of→若干

5. criteria 的单数为 criterion。-ion 结尾的词复数大都为 -ia

TRANSLATION TEST (2) (30 minutes)

Directions: Translate the following passage into English and write your version in the corresponding space in your ANSWER BOOKLET.

这所大学的任务是培养德智体全面发展，能熟练运用外语从事外事和文化交流工作的合格人才。本科生分四年制和五年制两种，学生毕业考试及格并且通过论文后，即可获得学士学位。通用语种的学生，在能熟练使用外语后，还要接受诸如外事翻译、语言学、文学、新闻、国际文化交流等方面的专业训练。这样，毕业生在掌握一门外语之外还具备上述专业的基础知识。

分析:

一、这所大学的任务是培养德智体全面发展，能熟练运用外语从事外事和文化交流工作的合格人才。

译文 1: The task of this university is to train qualified personnel for foreign affairs and cultural exchange, (who are morally, intellectually and physically qualified and have a good command of foreign languages).

译文 2: The objective of the university is to cultivate qualified personnel/human resources who are morally, intellectually and physically qualified for foreign affairs and cultural exchange with proficient use of English.

考点: 1. 换序译法: 如上图分析，＿＿＿是句子的主语，＿＿＿是句子的谓语，＿＿＿是句子的宾语，( )里是句子的定语，明确以上部分的架构后，采分点就被清晰地体现出来，考生不必因不会翻译"德智体"或"外事"等词汇而哀叹不已了。

     2. 转性译法: 名词→副词 德智体→morally, intellectually and physically

二、本科生分四年制和五年制两种，学生毕业考试及格并且通过论文后，即可获得学士学位。

译文 1: It has both 4-year and 5-year undergraduates programs. Those who have passed the graduation examination and have written an acceptable thesis are awarded/given a Bachelor's degree.

译文 2: Undergraduate program lengths vary from 4 years to 5 years. The undergraduates are awarded a Bachelor's degree after passing the graduation examination and accomplishing a thesis.

考点: 1. 具体译法: 本科生→本科生(学习)→undergraduate study

     2. 转态译法: 主被交换: 获得学士学位→be awarded a Bachelor's degree，如翻译成 get a Bachelor's degree，在词汇部分不会扣分，而在 paraphrasing nativeness 上就要被扣去 1 分，因为"拿学位"不能主动。

三、通用语种的学生，在能熟练使用外语后，还要接受诸如外事翻译、语言学、文学、新闻、国际文化交流等方面的专业训练。

译文: Students of commonly used foreign languages, after acquiring the ability to use language efficiently, receive special training in such fields as foreign affairs translation, linguistics, literature, journalism, intercultural communication.

考点: 1. 专业名词的翻译:

通用语种→commonly used foreign languages   语言学→linguistic

文学→literature   新闻→journalism

国际文化交流→intercultural communication

这句句子集中了大量的专业名词,专业名词在评分中十分严格,稍有不同就算失分。考生应注意平时对专业语汇的积累,这是翻译技能不能补救的。

2. 增词译法:在能熟练使用外语后→after acquiring the ability to use language efficiently,其中 ability 是在翻译中新增的词汇。

3. "等等"的翻译:"等等"在中级翻译中最好处理成 and so on,不要写简写形式 etc.。这里因为使用了 such as,可省略不译。

四、这样,毕业生在掌握一门外语之外还具备上述专业的基础知识。

译文 1: So that the graduates will have a basic knowledge in those fields in addition to their mastery of a foreign language.

译文 2: Therefore, the graduates will have a basic knowledge in those fields in addition to their mastery of a foreign language.

考点: 转性译法:动词→名词   掌握→mastery

第四节   1998 年 9 月考题

TRANSLATION TEST (1) (30 minutes)

Directions: Translate the following passage into Chinese and write your version in the corresponding space in your ANSWER BOOKLET.

BBC World Service is the world's biggest radio network, with 140 million listeners across the globe, broadcasting in 44 languages, heard on short-wave, medium-wave, FM and satellite. We have an ambitious plan for the brand new technology of Digital Broadcasting by Satellite, due to start next year. The appearance of the Internet has taken us broadcasters all by surprise. The Internet has enabled any radio station anywhere to become an international broadcaster with only a minor investment. Although its sound quality is far from perfect, it excels that of short-wave. Internet radio does not only mean competition but also great opportunities. The BBC is taking the Internet very seriously, for it's a cheap way of getting a reasonable quality signal to places in the world that even our short-wave transmitters can't adequately reach. Very recently, we launched

"BBC On-Line", which incorporates a 24-hour news service. And the users can hear programmes in Mandarin, Arabic, Spanish and Russian.

分析:

一、BBC World **Service** is the world's biggest radio network, **with** 140 million listeners across the globe, broadcasting in 44 languages, heard on **short-wave, medium-wave, FM** and satellite.

译文： 英国广播公司国际广播电台是世界上最大的广播网，在全球拥有 1.4 亿听众，通过短波、中波、调频和卫星以 44 种语言广播节目。

考点： 1. service 一词多义：许多学生看到 service 马上先想到"服务"，这种条件反射是要不得的，况且 service 在中口笔试中经常不解释为"服务"。考生需要掌握 service 的大致用法如下：

1）供职（如在军队、政府、公司）

eg. He retired after many years of faithful service to the company.
他在这公司效力多年，直到退休。

2）政府机构或公务部门

eg. National Health Service→国家卫生局
the Civil Service→政府的文职机构

3）帮助；贡献（pl.）

eg. You did me a great service by showing me around the campus.
你带我看了一下校园，这对我是很大帮助。

eg. Her services to the community have been tremendous.
她对社区的贡献很大。

4）（商业）服务行业（供给、但不生产产品）

eg. Banking and insurance services→银行和保险业务

eg. The tertiary industry is mainly composed of the service industry.
第三产业主要是由服务行业构成。

此处 service 选取了第二个意思。

2. 转性译法：介词→动词 with→拥有

3. 转态译法：被主转换 heard on→通过……广播

4. 换序译法：本来 broadcasting in 44 languages 在前面，应先翻译，不过由于"通过短波、中波、调频和卫星"句子较长，因此把"以 44 种语言广播"置于后面进行翻译。

二、We have an **ambitious** plan for the **brand new** technology of Digital Broadcasting by Satellite, due to start next year.

译文： 我们有一项雄心勃勃的计划，即明年起使用全新的卫星数码技术进行广播。

考点： 1. 褒贬译法：ambitious→雄心勃勃的

2. due to 在这里不再解释为"由于"，而相当于 about to。

3. brand new = completely new

4. 转性译法：介词→动词　　for→使用

三、The appearance of the Internet has taken us broadcasters all by surprise.

译文： 国际互联网的出现使我们(广播人)措手不及。

考点： 1. us 和 broadcasters 为同位语。

2. 具体译法：take...by surprise→使……措手不及

四、The Internet has enabled any radio station anywhere to become an international broadcaster with only a **minor** investment.

译文： 国际互联网可以使位于世界任何一个地方的广播电台以很小的投资便可成为一家国际广播站。

考点： 换序译法：with only a minor investment 介词短语应置于 to 短语前进行翻译。

五、Although its sound quality is far from perfect, it **excels** that of short-wave.

译文： 虽然互联网广播的音质远非完善，但却胜于短波。

考点： 省词译法：it excels that of short-wave→但却胜于短波(的音质)

六、Internet radio does not only mean competition but also great opportunities.

译文 1： 互联网电台的出现不仅意味着竞争，同时也意味着机会。

译文 2： 互联网电台的出现不仅意味着竞争，同时也提供了机遇。

考点： 增词译法：Internet radio→互联网电台的出现

　　　　　　but also 后省略了动词 mean，在翻译中应补齐。

七、The BBC is taking the Internet very seriously, **for** it's a cheap way of getting a **reasonable** quality signal to places in the world (that even our short-wave **transmitters** can't adequately reach).

译文： 英国广播公司非常认真地对待互联网广播一事，因为互联网广播可以将音质不劣的信号传送到短波都无法达到的地区，且耗资少。

考点： 1. 意译：reasonable quality→音质不劣

2. 定语从句的翻译：前置法

3. 转性译法：名词→动词　　transmitters→传送

如翻译成"将音质不劣的信号传送到短波传输器都无法达到的地区"，那么就发生误解，因为不是短波传输器移动，而是短波移动，这句话极易造成考生的误译。因此必须采取转性译法。

八、Very recently, we launched "BBC **On-Line**", which **incorporates** a 24-hour news **service**.

译文： 最近，我们开通了一条包括 24 小时新闻联播(服务)在内的英国广播公司联网/在线(频道)。

考点： 1. 定语从句的翻译：前置法

2. service 的翻译: 取了前面讲过的第四个含义→服务(部门)

九、And the users can hear programmes in **Mandarin**, Arabic, Spanish and Russian.

译文: 用户可以收听到汉语、阿拉伯语、西班牙语和俄语的广播节目。

考点: 换序译法: in 短语应提前翻译

TRANSLATION TEST（2）(30 minutes)

Directions: Translate the following passage into English and write your version in the corresponding space in your ANSWER BOOKLET.

深圳作为全国最早的特区，与内地经济往来极为密切，特别是在香港回归祖国以后，人员往来大为增加，深圳机场是全国十大机场之一。由于深圳地处亚热带，与北方温差较大，从北方来的旅客，为了适应深圳的气候，走下飞机的第一件大事就是脱掉身上过多过厚的衣服。

深圳机场为方便旅客，设置了4间更衣室。室内设备齐全。旅客可以在轻松愉快的环境中更换衣服，整理仪容，给前来迎接的亲朋好友留下良好的第一印象。

分析:

一、深圳作为全国最早的特区，与内地经济往来极为密切。

译文: As the nation's earliest (established) special economic zone, Shenzhen has very close economic contacts with the innerland provinces.

考点: 1. "作为"的译法: 一般用 as 去翻译。如: Make yourself at home and treat me as a friend. 这里必须用 as，如用 like，解释为"好像"，语义效果极差，似乎我"像"一个朋友，而不是一个真正的朋友。

   - 注意翻译"作为"时，如果后跟"一个"，在翻译成英语时别忘了用 one of ...，结尾别忘了加复数，当然如原文中的最高级，自然不必加。
   - as 作为介词翻译时，考生切忌都翻译成"作为"。下面两个例句从形式上分析，考生容易翻译成"作为"，但细想下都有另外的涵义。
   1) As her private secretary, he has access to all her correspondence.
      由于他是她的私人秘书，他有机会接触她所有的信件。
   2) As a child, she was sent to seven different schools.
      (当)她小时候曾上过七所不同的学校。

   2. 增词译法: 特区→special economic zone 这里的特区其实是指"经济特区"，因此补充 economic。

二、特别是在香港回归祖国以后，人员往来大为增加，深圳机场是全国十大机场之一。

译文 1: Especially after the returning of Hong Kong to the motherland, the number of passengers coming to and leaving Shenzhen is increasing rapidly. Shenzhen Airport claims to be one of the ten largest airports in the country.

译文 2: Especially after Hong Kong's return to the motherland, there is a dramatical increase in the number of passengers coming to and leaving Shenzhen. Shenzhen Airport claims to be one of the ten largest airports in the country.

考点: 转性译法: 回归祖国→return to the motherland, 一些词既可以做名词也可以作动词, 翻译时形式可以灵活一点, 根据需要处理成动词或名词, 如"回归"、"加入"、"反对"等。请看下面的例子: 1) China's entry into the WTO; 2) China's objection to USA's interference in other countries' internal affairs.

三、由于深圳地处亚热带, 与北方温差较大。

译文: Since Shenzhen is located in the subtropical zone, there exists quite big temperature difference between the city and northern areas in China.

考点: 专有名词的翻译: 对于专有名词的翻译, 考生应在考前积累相关十大场景的词汇和句型。在实战考试时如遇到专有名词不会翻译, 应立即放弃, 不要苦思冥想, 浪费时间。因为专有名词在判卷时是十分严格的, 有绝对的讲法, 不存在 paraphrase 的可能性, 因此不能翻译不必勉强, 最多扣去词汇的 1 分。

相关词汇:

热带→tropical/torrid zone 亚热带→subtropical/subtorrid zone

温带→temperate zone 北温带→the north temperate zone

南温带→the south temperate zone 寒带→frigid zone

亚寒带→subfrigid zone 半球→hemisphere

南极→South Pole 北极→North Pole

南极圈→Antarctic Circle 北极圈→Arctic Circle

经度→longitude 纬度→latitude

海拔高度→altitude 北回归线→Tropic of Cancer

南回归线→Tropic of Capricorn 本初子午线→prime meridian

四、从北方来的旅客, 为了适应深圳的气候, 走下飞机的第一件大事就是脱掉身上过多过厚的衣服。

译文: So first thing after landing the passengers from the north take off their extra warm clothes in order to adapt themselves to the local temperature.

考点: 1. 换序译法: 翻译句序: 1)第一件大事 2)走下飞机 3)从北方来的旅客 4)脱掉身上过多过厚的衣服 5)为了适应深圳的气候

2. 意译: 过多过厚→extra warm clothes

3. 非专有名词的翻译: 和前面专有名词的翻译不同, 考生在实战中如遇到陌生的非专有名词, 千万不要轻易放弃, 因为非专有名词并不只有惟一的讲法, 大可用自己的方式试着去解释翻译一下, 如上文中"过多过厚的衣服", 这种语汇考生可能不熟悉, 但根据字面意思可 paraphrase 成"重、麻烦"的意思, 可用 heavy and cumbersome 去翻译, 也得到了词汇部分的分数。

五、深圳机场为方便旅客，设置了4间更衣室。室内设备齐全。

译文： For the convenience of the passengers, Shenzhen Airport (Administration) set up 4 well-furnished changerooms.

考点： 1. 转性译法：动词→名词　方便→convenience

　　　　2. 换序译法："设备齐全"译成 well-furnished，修饰前面的更衣室。

六、旅客可以在轻松愉快的环境中更换衣服，整理仪容，给（前来迎接）的亲朋好友留下良好的第一印象。

译文： The passengers can change their clothes and tidy themselves up in the easy and pleasant surroundings so as to leave a good first impression on the relatives and friends who come to meet them at the airport.

考点： 定语从句的翻译：前置法

第五节　1999年3月考题

TRANSLATION TEST（1）（30 minutes）

Directions: Translate the following passage into Chinese and write your version in the corresponding space in your ANSWER BOOKLET.

On August 6, 1991, when 55,000 people gathered in Hiroshima to commemorate the 46th anniversary of the devastating bombing that killed an estimated 140,000 people and brought World War II to a sudden halt, the city's newly elected mayor broke with tradition by adding a few uncustomary lines to the annual Peace Declaration. It should also be recalled, he declared, that "Japan inflicted great suffering and despair on the peoples of Asia and the Pacific during its reign of colonial domination and war. For this we are truly sorry." Noting that this year marks the 50th anniversary of the Japanese assault on the U. S., he added, "Remembering all too well the horror of this war, starting with the attack on Pearl Harbor and ending with the atom-bombings of Hiroshima and Nagasaki, we are determined anew to work for world peace."

Usually, in Japan, when people discuss the war at all, they speak of victimization: their own victimization by the militarists who led the country into battle and by the Americans who bombed their cities. The suffering inflicted by the imperial army on the peoples of Asia is ignored, as is Japan's aggression in China and at Pearl Harbor. The appealing image of Japan the victim has no room for the underside of Japan the aggressor.

分析：

一、On August 6, 1991, when 55,000 people gathered in **Hiroshima** to **commemorate** the 46th **anniversary** of the **devastating** bombing （that killed an **estimated** 140,000 people） and brought World War II to a sudden **halt**, the city's newly elected mayor **broke with** tradition by adding a few **uncustomary lines** to the annual Peace Declaration.

译文1: 1991年8月6日，55000人在广岛集会，纪念原子弹（轰炸）事件46周年。毁灭性的原子弹致使约14万人丧生，平息了第二次世界大战的战火。广岛市新当选的市长打破传统，在年度《和平宣言》中增加了不寻常内容。

译文2: 1991年8月6日，55000人在广岛集会，纪念原子弹（轰炸）事件46周年。毁灭性的原子弹致使约14万人丧生，同时也使第二次世界大战戛然而止。集会上，广岛市新当选的市长打破传统，在年度《和平宣言》中增加了一些非同寻常的话语。

考点: 1. 时间日期的翻译: 英语中对于日期的常见处理方式为 month date, year 或 date month, year。如 Aug 6, 1998，也可写成 Aug 6th, 1998，但前者较简便，建议使用。

2. 地名的翻译: 和人名一样，一般地名只需要音译即可，如 Gambia→冈比亚，但是绝大多数情况出现的是耳熟能详的地名，考生一般一定知道，但此句中 Hiroshima→广岛的翻译，应该说是超过了一般考生的知识范围。

3. 定语从句的翻译: 省略法

4. 转性译法: 名词→动词   halt→平息

二、It should also be recalled, he declared, that "Japan **inflicted** great suffering and **despair on** the **peoples** of Asia and the Pacific during its reign of **colonial** domination and **war**. For this we are truly sorry."

译文1: 他表示人们不应忘记"日本在对亚洲和太平洋地区实行侵略和殖民统治期间，给这些地区的人民带来了苦难和绝望，为此我们深感内疚"。

译文2: 他表示人们不应忘记"日本在对亚洲和太平洋地区实行殖民统治和战争期间，给这些地区的人民带来了痛苦和绝望，为此我们深感内疚"。

考点: 1. 转态译法: 形式主语法 It should also be recalled→人们不应忘记

2. 意译: war→侵略

三、Noting that this year marks the 50th anniversary of the Japanese **assault** on the U. S., He added, "Remembering all too well the **horror** of this war, starting with the attack on Pearl Harbor and ending with the atom-bombings of Hiroshima and **Nagasaki**, we are determined **anew** to work for world peace."

译文: 谈及50年前日本袭击美国事件，他补充道："从日本偷袭珍珠港开始，到广岛、长崎原子弹爆炸告终，可怕的二战的每一幕仍历历在目，我们决心为世界和平继续奋斗。"

考点: 1. 意译: 句子 this year marks the 50th anniversary of the Japanese assault on the U. S. 按照直译为"今年是日本袭击美国事件的50周年"，这种翻法欠妥当，因为这个事件并不是一个值得庆祝的事件，因此把 anniversary 就省去不译了,意译成"50 年前"。

2. 转性译法: 名词→动词　　　　　　assault→袭击

名词→形容词　　　　　　horror→可怕的

副词→动词　　　　　　　anew→继续;重新

3. anew 是个副词,解释为"重新;再次"的意思,表示强调。如:

Our efforts to pass the intermediate interpretation test must begin anew.

我们必须重新努力来通过中级口译的考试。

四、Usually, in Japan, when people **discuss** the war **at all**, they speak of **victimization**: their own **victimization** by the **militarists** (who led the country into battle) and by the Americans (who bombed their cities).

译文 1: 通常在日本,只要一提到战争,就会讲到受害,讲他们是军国主义的受害者,军国主义把国家引入战争;他们是美国的受害者,美国向他们的城市投掷了原子弹。

译文 2: 在日本,通常人们只要谈到第二次世界大战,就只讲日本是受害者,是军国主义分子把国家引向战争,是美国人轰炸了他们的城市。

考点: 1. 意译: discuss→提到

2. at all 的翻译: 一些考生只要提到 at all,就会想到"一点不",确实,at all 经常和否定词连用来强化否定,但也可跟于肯定句后,表示"in any way; to any extent",在翻译中较灵活,在动词后常翻译成"究竟",在条件状语从句或时间状语从句后,常翻译成"只要"。如:

Are you at all worried about the forecast?

对那项预测,你究竟担心不担心?

If you promise to leave me alone at all, I would give you $500.

只要你答应别来烦我,我就给你 500 美元。

3. 具体译法: 加字法 victimization→受害者

4. 定语从句的翻译: 重复法

5. 增词译法: by the Americans who bombed their cities 前省略了 their own victimization,因此在翻译中要补全"他们是美国受害者"。

五、The suffering inflicted by the **imperial army** on the peoples of Asia is ignored, **as is** Japan's **aggression** in China and at Pearl Harbor.

译文: 然而他们闭口不谈皇军给亚洲人民带来的灾难,也不谈对华侵略和偷袭珍珠港。

考点: 1. 转态译法: 被主转换 is ignored →他们闭口不谈

2. 意译: ignore→闭口不谈

3. 定语从句的翻译: 综合法 as is Japan's aggression

六、The **appealing** image of Japan the victim has no room for the underside of Japan the aggressor.

译文 1: 日本作为战争的受害者,形象似乎很感人,从而掩盖了其侵略者的一面。

译文 2: 日本作为战争的受害者,其乞怜形象掩盖了其侵略者的一面。

考点: 1. 正反译法: appealing→乞怜的

2. 转性译法: 名词→动词　　no room→掩盖了

room 在这里解释为"空间",no room 表示"没有空间",即"掩盖了",如:

There is no room for justice and truth in a world of bureaucracy.

在官僚主义的世界里,公正和事实往往被掩盖。

3. 同位语的翻译: Japan 和 the victim, Japan 和 the aggressor 都是同位语,在这里加了"作为"的意思。

TRANSLATION TEST (2) (30 minutes)

Directions: Translate the following passage into English and write your version in the corresponding space in your ANSWER BOOKLET.

澳门,南海之滨一颗闪耀的明珠,以她的风采、沧桑和辉煌,更以 1999 年 12 月 20 日这个不同寻常的日子,吸引着全世界的目光。

自古以来,澳门就是中国的领土,中华儿女世世代代在这里繁衍生息。

早在 80 年代,世纪伟人邓小平就提出了"一国两制"的伟大构想。1997 年 7 月 1 日,中华人民共和国恢复对香港行使主权。今年,澳门又将彻底结束外国管治,回到祖国怀抱,这是中华民族的又一件历史盛事。它标志着中国人民向着祖国统一的伟大目标又迈出了重大的一步。澳门的明天一定会更加美好。

分析:

一、澳门,南海之滨一颗闪耀的明珠,以她的风采、沧桑和辉煌,更以 1999 年 12 月 20 日这个不同寻常的日子,吸引着全世界的目光。

译文: The very date of December 20, 1999 gives the world of limelight to Macao, a sparkling pearl on China's south coast well known for her natural charm, vicissitudinous history and splendid achievement.

考点: 1. "南海之滨"和"南海"并没有什么关系,有不少考生翻译成 the south sea 就错了,文中意思实为"南部的滨海地区/海岸",应翻译成 the south coast。

2. "引人注目"的翻译方法: noticeable, conspicuous, spectacular, distinct, plain, perceptible, appreciable, obvious, apparent, eye-catching, catch one's eye, catch the attention of, draw one's attention, etc. ,请考生根据不同的上下文和语境选择使用。

二、自古以来,澳门就是中国的领土,中华儿女世世代代在这里繁衍生息。

译文: Macao has been the territory of China ever since ancient times. The Chinese people have been living and working there for generations.

考点： 1. 时态问题：此句中使用了现在完成进行时，表示动作状态一直持续到说话时。

2. 意译：繁衍生息→live and work

三、早在 80 年代，世纪伟人邓小平就提出了"一国两制"的伟大构想。

译文 1： Early in the 1980s, Mr. Deng Xiaoping, one of the great figures of the century, put forward the bold concept of "One Country, Two Systems".

译文 2： As early as 1980s, Mr. Deng Xiaoping, a great statesman of the century, put forward the bold concept of "One Country, Two Systems".

考点： 1. ×年代→in the ×s 如：30 年代→in the 30s，原文中最好处理成 in the 1980s，因为现在已经是 21 世纪了，如写成 80s，就可能理解成 21 世纪 80 年代。

2. 同位语的翻译：世纪伟人邓小平→Mr. Deng Xiaoping, one of the great figures of the century 或者 Mr. Deng xiaoping, a great statesman of the century 这里 statesman 解释为：person who plays an important part in the management of state affairs, esp. one who is skilled and fair; wise political leader. 政府高级要员（有才干的、公正的）；政治家；英明的政治领袖。

3. 增词译法：上句中加了 one of 的架构，考虑到"世纪伟人"并不是只有一个人，邓小平为世纪伟人之一，因此译出了"之一"的涵义。

4. 专有名词的译法：本句出现了两个专有术语，一国两制→One Country, Two Systems；伟大设想→bold concept。对于这两个短语在评分时不允许有其他讲法。

四、1997 年 7 月 1 日，中华人民共和国恢复对香港行使主权。

译文： On July 1, 1997, the People's Republic of China resumed her sovereignty over Hong Kong.

五、今年，澳门又将彻底结束外国管治，回到祖国怀抱，这是中华民族的又一件历史盛事。

译文： Another great historical event for the Chinese people this year is Macao will end the rule of foreign administration and return to the embrace of the motherland.

考点： 1. 结束→end；get rid of

2. 省词译法：回到祖国怀抱→return to (the embrace of) the motherland

六、它标志着中国人民向着祖国统一的伟大目标又迈出了重大的一步。

译文 1： It symbolizes another big/significant step for the Chinese people on their way towards the great goal of the nation's reunification.

译文 2： It symbolizes another big/significant step for the Chinese people to reach the great goal of the country's reunification.

考点： 转性译法：介词→动词 向着→reach

七、澳门的明天一定会更加美好。

译文 1： Macao is sure to have a better tomorrow.

译文 2： Macao's tomorrow will be better.

第六节 1999年9月考题

TRANSLATION TEST (1) (30 minutes)

Directions: Translate the following passage into Chinese and write your version in the corresponding space in your ANSWER BOOKLET.

Those people whose only experience of Helen Keller is *The Miracle Worker* will be surprised to discover her many dimensions. "My work for the blind," she wrote, "has never occupied a center in my personality. My sympathies are with all who struggle for justice." She was a tireless activist for racial and sexual equality. She was complex. Her main message was and is, "We're like everybody else. We're here to be able to live a life as full as any sighted person's. And it's O. K. to be ourselves."

That means we have the freedom to be as extraordinary as the sighted. Helen Keller loved an audience and wrote that she adored "the warm tide of human life pulsing round and round me." That's why the stage appealed to her, why she learned to speak, to deliver speeches and to feel the vibrations of music, of the radio, of the movement of lips.

分析:

一、Those people (whose only **experience** of Helen Keller is *The Miracle Worker*) will be surprised to discover her many **dimensions**.

　　译文: 对于那些仅仅通过《奇迹创造者》了解海伦·凯勒的人们,她各方面的性格特点将令他们大吃一惊。

　　考点: 1. 定语从句的翻译:前置法

　　　　　2. 转性译法:名词→动词 experience→了解

　　　　　3. 书名的翻译: *The Miracle Worker*→《奇迹创造者》
　　　　　英语中没有书名号,因此遇到书名号,一般可以用斜体或加下划线表示,如 *Gone with the Wind*, the Lord of the Rings

　　　　　4. 具体译法:加字法: dimensions→性格特点

　　　　　5. 换序译法: be surprised to discover her many dimensions→她各方面的性格特点将令他们大吃一惊

二、"My work for the blind," she wrote, "has never occupied a **center** in my **personality**. My **sympathies** are with all (who struggle for **justice**)."

　　译文: "我为盲人所做的工作,"她写道,"从未在我的人生中(我身上)占据中心地位。我的同情心是向着所有为正义而斗争的人们的。"

　　考点: 1. the + adj. 表示一类人,因此在翻译"……人"时,可以考虑用 the + adj. 的形

式。如:

the poor/rich,the young/elderly

the sick/healthy,the disabled/handicapped

the underprivileged/predominant

2. 具体译法: 加字法: center→中心地位,sympathies→同情心

3. personality→人生

personality 在这里解释为"性格;特征;个性"都不合适,其含义相当于 life,考生以后在翻译 personality 时,要特别注意其另外两个比较冷门的意思。如:

1) We need someone with lots of personality to organize the party.

我们需要一位非常有魅力的人来组织晚会。

2) Let's keep personalities out of it, which means avoiding criticizing individual people.

咱们不要对他品头论足。

4. 定语从句的翻译: 前置法

三、She was a **tireless** activist **for** racial and sexual equality. **She** was **complex**.

译文1: 她是一个孜孜不倦的活动家,提倡种族和男女平等。她的思想丰富而深邃。

译文2: 她是一个孜孜不倦地提倡种族和性别平等的活动家。她的思想丰富而深邃。

译文3: 她是一个提倡种族和性别平等的不倦的活动家。她丰富而深邃。

考点: 1. 转性译法: 形容词→副词 tireless→孜孜不倦地

介词→动词 for→提倡

2. 换序译法: She was a tireless activist for racial and sexual equality. 这句话可以在 activist 后断句,然后从 for 后再成为一个小分句;也可成为一个较长的定语从句,如译文 2 和译文 3,相比而言,译文 1 的翻译方式较妥。

3. 增词译法: she→她的思想

四、Her main message was and is, "We're like everybody else. We're here to be able to live a life as **full** as any **sighted** person's. And it's **O. K.** to be ourselves."

译文: 她(传递)的信息过去是、今天依然是,"我们和别人一样。我们在这个世界上能够和视力正常的人一样过上充实的生活。我们成为盲人没有什么不好。"

考点: 1. 增词译法: Her main message was and is→她传递的信息过去是、今天依然是,这句话中过去时和现在时在翻译中分别加上了"过去"和"现在",使句意更加明确。

2. 比较级的翻译: live a life as full as any sighted person's = live as full a life as any sighted person's life

3. OK 除了是打招呼用语外,其基本意思是 all right; satisfactory→不错的;令人满意的, 如: I think I did OK in the exam. →我觉得自己这次考试考得不错。

五、That means we have the freedom to be as **extraordinary** as the sighted.

译文 1：这意味着我们拥有和视力正常者一样的成为非凡者的自由。

译文 2：这意味着我们拥有和视力正常者一样出色的自由。

考点：1. 比较级的翻译 as...as→和……一样

2. 转性译法：形容词→名词 extraordinary→非凡者

六、Helen Keller loved an audience and wrote that she **adored** "the **warm tide** of human life **pulsing** round and round me."

译文：海伦·凯勒热爱听众，她写道她非常喜欢"在我周围涌动着的人类生命的暖流"。

考点：人名的翻译

七、That's why the **stage appealed to** her, why she learned to speak, to deliver speeches and to feel the **vibrations** of music, of the radio, of the movement of lips.

译文：这就是为什么讲坛对她有（如此的）吸引力，她为什么去学习说话，学习演说，学习去感觉（受）由音乐、收音机、（人的）嘴唇嚅动（所）发出的颤动的原因。

考点：1. stage→讲坛。

许多考生看到 stage，不假思索地翻译成"舞台"，这种失误是十分低级的，在翻译了大段文章后居然认为海伦·凯勒是演员，翻译成"舞台"。

2. 转性译法：动词→名词 appeal to→吸引力

3. 增词译法：

1) why she learned to speak, to deliver speeches and to feel... 这句句子中后两个 to 前都省略了 learned，在翻译中应补全"学习"的意思。

2) feel the vibrations of music, of the radio, of the movement of lips 这句句子中 of the radio, of the movement 两个 of 前也都省略了 vibrations，翻译时也应补全。

3) vibrations→颤动的原因

TRANSLATION TEST (2) (30 minutes)

Directions: Translate the following passage into English and write your version in the corresponding space in your ANSWER BOOKLET.

　　正在建设之中的浦东国际机场位于长江入海口南岸的濒海地带，占地约 32 平方公里。根据上海社会经济发展对航空业务量的需求，浦东国际机场的最终设计能力是年旅客客运量 8000 万人次，货运量 500 万吨。机场全部建成后，绿化覆盖率将达到 50% 以上。浦东国际机场是一扇向天空开启的大门，是一条与世界联系的纽带。人类即将进入 21 世纪，人、自然、环境和建筑必将和谐、持续地发展。

分析：

一、正在建设之中的浦东国际机场位于长江入海口南岸的濒海地带，占地约 32 平方公里。

译文: Pudong International Airport, now under construction, is located on the south bank of the Yangtze/Changjiang estuary, covering/with an area of approximately 32 square kilometers.

考点: 1. "大约"的翻译: about 后跟比较模糊的整数,即"几百几千",如 about 1200。根据精确程度,"大约"的翻译如下(从较模糊到较精确):

about> roughly> around> nearly> approximately> circa

2. 度量衡的翻译: 中口翻译中需要掌握的度量衡单位包括如下:

1)	Linear Measurement	长度单位
	inch(es)	英寸
	foot/feet	英尺
	yard	码
	mile	英里
	millimeter	毫米
	centimeter	厘米
	metre	米
	kilometer	公里
2)	Area Measurement	面积单位
	square	平方
	acre	英亩
	hectare	公顷
3)	Volume Measurement	容(体)积单位
	cubic	立方
4)	Liquid Measurement	液体测量单位
	pint	品脱
	quart	夸脱
	gallon	加仑
	litre	升
5)	Weight Measurement	重量单位
	ounce	盎司
	pound	磅
	ton	吨
	grams	克
	kilo(gram)	千克,公斤
	metric ton	公吨
6)	Measurement of Temperature	

Celsius   摄氏
        Fahrenheit   华氏

二、根据上海社会经济发展对航空业务量的需求,浦东国际机场的最终设计能力是年旅客客运量 8000 万人次,货运量 500 万吨。

译文 1: To meet the demands of Shanghai's social and economic development for aviation services, the maximum design capacity of the airport is 80 million passengers and 5 million tons of freight annually.

译文 2: According to the demands of Shanghai's social and economic development for airline business, the maximum design capacity of the airport is 80 million passengers and 5 million tons of freight annually.

考点: 业务量→services,最终→maximum,能力→capacity

这里"最终"并不能翻译成 final,因为根据后面的数字其实表示"最大的"意思,capacity 与其表示"能力",还不如解释为"容量"。比如 a hall with a seating capacity of 2000→可坐两千人的大礼堂。考生应掌握 capacity 的一个重要含义:the ability to produce, experience, understand or learn sth. 生产、感受、理解或学习的能力。如:

Some people have a greater capacity for happiness than others.

有些人比别人更善于体会幸福。

This book is beyond the capacity of younger readers.

较年轻的读者难以理解这本书。

三、机场全部建成后,绿化覆盖率将达到 50% 以上。

译文: The completion of the airport (project) will bring the ratio of green space coverage to the total area above 50%..

考点: "达到"的翻译:

1) 如果是达到某个数字(非百分比),一般可以用 reach, arrive at, amount to, come to, add up to, total, equal 等。

2) 如果是达到百分比,一般可以用 cover, occupy, take up, account for 等。

四、浦东国际机场是一扇向天空开启的大门,是一条与世界联系的纽带。

译文: Pudong International Airport is a gate open to the sky and a link connecting (different parts of) the rest of the world.

五、人类即将进入 21 世纪,人、自然、环境和建筑必将和谐、持续地发展。

译文: The upcoming 21st century will witness a sustained development of man, nature, environment and construction as well as a harmonious relationship among them.

考点: 转性译法: 副词→形容词,动词→名词,和谐、持续地发展→a sustained development, a harmonious relationship

第七节 2000 年 3 月考题

TRANSLATION TEST (1) (30 minutes)

Directions: Translate the following passage into Chinese and write your version ın the corresponding space in your ANSWER BOOKLET.

Information and communications are central to modem society and organizations. One approach to understand the working environment is to consider an organization as a communications system. An organization that has open lines of communication with valid, honest information going up, down, and throughout the organization will be much more effective and a much better place to work in than the organization that attempts to restrict the flow of information or distort and deceive. When leadership attempts to keep workers in the dark, workers tend to become distrustful. This undermines their cooperation.

It is easy to understand the value and importance of open, honest communications and valid information. Yet, few organizations are able to function in this manner. In the long run, poor communication will undermine the entire organization. Restricting communication and distorting information are symptoms of short-range thinking. We must avoid these stupid, short-sighted traps and constantly strive for an open communications system with objective information.

分析:

一、Information and **communications** are central to modern society and **organizations.**

译法: 信息和沟通/交流对于现代社会和企业组织来说至关重要。

考点: 1. organization 常解释为"公司;企业"或"组织",这篇文章其实属于 Management
板块,应解释为"企业"。

2. 具体译法: 成语法: central→至关重要

二、One approach to understand the working environment is to consider an organization as a communications system.

译文 1: 把企业看作是一个沟通体系,这是了解工作环境的方法之一。

译文 2: 了解工作环境的一个方法是把企业看作是一个沟通体系。

三、(1) An organization (that has **open lines** of communication with **valid, honest** information going up, down, and throughout the organization) (3) will be much more effective and a much better place to work in (2) than the organization (that attempts to restrict the flow of information or distort and deceive).

译文: 如果一个企业具备公开的传播渠道,企业内部信息传播流畅、内容真实可信,
比起那些试图封闭信息,歪曲甚至欺骗的企业来说,将会有更高的工作效率,更

好的工作环境。

考点： 1. 定语从句的翻译：第一句用了省略法，第二句用了前置法。

2. 换序译法：翻译顺序：(1)(2)(3)。这是一句较长的句子，但是句子结构并不复杂，考生可以发现整句句子是一个比较级，谓语部分是 will be much more effective and a much better place to work，不过两个企业的后面都各有一个长句进行修饰，特别是第一个企业。因此在翻译时先把主语的情况交待完毕，然后用"比"连起后面的比较部分，其定语并不长，可以前置，最后再翻译谓语。

3. 意译：这句句子意译的成分相当多，可以说是中级口译翻译到现在为止意译考点最多的地方了。

going up, down, and throughout   →机构内上下（直译）

  →（内部传播）流畅（意译）

restrict the flow of information   →限制信息的流通（直译）

  →封闭信息（意译）

4. 转性译法：形容词→名词   effective→效能

       形容词→动词   better→适宜于

四、When **leadership** attempts to keep workers in the dark, workers **tend to** become **distrustful**.

译文1： 如果领导层让员工蒙在鼓里，员工很难信任领导。

译文2： 领导如果什么事情都不对员工讲，员工就会不信任领导。

考点： 1. 具体译法：加字法：leadership→领导层

           成语法：keep workers in the dark→让员工蒙在鼓里

2. 转性译法：形容词→动词 distrustful→不信任

五、This **undermines** their cooperation.

译文： 由此破坏他们之间的合作。

六、It is **easy** to understand the value and **importance** of **open, honest** communications and **valid** information.

译文1： 开诚布公的沟通和无误的信息，它们的价值和重要性是显而易见的。

译文2： 懂得公开真诚的交流和可靠信息的价值和重要性是不难的。

考点： 1. 具体译法：加字法：importance→重要性

           成语法：open, honest communications→开诚布公的沟通

2. 正反译法：easy→不难的 valid→无误的

七、Yet, **few** organizations are able to **function** in this manner.

译文1： 然而能够做到这点的企业并不多见。

译文2： 然而很少有企业能够这样做。

考点： 正反译法：few→不多见

八、**In the long run, poor** communication will **undermine** the entire organization.

译文： 不良沟通从长远上讲就会危害整个企业.

考点： 正反译法：poor→不良的

九、Restricting communication and distorting information are **symptoms** of short-range thinking.

译文 1： 限制沟通和歪曲信息会使企业成为井底之蛙。

译文 2： 限制沟通和歪曲信息会使企业鼠目寸光。

译文 3： 限制沟通和歪曲信息会使企业缺乏远见。

译文 4： 限制沟通和歪曲信息是思想狭隘的表现。

考点： 具体译法：成语法：short-range thinking→井底之蛙；鼠目寸光

　　　　　正反译法：short-range thinking→缺乏远见

十、We must avoid these stupid, **short-sighted traps** and constantly **strive for** an open communications system **with** objective information.

译文： 我们必须摆脱这些愚蠢、短浅的思想羁绊，不断努力，营造一个确保客观信息公开交流的系统。

考点： 1. 正反译法：short-sighted→缺乏远见

　　　　　2. 意译：traps→羁绊

　　　　　3. 转性译法：介词→动词 with→确保

TRANSLATION TEST（2）（30 minutes）

Directions: Translate the following passage into English and write your version in the corresponding space in your ANSWER BOOKLET.

　　中华民族历来爱好自由和和平，中国人民始终希望天下太平，希望各国人民友好相处。中国人民在近代饱受战争和侵略的痛苦,更深感自由与和平的珍贵。任何一个国家建设和发展，都需要一个和平稳定的国际国内环境。任何一个国家和民族的自由，都是一切个人自由的前提和基础。我们希望各国人民都生活在没有战争和暴力的世界里,希望各国人民都能享有不被人压迫，歧视和欺凌的自由。

分析:

一、中华民族历来爱好自由和和平。

　　译文 1： Traditionally, the Chinese nation has been a peace-loving country that values freedom.

　　译文 2： The Chinese people have a tradition to love peace and freedom.

　　考点： 换序译法："历来"前置翻译→Traditionally

二、中国人民始终希望天下太平,希望各国人民友好相处。

　　译文： The Chinese people always seek the global peace and friendship among all nations.

　　考点： 转性译法：副词→名词　友好→friendship

三、中国人民在近代饱受战争和侵略的痛苦,更深感自由与和平的珍贵。

译文 1: Having suffered from the pains of wars and invasion in recent times, the Chinese people have cherished the value/preciousness of freedom and peace than ever.

译文 2: Having suffered from wars and foreign aggression in recent times, the Chinese people treasure freedom and peace all the more.

考点: 换序译法:"中国人民"后置翻译。

四、任何一个国家建设和发展,都需要一个和平稳定的国际国内环境。

译文 1: The construction and development of any country requires/demands a peaceful and stable international and domestic environment.

译文 2: Every nation needs a peaceful and stable international and domestic environment for its construction and development.

五、任何一个国家和民族的自由,都是一切个人自由的前提和基础。

译文: The freedom of any country or nation is the prerequisite and foundation/basis of that of any individual.

六、我们希望各国人民都生活在没有战争和暴力的世界里,希望各国人民都能享有不被人压迫,歧视和欺凌的自由。

译文: We sincerely hope people of all nations live in a world free from wars and violence and enjoy a freedom without oppression, discrimination and humiliation.

考点: 换序译法:"没有战争和暴力的"和"不被人压迫、歧视和欺凌的"后置到所修饰主体名词后翻译。

第八节　2000 年 9 月考题

TRANSLATION TEST (1) (30 minutes)

Directions: Translate the following passage into Chinese and write your version in the corresponding space in your ANSWER BOOKLET.

Both language and culture are learned by children without special organized programs of instruction, but motivation to learn is very high since language is the most effective means for a child to obtain what he or she wants. If the learning of a new language begins before lower adolescence, one is likely to be able to speak such a language with complete naturalness, but if learned after upper adolescence some hangover of a mother-tongue feature is very likely to persist. But not only do languages exhibit such learning patterns, but so do cultural traits, for example, shaking hands, kissing, and embracing.

Although many persons assume that languages exist in dictionaries and grammars, in fact they only exist in people's heads. But this is equally true of cultural traits, which indicate clearly a person's value system when crucial decisions need to be made before there is any time to think about alternatives, for example, diving into a flooding stream to rescue a drowning child.

分析:

一、Both language and culture are learned by children without **special organized programs of instruction**, but **motivation** to learn is very high since language is the most effective means for a child to **obtain (what he or she wants)**.

译文 1: 语言和文化学习,对儿童来说并不存在特定的程序和计划,但是由于语言是儿童得偿所愿最有效的方式,因而他们学语言的积极性是很高的。

译文 2: 儿童学习语言和文化,无需专门编制的教学计划,但他们的学习积极性很高,因为他们若要获得想要的东西,语言乃是最有效的手段。

考点: 1. 转态译法:被主交换:are learned by children→儿童学习

2. special organized programs of instruction→特定的程序和计划

3. 具体译法:成语法:obtain what he or she wants→得偿所愿

4. 换序译法:since 从句先译

二、If the **learning** of a new language begins **before lower adolescence**, one is likely to be able to speak such a language with complete **naturalness**, but if learned **after upper adolescence** some **hangover** of a mother-tongue feature is very likely to persist.

译文 1: 如果一个人在少年时期就学一门新的语言,那么(将来)很可能说得很流利。但如果成年还没有学语言,母语的一些习惯特征就会根深蒂固。

译文 2: 如果一个人十来岁开始学习一门新的语言,日后他就有可能轻松自如地说这门语言。但如果到十六、七岁才学,那么他说话时多半会夹杂一些母语的痕迹。

考点: 1. 转性译法:名词→动词　　　　learning→学习

　　　　　　　　动词→形容词　　　persist→根深蒂固

　　　　　　　　名词→副词　　　　naturalness→轻松自如地;流利

2. before lower adolescence→少年时期;十来岁

after upper adolescence→到成年;十六、七岁

hangover→痕迹

adolescence 在英语中表示"青春期",一般指成年以前从 13 到 15 岁的发育期。在翻译 before lower adolescence 时,不能简单处理成"青少年时期的早期",既累赘,语义又晦涩。可以翻译成"少年时期",因为"青少年时期的早期"即"少年时期",也可根据 adolescence 的年龄范围处理成"十几岁"。当然 after upper adolescence 直译为"在青春期后",即"十六、七岁",此阶段离"成年"不远。

3. 正反译法:if learned after upper adolescence→如果成年还没有学语言

4. 转态译法: 被主交换 but if learned after upper adolescence→如果成年还没有
学语言

5. 具体译法: 成语法: persist→根深蒂固

三、But not only do languages **exhibit** such learning **patterns**, but so do **cultural traits**, for example, shaking hands, kissing, and **embracing**.

译文 1: 不仅语言体现了这种学习方式,文化特征也是如此,诸如握手、接吻和拥抱。

译文 2: 不仅语言学习呈现这种模式,文化特征,如握手、接吻和拥抱,也同样如此。

考点: 倒装句的翻译

四、Although many persons **assume** that languages exist in dictionaries and **grammars**, in fact they only exist in people's heads.

译文: 尽管许多人认为语言只存在于字典和语法书中,其实它只存在于人的头脑里。

考点: 具体译法: 加字法: grammars→语法书

前文有"字典", grammar 如翻译成"语法", 和"字典"无法并列, 因为"语法"是一
个抽象的东西, 而"语法书"是一个具体的出版物, 因此应翻译为"语法书"。

五、But **this is** equally **true of** cultural traits, (which indicate clearly a person's value system) when crucial decisions need to be made before there is any time to think about **alternatives**, for example, diving into a **flooding stream** to **rescue** a **drowning** child.

译文 1: 文化特征何尝不是如此? 有时候, 人们来不及思索就必须做出关键决定, 比如
说跳进湍急的水流中救一个溺水儿童, 那么这种情况下一个人的文化特征就
清晰地折射出他的价值体系。

译文 2: 文化特征亦然。在没有时间考虑何取何舍而必须做出关键性决定时, 如跳进
湍急的水流中去救一个溺水的孩子, 文化特征会清楚地表现出一个人的价值
体系。

考点: 1. This is true of/in... 表示以上情况也适用于 of 后的宾语, 翻译时可用"何尝
不是如此"、"亦然"、"也是这样"等表达。如:

In Mac, you can enjoy the food in a comforting atmosphere with instant and
professional service. This is also true in KFC.

麦当劳的用餐环境舒适, 服务专业迅捷。肯德基何尝不是如此?

2. 定语从句的翻译: 重复法→which...

3. 换序译法: (1) But this is equally true of cultural traits, (5) which indicate clearly
a person's value system (3) when crucial decisions need to be made (2) before
there is any time to think about alternatives, (4) for example, diving into a
flooding stream to rescue a drowning child.

翻译顺序如上。这是一句非常复杂的句子, 表面上不难理解, 但翻译的顺序
很有讲究。除了第(1)句, 后面有两句相连环的定语从句, which 是一句非限制
性定语从句, when 是一句限制性定语从句, 由于较长, 不可能翻译成"清晰

地展现了当……的价值体系"。因此可以把 when 这句定语从句当成是时间状语从句去处理,单独断句。不料在 when 这句中又有 before 真正的时间状语从句,这时有两种翻译方法:一种是把它翻译成一般的时间状语从句,或是把它处理成较简单的表达,作定语去修饰 decisions,两种方法都需要前置。翻译完后再紧跟第(4)句作为例子,趁热打铁。最后再回到上面处理第(5)句,不过由于当中隔离许多内容,读者对 which 所指代的 cultural traits 已经没有印象,需要在翻译时再次提起。

4. 转态译法:被主交换: crucial decisions need to be made→人们不得不做出关键决定

5. before there is any time to think about alternatives→不假思索地

6. flooding stream 极易翻错,不解释为"洪水",因为"洪水"为 flood,在这里 flooding 为形容词,修饰 stream,表示"湍急的水流"

TRANSLATION TEST (2) (30 minutes)

Directions: Translate the following passage into English and write your version in the corresponding space in your ANSWER BOOKLET.

中国政府在宣布实行和平统一的方针时,是基于一个前提,即当时的台湾当局坚持世界上只有一个中国,台湾是中国的一部分。同时,中国政府考虑到美国政府承认了世界上只有一个中国,台湾是中国的一部分,中华人民共和国政府是中国的惟一合法政府。

中国政府在实行和平统一方针的同时始终表明,以任何方式解决台湾问题是中国的内政,并无义务承诺放弃使用武力。

分析:

一、中国政府在宣布实行和平统一的方针时,是基于一个前提,即当时的台湾当局坚持世界上只有一个中国,台湾是中国的一部分。

译文 1: The Chinese government proclaimed/declared to adopt/implement the policy of peaceful reunification on the premise that the then Taiwan authorities maintained that there is but one China in the world and Taiwan is a part of China.

译文 2: The declaration by the Chinese government to implement the policy of peaceful reunification was based on the prerequisite that the then Taiwan authorities insisted that there is but one China in the world and Taiwan is a part of China.

考点: 1. 政府在"宣布"时宜使用较正式的词语,比如 maintain, declare, state, affirm, avow, assert, attest, aver 等,比 announce, believe 等单词更为合适。

2. 转性译法:动词→名词 宣布→declaration

3. "前提"的翻译:"基于一个……的前提"是翻译中的常见句型,考生可以根据表达的需要,选取以下表达: on the premise/ground that; based on the pre-

requisite/proposition/hypothesis/assumption/presupposition 等

4. "当时的"的翻译：在外交的翻译中，经常要遇到"当时的"的翻译，请考生使用 the then+noun 的表达方法。如：当时的政府→the then government

5. 褒贬译法：坚持→insist（褒义译法）

→persist（贬义译法）

二、同时，中国政府考虑到美国政府承认了世界上只有一个中国，台湾是中国的一部分，中华人民共和国政府是中国的惟一合法政府。

译文： Meanwhile, the Chinese government took into account/consideration that the US government acknowledged/recognized that there is only one China in the world, (that) Taiwan is a part of China and (that) the Government of People's Republic of China is the sole legitimate government representing China.

三、中国政府在实行和平统一方针的同时始终表明，以任何方式解决台湾问题是中国的内政，并无义务承诺放弃使用武力。

译文： Adopting the policy of peaceful reunification, the Chinese government always makes it clear that it is China's internal affair to solve the Taiwan issue by whatever means and China is under no obligation to undertake to give up military force.

考点： 转性译法：动词→介词　无义务→under no obligation

第九节　2001年3月考题

TRANSLATION TEST (1) (30 minutes)

Directions: Translate the following passage into Chinese and write your version in the corresponding space in your ANSWER BOOKLET.

　　Twenty years ago, Motorola looked upon the Japanese with something close to fear. The Chicago company's television-manufacturing division had been large and profitable in the 1960s. By the early 1970s, however, high costs and a rising tide of inexpensive Japanese TVs were taking a heavy toll. "The Japanese were very aggressive," recalls Motorola spokesman Mario Salvadori. "They wanted to get market share." With cutthroat pricing, they did eventually run nearly every US electronic company out of the TV business. Motorola sold its Quasar TV unit to a Japanese company in 1974. But while other US companies were floored for foreign competition, Motorola refocused its energies. It turned to wireless communications—an industry it had pioneered (with mobile radios and walkie-talkie) in the 1920s. It was a prescient move.

分析：

一、Twenty years ago, Motorola **looked upon** the Japanese with **something** close to fear.

译文： 20 年前，摩托罗拉公司带着近乎害怕的心理看待日本企业。

考点： 意译：something→某事；某物（直译）

　　　　　　　　→联系后文 something close to fear, 翻译为心理（意译）

二、The Chicago company's television-manufacturing **division** had been large and profitable **in the 1960s**.

译文： 在 20 世纪 60 年代，其在芝加哥的电视制造分公司规模大，利润高。

考点： 增词译法：in the 1960s→在 20 世纪 60 年代

　　　　　　had been large and profitable→（规模）大，（利润）高。

三、By the early 1970s, however, high costs and a rising **tide** of **inexpensive** Japanese TVs were taking a **heavy toll**.

译文： 但在 20 世纪 70 年代初，生产成本上升，而日本廉价电视机数目日趋增长，其市场份额遭受重创。

考点： 1. 正反译法：inexpensive→廉价的

　　　　 2. 意译：

　　　　　 toll→ a fixed charge or tax for a privilege, especially for passage across a bridge or along a road（直译）

　　　　　　 eg. toll on long-distance telephone calls→长途电话费用

　　　　　 → the amount or extent of loss or destruction, as of life, health, or property, caused by a disaster（意译）

　　　　　　 eg. Automobile accidents take a heavy toll of human lives.

　　　　　　 许多人在车祸中丧生。

四、"The Japanese were very **aggressive**," recalls Motorola spokesman Mario Salvadori. "They wanted to get market share."

译文 1： "日本人非常嚣张，"摩托罗拉公司发言人马里奥·萨尔瓦多瑞回忆道，"他们想分享市场。"

译文 2： "日本人可谓野心勃勃，"摩托罗拉公司发言人马里奥·萨尔瓦多瑞回忆道，"他们想要市场份额。"

考点： 1. 褒贬译法：aggressive→嚣张；野心勃勃（贬译）

　　　　 2. 转性译法：名词→动词　　share→分享

　　　　 3. 人名的翻译：音译法：Mario Salvadori→马里奥·萨尔瓦多瑞

五、With **cutthroat** pricing, they did eventually **run** nearly every US electronic company **out of** the TV business.

译文 1： 通过残酷无情的价格战，他们最终把几乎所有美国电子公司赶出了电视机行业。

译文 2： 通过残酷无情的价格战，他们如愿以偿，电视机行业所剩的美国电子公司寥寥无几。

考点： 1. cutthroat: →relentless or merciless in competition 残酷无情的

　　　eg. a cutthroat business→一笔残酷无情的生意

　　2. 具体译法：

　　　加字法: pricing→价格战

　　　成语法: run nearly every US electronic company out of the TV business→

　　　　　电视机行业所剩的美国电子公司寥寥无几

六、Motorola sold its Quasar TV unit to a Japanese company in 1974.

　　译文： 1974 年，摩托罗拉公司将其在 Quesar 的电视生产厂卖给了一家日本公司。

　　考点： 换序译法：将 in 1974 提前到句首翻译。

七、But while other US companies were **floored** for foreign competition, Motorola refocused its **energies**.

　　译文： 但是当其他美国公司被外国竞争者淘汰出局时，摩托罗拉公司重新调整了产业方向。

　　考点： 意译: floor 　→ to knock down 击倒（直译）

　　　　　　　　　　　→ to stun; overwhelm 使败北，击败；使震惊，使不知所措（意译）

　　　　　　energies → 能量；活力；精力（直译）

　　　　　　　　　　　→ 产业方向（意译）

八、It turned to **wireless communications—an industry it had pioneered** (with **mobile** radios and **walkie-talkie**) in the 1920s.

　　译文： 无线通讯是它在 20 世纪 20 年代开拓的新产业（主要产品包括随身听收音机和步话机）。

　　考点： 换序译法: in the 1920s 前置修饰 industry

九、It was a **prescient move**.

　　译文： 此举确有先见之明。

　　考点： prescient→having knowledge of actions or events before they occur; having foresight

　　　　　　　有先见的

　　　　　move→an action taken to achieve an objective; a maneuver 采取的行动／步骤

　　　　　eg. What's our next move?

　　　　　　我们下一步怎么做？

TRANSLATION TEST (2) (30 minutes)

Directions: Translate the following passage into English and write your version in the corresponding space in your ANSWER BOOKLET.

　　据调查，我国有 40% 的青少年除了课本以外不看其他书籍。对此，我感到极为震惊。虽然有关人士声称调查具有科学性，我仍不敢相信。不过尽管怀疑，事实却是，越来越多的年轻人在业余时间已不再读书，而是看电视，跳舞，打电子游戏机，或者侃大山。高尔基说过:"书籍是人类进步的阶梯。"众所周知,书籍是人类智慧的结晶。尽管现代传媒(如电视、计算机)在信息的传播速度上有许多优势,但到目前为止,还没有哪一种在传播知识的深度方面能取代书籍。

分析:

一、据调查,我国有 40% 的青少年除了课本以外不看其他书籍。对此,我感到极为震惊。

> **译文:** According to survey, (about) 40% of the youth in our country do not read any books other than their textbooks, which takes me by great surprise.

> **考点:** 定语从句的翻译:重复法

二、虽然有关人士声称调查具有科学性,我仍不敢相信。

> **译文:** I remain suspicious of the survey, though the people concerned claimed it to be scientific.

> **考点:** 1. 让步状语从句的翻译
>
> 2. 有关人士→the people concerned 有关方面→the relevant party
>
> 3. 正反译法:不敢相信→suspicious
>
> 4. 转性译法:名词→形容词 科学性→scientific

三、不过尽管怀疑,事实却是,越来越多的年轻人在业余时间已不再读书,而是看电视,跳舞,打电子游戏机,或者侃大山。

> **译文:** Despite my suspicion, there is virtually an increase in the number of the young adults who spend their spare time watching TV, going to dance parties, playing video games or chitchatting instead of reading books.

> **考点:** 1. 意译:跳舞→dance(直译)
>
>   →go to dance parties(意译)
>
> 2. 让步状语从句的翻译:不过尽管怀疑→despite my suspicion
>
> 3. 事实却是→副词:virtually,或处理成同位语从句:the fact is that

四、高尔基说过:"书籍是人类进步的阶梯。"

> **译文:** Gorgy once said, "Books are steps toward human progress."

> **考点:** 1. 人名的翻译:高尔基→Gorgy,音译
>
> 2. 名人名言的翻译

五、众所周知,书籍是人类智慧的结晶。

> **译文 1:** As we all know, books are a crystallization of human wisdom.

> **译文 2:** It is well known that books are a crystallization of human wisdom.

> **考点:** 转态译法:形式主语法:众所周知→It is well known

六、尽管现代传媒(如电视,计算机)在信息的传播速度上有许多优势,但到目前为止,还没有哪一种在传播知识的深度方面能取代书籍。

> **译文:** Despite the advantage of modern media such as TV and computers in the speed of

information dissemination/delivery, so far none of them can replace books in respect of the depth of knowledge being spread.

第十节　2001 年 9 月考题

TRANSLATION TEST (1) (30 minutes)

Direction: Translate the following passage into Chinese and write your version in the corresponding space in your ANSWER BOOKLET.

By the middle of this century, some two thirds of the world's nation, with at least five billion people, will enjoy a standard of living, which only the advanced economies now have. Some three billion of these people will live in Asia. Collectively, the Asian Countries will have a larger economy than the rest of the world put together.

The rest of the world will have to react to this millennial economic shift to Asia, and to the rising power of China. The rest of the world will be divided between the Euro-American countries, and the two big peripheral powers, Japan and Russia. Russia is a huge geographical country, with well educated people, and will eventually recover.

In terms of nations, it will be a world of much greater economic equality. Although there will still be poor countries, most will be quite rich. Inside these nations there will be mass prosperity, but with a large minority in serious poverty, and a small number who are very rich.

分析:

一、By the middle of this century, **some** two thirds of the world's nation, with at least five billion people, will enjoy **a standard of living**, (which only the advanced **economies** now have).

译文 1: 到本世纪中叶,世界上约三分之二的国家,至少 50 亿人口,将会过上当今发达经济体所享有的生活。

译文 2: 到本世纪中叶,世界上约三分之二的国家,至少 50 亿人口,将享受到目前只有经济发达国家才享有的生活水准。

考点: 1. some 在这里表示"大约",与数字连用。如: He spent some twenty years of his life in Africa.

　　 2. 定语从句的翻译: 前置法: 尽管这句定语从句为非限制性定语从句,但意思较简单,因此前置。

二、**Some** three billion of these people will live in Asia.

译文: 其中约 30 亿人口居住/生活在亚洲。

三、**Collectively**, the Asian Countries will have a larger **economy** than the rest of the world **put together**.

译文：亚洲国家的整体经济规模，将超过其他国家和地区(经济规模)的总和。

考点： 1. 转性译法：副词→形容词 collectively→整体的

collectively 本为副词，表示"集中起来"，如在一开始翻译，就会产生无主句的情况，令人匪夷所思。如翻译成"亚洲国家的经济规模集中起来"，也不是最佳。因此翻译成"亚洲国家的整体经济规模"，把 collectively 处理成"整体的"。

2. 具体译法：加字法：economy→经济体；经济规模

考生在翻译 economy 这个单词时，应注意其经常会出现具体译法而不解释为"经济"，可能会解释为"经济制度/现象/体/规模等等，总之考生应看清 economy 在语境中的含义，翻译成"经济××"。

3. 增词译法：整句在 than 之后其实省略了 the economy of，在翻译中应补全。

4. 换序译法：collectively 置于 the Asian Countries 后翻译

四、The rest of the world will have to **react to** this **millennial** economic **shift** to Asia, and to the rising power of China.

译文1：其他国家将不得不面对新千年吹向亚洲的经济东风和中华民族的迅速崛起。

译文2：在新千年，经济重心将向亚洲转移，中国的力量将日益强大，世界其他地区将不得不对此做出反应。

考点： 1. 意译：react to→面对，economic shift→经济东风

2. 换序译法：由于 react to 后的宾语偏长，因此可先翻译宾语的情况，再翻译主谓。

五、The rest of the world will be divided between the Euro-American countries, and the two big **peripheral powers**, Japan and Russia.

译文：它们被划分为欧美国家及两大边缘势力国家，日本和俄罗斯。

考点： 1. 省词译法：前句 the rest of the world 已经交待过，且主语相同，这里用"代词"简单重复即可。

2. peripheral powers→边缘势力国家；外围大国

六、Russia is a huge geographical country, with well educated people, and will eventually **recover**.

译文1：俄罗斯人杰地广，全面复苏只是时间问题。

译文2：俄罗斯人杰地广，东山再起指日可待。

译文3：俄罗斯幅员辽阔，国民素质良好，最终将东山再起。

考点：具体译法：成语法：Russia is a huge geographical country, with well educated people→俄罗斯人杰地广

七、**In terms of** nations, it will be a world of much greater economic equality.

译文1：就(每个)国家而言，各国的经济发展将实现更大程度的平等。

译文2：就(每个)国家而言，世界各国经济将越发不相上下。

考点: 转性译法: 名词→动词 economic equality→经济平衡,经济不相上下

八、Although there will still be poor countries, most will be quite rich.

译文 1: 尽管贫穷的国家还将继续存在,但大多数国家将会变得富足。

译文 2: 尽管仍有穷国,但大多数国家将相当富有。

九、Inside these nations there will be **mass prosperity**, but with a large minority in serious poverty, and a small number who are very rich.

译文: 这些国家呈现出欣欣向荣的态势,但是将出现两极分化,为数不少的弱势群体将极端贫穷,一小部分人则极端富有。

考点: 1. 具体译法: 成语法: mass prosperity→欣欣向荣

2. 转性译法: 名词→形容词 prosperity→欣欣向荣,poverty→贫穷

3. 增词译法: 在"极少数国家"后增加"两极分化",意思更加明确。

TRANSLATION TEST (2) (30 minutes)

Direction: Translate the following passage into English and write your version in the corresponding space in your ANSWER BOOKLET.

本届会议将围绕"新世纪、新挑战: 参与、合作、促进共同繁荣"的主题,审议五个方面的议题,以期促进亚太地区和全球经贸的发展。

今年的亚太经济贸易合作组织会议将主要侧重两个方面: 一是加强亚太经合组织成员之间的合作,共同应对可能出现的经济衰退,重树信心;二是继续推进亚太经合组织贸易投资自由化进程,推动世界贸易组织尽早开始新一轮谈判。

分析:

一、本届会议将围绕"新世纪、新挑战: 参与、合作、促进共同繁荣"的主题,审议五个方面的议题,以期促进亚太地区和全球经贸的发展。

译文 1: This meeting will discuss the topic of "new century, new challenge: participate, cooperate and promote common prosperity" covering 5 areas with a view to enhancing the development of economy and trade between the Asia-Pacific region and the rest world.

译文 2: This meeting will, centering round the theme of "Meeting new challenges in the new century: achieving common prosperity through participation and cooperation", reviewing the agenda under 5 heads with a view to promoting the economic and trade development in the Asia-Pacific region and the world at large.

考点: 1. 意译:"新世纪、新挑战: 参与、合作、促进共同繁荣"如译文 1 翻译纯粹采取直译,把字面意思翻译出来,而译文 2 把这句话的含义翻译出来,值得推荐。

方面→head

2. 转性译法: 动词→名词 参与→participation, 合作→cooperation

二、今年的亚太经济贸易合作组织会议将主要侧重两个方面：一是加强亚太经合组织成员之间的合作,共同应对可能出现的经济衰退,重树信心;二是继续推进亚太经合组织贸易投资自由化进程,推动世界贸易组织尽早开始新一轮谈判。

译文： The APEC meeting in this year will focus mainly on two aspects: one is on strengthening the cooperation among all the APEC members in confronting the possibly occurring economic recession with rebuilt-up confidence; the other is on facilitating the development of free trade and investment among all APEC members for the start of a new round of negotiations for WTO.

考点： 增词译法："一是加强"→one is on strengthening,因为前接 focus mainly on,因此增加 on 介词。

第十一节　2002年3月考题

TRANSLATION TEST (1) (30 minutes)

Directions: Translate the following passage into Chinese and write your version in the corresponding space in your ANSWER BOOKLET.

Foundations are tax-free institutions that are created to give grants to both individuals and nonprofit organizations for activities that range from education, research, and the arts to support for the poor and the upkeep of exotic gardens and old mansions. They provide a means by which wealthy people and corporations can in effect decide how their tax payments will be spent, for they are based on money that otherwise would go to the government in taxes. From a small beginning at the turn of the century they have become a very important factor in shaping developments in higher education and the arts.

Think tanks and university research institutes are nonprofit organizations that have been developed to provide settings for experts in various academic disciplines. In this way, they may devote their time to the study of policy alternatives free from the teaching and departmental duties that are part of the daily routine for most members of the academic community. Supported by foundation grants and government contracts, they are a major source of the new ideas that are discussed in the policy-formation groups.

分析：

一、Foundations are tax-free institutions (that are created to **give grants to** both individuals and nonprofit organizations for activities (that **range from** education, research, and the arts to support for the poor and the **upkeep** of **exotic gardens and old mansions**)).

译文： 基金会是免税组织，其设立的目的是赞助一系列个人或非赢利性组织的活动，包括教育、调研及美术/艺术,以及扶贫和对奇园古宅进行养护。

考点: 1. 层次断句: 这句话相当复杂。句中套了两句定语从句,一句修饰主句中的 institutions,另一句修饰 activities,另一个难点是 support 前的 to 到底承接哪里,其实它和前面的 from 构成了 from...to... 的短语,判断了 to 的结构后,就不会把 to 后的内容理解成目的了。

2. 定语从句的翻译:
第一句是重复法,Foundations are tax-free institutions that are created to...→基金会是免税组织,其设立……
第二句是省略法,activities that range from education, research, and the arts→活动,包括教育、调研及艺术

3. 转态译法: 省略被动词 that are created to→其设立

4. the arts 的翻译: the arts 对于词汇较好的考生来说极易理解成"人文学科;文科"等,不过不知大家有没有注意到定冠词 the,原来 arts 解释为"人文学科;文科",但 the arts 相当于 fine art,解释为"美术;艺术"。

5. 转性译法:
形容词→名词
support for the poor→扶贫
the poor→穷人(the + 形容词 表示一类人)
名词→动词 the upkeep of→进行养护

6. 具体译法: 成语法: exotic gardens and old mansions→奇园古宅

二、They provide a means (by which) **wealthy** people and corporations can in effect decide how their tax payments will be spent, for they are based on money (that otherwise would go to the government in taxes).

译文: 通过基金会,有钱人和大公司能实际支配缴纳税款的用途,因为这些税款如果不用于基金会,就会划并到政府税收中去。

考点: 1. wealthy people 翻译成"有钱人"可以,但 wealthy corporations 翻译成"有钱的公司"语义就不明确了,可以翻译成"大公司"。

2. 定语从句的翻译: 省略法:
They provide a means by which wealthy people...→
基金会提供了一种方式可以让有钱人……
for they are based on money that otherwise would go to the government in taxes→因为这些税款如果不用于基金会,就会划并到政府税收中去。

三、**From a small beginning** at the turn of the century they have become a very important factor in **shaping** developments in higher education and the arts.

译文: 本世纪初,基金会数量并不多/比较少,而现在已在高等教育和艺术发展的格局中显得举足轻重了。

考点： 1. 转性译法：动词→名词 shape→格局

2. 正反译法：small→不多

3. 增词译法：From a small beginning 这句话许多考生在翻译时根本没有注意到，有人理解成和 at the turn of the century 相同的意思，其实在 small 后面省略 number，表示基金会数量在本世纪一开始不多。在翻译时应补充"数量"。

4. 换序译法：at the turn of the century 在句首翻译

四、**Think tanks** and university research institutes are nonprofit organizations (that have been developed to provide **settings** for experts in various academic **disciplines**).

译文1： 智囊团和大学中的研究机构是非赢利性组织，为不同学术领域的专家提供了舞台。

译文2： 智囊团和大学中的研究机构是不同学术领域专家栖息的非赢利性组织。

考点： 1. think tanks: organization or group of experts providing advice and ideas on national or commercial problems 为国家或商业问题提供建议、解决方法的专家小组或组织；智囊团

2. 定语从句的翻译：省略法

3. 意译：settings→舞台

4. 转态译法：省略不译

5. 转性译法：名词→动词 settings→栖息

五、In this way, they may **devote** their time **to** the study of policy **alternatives free from** the teaching and **departmental duties** (that are part of the daily routine for most members of the **academic community**).

译文： 正因为如此，这些专家就可以从大多数学术人士习以为常的日常教学和科系公务中脱离出来，全身心地投入到政策的研究中去。

考点： 1. alternative 的翻译：alternative 作为名词有以下常见解释：

- 两者（或两者以上）择其一

  eg. People above 30 have the alternative of marrying or remaining a bachelor.

  30 岁以上的人可以选择结婚，也可以选择独身。

- 数种可能性（解决办法）之一

  eg. One of the alternatives open to you is to resign.

  你面前的一项选择就是辞职。

- （选择题的）选项

  eg. In each question, you have 4 alternatives to choose, among which there is only one correct answer.

  每道问题有四个选项，其中只有一个是正确答案。

- 替代品

  eg. In modern society, we must find some biodegradable alternatives to plastics in order to avoid environmental pollution.

在现代社会中，我们必须找到一些可降解的材料来代替塑料，从而避免环境污染。

2. free from 的翻译：文中的 free from 相当于 without 的意思，表示"脱离；没有"等意思，其同义词有 lacking, short of, excluding, immune to 等

3. 换序译法：从原文分析，"脱离教学和公务"在前，而"投入政策研究"在后，两者是时间的先后关系。因此可以先翻译 free from 的部分，然后再翻译 devote their time to the study of policy alternatives。

4. 定语从句的翻译：前置法

5. 转性译法：形容词→动词　free→脱离

名词→动词　routine→习以为常

六、Supported by foundation **grants** and government contracts, they are a major source of the new ideas (that are discussed in the policy-formation groups).

译文： 有了基金会的资助和政府的合约（保护），这些专家就能够为政策的制定提供源源不断的新思维。

考点： 1. 转性译法：名词→形容词 source→源源不断的

2. 定语从句的翻译：综合法

TRANSLATION TEST (2) (30 minutes)

Directions: Translate the following passage into English and write your version in the corresponding space in your ANSWER BOOKLET.

我总以为，在中国效率最高的会议要数学校召集的家长会。家长会完全符合"廉政建设"的要求，与会的家长绝不会像参加行业、单位的一些会议，先看看会议地点是不是设在风景旅游区，会后发不发纪念品之类，然后方决定是否参加。其他会议都难得准时，惟有家长会绝对正点召开。在家长会上，家长们个个全神贯注地倾听、记录，生怕漏掉一点内容。不少会议都可列入可开可不开之列，但对于学校和家长而言，家长会则是必不可少的。

分析：

一、我总以为，在中国效率最高的会议要数（学校召集的）家长会。

译文： I always believe that the most efficient meeting in China is the parents' meeting called by the school.

考点： 1. "家长会"的翻译："家长会"翻译成 the parents' meeting，而不是 the parent's meeting，有人认为家长会一般只是一位家长参加，应用 parent 单数，不过这是专业表达方法。关于会议集锦请参考 1997 年 9 月试题汉译英部分（第四章第二节）。

2. 比较级的翻译：最高级：效率最高的→most efficient

3. 定语从句的翻译：前置法

二、家长会完全符合"廉政建设"的要求，与会的家长绝不会像参加(行业、单位的)一些会议,先看看会议地点是不是设在风景旅游区,会后发不发纪念品之类,然后方决定是否参加。

译文： The parents' meeting is in full conformity with the requirements for "building an honest and clean government". Before making a decision whether to attend the meeting or not, nobody will be interested in knowing whether the meeting place is located in a tourist area and whether gifts or souvenirs will be handed out after the meeting while these factors are commonly considered in the case of attending meetings organized by a certain trade or unit.

考点： 1. 专业名词的翻译：廉政建设→building an honest and clean government

2. 转性译法：发纪念品→gifts or souvenirs will be handed out

3. 省词译法：原文中"与会的家长",不少的考生把它翻译成 the parents who attend the meeting, 其实犯了一个逻辑错误,因为后面提到"方决定是否参加",说明参加不参加不一定,因此前面就不能讲"已经参加了",所以"与会的家长"中"与会的"就不必翻译了。

三、其他会议都难得准时,惟有家长会绝对正点召开。

译文： While other meetings are rarely convened on time, the parents' meeting absolutely／invariably starts with punctuality.

考点： 1. 正反译法：绝对→invariably

2. convene: summon (people) to come together; arrange (a meeting, etc.) 召集；召开(会议)

四、在家长会上,家长们个个全神贯注地倾听、记录,生怕漏掉一点内容。

译文 1: At the parents' meeting, every parent is devoted to／concentrated on listening and taking notes so as not to miss anything.

译文 2: At the parents' meeting, every parent is devoted to／concentrated on listening and taking notes for fear that he or she might miss anything.

考点： 1. 转性译法：副词→名词　　全神贯注地→attention

动词→连词　　生怕→lest

2. lest 的翻译: lest 是一个较正规的连词,可以翻译成"惟恐；以免；生怕"。

五、不少会议都可列入可开可不开之列,但对于学校和家长而言,家长会则是必不可少的。

译文： It does not really matter whether some meetings are to be held or not, however, the parents' meeting is absolutely necessary／indispensable to the school and the parents.

考点: 正反译法: 必不可少的→necessary(正译)
　　　　　　　　　　→indispensable(反译)

第十二节　2002 年 9 月考题

TRANSLATION TEST（1）（30 minutes）

Direction: Translate the following passage into Chinese and write your version in the corresponding space in your ANSWER BOOKLET.

　　If the Immigration and Naturalization Service (INS) thinks it can largely curtail the nation's terrorism problems by focusing on college students, we all should worry.

　　Identification cards already are required here for most persons to enter their workplace, take an airplane flight or go into a public building, including my campus library. The idea of a national ID, however, was locked out of earlier drafts of legislation by a coalition of civil rights and ethnic groups, who opposed a requirement that all non-citizens carry identifying documents. In some degree, they have a point.

　　We must face the fact — and benefit from realizing—that no one can drive, or fly, or enter many private and public buildings without a picture ID, usually a driver's license or passport. That means that practically all Americans already must have what in effect is a national ID card.

　　We already routinely screen people. If we would just make good use of the national ID cards we have — and improve them—we could enhance our safety, avoid discrimination and not spend millions on another system.

分析:

一、If the **Immigration and Naturalization Service** (INS) thinks it can largely **curtail** the nation's terrorism problems by **focusing on** college students, we all should worry.

　　译文: 如果移民归化局认为，它能够通过对大学生进行重点管理，大体上减少在美国的恐怖主义活动，我们大家都应当为此担心。

　　考点: 1. Immigration and Naturalization Service→移民归化局
　　　　　　service 在前面已经提过,表示一个机构。Naturalization 不解释为"自然化",此涵义考生可能比较模糊,其动词 naturalize 表示 make (sb. from another country) a citizen (of the specified country) 使加入……国籍;使成为……国公民;使归化。
　　　　　2. 意译: focus on→将注意力集中在(直译)
　　　　　　　　　　→对……进行重点管理(意译)
　　　　　　problem→问题(直译)
　　　　　　　　　　→活动(意译)

二、Identification cards already are required here for most persons to enter their workplace, take an airplane flight or go into a public building, including my campus library.

译文：在美国，现在大多数人进入工作场所，乘飞机或进入公共大楼，包括我所在大学的图书馆，已经需要出示身份证。

考点：1. 转态译法：

被主交换：Identification cards already are required→已经需要出示身份证

2. 换序译法：Identification cards already are required 在最后翻译

三、(4) The idea of a **national ID**, however, (3) was **locked out of** earlier **drafts** of legislation by (1) a **coalition** of **civil rights** and **ethnic groups**, (2) (who opposed a requirement that all **non-citizens** carry identifying documents).

译文：然而，公民权利维护团体和少数民族结成联盟共同反对要求非美国公民必须随身携带身份证的提案，因此，最初的几次立法草案都未收录关于实施全国统一身份证的主张。

考点：1. 换序译法：翻译顺序如上句所示：(1)(2)(3)(4)

2. 定语从句的翻译：省略法

3. 同位语从句的翻译：requirement that all non-citizens carry identifying documents 中 that 引导的是一句同位语从句，表示 requirement 的内容。

4. 转态译法：被主交换：was locked out of→推翻

5. 转性译法：名词→动词 coalition→结成联盟

四、In some degree, they have a **point**.

译文：在某种程度上，他们是有道理的。

考点："在某种程度上"一般可以翻译成 to a certain extent, to some extent, in some degree 等

五、We must face the fact — and benefit from realizing—that **no** one can drive, or fly, or enter many private and public buildings **without** a **picture** ID, usually a driver's license or passport.

译文：我们必须面对这一事实，并因认识到这一事实而获益，即每一个人驾车、乘飞机或进入许多私人大楼或公共大楼，都必须出示有照片的身份证，通常是驾驶执照或护照。

考点：1. 同位语从句的翻译：We must face the fact. . . that

2. 正反译法：双重否定 no one can. . . without→每一个人都必须……

3. picture 在这里解释为"照片"，比如说 take pictures→拍照片

六、That means that **practically** all Americans already must have (what **in effect** is a national ID card).

译文：这意味着，实际上所有美国人早就持有事实上的全国通用的身份证。

考点：定语从句的翻译：

省略法: have what in effect is a national ID card→持有事实上的全国通用的身份证,这里 what 相当于 sth. that。

七、We already routinely **screen** people.

译文 1: 对人们进行甄别,在我们这儿早就是例行公事。

译文 2: 对人们进行检查,在我们这里早就是家常便饭。

考点: 1. screen 作动词,请考生掌握以下两大重要意思:

- to examine (a job applicant, for example) systematically in order to determine suitability

eg. The applications were carefully screened in case any of them contained false information.

对申请书进行了仔细检查,以防止弄虚作假。

eg. Government employees are often screened by the security services.

政府雇员经常受到安全部门甄别。

- to test or examine for the presence of disease or infection

eg. screen blood for the presence of a virus; screen patients in an epidemic zone

2. 转性译法: 副词→名词　routinely→例行公事;家常便饭

3. 具体译法: 成语法: routinely→家常便饭

八、If we would just **make** good **use of** the national ID cards (we have) — and improve them— we could enhance our safety, avoid discrimination and not spend **millions** on another system.

译文: 只要好好利用大家已持有的全国通用身份证,并加以改进,就可以增强安全,避免歧视,而不必在另一个系统花上数百万美元。

考点: 1. 定语从句的翻译: 前置法

2. 具体译法: 加字法: millions→数百万美元

TRANSLATION TEST (2) (30 minutes)

Directions: Translate the following passage into English and write your version in the corresponding space in your ANSWER BOOKLET.

到 2007 年,上海市人均国内生产总值预计达到 7,500 美元。这一目标的实现,最直接的应该是老百姓住得更宽敞,更舒服了。因为从市民的衣、食、住、行消费来讲,住房是一个重要的因素,而且占了大头。届时,上海人均住房面积会大幅增加。除此以外,老百姓的服务性消费,如教育、信息、旅游等消费也会大量增长。用一句话来说,那便是未来老百姓的生活会更好,那时的老百姓的生活将和中等发达国家的居民一样。

分析:

一、到 2007 年,上海市人均国内生产总值预计达到 7,500 美元。

译文: By 2007, the per capita GDP in Shanghai is expected to reach 7,500 US dollars.

考点: 1. "人均"的翻译: 在这里"人均"如处理成 every person,在翻译自然度和专业度上一定会扣分。应翻译成 per capita,考生还应注意以下与 per capita 有关的语汇:

per capita productivity→人均产量

per capita ceiling principle→国民平均最高限额原则

per capita consumption→人均消费量

per capita levy→居民人均税额

per capita production→按人口计算的生产

per capita real output→人均实际产量

2. 缩略语的翻译: 国内生产总值→GDP,以下一些常见缩略语也应掌握:

GNP = Gross National Product 国民生产总值

GDP = Gross Domestic Product 国内生产总值

MNC = Multi-National Corporation 跨国公司

SOE = State-Owned Enterprise 国有企业

EEC = European Economic Community 欧洲经济共同体

EU = European Union 欧盟

ASEAN = Association of Southeast Asian Nations 东南亚国家联盟

NATO = North Atlantic Treaty Organization 北大西洋公约组织

CENTO = Central Treaty Organization 中央条约组织

FAO = Food and Agriculture Organization 联合国粮食与农业组织

IATA = International Air Transport Association 国际航空运输协会

ILO = International Labour Organization 国际劳工组织

CPIT = Committee for the Promotion of International Trade 国际贸易促进会

IMF = International Monetary Fund 国际货币基金组织

IBO = International Broadcasting Organization 国际广播组织

IOC = International Olympic Committee 国际奥林匹克委员会

IDA = International Development Association 国际开发协会

ISO = International Standards Organization 国际标准组织

OPEC = Organization of Petroleum Exporting Countries 石油输出国家组织

APEC = Asia-Pacific Economic Cooperation 亚太经合组织

SAR = Special Administrative Region 特别行政区

UN = United Nations 联合国

WTO = World Trade Organization 世界贸易组织

WHO = World Health Organization 世界卫生组织

WB = World Bank 世界银行

UNICEF = United Nations International Children's Emergency Fund 联合国儿童基金会

CIA = Central Intelligence Agency（美）中央情报局

FBI = Federal Bureau of Investigation（美）联邦调查局

NBA = National Basketball Association（美）全国篮球协会

EMS = Express Mail Service 速递公司

R&D = Research and Development 研究与发展/研发

OTC = Over The Counter 非处方药

3. 时态问题：本句中出现 by 2007，原本谓语应使用将来完成时，但是由于动词是"预计"，反映现在的动作，因此还是使用一般现在时，如原文为"到 2007 年，上海市人均国内生产总值将达到 7,500 美元"，译文则为：By 2007, the per capita GDP in Shanghai will have reached 7,500 US dollars.

二、(3)这一目标的实现，(2)最直接的应该是(1)老百姓(4)住得更宽敞，更舒服了。

译文 1: The goal's direct result is that common people will live more spaciously and comfortably.

译文 2: Common people will enjoy larger living space and greater comfort, benefiting most directly from the attainment of the goal.

考点： 1. 换序译法：这句话有两种翻译顺序：(1)(2)(3)(4)

  (1)(4)(2)(3)

2. 转性译法：形容词→副词 宽敞→spaciously，舒服→comfortably

三、因为从市民的衣、食、住、行消费来讲，住房是一个重要的因素，而且占了大头。

译文： As an important factor for living, housing takes a lion's share in the total budget covering clothing, food, shelter and transportation.

考点： 1. 具体译法：占了大头→a lion's share

2. 换序译法："住房是一个重要的因素，而且占了大头"可以先翻译

四、届时，上海人均住房面积会大幅增加。

译文： At that time, the average per capita living space will surge dramatically.

考点： 翻译的多样性：

住房面积→living space/dwelling area

大幅增长→increase/surge sharply/dramatically/

  considerably/significantly/immensely/

  tremendously/substantially

  →soar/rocket

  →increase by a large margin

五、除此以外，老百姓的服务性消费，如教育、信息、旅游等消费也会大量增长。

译文： In addition/Bcsidcs, this is also the case with civic expenditure on such services as education, information and traveling.

考点： 省词译法：考生应该发现此句中的"也会大量增长"与前句最后重复，因此在翻译时可以不再重复，用 This is the case with sth，表示以上陈述描写也适用于 with 后的宾语。

六、用一句话来说，那便是未来老百姓的生活会更好，那时的老百姓的生活将和中等发达国家的居民一样。

译文： In a word/nutshell, the citizens will live a better life, a life of the same standard enjoyed by those in the middle-ranking developed countries.

考点： 1. 具体译法：用一句话来说→in a nutshell
　　　　　 2. 比较级的翻译

第十三节　2003 年 3 月考题

TRANSLATION TEST（1）（30 minutes）

Directions: Translate the following passage into Chinese and write your version in the corresponding space in your ANSWER BOOKLET.

If there's a threat of dangerous deflation—a general fall in prices—the causes lie as much in Europe and Japan as in the United States. The inevitable collapse of America's speculative boom would not have been especially damaging if the world's other advanced economies were healthy. Their expanding appetite for imports would have bolstered the United States and so-called emerging-market countries, from Brazil to South Korea. The trouble is that other advanced economies aren't healthy.

Deflation could emerge from simultaneous slumps in the world's three major economies. Prices drop because there's too little global demand chasing too much global supply—everything from steel to shoes. Japan's ills are well known. Its banks are awash in bad loans. Less understood (at least in the United States) is the fact the Europe's troubles stem significantly from Germany. Germany is Europe's "sick man", just as Japan is Asia's. Only 15 years ago, these countries seemed poised to assume leadership of the world economy. Now they are dragging it down.

分析:

一、If there's a threat of dangerous **deflation**—**a general fall in prices**—**the causes lie as much in Europe and Japan as in the United States.**

译文： 如果全球经济中出现通货紧缩的危险信号——即消费品价格普遍下跌的现象，

那么欧洲、日本以及美国都难辞其咎。

考点: 1. 增词译法:本句在"价格普遍下跌"前后分别加了"消费品"和"的现象",如不指明主语是"消费品",一、读者可能会觉得句意不清,二、deflation 的定义为: a persistent decrease in the level of consumer prices or a persistent increase in the purchasing power of money because of a reduction in available currency and credit,表示主要是消费品价格下跌,这也是通货紧缩的定义对翻译的一个增词要求。后面不增加"的现象",句意不完整。

2. 比较级的翻译: as much in Europe and Japan as in the United States 这句中考生请注意其语义断开的位置,Europe and Japan 是一个词群,the United States 是另一个词群,因此不能简单处理成"欧洲、日本和美国",应稍强调一下美国,翻译成"欧洲、日本以及美国"。

3. 意译: the causes lie... →难逃其咎

二、**The inevitable** collapse of America's **speculative boom** need not have been especially damaging if the world's other advanced **economies** were healthy.

译文: 如果世界上其他发达经济体保持良好态势,(即使)美国投机热不可避免地覆灭,(也)不会带来特别的危害。

考点: 1. 转性译法:名词→动词　　collapse→覆灭
　　　　　　　 形容词→名词　　damaging→危害

2. 增词译法:即使……也……,这对让步词组的增加可以使句子的涵义更加清晰。

3. 换序译法:先翻译条件从句,再翻译主句。

4. 具体译法:加字法: economy→经济体;经济制度

三、Their expanding appetite for imports would have **bolstered** the United States and so-called **emerging** market countries, from Brazil to South Korea.

译文: 那些国家热衷于进口,确实给美国和一些所谓新兴市场国家如巴西、韩国打了一针强心剂。

考点: 1. 转性译法:名词→动词 appetite→热衷于

2. 意译: bolster→支持;助长;援助(直译)
　　　　　→给……打了一针强心剂(意译)
　　　 from Brazil to South Africa→从巴西到韩国(直译)
　　　　　　　　　　　　→如巴西、韩国(意译)

"从巴西到韩国"有歧义,似乎包括从巴西到韩国所有地域的国家,其实这里只是举了两个新兴国家的例子,可以用"如……"来翻译。

四、The trouble is that other advanced **economies** aren't healthy.

译文 1: (不过)问题在于其他发达经济体并不完善。

译文 2: (不过)问题在于其他发达经济体存在弊端。

考点： 1. 具体译法：加字法：economy→经济体；经济制度

         2. 正反译法：other economies aren't healthy→其他发达经济体并不完善（正译）

                                                →其他发达经济体存在弊端（反译）

五、Deflation could emerge from **simultaneous slumps** in the world's three major economies.

译文： 如果全球三大经济体同时下滑，通货紧缩就会产生。

考点： 1. 具体译法：加字法：economy→经济体；经济制度

         2. 转性译法：名词→动词 slump→下滑

六、(3) Prices drop (2) because there's too little global demand chasing too much global supply—everything from steel to shoes.

译文： 从钢铁业到鞋业，全球需求急剧萎缩，而供给却源源不断，从而/这样就会导致商品价格下跌。

考点： 1. 换序译法：翻译顺序为：(1)(2)(3)

         2. 具体译法：加字法：steel→钢铁业，shoe→鞋业

         3. 转性译法：形容词→动词 little→萎缩，much→源源不断

七、Japan's **ills** are well known. Its banks are **awash** in **bad loans**.

译文： 众所周知的是，日本的症结在于银行不良贷款的冲击。

考点： 1. 意译：ills→病（直译）

               →症结；弊端（意译）

           awash→被海浪冲平或洗刷的（直译）

               →充斥，冲击

         2. 转性译法：形容词→名词 awash→冲击

八、Less understood（at least in the United States）is the fact the Europe's troubles **stem** significantly **from** Germany.

译文： 但有一点全世界（至少美国）搞不太明白，即欧洲国家的经济问题主要由德国引起。

考点： 1. 具体译法：加字法：troubles→经济问题

         2. 转态译法：被主交换：less understood→搞不太明白

         3. 增词译法：被主交换后缺乏主语，应为"全世界"，应补齐翻译。

         4. 比较级的翻译：less understood，跟前句的 are well known 相比，表示大家对此并没有做到达成共识，但也不是完全不懂，因而不能翻译成"搞不明白"，可译成"搞不太明白"。

九、Germany is Europe's "**sick man**", just as Japan is Asia's.

译文： 德国是欧洲的病根，就像日本是亚洲的病根一样，

考点： 1. sick man→病人（直译）

               →病根（意译）

         2. 比较级的翻译：just as→和……一样

3. 增词译法: just as Japan is Asia's→就像日本是亚洲的病根一样

十、Only 15 years ago, these countries seemed poised to **assume** leadership of the world economy. Now they are **dragging it down**.

译文: 仅仅 15 年前,这些国家曾信誓旦旦地想要争做全球经济的领头羊,而现在却在拖后腿。

考点: 具体译法: 加字法: leadership→领头羊

成语法: poised→信誓旦旦, drag it down→拖后腿

TRANSLATON TEST (2) (30 minutes)

Directions: Translate the following passage into English and write your version in the corresponding space in your ANSWER BOOKLET.

中国改革开放以来,国民经济年均增长速度达到 9.7%。中国已经发展成为一个全球极富吸引力的大市场。世界各国和地区不少有远见卓识的企业家,都将目光投向了中国,投向了西部,并从投资活动中获得了丰厚的回报。中国加入世贸组织后,外商参与中国西部开发的机会越来越多。西部大开发一定能成为沟通世界各国和中国的一座桥梁,促进中国和世界经济共同发展,共同繁荣。

分析:

一、中国改革开放以来,国民经济年均增长速度达到 9.7%。

译文: Since the adoption of opening and reform policy, China's annual growth of national economy has reached 9.7%.

二、中国已经发展成为一个(全球极富吸引力的)大市场。

译文 1: China has developed into a big market attractive to the rest of the world.

译文 2: China has developed into an attractive big global market.

考点: 1. 换序译法: 如像译文 2 般的三个形容词累加堆砌,句子侧重点有所削弱。可以首先翻译出"大市场",然后"对全球富有吸引力",中间把语义断开,如译文 1 所示。

2. 形容词修饰的位置: 如像译文 2 那样翻译,考生请注意形容词修饰的先后关系,英语中形容词之间存在优先关系,大致如下: 定冠词〉一般形容词〉大小形状的形容词〉国籍形容词〉颜色形容词〉材料质地形容词〉分词。请看实例: a beautiful giant Indian amber wooden eating table→一张漂亮的琥珀色的木质印度大饭桌,考生可以感觉到中英在选择形容词的顺序上有很大的区别。

3. 定语从句的翻译: 前置法: 全球极富吸引力的大市场→a big market which is attractive to the rest of the world

三、世界各国和地区不少有远见卓识的企业家,都将目光投向了中国,投向了西部,并从投资活动中获得了丰厚的回报。

译文: Numerous/A number of entrepreneurs of foresight around the world have cast their eye on China, especially the west China and gained abundant profit/profitability from investment.

考点： 1. "有远见卓识的"可以翻译成 far-sighted，也可以翻译成 of foresight

2. 转性译法：形容词→名词 有远见卓识的→foresight

3. 直译与意译："将目光投向了中国"→cast their eye (eyes ×) on China (直译)

→China draws the attention of... (意译)

→China catches the eye of... (意译)

4. 抽象译法：减词法：投资活动→investment

四、中国加入世贸组织后，外商参与中国西部开发的机会越来越多。

译文： After China's entry into the WTO, there are more and more opportunities for foreign businessmen to join in the development of China's West.

考点： 1. 转性译法：动词→名词 加入→entry

2. 词组辨析："参与"有多种译法。join 指参加政党、军队、俱乐部、战争等正式组织或活动；take part in 指参加一些非正式的活动或会议，其同义词有 attend 和 participate；join in 指和某人一起做某事，有"加入"的意思；enroll 指"入会；入学"，可以解释为"注册"；enlist 特指"入伍；参军"。

五、西部大开发一定能成为沟通世界各国和中国的一座桥梁，促进中国和世界经济共同发展，共同繁荣。

译文： The Great Development of China's West is sure to be a bridge between China and the rest of the world, which promotes/promoting the common development and prosperity of China and the world.

考点： 定语从句的翻译：省略法

第十四节 2003 年 9 月考题

TRANSLATION TEST (1) (30 minutes)

Directions: Translate the following passage into Chinese and write your version in the corresponding space in your ANSWER BOOKLET

The expansion of the universities since the beginning of World War II and the great increase in number of college graduates and Ph. D. s have produced a corps of technicians, aides, speechwriters, symbol manufacturers, investigators, and policy proposers who are now employed by practical men in all institutions. These people, called intellectuals in the sense that they deal with symbols and ideas, have become professionalized in exactly the same sense as the engineer. Unlike the engineer, however, these professional intellectuals are free from much of the routine grind of daily work: they carry light teaching load and enjoy government and foundation grants and subsidies for their research.

The professor's project budget is the initial economic base that supports his independence within the university. The project budget sustains both the existence of graduate students and the fiscal solvency of the university, which takes a percentage "overhead" out of every project budget. The major feature of project money, whether its source is government or business, is that it is given on a contractual basis, a different contract for each project, so that the investigator's independence rests upon his capacity to secure a succession of contracts. The ability to secure contracts is a genuine talent among professional intellectuals.

分析:

一、(2) The expansion of the universities (1) since the beginning of World War II and (3) the great increase in number of college graduates and **Ph. D. s** have **produced** a **corps** of **technicians, aides, speechwriters, symbol manufacturers, investigators,** and **policy proposers** (4)(who are now employed by practical men in all institutions).

译文: 第二次世界大战以来，大学的数目不断增长，本科、甚至是博士毕业生也与日俱增，从而诞生了大批的技术人员、助手、演讲稿撰写人、徽章生产商、调查人员和政策研究员，他们效力于各类务实的机构中。

考点: 1. 转性译法：名词→动词　expansion→不断增长，increase→与日俱增

2. 换序译法：翻译顺序：(1)(2)(3)(4)

3. produce→诞生

a corps of→大批的

corps 的含义: a body of persons acting together or associated under common direction

eg. the press corps 记者团

4. 难词的翻译：这里从 technician 到 policy proposers 共六个单词都不是很好翻译，考生请注意平时的积累。

5. 定语从句的翻译：重复法

6. 转态译法：被主交换: who are now employed→效力于

7. 省词译法: who are now employed by practical men in all institutions 这句中 practical man 解释为"实干家"，但整句翻译成"他们被各类研究所里的实干家雇佣"，略显累赘，因此可以把 man 在翻译中省略，译成"他们效力于各类务实的机构中"即可。

二、(4) These people, called intellectuals **in the sense** that (1) they **deal with** symbols and ideas, (3) have become professionalized (2) in exactly **the same** sense **as** the engineer.

译文: 这些人员主要与符号和概念打交道，所以人们把他们称为知识分子，他们已经与工程师几乎一样高度专业化。

考点： 1. in a sense 解释为"在某种意义上"。如：What you've said is in a sense a great insult to his dignity. →你的话语在某种程度上对他的尊严是一种侮辱。

2. 意译：deal with→对付；处理（直译）

　　　　　　　　→打交道（意译）

3. 换序译法：翻译顺序：(1)(2)(3)(4)

4. 比较级的翻译：exactly the same sense as the engineer→与工程师几乎一样

5. 转态翻译：被主交换：called intellectuals→人们把它们称为知识分子

三、Unlike the engineer, however, these professional intellectuals are free from much of the routine **grind** of daily work: they carry **light** teaching load and enjoy government and foundation **grants** and **subsidies** for their research.

译文： 然而这些人员与工程师还有所不同——他们不需从事繁重的日常例行工作，仅承担少量教学工作，同时享受政府研究津贴或补贴。

考点： 1. 正反译法：free from→不需

2. 转性译法：形容词→动词　　free from→不需从事

　　　　　　　名词→形容词　　grind→繁重的

grind（n.）：a laborious task, routine, or study 苦力，苦差；费力的任务、日常工作或学习

3. light：easy to carry out or perform

eg. Since her accident, she can only do light work.

四、The professor's **project budget** is the **initial** economic base (that supports his independence within the university).

译文： 项目预算是教授在大学里保持独立的基本前提。

考点： 定语从句的翻译：前置法

五、The project budget sustains both the existence of graduate students and the fiscal **solvency** of the university, (which takes a percentage "**overhead**" out of every project budget).

译文： 研究生的存在，大学的资金偿还能力，这些都依靠项目预算。大学的资金偿还在每个项目预算中都占有重要比例。

考点： 1. 意译：sustain：maintain; keep the existence of→维持。由于"维持"后的宾语较长，可以先把宾语译出，把"项目预算"作为宾语，用谓语"依靠"连接，句子就比较平衡。

2. 转性译法：名词→动词 existence→存在

3. 定语从句的翻译：重复法

六、The major feature of project money, whether its source is government or business, is that it is given on a **contractual** basis, a different contract **for** each project, **so that** the investigator's independence **rests upon** his capacity to **secure** a succession of contracts.

译文： 无论来自于政府或商界，项目资金的重要特点是其建立在契约上，即不同的项

目可以争取不同的项目资金，因此调研人员要取得独立，就必须得到连续的研究项目。

考点： 1. 转性译法：形容词→名词　contractual→契约

介词→动词　for→争取

2. 具体译法：加字法：project→项目资金

3. contract→合同（误译）

→项目；研究项目（正译）

secure→保护（误译）

→得到（正译）

4. 意译：rest upon→建立在……的基础上（直译）

→必须（意译）

5. so that 的翻译：表示结果

so that 和 so...that... 在翻译中一般不是表示"目的"，就是表示"结果"。前者可以翻译成"以此"，后者可翻译成"从而"，不过有时两者的区别并不明显。如：

- She worked hard so that everything would be ready before 5 o'clock.（目的）
- Nothing was heard from him so that we began to wonder if he was dead. （结果）

七、The ability to secure contracts is a genuine talent among professional intellectuals.

译文： 获得研究项目是知识分子的一种真正才能。

TRANSLATION TEST (2) (30 minutes)

Directions: Translate the following passage into English and write your version in the corresponding space in your ANSWER BOOKLET.

经过 20 多年的快速发展，中国西部地区已奠定了一定的物质技术基础，社会保持稳定，市场经济体制正在逐步建立和完善，为西部经济持续快速增长创造了有利的市场环境。中国政府坚持实行以扩大内需为主的发展方针，并把扩大内需与调整经济结构，推动科技进步，促进对外开放结合起来。随着西部大开发战略的稳步推进，西部地区的资源优势，经济优势将得到充分发挥，经济增长的质量和水平将进一步提高。

分析:

一、经过二十多年的快速发展，中国西部地区已奠定了一定的物质技术基础。

译文: Thanks to the rapid (economic) development in the past 20-plus years, a relatively solid foundation in terms of material wealth and technology was laid in the western region of China.

考点: 1. 转态译法：主被交换

2. 经过二十多年的快速发展→Having experienced the rapid development for more than 20/a score years(直译)，这种译法也可，而且更易为广大考生所接受，不过后面的逻辑主语必须是"中国西部地区"，因此后面可以译成 the western region of China has witnessed a relatively solid foundation in terms of material wealth and technology，跟原译文相比，意思有些改变，因此最好的方式是把"经过"处理成"由于"的意思,而主句使用被动语态。

二、社会保持稳定，市场经济体制正在逐步建立和完善，为西部经济持续快速增长创造了有利的市场环境。

译文： The society maintains a rather satisfactory stability. The market economic system is in the process of establishment and healthy development. All these combined to provide a favourable market environment for the western region to maintain the economy's sustained and fast growth.

考点： 增词译法：为西部经济持续快速增长→for the western region to maintain the economy's sustained and fast growth

三、中国政府坚持实行以扩大内需为主的发展方针，并把扩大内需与调整经济结构，推动科技进步,促进对外开放结合起来。

译文： While focusing on its policy of raising domestic demand, the Chinese government also attaches rather great importance to the restructuring of the economy, the promotion of the scientific and technological development, the deepening of the opening-up policy as well.

考点： 转性译法：名词→形容词　　科技→scientific and technological

　　　　　动词→名词　　　　调整→restructuring

　　　　　　　　　　　　　推动→promotion

　　　　　　　　　　　　　促进→deepening

四、随着西部大开发战略的稳步推进,西部地区的资源优势,经济优势将得到充分发挥,经济增长的质量和水平将进一步提高。

译文： The development strategy of the western region, in the advancement, will give full play to its economic advantage in resources and thus further improving the quality and standard of the economic growth.

考点： 转态译法：主被交换：将得到充分发挥→will give full play to

第十五节　　2004 年 3 月考题

TRANSLATION TEST (1) (30 minutes)

Directions: Translate the following passage into Chinese and write your version in the corresponding space in your ANSWER BOOKLET.

For 8 years, students at Michigan State University borrowed tuition money directly from the federal government. But last spring, university officials shucked that arrangement and signed up with private lenders and a state agency that provides loans under a separate federal plan. They guaranteed a profit to the university—something the federal government could not do. Sounds sweet for Michigan State, but it's not so terrific for federal taxpayers, who will almost certainly wind up shelling out $23. 5 million more each year as a result of the charge.

Michigan State is not unique. Today, dozens of colleges and universities are abandoning the Department of Education's direct-loan plan, lured by the promise of a quick buck from banks, state lending agencies, and most significantly, Sallie Mae, the giant private lender based in Reston, Virginia. In all, 62 colleges and universities have dropped out of the Education Department's direct-loan program since 2000, and the list is growing. Sallie Mae has won over $1 billion in loan business from former direct-loan schools.

分析:

一、For 8 years, students at Michigan State University borrowed tuition money directly from the federal government.

译文: 密歇根州立大学的学生直接向联邦政府贷款支付学费，这种情况已经维持了8 个年头。

考点: 1. 增词译法: borrowed tuition money→贷款支付学费

2. 换序译法: for 8 years→这种情况已经维持了8个年头

二、But last spring, university officials shucked that arrangement and signed up with **private lenders** and a **state agency** (that provides loans under a separate federal plan).

译文: 但去年春季开始，大学的行政官员废止了这项安排，与私贷方和本州贷款机构 签订了协议，后者遵照另一项联邦计划提供贷款。

考点: shuck→剥去……的外皮或外壳(直译)

→废止(意译)

三、They guaranteed a profit to the university—**something** the federal government could not do. Sounds sweet for Michigan State, but it's not so terrific for federal taxpayers, (who will almost certainly **wind up shelling out** $23. 5 million more each year as a result of the charge).

译文 1: 这些机构承诺学校受益——这点联邦政府可做不到。密歇根州可谓春风得 意，可对于联邦纳税人却是悲喜两重天，因为这项收费，他们每年几乎肯定要 多支付2,350万美元。

译文 2: 这些机构承诺学校受益——这点联邦政府可做不到。密歇根州可谓得到了好 消息，但联邦纳税人却笑不起来，因为这项收费，他们每年几乎肯定要将多支 付2,350万美元。

考点: 1. 转性译法: 名词→动词 profit→受益

2. 代词的翻译: something→这点

3. 具体译法:

    成语法: sounds sweet→春风得意

             it's not so terrific→悲喜两重天

4. 定语从句的翻译:综合法:做因果状语从句

四、(1) Michigan State is not unique. (5) Today, dozens of colleges and universities are abandoning the Department of Education's direct-loan plan, (2) lured by the promise of a quick **buck** from banks, state lending agencies, and most significantly, (4) Sallie Mae, the **giant** private lender (3) based in Reston, Virginia.

译文: 无独有偶的是,由于受到银行、本州贷款机构,最主要的是弗吉尼亚州莱斯登的私营贷款业巨头赛里·梅伊快速发放贷款许诺的诱惑,如今,好几十家学院和大学都在考虑放弃教育部的直接贷款计划。

考点: 1. 具体译法: unique→无独有偶

       2. 换序译法: 翻译顺序: (1) (2) (3) (4) (5)

       3. 转态译法: 采用多种被动词 lured by→受到……的诱惑

       4. buck→美元(误译)

            →贷款(正译)

       5. 专有名词的翻译: 本句中除了 Virginia 必须翻译成"弗吉尼亚",其他的 Reston 和 Sallie Mae 可以保留原文形式不译。

五、(2) **In all,** (3) 62 colleges and universities have **dropped out** of the Education Department's direct-loan program (1) since 2000, and the list is growing.

译文: 从2000年至今,总共已有62所高校陆续退出教育部的直接贷款计划,而且数量仍在与日俱增。

考点: 换序译法: 翻译顺序: (1) (2) (3)

六、Sallie Mae has won over $1 billion in loan business from former direct-loan schools.

译文: 赛里·梅伊因向先前接受直接贷款学校发放贷款已获利10亿美元。

TRANSLATON TEST(2)(30 minutes)

Directions: Translate the following passage into English and write your version in the corresponding space in your ANSWER BOOKLET.

    中华民族历来珍惜和平。中国的崛起,是和平的崛起,是依靠自己力量来发展自己。对外关系中,我们一贯主张以邻为伴、与人为善,同各国发展友好合作关系。

    中国现在是、今后相当长时间内仍将是一个发展中国家。中国有13亿人口,这是最大的国情。中国国内生产总值已居全球第六位,但人均水平却排在138位。我们还面临不容忽视的失业、贫困和发展不平衡等问题。中国要赶上发达国家,还需要几代人,十几代人的艰苦努力。

分析:

一、中华民族历来珍惜和平。

　　译文 1: The Chinese nation has always been cherishing the value of peace.

　　译文 2: The Chinese people always cherish the value of peace.

　　考点: 时态: 考生可以发现, 这篇文章与 2000 年 3 月所考的一篇汉译英文章的内容题材有些许的雷同。此句句子与那篇文章的开篇之句更是如出一辙,因此选用现在完成进行时和一般现在时都是可以的。

二、中国的崛起,是和平的崛起,是依靠自己力量来发展自己。

　　译文: The rise of China is a peaceful rise with development based on its own strength.

　　考点: 1. 转性译法: 动词→名词

　　　　　　　　　　发展→development

　　　　2. "崛起"的翻译: "中国的崛起"可以翻译成 the rise of China, 也可以译成 the rising power of China, 这句句子在 2001 年 9 月的汉译英考试中出现在第二段的第一句: The rest of the world will have to react to this millennial economic shift to Asia, and to the rising power of China. 当时翻译成 "中华民族的崛起"。"崛起"在这里翻译成 springing 也可, 但如翻译成 growing up, growth, launching, raise 等都算错误。

三、对外关系中,我们一贯主张以邻为伴、与人为善,同各国发展友好合作关系。

　　译文: As to/for foreign relations, we always assert to build a good neighbourly relationship and partnership with other countries, aiming at building amity and copperation with all the other countries.

　　考点: 成语翻译: 细心的考生可能会发现从 2004 年 3 月的考试开始, 在中级口译汉译英部分也开始出现一定数量的成语翻译,这在以前的汉译英翻译中几乎是从未出现过的。这就给将来的中级口译的考生一个信号: 以前往往在高级口译中翻译部分出现的连串成语, 现在和将来也会逐渐有步骤地移植到中级翻译上去。因此这对中级考生的语汇积累又提出了一个更高的要求,考生在重视翻译场景的基础上也应掌握一些基本的成语谚语,彻底锻炼 "基本功",适当地掌握这些 "高级语言" 对于将来的口语和口译部分也是有利的,因此对于成语谚语的积累还是有相当高的 "性价比" 的。正可谓 As you sow, so shall you reap.

四、中国现在是、今后相当长时间内仍将是一个发展中国家。中国有 13 亿人口,这是最大的国情。

　　译文: China is and will remain a developing country in the foreseeable future. Having a population of 1. 3 billion is China's most obvious national condition.

五、中国国内生产总值已居全球第六位,但人均水平却排在 138 位。

　　译文: China's GDP ranks 6th in the world while its per capita GDP ranks 138th.

　　考点: 1. "国内生产总值"已经不是第一次考到了,说明常见的一些缩略语还将继续成为今后的考点。"人均水平"应译为 per capita GDP，但许多考生误译为 average living standard, average output 等。

2. "居……第几位"可译成 rank + 序数词。

六、我们还面临不容忽视的失业、贫困和发展不平衡等问题。

译文： We are also confronted with the problems which we can not afford to ignore, such as unemployment, poverty and imbalance in development.

考点： 1. 定语从句的翻译：前置法：不容忽视的→which we can not afford to ignore，有些基础较好的考生在这一短语的翻译上反而表现不好，用一些比较晦涩的形容词如 unignorable, disnegligible，其实这些单词都是不存在的。

2. "面临"的翻译：除了译文的翻译，也可用 face up to→正视

七、中国要赶上发达国家，还需要几代人、十几代人的艰辛努力。

译文： A developed China shall take generations or even ten generations of hard efforts.

附 录

附录一　常用词语表

A	
a long face	愁眉苦脸
a stab in the back	暗害
all ears	聚精会神地听
adapt oneself to	使自己适应……
above all	首先,首要,尤其是
after all	毕竟,终究
ahead of	在……前面,先于
all but	几乎,差一点;除了……都
all of a sudden	忽然
all over	到处,遍及;全部结束
in all	总共,共计
all the same	仍然,照样地
all the time	一直,始终
apart from	除……之外(别无);除……之外(尚有)
as far as	远到;就……而言,至于
ask after	问候(身体健康)
ask for leave	请假
as long as	只要,如果;既然,由于
as to	至于,关于
at a loss	困惑不解,茫然不知所措

at all costs	不惜任何代价,无论如何
at all events	不管怎样,无论如何
at any rate	无论如何,至少
at ease	舒适(地),安逸(地)
at hand	近在手头,在附近
at no time	从不,决不
at the cost of	以……为代价
at the sight of	一看见……就

B

back and forth	(前后)来回地,反复地
back up	支持;倒退
bark up the wrong tree	攻击错了目标
be in favor of	支持
be made up of	由……组成,由……构成
be short of	缺少,不足;未达到
bear. . . in mind	记住(某事)
before long	不久以后
below the belt	残酷的,不公平的
be worth doing sth	值得做某事
beyond the question	毫无疑问,确定无疑
born with a silver spoon in one's mouth	生来富贵
break down	损坏,抛锚
break in	破门(窗)而入;打断,插嘴
break into	强行闯进
break off	中断,中止
break out	(战争等)爆发;使逃脱,使逃走
break through	突破,突围
break the back of something	完成工作中最困难的部分
break the ice	打破僵局,消除拘谨
break up	打碎;终止,结束
bring about	带来,引起,导致
bring forward	提出(建议等)
bring into effect	使生效,实行
bring to operation	使……实施;使运行

bring out	使……显示出来;出版
bring up	教育,培养
build up	逐步建立,增强,增进
but for	倘没有,要不是
burn down	烧毁,烧掉
burn out	烧光;熄灭;疲乏
burn up	烧尽;烧旺
by accident	偶然
by air	通过航空途径;用无线电
by all means	尽一切办法,务必
by and by	不久,迟早
by chance	偶然,碰巧
by means of	用,凭借
by no means	决不,并没有
by oneself	单独地,独自地
by the way	顺便地,附带地说说
by way of	经过,经由;通过……的方法

C

call for	要求,需要;邀请
call off	取消
call on	访问,拜访;呼吁,号召
call up	打电话;召集
cannot help doing	禁不住,忍不住
capable of	有……能力(或技能)的;能……的
cannot... too...	越……越好,再……也不过分
care for	照顾,照料;喜欢
carry forward	发扬;进行
carry off	拿走,夺去……的生命
carry on	继续
carry out	执行,贯彻;进行(到底)
catch sight of	看到,发现
catch up with	赶上
check in	办理登记手续,报到
check out	结账后离开,办妥手续离开

cheer up	高兴起来,振作起来
clear up	清理;(天气)放晴
come around	苏醒;顺便来访
come in handy for sth	某物迟早有用
come on	(表劝说,鼓励等)来吧,走吧;开始
come out	出版,发表;显现,出现;结果是
come through	经历……仍活着
come to	苏醒;共计,达到
come to an end	结束
come true	实现
come up	出现,走上前来
come up with	追上,赶上;提出
compare... to	把……比作,把……与……比较
count for little	轻视
count on	依靠,指望
count up	算出……总数,总计
cut down	砍倒;消减;缩短
cut in	打断,插嘴
cut off	切掉;切断;阻隔
cut out	删掉,割去
cut short	缩短,删节

D

deal with	做买卖;处理;涉及
dead wood	无用的人
decide on	考虑后选定或决定
die out	消失,灭绝
do away with	废除,去掉
do... a favour	帮助某人
draw in	(火车、汽车)进站
draw up	起草,制订
dream of	梦到;梦想,向往
dress up	穿上盛装,精心打扮
drop by / in	顺便(非正式)访问
drop out	退学,退出

due to	由于,因为

E	

end up	结束,告终
every now and then	时而,偶尔
every other	每隔一个

F	

face to face	面对面(的)地;对立地
fail to do...	没能做……
fall behind	落后
fall in with	同意,依从
fall out	争吵;脱落
fall through	落空;失败
fall on / turn a deaf ear	充耳不闻
follow your nose	凭直觉行事

G	

get along	过活;相处(with);进展
get down	从……下来;着手进行;写下
get into	对……发生兴趣;卷入;进入
get off	(从……)下来;逃脱惩罚
get on	骑上,登上(车、船、飞机等);有进展
get on with	与……友好相处;继续干
get out	离去,退出(组织等);(消息等)泄漏
get over	克服;从(疾病、失望等)中恢复过来
get rid of	处理掉;摆脱
get through	完成;打通电话;通过(考试)
get up	起床;起立
give in	屈服;让步
give off	发出/放出(蒸气等)
give out	分发;发出(气味等)
give up	放弃;投降
give way to	让位于;给……让路
go after	追逐,追求;设法得到
go along with	赞同,附合,支持

go around	(消息)流传;足够分配
go down	下去;(船等)下沉;下降
go into	进入;调查;从事
go into action	开始行动
go into effect	实施,生效
go on	继续下去,进行
go out	熄灭,停止运转;过时
go over	检查;复习
go through	遭受,经历;检查,审查
go up	上升,(物价等)上涨;被炸毁,被烧毁
go wrong	出错;发生故障,出毛病
grow up	成熟;成年;发展

H

hand in	交上;递上
hand out	分发,散发
hand over	交出,移交
hang on	抓紧不放;坚持下去;(电话不挂) 等一会
hang up	把……挂起来;挂断(电话)
have an advantage over	胜于,优于
have in mind	记在心里;考虑到,想到
have nothing to do with	和……毫无关系
have (something) to do with	和……(有点)关系
have ants in one's pants	焦躁不安
have one foot in the grave	快要死了
head for	朝……方向走去
help oneself	自取所需(食物等)
hold back	踌躇,退缩不前;阻止
hold sth back from sb	向某人隐瞒某事
hold on	握住不放;坚持;(打电话用语) 等一会
hold on to	紧紧抓住;控制,克制
hold up	举起;耽搁;延迟
hurry up	(使)赶快;匆匆完成
hurt one's feelings	伤害某人感情

if only	只要;要是……就好
in a hurry	急于,忙于
in a sense	从某种意义上
in a way	在某种程度上,从某一点上看
in a word	简而言之,一句话
in addition to	除……之外(还)
in advance	预先,事先
in any case	无论如何,不管怎样
in brief	简单地说
in case of	假如,如果发生;防备
in charge of	负责,主管
in common	共有的,共用的
in debt	欠债
in detail	详细的
in effect	实际上,事实上
in fact	事实上,其实
in favour of	支持,赞成
in front of	在……前面
in general	一般说来,大体上
in half	成两半
in honour of	向……表示敬意;为纪念,为庆祝
in no case	无论如何不,决不
in no time	立即,马上
in no way	决不
in order	按顺序;整齐
in other words	换句话说,也就是说
in part	部分地
in particular	特别,尤其
in person	亲自
in proportion to	与……成比例
in public	公开地,当众
in question	正在谈论的
in relation to	有关,涉及

in return (for)	作为(对……的)回报、交换
in short	简言之,总之
in sight	看得见,在视线之内;在望
in that	因为
in the course of	在……期间,在……过程中
in the end	最后,终于
in the face of	……前面;不管,即使
in the way	挡道,妨碍某人
in time	及时;最后,终于
in touch	联系,接触
in turn	依次地,轮流地;转而,反过来
in vain	徒劳,白费力

J

just now	刚才,才不久;现在,眼下
join in	参加,加入;和……在一起

K

keep an eye on	留意,照看
keep a straight face	板着面孔
keep in mind	记住
keep in touch with	与……保持联系
keep it up	坚持
keep on	继续进行,反复地做
keep one's word	守信用
keep sth in one's mind	牢记某事
keep to	坚持;固守(习惯等)
keep up with	跟上,不落后
keep your nose clean	不卷入是非
kill off	消灭,杀光
knock down	撞倒;击倒
knock out	(拳击中)击倒,击昏

L

laugh at	因……而发笑;嘲笑
lay aside	把……搁置一旁;留存,储存

lay down	放下;铺设(铁路);制定(计划等)
lay out	布置,安排,设计;摆出,展开
lead to	通向;导致,引起
learn by heart	记住,背诵
leave behind	丢弃;留下;忘记携带
leave off	(使)停止,停下来
leave out	忽略,遗漏;省略
let alone	更别提;不打扰
let off	排放;放(炮),开(枪)
let out	放掉(水等),发出
lie in	在于
line up	排队,使排成一行
live on	靠……生活;以……为食
live through	经历过;度过;经受住
live up to	无愧于;做到;符合
long for	渴望
look after	目送;照料,照顾
look down on/upon	蔑视,看不起
look into	观察;调查;查阅
look on	旁观;观看
look out	留神,注意
look over	仔细检查,细看;察看,巡视
look through	(从头至尾)浏览;详尽核查;温习

M

make fun of	嘲笑;开……玩笑
make one's way	去,前进,前往
make out	写出,开列;看出,辨认出
make sense	讲得通,有意义,言之有理
make sure	查明,务必要做到
make up	组成,构成;编造,虚构;化妆
make up for	补偿,弥补
make up one's mind	下定决心,打定主意
make use of	使用,利用
mix up	拌和;混淆

more or less	或多或少,左右;有点儿

N

no doubt	无疑地
no less than	不少于,多达
no longer	不再,已不
nothing but	只有;只不过
now and then	时而,不时
now that	既然,由于

O

of course	当然,自然
off duty	下班
on a small/large scale	小(大)规模地
on account of	由于,因为
on average	平均;通常;普通
on bended knees	恭敬地
on board	在船(或车、飞机等)上
on business	因公出差
on duty	值班,当班
on earth	究竟,到底
on foot	步行
on guard	站岗,警戒
on occasion(s)	有时,间或
on one's own	独立地,靠自己地
on purpose	故意,有目的地
on sale	出售;廉价出售
on the contrary	正相反
on the spot	在现场,当场
on the whole	总的来说,大体上
on time	准时
once in a blue moon	千载难逢,机会难得
once again	再一次
open fire	开火
or else	否则,要不然
or so	大约,左右

other than	不同于;除了
out of breath	喘不过气来
out of control	失去控制
out of date	过时的,不用的
out of doors	在户外
out of the question	毫不可能
out of work	失业
over and over	一再地,再三地

P

pass away	去世
pay off	还清(债款);取得成功
pick out	选出,挑出;辨认出,分辨出
pick up	捡起;(车等)中途搭人;学会
play a part (in)	(在……中)扮演角色;(在……中)起作用
point out	指出,指明
prior to	在前,居先,比……在先
pull in	(车)进站;(船)到岸
pull into	(车等)进入,驶入
pull out	拔出,抽出;(车、船等)驶出
put aside	储存,保留
put away	把……收起,放好
put down	记下;放下;镇压
put forward	提出(要求、事实等)
put into practice	实行,实施
put off	推迟,拖延
put on	穿上;上演
put out	熄灭;关(灯);公布,出版
put to use	使用
put up	举起;建造;张贴
put up with	忍受,容忍(讨厌的人)

Q

| quite a few | 相当多,不少 |

R

regardless of	不顾,不惜
remind sb of sth	提醒某人某事
result from	是(由)……造成
result in	引起,导致;结果是
right away	立即,马上
ring off	挂断电话;停止讲话
ring up	打电话
rob sb of...	抢劫某人……
run into	偶然碰见;遇到(困难等);共计
run to (of)	用完,耗尽
run out of steam	精疲力尽;泄气
run over	(跑)过去、撞倒;溢出
run through	跑着穿过;刺穿;贯穿

S

see... off	为某人送行
see... through	看破,看穿
see eye to eye	意见一致
see to	注意,负责,照料
send for	派人去请;召唤;索取
send off	寄出;为……送行;解雇
set about	开始,着手
set a fire to...	给……烧把火
set apart	使分离;使显得突出
set aside	留出,拨出;不理会,置于一边
set back	推迟,延缓,阻碍;使花费
set down	制订……;放下……
set free	释放
set off	出发,起程;激起,引起
set out	动身,起程;开始
set up	创立,建立,为……作好准备;建造
settle down	定居;安下心来
shake a leg	赶快
show off	炫耀,卖弄

show up	来到,露面
side by side	肩并肩地,一起
slow down/up	放慢速度;减速
so... as to	如此……以至于
so far	迄今为止;到这种程度
so/as far as... (be) concerned	就……而言
so long as	只要,如果;既然,由于
sooner or later	迟早,早晚,或迟或早
stand for	代表,意味着;是……的缩写,主张,支持
stand out	引人注目;杰出,出色
stand up	起立;(论点、证据等)站得住脚
stick to	粘贴在……上;紧随;坚持;忠于;信守
a storm in a teacup	小题大做
such as	例如,诸如
sum up	总结,概括
switch off/on	(用开关)关掉/开启

T

take... for	把……认为是,把……看成是
take... for granted	想当然,认为理所当然
take advantage of	利用,趁……之机
take after	(在外貌、性格方面)与(父、母)相像
take apart	拆卸,拆开
take away	拿走;减去
take down	取下;记下;拆卸
take for	把……认为是,把……看作是
take for granted	认为,理所当然;对……不予以重视
take in	欺骗;领会,理解
take into account	把……考虑进去
take off	脱下(衣帽等);起飞
take on	承担,呈现(面貌)
take one's time	不着急,不慌忙
take out	扣除
take over	接受,接管;借用,承袭
take part in	参加,参与

take place	发生,进行,举行
take the place of	代替,取代
take turns	依次,轮流
take up	开始从事;占去,占据
taste blood	因初次胜利而尝到甜头
tell...from	辨别,分辨
thanks to	由于,多亏
the tip of the iceberg	事物的表面小部分,端倪
think over	仔细考虑
throw away	扔掉,抛弃
throw one's hat in the air	欣喜若狂
to a certain degree/extent	某种程度
to the point	切中要害,切题
touch on	谈及,提及
try on	试穿
try one's best	尽力,努力
try out	试用,试验
turn down	拒绝;关小,调低
turn in	上床睡觉;交还,上交
turn...into	使变成,使成为
turn off	关(水源等);拐弯
turn on	开,旋开(电灯等)
turn one's back on	不理睬
turn out	关掉;生产,制造;驱逐;结果是
turn over	仔细考虑
turn to	变成;求助于,借助于
turn up	出现,来到;开大,调大

U

under control	处于控制之下
under the circumstances	在这种情况下,(情况)既然如此
under the sun	天下,世界上,到底,究竟
up to	(数量上)多达;(时间上)直到;取决于
up to date	现代化的,切合目前情况的
use up	用完,耗尽

V	
vote down	否决
vote for	投票赞成
vote on	就……表决

W	
walls have ears	隔墙有耳
wait on	服侍(某人)
warm up	(使)暖起来;(使)变热
wash up	洗餐具;洗手洗脸
watch out for	密切注意;戒备,提防
wear out	穿破,用坏;(使)疲乏,(使)耗尽
wipe out	彻底摧毁,消灭
within reach	伸手可及
with the exception of	除……之外
without question	毫无疑问,毫无异议
work out	算出;想出,制定出

附录二　英语美语常用词区别对照

单词含义	美　　语	英　　语
零用钱	allowance	pocket money
律师	attorney	barrister
公寓楼	apartment	flat
汽车	automobile	car
行李	baggage	luggage
酒吧	bar	pub
皮夹	billfold	wallet
出租车	cab	taxi
罐头	can	tin
糖果	candy	sweets
手机	cellular phone (cell phone)	mobile phone
账单	check	bill (restaurant)
小饼干	cookie	biscuit
疯狂的	crazy	mad
驾驶执照	driver's license	driving licence
电梯	elevator	lift
橡皮	eraser	rubber
秋天	Fall	Autumn
一楼	first floor	ground floor
手电筒	flashlight	torch
高速公路	freeway, expressway	motorway
薯条	French fries	chips
汽油	gas, gasoline	petrol
垃圾桶	garbage can, trashcan	dustbin
垃圾	garbage, trash	rubbish
十字路口	intersection	crossroads
数学	math	maths
邮寄	mail	post
邮箱	mailbox	postbox
邮递员	mailman	postman
发动机	motor	engine
电影	movie	film
单程票	one-way	single

单词含义	美 语	英 语
长裤	pants	trousers
钱包	purse	handbag
铁路	railroad	railway
时间表	schedule	timetable
短裤	shorts	pants
人行道	sidewalk	pavement
餐具	silverware	cutlery
商店	store	shop
地铁	subway	underground
卡车	truck	lorry
电影院	the movies	the cinema
假期	vacation	holiday
挡风玻璃	windshield	windscreen

附录三　英美拼写主要区别

词　　意	美　语	英　语
-m／mme		
公斤	kilogram	kilogramme
方案	program	programme
-g／gue		
目录	catalog	catalogue
对话	dialog	dialogue
序言	prolog	prologue
-or／our		
举止	behavior	behaviour
颜色	color	colour
喜爱的	favorite	favourite
风味	flavor	flavour
荣誉	honor	honour
劳动	labor	labour
-er／re		
中心	center	centre
纤维	fiber	fibre
公尺	meter	metre
剧场	theater	theatre
-ense／ence		
防御	defense	defence
冒犯	offense	offence
执照	license	licence
伪称	pretense	pretence
-ize／ise		
批评	criticize	criticise
组织	organize	organise
实现	realize	realise
使标准化	standardize	standardise
辨认	recognize	recognise
-l／ll		
顾问	counselor	counsellor
珠宝商	jeweler	jeweller

词　意	美　语	英　语
奇异的	marvelous	marvellous
旅行	traveling	travelling
其他		
支票	check	cheque
小胡子	mustache	moustache
犁	plow	plough
睡衣裤	pajamas	pyjamas
怀疑的	skeptical	sceptical

附录四 常见逻辑关系列表

转折关系

- but
- on the contrary
- though
- nevertheless
- while
- even though

- however
- albeit
- despite
- nonetheless
- regardless
- yet

- otherwise
- although
- in spite of
- notwithstanding
- even if

因果关系

- because
- therefore
- consequently
- so...that
- when...then

- in that
- thus
- given
- so...as to
- as long as

- for
- accordingly
- hence
- if...then

对比(比较)关系

- in contrast
- on the other hand
- not...but

- on the contrary
- rather than
- more...than

- far from
- instead of

举 例

- for example
- like

- take...as an example
- such as

- for instance

条 件

- if
- otherwise

- if so
- in that case

- unless

列 举

- firstly...secondly...thirdly...finally
- moreover

- next/after

- besides
- in addition

作者简介

邱政政

上海新东方学校英语综合能力培训部主任，著名英语听力、口语、电影教学专家，首创"M7英语听说教学法"。毕业于北京语言大学语言文学系对外汉语专业，致力于第二语言教学与习得（汉/英）方面的研究。著有《TOEFL听力新思维》、《美音纠音、透析与突破》、《美国签证口语指南》、《美国口语超强纠错》、《"美国情景喜剧"俚语百分百》等多部畅销书。1999年加盟新东方学校。

徐 兰

上海外国语大学英语语言文学硕士，新东方口译教研组资深听力教学专家，美国政府特聘同声翻译，美国 New York University 法学硕士，美国纽约州注册律师，中国执业律师。

张驰新

新东方口译教研组资深笔译教学专家，口译教研组翻译课题组组长，高级翻译。多次担当大型国际商务会议同声翻译，澳大利亚 IDP（澳洲教育开发署）悉尼总部会员。首创"翻译字母理论"、细化"笔译阅卷流程"，深谙中高级口译考试机理，对考试趋势的把握独到、精确。

David Qian

新东方口译教研组资深阅读教学专家，高级翻译，毕业于加拿大名校 York Univ，曾任 York University MBA 助教。